RANCH WITHOUT COWBOYS

RANCH WITHOUT COWBOYS

Recovery, Romance, and a Second Chance
A Novel

JAMES R. DAVIS

SUNSTONE
PRESS

SANTA FE

Sunstone books may be purchased for educational, business, or sales promotional use.
For information please write: Special Markets Department, Sunstone Press,
P.O. Box 2321, Santa Fe, New Mexico 87504-2321.
Design › R. Ahl
Printed on acid-free paper

eBook 978-1-61139-625-6

Library of Congress Cataloging-in-Publication Data

Names: Davis, James R., 1936- author.
Title: Ranch without cowboys : recovery, romance, and a second chance : a
    novel / by James R. Davis.
Description: Santa Fe, New Mexico : Sunstone Press, [2021] | Includes
    readers' guide. | Summary: "A Kansas dairy farmer's daughter is raped
    and banished from home by her father, but with the help of strong women
    and real men, she survives with her baby on a guest ranch and bison
    reserve in Southern Colorado-the ranch without cowboys"-- Provided by
    publisher.
Identifiers: LCCN 2021030490 | ISBN 9781632933317 (paperback) | ISBN
    9781611396256 (epub)
Subjects: LCGFT: Novels.
Classification: LCC PS3604.A9587 R36 2021 | DDC 813/.6--dc23
LC record available at https://lccn.loc.gov/2021030490

WWW.SUNSTONEPRESS.COM
SUNSTONE PRESS / POST OFFICE BOX 2321 / SANTA FE, NM 87504-2321 /USA
(505) 988-4418 / FAX (505) 988-1025

To Adelaide B. Davis

This is far more than the typical "thanks, honey" dedication to a spouse. Adelaide encouraged the first visit to the guest ranch that inspired the setting and led to the story. She offered plot ideas, edited the Spanish, read every word, caught the typos, took the cover photo, provided significant computer support, and insisted that I try to find a publisher. Don't I owe my Brazilian sweetheart at least one more vacation at that gorgeous guest ranch under the cottonwoods at the base of the Sangre de Christo Mountains?

I respect any man who can heal a heart he didn't break...
and raise a child he didn't make.
    —Unknown

CONTENTS

PREFACE

Ilive in Colorado, and I've traveled around enough to know that Colorado has some fantastically beautiful scenery year-round. One summer, my wife and I booked a few days at Zapata Ranch, a cattle and bison guest ranch in Southern Colorado near the Great Sand Dunes National Park at the foot of the snow-capped Sangre de Christo mountains. When we stepped out into the parking lot near the lodge, looked around, and listened to the silence under the hundred-year-old cottonwoods, we turned to each other to say, almost at the same instant, that we'd never seen anything quite like it. It's a place to inspire a story, and it did.

I started to write a short story when I arrived back home, but the short story grew into a long story and then a novel. When I finished it, my writing consultant said it wasn't finished, so I wrote a little more. The reason the story grew is the fascination with the main character, Molly O'Reilly, not only her sad situation of being rejected by her own father and banished from home, not only her loneliness and confusion at the ranch without cowboys, but Molly's grit and resilience, her continuing determination to move from a naive high school grad to a "me-too" young woman. She was in a tough spot, and she needed strong women like Rainbow and Jersey, and kind men like Wayne and Carlos, to help her heal her broken spirit. So, the short story became a coming-of-age novel and present-day Western romance.

I invite you to jump into the passenger side of the old crew cab pick-up truck and join Molly on her journey as she leaves the Kansas dairy farm, the only home she has known, to drive west to Colorado to begin a new life at the fictional Horseshoe Ranch. And when you get there, stay close by Molly's side, and look over her shoulder to share her joys and miseries, her search for a new home, and her eventual love for Carlos Ouray, a descendent of Old Spanish settlers and Ute Indians from the San Luis Valley.

—James R. Davis
Lakewood, Colorado, 2021

1

MOLLY O'REILLY ARRIVES AT HORSESHOE RANCH

A column of swirling dust trails along behind the old Ford truck on the road that leads from the O'Reilly farm to the main highway. In the cracked rear-view mirror, Molly sees the dust and the orange sun edging up over the grove of maple trees at the back of the property. It makes her sad, driving away and looking back like that on the silhouette of the house and barns, knowing the way she is leaving home. She's getting an early start, early even for a Kansas dairy farmer's daughter, because she has a long way to go to get to Horseshoe Ranch before sunset. She has her maps, a cooler of sandwiches and homemade lemonade, a full tank of gas, and enough cash in her purse to get there—her mother made sure of that—but she's a little spooked about the trip. She's never been on the road by herself for a trip as long as this one to Colorado's going to be. Molly's not exactly overflowing with confidence, but there's more to it than that.

South on 83 to join Route 50 going west: those are the directions for the first leg of the journey. As soon as she gets on 50, she begins to see signs for Holcomb, that little town made famous in Truman Capote's book *In Cold Blood*. She finished reading it for Honors English class back in January, and she remembers how scared she got, thinking that killers like that could just come through an unlocked door and murder that whole Clutter family. Evil men on the loose and so close to home, too. And then...she can't even think about that.

She's glad to get past Holcomb, but then the road is no longer familiar. She's on her own. Knowing that in western Kansas all she's likely to see is wheat, corn, and cattle for mile after flat mile—open fields punctuated by an occasional grain elevator—she settles in for a long stretch of nothing before the Colorado border. The blue sky is calming, full of puffy white clouds of all different shapes floating carefree just above the horizon as if they had drifted in from a painting. Maybe the drone of the tires and the whistle of the wind will blot out the ugly names she was called, but so far, they keep coming back like a dog you're trying to send home, only he won't go. It's difficult to forget such language from your own father.

After crossing the state line into Colorado, Molly passes through Lamar and Las Animas before gassing up in La Junta, seeing from the map that there is absolutely nothing ahead on Route 10, not even the tiniest jerkwater town before Walsenburg. She pulls into a Sinclair station, finds a vacant pump, and slips in her credit card. Her mother told her to swipe her card as needed and she would see to it that the bill was paid because she does the bills each month. Paying the bills seems completely out of place for her mother considering how her father never lets them forget his number one position in the pack as head of the household. Maybe he isn't so good with math after the number one.

She retrieves a bottle of lemonade and a tuna sandwich from the cooler in the cab and transfers them to the passenger seat for later. It looks like her mom has thrown three novels in next to the cooler. Her mom loves novels. Maybe her only escape. As Molly unscrews the gas cap and inserts the nozzle, she tries to remember a time without this truck, but she can't. It seems like it's always been part of the family. Not anymore. At one time it must have been really something to own a crew cab short bed truck like this. While the gas is pumping, she hears a voice. "Is there anything I can help you with, young lady?"

A numbing sense of panic comes over her, but she manages to say, "No thank you, sir." She sneaks a guarded glance around the pump to see where the voice is coming from and notices a handsome guy who looks to be in his thirties filling his Camaro.

"Everything okay?" he asks.

"I'm fine," she says with a voice that betrays that she's not. She hauls in a deep breath.

Thank god she's finished pumping, so she jumps back into the truck and pulls away. Why is it that these older guys are attracted to her? She hurries along right at the speed limit, but then she realizes that someone driving a Camaro could easily catch up with her, so she watches in the rear-view mirror for a while to make sure he isn't following her as she goes through town. He's not, but she tells herself that he could be. Maybe he lives in La Junta? How could anyone live in this town? She finds her turn onto Route 10 and heads southwest. She keeps checking the mirror for the Camaro. That's how to stay awake without caffeine: worry about some jerk following you.

Some miles pass and she's calm enough now to admit her overreaction; his question was probably nothing more than a friendly gesture. She notices the unopened bottle of lemonade next to her, wiggles off the top with one hand, and takes a sip. That's better. Stay calm. Now she's ready for her sandwich. She's going to miss her mom's tuna sandwiches.

Eventually, after a long stretch of prairie, she thinks she spots snow-capped mountains off in the distance, hoping they're not a mirage. When she passes into those mountains, she knows she will be trading in her old life for something completely unknown. The past is behind her and the future is on a ranch beyond that mountain range. She'll just have to wing it for a while and see what happens. Survive somehow.

Does she stay on 10 or catch a new route in Walsenburg? *Pull over to use your phone or check the map, dear,* she hears her mother's voice reminding her, so she does. She doesn't need to drive smack into a telephone pole looking up something on a road map although she wonders momentarily if that might be the easiest solution. She finds Highway 160 going out of town and heads uphill for a long stretch, eventually reaching what the sign says is 9,413 feet in elevation at La Veta Pass. Pulling over next to the sign, she hops out to stretch her legs and see what the air is like at this altitude. She walks over and takes a selfie by the sign and draws in a few deep breaths. The road cuts through a dense evergreen forest below tree line, and gazing into that vast silent forest scares her a little, as if she is gazing into a dark infinity.

Suddenly, feeling a little lightheaded—maybe it's the thin air—she is overcome by an unexpected sensation of loneliness. So far away from anything familiar: no cornfields, no cows. How could she be missing dairy cows and Kansas cornfields? The sharp call of a bird catches her attention and she looks up to see a big black-and-white magpie flitting from tree to tree with outstretched wings flashing as if to get a better view of her. Could he be watching her? The bird cries out again. Not the friendly chirp of the sparrows back home. She misses home already, her mom and her younger brother, her friends at school, and her English teacher Mrs. Braxton. Under the circumstances of her leaving, she wasn't even able to say good-bye to the other cheerleaders and yearbook staff. She wonders what she is doing here at La Veta Pass on the last Friday in May when she's really supposed to be at The Colby High graduation ceremonies. She wants to turn around and drive home, but she knows she can't do that.

Molly circles the truck once, checking out all four tires. The old clunker seems to be holding together so maybe what she needs to do is get the heck out of this lonely place. She grabs another sandwich and more lemonade. Once she's behind the steering wheel she begins to feel like her old self again, but what a strange sensation that was being all alone on the edge of that dark forest. Now that she's over the pass, it shouldn't be long now, but when she glances at the map, she sees that it is, and she's facing that glaring globe in the west. She starts up the engine and as she pulls away, she cranks down the window to let in some of the cool mountain air to help keep her awake.

Horseshoe Ranch, the sign says, and it is right next to the mailboxes just as Wayne's directions said it would be. Now it's only six-tenths of a mile on the unimproved dirt road to the turn for the lodge. Molly jukes around the rocks and potholes. She's good at that. The road twists one more time and she finds herself coming to rest in the gravel parking lot. She sits for a moment, looking around in amazement at the quaint set up tucked back in here like something out of a storybook. Bathed in peaceful shade, the log cabin lodge sits under a canopy of tall old cottonwoods and is surrounded by entirely natural landscaping except for two cultivated beds of freshly planted petunias and marigolds. A broad lawn, neatly tended for a fifty-foot perimeter around the building, ends in pale green sagebrush, fallen limbs, and acres of grassland stretching off into the distance. It's a ranch not a farm, she reminds herself.

Molly pushes her sunglasses up on her head and checks her appearance in the cracked rearview mirror. Are there two of her in there or are her tired eyes seeing double? She smooths her eyebrows with her fingertips and applies a new layer of lip gloss. Funny how her perfectionist father would tolerate something like that cracked mirror. Glancing at herself again, she is thankful for her straight nose and wide set blue eyes, but her oval face appears to her a bit round, more than usual today. Her mom always said that her face was quick to take on a smile, but she hasn't had much to smile about lately.

She needs to stop looking in the stupid mirror at her appearance and get out of this truck to face the world. Sliding down from the seat, stiff from being scrunched up so long, she presses her elbows back a few times, rotates her neck in circles, and stretches out her gangling cramped legs. She tucks the tail of her blouse into her jeans, gives them a tug, and resets her pony tail of red ringlets. There's no sound but the twitter of birds and the air is so fresh she keeps taking deep breaths. It's so quiet here she wants to speak in a whisper. Someone is coming toward her. She's not really fond of meeting new people, but she better get ready. Now it begins.

"You must be Molly O'Reilly." She is greeted by a young woman with a strong voice.

"That's me, freckles and all." She runs a hand self-consciously over her forearm. "Can't get much more Irish than that, wouldn't you say?"

"Long trip?"

"From Kansas? For sure." She shakes her head slowly, deliberately. "Long and definitely boring."

The young woman who meets her is tall and attractive, scrubbed and neat in her appearance, and she looks to be a few years older than Molly is. Seems like she has a touch of a Southern accent.

"Once you get here though," the greeter says, "it's seriously beautiful. I mean, take a look at these mountains." She sweeps a long arm toward a prominent range of snow-capped peaks. Molly notices that the sun is beginning to set, casting slanted rays back that give the peaks a golden tinge. Wow! The sky is so blue.

"They're called the Sangre de Cristo Mountains, and that one to the south there is Blanca Peak, what the folks out here call a 'fourteener' because it's more than 14,000 feet above sea level. And over this way if you look beyond the cottonwoods, you can see the sand dunes lying along the foot of the mountains there to the north."

The sun is making a display of light and shadow on the twisting dunes. Molly takes in the panoramic view, noticing how clear and dry the atmosphere is and how the majestic mountains are so distant and yet so distinct.

"And the locals insist that these prairie grasslands have a haunting beauty, too," the young woman continues.

"Well, I don't need the haunting part." They exchange half-smiles and nods of agreement, trying to break the ice. Molly isn't sure what to say next. It's so quiet here that her words seem to get lost in the vast expanse of atmosphere. She raps on the hood of the truck. "At least this old junker held up." She's truly grateful that there weren't any breakdowns on those long stretches of desolate highways. "Now it can rest until November."

"Definitely. Once you're here, there's really no place to go."

Molly can't tell whether the young woman likes that or not. "How about you? Where did you come from?"

"I got to see, like, the whole great State of Texas east to west on Interstate 20. Drove in from Louisiana." She says *Lou-zee-an-a* like they do down there.

"Are you the intern?"

"Wildlife Management and Fisheries major. LSU." She points to the letters on her sweatshirt.

"Then you must be my bunkmate. They said I was rooming with the intern. College student. I was hoping to go to college this fall." Molly glances down at her boots.

"You actually grew up on a farm?" The intern gives her an inquisitive squint.

"I know a little about it. Enough to get hired here, I guess. What did you say your name is?"

"I don't think I said. Savannah, like the city in Georgia where I was born. Hey, let me show you around. We'll unload your stuff later." Savannah starts right off telling her about the ranch, like she's a tour guide and Molly's a first-time guest. Maybe she's practicing her spiel on her.

Savannah explains that Horseshoe Ranch is both a working ranch and a guest ranch. Adjacent to the Great Sand Dunes National Park, it's comprised of 100,000 acres of grasslands bought at below market price in 1991 by a conservation organization primarily for the purpose of keeping and enlarging a herd of 2,000 wild Plains Bison, but also to maintain grass fed cattle using sustainable grazing methods. Some guests interested in ranching come to see how it's done. Others are vacationers who come to view the bison, ride horses, or take tours around the endless grassland acreage. Sometimes the lodge will be booked by organizations for retreats. People who want to take a break from life and get away from it all say they like it here because cell phone coverage is poor, internet access is shaky, and cable TV is non-existent.

Molly knows most of this, of course, from the website and she's seen the photos, but standing here now in the midst of such immense grandeur she can feel how special the place is with its overwhelming majesty. "I get the idea," Molly says, "that we are kind of out in the middle of nowhere."

"You've got that right, sis. You might as well put your phone away. But on the positive side, it's an awesome slice of nature, don't you think? My mom would say that this is where God comes for *His* vacation."

They amble toward the lodge. "This first little building," Savannah says, "is the office. It's like the main desk in a hotel, like where guests check in and out, and in the back there in that little room is Wayne's office although he's hardly ever in there."

"Wayne Weston? The boss?"

"Manager. Facilitator. FYI, he never bosses anyone."

Molly nods without comment, remembering how her dad bossed people, even his own son and daughter something terrible.

"To our left here is the main lodge." Savannah opens a screen and then struggles to unlatch a heavy old oak door with squeaky hinges. Molly steps into a lobby area with log walls, tile floors, and rugs with colorful Native American designs. Indian baskets sit on a small shelf. Above two leather easy chairs, on the wall, is a big painting of a Western mountain scene signed simply *Emily*. "Over here," Savannah continues, "is the main dining room, where they serve buffet or family style meals depending on the numbers." It has knotty pine paneling and ceiling boards and a stone fireplace. Several wood tables and curved spindle-back chairs sit on a polished oak floor. An additional row of chairs lines the back window. "Out beyond the kitchen yonder is where the staff eats, so remember that because I guarantee that you will consume double or triple your normal appetite during your stay here. Believe that."

Molly doesn't respond to what she is sure will be true. "What exactly will I do? Mr. Weston never said much about that in his letter, just regular ranch work and other duties as assigned."

"Wayne, Molly. He'll want you to call him Wayne, not Mr. Weston. I don't know the answer to specific questions like that because I just got here myself two weeks ago, but from what I understand we are cross-trained to do just about everything on the ranch. The two cooks just cook, but everything else—the care of the bison, the calving and branding of the cattle, the fences, the movement and containment of the herds—all that is done by the staff, interchangeably and as buddies or in teams."

"I guess I can learn that." Molly nods her head up and down and compresses her lips. "I can ride pretty good." She remembers her horse, O'Grady, and knows she will miss him for sure.

"As a matter of fact, now that the branding of the cattle is finished and we are fully staffed, a training session is scheduled for tomorrow morning right here in the guest dining room. We're not open for guests yet. That starts the second week of June."

From the dining room they exit onto a large deck filled with picnic tables. A big old cottonwood grows up through one side of the deck, or maybe the deck was built around it. "People love to sit out here and gab," she tells Molly.

With the tour of the lodge complete, Savannah jumps into the dilapidated truck next to Molly and points out the narrow, rutted, nearly overgrown road that she needs to take to get back through the copse of cottonwoods to a cluster of cabins where the transient staff is housed. "A few of the more permanent employees, mostly older women, like Rainbow and Jersey, live in nearby towns: Mosca, Hooper, even as far as Alamosa. They commute to the ranch from the big city," she chuckles, "but the summer help, we live here." The truck is bouncing up and down so bad over the rough terrain that Molly wonders if this is what it feels like to ride a bucking bull. "Whoa!" Savannah shouts. "Right here is our cabin under these big shade trees, only the two of us, so that's nice. I was getting kind of lonely with nobody to talk to. I can't even get my frickin' phone to work. Maybe that's why I'm bending your ear so bad just now."

Molly doesn't mind. Maybe she can get to know Savannah and then she'll have at least one friend out here. Savannah opens the door and Molly discovers a sizable room with four single beds, a bath, and half a kitchen with a microwave, a stove, and a fridge and freezer, maybe a good place for storing leftovers and snacks. It's in a log cabin style, too, with sharply pitched rafters and a ceiling of knotty pine. Big screened windows. "I hope you like fresh air, Molly, because I seriously like to throw open those windows at night." Savannah helps Molly lug in her duffle bag and backpack. "Just this?" she asks.

"Yeah, I left in kind of a hurry," Molly says, without further explanation. "Are those your fancy binoculars?" she asks. Savannah nods. "Wow! And are all these books yours, too?" She glances at the titles of a small library of textbooks perched on a shelf meant for towels.

"Just a few for reference. I'm designing a study with my advisor on how bison give birth. What I'm finding, though, is that most of the bison have already had their calves. They call them red dogs because of their reddish fur when they are born. I think that I'm a little late. I keep watching, but you can't get very close to them, you know, so I have to use the field glasses."

"That would be close enough for me," Molly jokes, squirming a little. "I've seen calves from our dairy herd born and it's not a pretty sight. One of our hired men had to reach up in and pull out an obstinate little calf once, but he lost his rubber glove up inside the cow and wouldn't go back for it."

"Not to worry. It might serve as a condom for the next bull." Savannah laughs hard at her own joke, but Molly doesn't think it's very funny, I mean, a cow going around with a glove up inside her.

Molly sleeps like a baby after that long drive from Kansas to Colorado, what with the silence and that cool fresh air blowing in all night. Savannah is up early and after her shower she awakens Molly. "Don't forget the training. Eight o'clock sharp."

After breakfast—man, they have a good breakfast here—everyone assembles in the guest dining room, chattering away like old friends, but when Wayne Weston comes in, the room grows hushed. He lays his felt cowboy hat on the table and runs a hand through his sandy hair. He has the weather-beaten face of a cowboy. Late forties or early fifties? Jeans. Light blue soft denim shirt. Very handsome still and with that shy way of being that makes a man attractive. All Molly knows about Wayne is that he's the boss and he interviewed her on the phone.

She was urgently looking for work in a restaurant or inn out West and she found the Horseshoe Ranch website listed with small hotels on a bed and breakfast directory. She thought working on a ranch would be more to her liking than being a maid or waiting tables, so she called the office and Wayne happened to pick up the phone. She told him about growing up on a dairy farm in Kansas, and that she'd helped with the milking and had her own horse. He asked what she had done in high school besides study, and when she said she was a cheerleader he chuckled, but then he said "that's okay." She told him how she was looking for a job, and after she dodged a few questions about why she wanted to work on a bison ranch, not knowing much about bison, he told her he still had one position to fill and to send him a brief letter. Wayne must have liked it. Three days later she got a contract in the mail, which she signed and sent back, and a map along with printed directions, but it all happened so fast and at the last minute that she's not sure how she got the job or what it really is.

Sitting alone, Molly is watching Wayne closely this morning to try to figure out who he is and what he's like, because he's the boss and that's important no matter what Savannah says about his not bossing. He's going on about values: the conservation and sustainability principles that guide the work of the ranch, which she takes to mean preserve things in their natural state and don't let the place run down. Wayne talks about prescriptive grazing plans and keeping a healthy ecosystem. Then he turns philosophical and says you can learn a lot from the cattle, the owls, and even the spiders by watching them closely. He tells the staff to be gentle to each other and to the horses and to observe the bison closely because they know things instinctively that we humans have trouble learning. He says not to forget that the dominant life form on this planet is insects not humans, which provides a perspective she hadn't considered.

The truly remarkable thing she notices, though, is that Wayne is the only guy in the room, the rest are all women. How can you run a ranch without cowboys? When she glances around, she notices that the women are all strong, really muscular, the toughest bunch of cowgirls imaginable. From the questions they ask, they seem to know what's involved in ranching. So, what is this, some kind of ranch for liberated women who are anxious to prove that they don't need a man around to repair a barbwire fence? Seems odd. She bites a thumbnail.

Then she harbors some darker thoughts that start to make her nervous. Is this guy some sinister sultan and is she now a member of his harem? Are these his hand-picked beauties? She notices that most of these women are not just strong but good looking as well. Savannah with her long auburn hair and narrow black plastic-rimmed glasses looks like a fashion model for expensive handbags. Did Wayne think she was attractive because she was a cheerleader? Is that how she got the job? What are those "other duties as assigned"? Good Lord, what has she gotten herself into? She starts to twirl the dangling hair in her pony tail around and around in a ringlet, like babies do with the hair at the crown of their head when they're taking a bottle. She knows it's a mania, and for sure her mom has harped on her to stop it, but she's usually not aware of when she's doing it.

She glances around the room to see how the other women interact with Wayne. They don't seem to be under any particular stress, no one hostile or challenging. In fact, they seem to worship him, but maybe that's not so good either. Is he some kind of warped religious nut leading all of these beautiful women astray before the rapture? Has she landed in a commune like that wacky place in Waco years ago that she remembers her parents talking about at the dinner table? Will she meet a violent death here in a fusillade of bullets, shot dead by federal marshals? She keeps twirling her hair around faster now.

At the first coffee break out on the deck with the picnic tables, Molly rushes up to Savannah and pulls her aside. "What's going on that there aren't any men here?"

"Well, I had that disappointing thought, too, when I first arrived because I was hoping I might meet a wicked hot guy on my internship, but I asked around and everyone said that the absence of men is just the way it happens to be at Horseshoe Ranch. I guess Wayne just wants to give women a chance."

"What about, like, I mean, Wayne himself?" She stumbles, at a loss for the right words and is too panicky to ask directly what's on her mind. "Does he expect certain...ah...benefits, if you know what I mean?"

"Not that I know of and no one complains about him."

"Maybe he just has one or two special ones."

"If so, it's a well-kept secret." Savannah shakes her head slowly, looking puzzled by Molly's insinuations. "No, to tell the truth, everybody thinks that Wayne is just one of those totally nice guys, someone that respects women and keeps his own place."

Molly's eyes flit around and she rubs her forehead hard as if to smooth out the wrinkles of a frown. "So, it's not dangerous here?" She feels her racing heart returning to a normal beat and then racing again.

"Maybe your imagination is just galloping away from you right now and you need to rein it in a little. Slow down. Chill. You're going to be okay here."

"With no men around, maybe I should worry about the women?"

"Well, for sure not me, but geez, Molly, if you need to worry about something, that's better than worrying about Wayne. From my observations, he is definitely legit."

After the break, Molly settles back in her chair and starts watching Wayne again. She's still nervous, running a thumbnail between her lower teeth. Once her imagination starts running wild, it's hard to corral it. If it's true what Savannah says that she doesn't need to worry about him, then maybe she can just take him to be an ordinary person. But as she watches him, she concludes that he is anything but ordinary, at least compared to any other men she has known in her short grown-up life, not her brother, not her father, not the guys she knew in high school, and certainly not that ridiculous farmhand who said he loved her.

What is so attractive about Wayne? His wavy hair? His clean-shaven tanned face? It's not really anything physical. It's his gentle way of speaking and his attentive way of listening, his patience with the most trivial question, and the special look of kindness on his face. She's never seen a guy so charming. Do the women flirt with him? It seems like they don't and for sure he doesn't encourage it. Maybe that blond over in the corner does and the one in the back row of chairs, that one with the dark eyes, but really the flirting is more like what a daughter does with her dad as a little girl. Yeah, that's it, more of a father and daughter thing.

2

MEETING CARLOS AT PEPE'S CANTINA

And so, Molly's work at Horseshoe Ranch begins the next day and continues through the weeks ahead. She works around the main lodge at first, mowing, trimming, weeding, and adjusting the sprinklers. Everything grows natural here and the yellow dandelions are considered wild flowers. A stone wall has been built around the lodge and no one seems to know its purpose: maybe to keep wild animals out of what was once a garden. Molly begins to turn the soil with a shovel and asks Wayne about planting a few more flowers there behind the wall.

Wayne finds her a suitable horse and for a few days she rides boundaries with an older woman named Rainbow, looking for breaks in the fencing to repair. Molly likes fixing things and catches on to fences quickly. Rainbow shows her how to use a tester on the electric fence to see if the wire is still hot. They also check the salt blocks for the cattle and drop new ones as needed.

Today, Wayne has Molly assigned to mowing and trimming around the lodge again, because it's getting a little shabby looking and he says that last time she really spruced it up.

"Do you mind if I fix this mower first before I start the job? It's not running so good."

"Help yourself," Wayne says. "You can probably find most of what you need in the shop over in the main barn. You know where that is, right?"

"I do, and maybe when I'm done here you could give me a hand with the front door of the lodge. We could shim the hinges and it wouldn't squeak so bad and the latch would line up."

He raises his eyebrows and the corners of his mouth edge up. "Okay, if that's something you want to fix, look for me when you're done here."

So, Molly tackles the mower: changes the oil, puts in a new spark plug, and finds a file to use on the dull blade. Flipping the mower upright, she yanks the rope to start it and it takes off on the first pull. That's a lot better. Sounds good now. She can fix about anything thanks to her dad and her little brother, neither of whom ever treated her like a useless girl.

Today she is working alone, not a soul around to talk to, and completely undisturbed by the tall old cottonwoods and silent but imposing mountains.

When she's working by herself at a routine job, she always has at least half of her brain free to think about something else. Her mother taught her to whistle before she started school, a whistling prodigy she was, and she usually whistles while she works, but not a whole song, just a phrase, usually repeated over and over. She's careful where she whistles because she knows it can be irritating. What she discovers today with the free half of her brain is that even though her gangly young body left the farm to come west, her meandering mind and most of her feelings are stuck back there in Kansas. She finds it especially difficult to stop thinking about her father because sometimes she feels a special fondness for him and at other times, well, it's definitely not fondness.

For instance, she remembers how sweet it was that he showed her how to drive the John Deere, sitting up there on his lap while he guided her child's hands on the big vibrating steering wheel and helped her push the accelerator lever up and back with just the right amount of pressure. But then the next day he's chewing her out for leaving a shovel out in the rain, going on and on about rust, the cost of a shovel, and carelessness until she felt completely humiliated for having done such a terrible thing. She's not sure whether her relationship with her father during her early teen-age years was any better or worse than her friends was—they all started talking about their parents around about eighth grade—but she knows she had no intention of ever leaving home like this. No, as bad as things got, she knew she needed to hang in, because college was coming up and her father would be filling the gap between her scholarships and the bottom line for tuition, room, and board. She knew that if she could just be respectful to him things would work out, and it wouldn't be long until she went off to the university and left him behind on the farm. But of course, that never happened. It wouldn't be so bad remembering him if she could just love him or hate him, but this business of liking him and not liking him at the same time is pathetic.

Molly shuts down the mower, empties the catcher, and takes up the power trimmer to catch the spots around the trees and next to the wall while her mind keeps churning up memories. Making ice cream is another example, she recalls. Somehow, she became her father's preferred partner for making homemade vanilla ice cream. He never lifted a finger to help with cooking, anything having to do with food being her mother's responsibility. Some days it seemed like her mother never left the kitchen, and she remembers coming home after school, taking pity on her mother, and without saying anything just pitching in to scrub some of the greasy pots and pans because she could be sure that she would never see her father either cooking or cleaning up. But making ice cream was different, maybe because it had a mechanical aspect to it. That was his thing.

She had the recipe down by heart for the cream, sugar, and vanilla, which she took outside all mixed together in the big metal container that slid nicely into place—the electric version having replaced the hand crank after years of thinking about it—while her father layered in just the right amount of ice and salt. Because of the brine, it could get messy, so the ice cream was always made outside on a tarp, even though it involved hooking up the machine to an extension cord. Of course, it was the best ice cream in all of western Kansas, made from fresh dairy cream like that, and who could think of anything but eating it once it was made, preferably with a drizzle of her mother's chocolate sauce and a plateful of homemade chocolate chip cookies.

Well, the routine worked out pretty well until one day she brought the ice cream into the kitchen but left the maker outside to clean up later, only she forgot all about it later because the ice cream was so good it beckoned for a second and then a third helping, while she and her younger brother Danny got into a few giggling fits, so that pretty soon ice cream was coming out his nose. When father discovered the ice cream maker still outside an hour later, he exploded into one of his lectures on taking care of costly equipment, paying attention to what you're doing, and being responsible. So, you couldn't ever enjoy the good times completely without some scolding from dad to spoil it. She knows that he meant well for her, wanting her to grow up organized and responsible, but he sure had an awful way of going about it, crushing her confidence and self-esteem at a time when she had very little of either one.

She has a sudden pang of homesickness for Danny and the bunch of good times they had together as brother and sister. They finished their homework as quickly as possible without cutting corners, because they both wanted to watch one of the crimes shows together: CSI, LAPD, Miami Vice, sometimes new episodes, sometimes reruns or a whole series downloaded or on a CD. They both loved Law and Order: Special Victims Unit with all those sex-based crimes and child kidnapping cases full of intrigue. Wow! Danny. He'll be in eleventh grade this fall, a junior already, a young man.

Molly shakes herself out of her reverie, recognizing the danger in allowing herself to get too homesick. She checks over her work, gathers in her tools, and pushes the mower with her free arm. It's time to go find Wayne and fix the front door.

The next week, already mid-June, Molly is assigned to accompany Savannah to learn to be a tour guide for guests. She has to learn a speech about the age and size of the ranch, the climate, the basics about the bison herd, and the land use patterns that keep the property sustainable. There's a lot to remember. Some of it is interesting, though, and Savannah is a good teacher. Like she told her that at one time there were sixty million bison in North America, but they nearly became extinct, down to around 750 of them in 1880. Now the population is back to five hundred thousand. "Whatever you do," Savannah says, "don't say *buffalo*. Call them by their genus name, *bison*. Actually, they are called *bison bison* to distinguish them from Paleolithic bison. They are *bovid ruminants*." Molly is pretty sure she can omit the double bison and bovid ruminant part.

Then Savannah is assigned elsewhere and Molly becomes the tour guide. She's learned that there are two ranches of 50,000 acres each, side by side, one for the bison that are allowed to grow wild, and one for the Black Angus cattle that are carefully managed. Sometimes she takes the guests to one side of the ranch, sometimes to the other. Her favorite part of the tour is driving the Chevy Suburban and coming up slowly at a safe distance to see the bison. She hands around the binoculars to the guests to look out from the open windows, and they are astounded to see a long line of dark brown bison stretched along the horizon as far as the eye can see. Then she gets the guests out of the van and they walk fifty yards closer to get a better look. Sometimes she has to coax them, like a border collie with sheep. "It's okay. It's safe. Come on, people. Let's sneak up on Tatanka." They love it, especially the ones from the big cities back East. She found a little patch of bison fur and gave it to a New Yorker and he invited her to spend a week in Manhattan. She told him she'd already been to Manhattan, but she didn't mention that it was Manhattan, Kansas, to visit the university.

On Saturday night of that week, Savannah invites Molly to go out with some of the summer staff to a bar in Alamosa.

"Not for me," Molly says abruptly, holding up her palms.

"Oh, come on, the crepuscular canine carnivores will love a good looking one like you. We call them creeps for short."

"Night-feeding wolves?"

"Hey, have you been reading my books?" Savannah asks sharply.

Molly can't tell whether Savannah is upset or not, so she apologizes. "Oh, sorry. I guess I should have asked."

"Just kidding."

"To tell the truth, I would rather stay home and read your books than to..."

"Well, who knows, tonight we might even meet some next level guys. There's a college in that town, you know." She nods vigorously and her eyes widen behind the black frames of her glasses.

"I wouldn't know what to do with a college guy. I don't dance well, I don't know anything to talk about, and I shouldn't drink."

Savannah frowns. "Why not?"

Molly just nods until she remembers to say, "My age."

"That's right, you are a little youngish. Well, they won't card you for nachos."

Molly has struck up an acquaintance with Jessica and Verónica, the blond and the dark-eyed ones she thought were kind of flirting with Wayne at the training session on the first day. Those two are fun to joke around with and she often sits with them at meals, but they seldom talk about anything serious, so there's not much real sharing. She's not keen on going to a bar, but maybe this would give her an opportunity for a little socializing, so giving into the peer pressure, she decides to go. In a few minutes, all of the women who are going have piled into Savannah's Cherokee for a short drive that seems long and bumpy to Molly.

She finds herself entering through the bright blue door of an old adobe style bar that looks like *it* was imported from Mexico along with the tequila advertised in the lighted neon sign over the entry. Inside Pepe's Cantina, it is dark, stuffy, crowded, and loud, just what she expected it to be. Jeez, why does she let herself be talked into things like this? She finds a remote table and sits with her back against the wall where she can sip her lemonade without being noticed, hoping that no one will ask her to dance to that bouncy live Mexican music. She notices that the owner, bartender, and most of the waitresses look Mexican, and that adds to her uneasiness though she tells herself it shouldn't. Hey, it's their bar; she's the one who's out of place.

It doesn't take long for Savannah to attract a crowd of guys and pretty soon Jessica and Verónica and the rest of squad from Horseshoe Ranch are up dancing or hanging out with the guys, and Molly is left sitting there alone at the table, which is embarrassing but not as bad as having to fight off some amorous jerk. Oh, crap, there's one now, standing right in front of her, and when he asks her to dance, she tells him no, and when the next one comes up, she says, "I'd like to, but I'm not able just now." She knows she's not ready for anything like that.

Savannah sees what's happening and hollers over, "Come on, Molly, join in."

But Molly just sits, listens, and observes, feeling suddenly overcome with another bout of melancholy, alone in that noisy crowd just crunching her nachos. She's so lost in her sadness that she hardly hears the scrape of the chair or feels the arm that has been placed around her shoulder. She glances at a dangling hairy hand, and then looks back the other way into the pale, smirking face of an unkempt long-haired dude with bulging eyes leering at her, a gold chain around his neck. She tries to push the twerp away, but he just clings to her, so close she can smell the whiskey on his breath. Wondering how she's going to deal with this disgusting creep sends a jolt to her stomach and she suddenly feels the panic coming on. She tries again unsuccessfully to get free and then she screams, "Get away. What do you think you're doing?"

"I just came over to invite you to dance," he smirks.

She frowns and twists. "I don't want to dance."

"You were just looking so sad, and I thought it might cheer you up."

"I said I don't want to dance," she yells at him and she wiggles to get loose.

"Hey, hey, take it easy." He holds a finger to his mouth but clings tight to her with his other arm.

She notices that the bartender has heard her and is motioning with his head and his eyes to the owner and a couple of guys seated at the bar, like there's trouble brewing. Before the intruder can notice, he is being surrounded by strong dark men.

One of them says, "*Suficiente*, Sonny. Let's go."

The second one says, "Time for you to head on home, Sonny. *Vá para casa.* The young lady is asking you to let go of her. What part of that don't you understand?" He points toward the door.

Sonny swallows hard, stands up, bows slightly, mockingly, and lurches toward the exit.

"Thank you," Molly gasps. "I...I..." She's biting her thumbnail and she notices a slight tremor in her hand. Her heart is racing.

"You don't need to explain anything. Sonny's here most every night. It's Sonny who needs to explain." The young men have returned to the bar now, except the most handsome one, the guy who told Sonny to go home, like shooing a dog. This one has a square chin and high cheekbones and his face seems tan and sunburned at the same time. His raven black hair is neatly trimmed, neither too long or short.

"Thank you," she whispers, holding a hand over her chest, drawing in a deep breath, still too frightened to smile.

"My name is Carlos. You let me know if you need anything." He gives her a friendly glance and asks, "You work out at the Horseshoe?"

"Yes. Just for the summer. I'm Molly," she says, noting an especially kind look in his eyes, like he senses something isn't quite right with her. He studies her a little and quickly looks away. He keeps standing by her table but doesn't say anything more. Is he shy?

"I appreciate what you did just now," she says to break the silence. "I hope I didn't overreact." She doesn't think she did, but she's pretty confused these days about her actions, reactions, and overreactions.

"Sonny needs to learn to control himself," Carlos says.

"I guess we all do, but aggressive guys like that scare me."

"Nothing wrong with that. A woman needs to be careful."

Carlos is still standing there by the table, swaying from side to side, but the conversation is stalled. He's making a good impression on her, but the last thing in the world she needs right now is to have a guy interested in her. Normally, she would small talk with a guy like this, but tonight, after what just happened with that disgusting Sonny, she finds it difficult, so she says, "Thank you again. I'll remember what you did for me tonight."

She expects him to leave but he doesn't. He remains at her side for another moment, glancing at her and looking away in a manner that makes her uncomfortable although she reminds herself that there is nothing inappropriate in a man's quiet admiration. Before he turns to go back to the bar, he says, "We don't see young women like you very often in the Valley." Molly can't bring herself to speak, but she does smile.

On Friday night of the next week, after dinner, Savannah comes running into the cabin out of breath to say, "Molly, there's some seriously handsome guy here to see you."

"I can't think who that could possibly be. For me? Where?"

"Up at the lodge. I'm just saying he's asking for you."

To make herself presentable, Molly changes quickly from her sweatshirt into a clean blouse, refreshes her lip gloss, and resets her pony tail as she hustles up to the lodge, where she finds standing out front by the stone wall a nice-looking dark-haired guy in black chinos shifting nervously from one foot to the other.

"Remember me?" he asks. He's looking down like he's sure she doesn't.

She hates when people ask that, but she does remember. "From Pepe's.

You saved me from that sleazy Sonny creep."

"That's me. Carlos."

"Yeah, of course I remember you." Especially that smile. She pauses to look at him closely now, noting that kind look in his eyes again. She remembered him as short, but really, he is about as tall and lanky as she is. "What is it you want?"

"To see you. I had to find you because I couldn't get you out of my mind." He shakes his head. "So pretty..." but he doesn't finish whatever he was going to say. Instead, he makes a bashful shrug and looks away.

Pretty? She can't understand how any guy would think she is pretty with so many freckles and those unattractive reddish eyelashes that she thinks make her look like an albino. She feels her face getting hot and can't think what to say until she remembers the words *thank you*. Then she looks up at him with her head on a tilt, one arm on her hip, and tells him, "If you're looking for a girlfriend, I won't make a very good one, working so many hours out here at the ranch and living in a cabin like I do."

"I understand." He hesitates, as if he's trying to think of some way to overcome his shyness and her resistance. "Maybe we could just go into town once in a while for something to drink and get acquainted."

"It's a nice invitation," she says thinking it over, "but you might have noticed I don't drink."

"Maybe milkshakes?" He grins, gazing at her again, then looking away.

She suspects that the milkshakes are only a pretense. "I told you I'm not..."

Molly is not very encouraging to Carlos, but he comes to visit her again and soon a seed of friendship sprouts. He seems nice enough, and for sure she needs a friend. Savannah is right: he *is* handsome. And persistent.

No Fourth of July celebration at the ranch? Why not? Molly has observed that there is no flag pole at the ranch, no flags, not a sign of patriotism. Maybe some miniature American flags will appear as table decorations at the evening meal, but that's it. No fireworks. The dry and windy weather has elevated the fire danger to extremely high risk, and campfires are banned in the park and the surrounding counties. Vacationers throng the main road going past the ranch on the way into the Great Sand Dunes National Park today, the vans and cars and motorcycles making enough racket to remind the folks at the Horseshoe that there is a tumultuous world out there full of ornery and obstreperous people beyond the boundaries of this peaceful ranch. For the staff, it's just another workday, and their priority is to mind the animals and serve the guests courteously, in that order.

Molly has noticed that living on the ranch is like being isolated on an endless prairie surrounded by nothing but fresh air. It is as if Horseshoe Ranch is not located in the United States, is not even a part of Colorado, but stands as an entity unto itself, as they say, self-sufficient and oblivious to the rest of the world. Out here there is no cable news, no polarized arguments about politics, no reports of school shootings or police murders of a black child waving a toy gun or a presumed delinquent merely carrying, as it turns out, a cell phone. Most everyone likes the ranch that way, quiet and remote; after all, that's why visitors come here, to get away from the pressures of the real world, to breathe pure air deeply, and to see the bison grazing together in contentment. Molly is beginning to like the tolerant and peaceful atmosphere of the ranch and living life away from the world and close to the land.

So, on this Fourth of July, forgetting that she would be making homemade ice cream for her family, she finds herself working with Rainbow and Jersey. Rainbow Gallegos is her full name. Probably fifty, but in good shape. Natural look. Tan skin and short brown hair streaked with gray, plus intense green eyes that seem to notice everything. Her partner Jersey is younger, shorter, and stockier, not so experienced and knowledgeable as Rainbow, and sometimes a bit outspoken, as if she's trying to get your goat. *Provoking*, that's the word for Jersey. Molly's been on their team several times before, and today they are working on the cattle part of the ranch, riding through the herd to check for sick cows and calves, looking to see if they can spot a persistent cough, diarrhea, or a young one favoring a leg. If they see one, they rope it, pull it aside and give it antibiotics or a painkiller. This work takes some skill and finesse because the mothers are very protective of the calves, calling out to them with a loud moo if they sense intruders. Rainbow tells Molly that the purpose of the cattle ranch is to produce and raise the calves for eight or nine months and then ship them off to another ranch for further care until they are sent to market. Unlike the cattle, the bison are not sent to market, the goal being simply to increase the herd.

The three women work together through the morning, and then come into the corral to see what can be done there. Molly notices that the gate doesn't swing right so she adjusts the hinges and shores up the adjoining post to make everything functional and more secure. When the sun is at its zenith, Jersey suggests that while they eat lunch, they should enjoy some shade in an adjacent outbuilding that shelters bales of straw. They arrange the bales as if to construct a table and chairs, and they spread out their food. Molly has picked up one of the sack lunches provided for staff working too far away to come to the lodge, and Rainbow and Jersey have brought food from home. Molly has always wanted to ask Rainbow how she got her name, so she wiggles in sideways like a crab with the question "Did you grow up around here?"

The question was intended for Rainbow, but Jersey barges in first. "Not me. I'm from New Jersey." Then she repeats New Jersey as *New Joisey*. "But I lost my accent when I moved out here. I just had to break free from that dog-eat-dog world my parents were training me for, I mean you can't believe the lessons they enrolled me in as a kid—flute, ballet, soccer, gymnastics—so when I landed here, I said to myself: this is it, kiddo, you're free at last."

"So, you like it out West," Molly says, letting Jersey talk, knowing that she can come back to Rainbow later.

"What's not to like? Working outdoors on the land, short four-day weeks in the winter, the mellow people who live in the Valley."

"What about you, Rainbow?" Molly asks. "Are you from around here?"

"Not originally. I'm from California, the daughter of a genuine California hippie."

"Really? Where did you live?" she asks, expecting to hear a town she wouldn't know.

"On a commune," Rainbow says, as if it were the most natural thing in the world.

"A commune? I've heard of that but what exactly is a commune?" Molly asks.

Jersey jumps in with, "It's a place where no one owns anything but shares everything, including husbands and wives. Isn't that right, Rainbow?"

"Well, yeah, things were pretty free back then, I guess, but not as loose as the majority of people made it out to be."

"You grew up there? What was that like?" Molly asks, sitting forward on her bale of straw to hear the answer.

"We were at a place called Wheeler's Ranch in Sonoma County, more than 300 acres that sat on a ridge four miles from the ocean. My mom told me all about it when I got older. Snatches of her reminiscences passed on to me. And she has pictures of really long-haired bearded men with their fanciful hippie sweethearts in tie-dye dresses and beads, slinging a baby on one hip. Yep, I was one of those babies."

"Really?" Molly's eyes are bugged out and the image of a baby born in a commune is disturbing to her. "Did you have a house?"

"Alternative living structures is what they called them. A lot of people lived in tents, A-frames, and geodesic domes covered with canvas, but we had a house, if you can call it that, actually more of a board shack with a corrugated galvanized roof."

"A self-inflicted slum," Jersey chimes in. "Can you imagine choosing to live like that?"

"It wasn't so bad. Mom showed me the pictures. Unspoiled charm. Supposedly idyllic. We had a wood-fired cook stove and a small garden plot out back. She said there was always music, always singing and whistling, and jams most every night with guitar and fiddle."

"Tell me about your name, Rainbow," Molly ventures. "I love it."

"You do? Well, let me tell you it's not always fun being a forty-eight-year-old woman walking around with the moniker *Rainbow*. I've tried to shorten it to *Rain* or *Bow*, but neither one works because people keep expanding it back again to Raincoat or Elbow, or something more ridiculous than Rainbow. Part of the counter-culture rebellion against conventional society was to give their kids unusual names. When I'd get upset with my mom for naming me Rainbow, she would remind me that she was also considering *Arrow, Baby Willow,* and *Vishnu Krishna.*"

Jersey jiggles both knees up and down. "Well, next to those," she says, "Arabella sounds pretty tame."

"Who's Arabella?" Molly asks.

"Me," Jersey replies.

"Really?" Rainbow says. "Holy cow, I didn't know that was your name."

"When I came out here, people just started calling me Jersey, and I let it stick, realizing that at long last I could ditch Arabella."

Molly hasn't finished with Rainbow. She wants to know more about life in a commune. "How long did you live at Wheeler's Ranch? Do you remember it?"

"Only from my mom's recollections and photos. She told me we lived there until they tore it down."

Now Jersey is getting curious. "Destroyed it?"

"Bulldozed it. The place had always made the neighbors nervous and they were constantly harassing the Ridgefolk with drug busts and city ordinance violations and even law suits. The owner of the property, a musician who was on the road most of the time, he didn't care, because he was happy to provide space for the back-to-the-land people, as they were called; but the neighbors, they freaked out, so in nineteen seventy-three, mom said, they bulldozed what they could and burnt the rest."

"How awful. Where did you go?" Molly asks.

"My mother was fed up with commune life anyway so she moved back to Haight-Asbury, a part of San Francisco where she had lived before, and she got a part-time job in a local food co-op. Everything natural and local."

"And what about her husband, your father?" Molly asks.

"Husband? Are you kidding me? My hippie father? He left, too, but mom never found out where he went. Gone without a trace. Probably smoking grass and cultivating mushrooms somewhere, she told me."

"The kind that make you high." Jersey tells Molly with a nodding chin.

Molly is fascinated with the big sandwich that Rainbow is eating, heavy wheat bread slices filled with stacks of vegetables and topped off with avocado and bean sprouts. She takes big bites and chews fast during the breaks in her story.

"Would you like a bite?" Rainbow asks, noticing Molly's careful inspection of her sandwich.

"Oh, no. Sorry. I was just observing how healthful looking it is," Molly says, a little embarrassed.

"Well, yeah, with my mom working at the health food co-op I was raised on a steady diet of what's good for you: tofu, tempeh, black strap molasses, whole wheat flour, brown rice, lentils, legumes, and mung beans."

"I haven't heard of half of that stuff," Molly admits. "My dad insisted on meat and potatoes. Is it good?"

"Not so much good as good for you. And look at me, I grew into a pretty strong woman eating that hippie food, wouldn't you say?"

Jersey says, "My mom was into some of those diets, but mostly reading about them and taking supplements. She swore by that *Prevention Magazine.*"

"That's another thing," Rainbow says. The books. We had stacks of books about food in our house, each diet claiming to be more nutritious than the last. So, my mom would make me read these books for my book reports in high school. I got an A on *Diet for a Small Planet* and an A plus on Rachael Carson's

Silent Spring, you know, one of the first books on polluting the environment. But tell me, how the hell was I supposed to write a book report on the *Tassajara Bread Book?"*

When lunch is over, Molly saunters over to check her work on the gate she fixed, but as she turns around to see where the others are headed, she notices them standing close together by the out-building, looking at her as if to observe her closely, whispering to each other. That makes Molly nervous.

3

A DARK SECRET REVEALED

In the second week of July, Savannah tells Molly that the others are talking about her and want to know if it's true.

"Who?"

"Rainbow, Jersey, Verónica, Jessica. Everybody. Even the cooks."

"The cooks?"

"Thelma and Jolene. I've been telling them that I don't know anything, but they expect me to know because we're roommates."

"Know what?"

"Don't jerk me around, Molly. They're observing you and commenting. Asking if you're pregnant."

"Could be that I'm just putting on a little weight with the good food here."

"Could be, all right, but very unlikely. So, let's have the truth because I'm no mid-wife and wouldn't know jack shit about trying to deliver a baby. I'm just a student of bison birthing behavior. The theory part."

Molly is silent for a while, clutching the last remnant of the cool disguise she has been wearing these many weeks. She twirls the ringlets in her ponytail. Then she begins to shake violently like she's sitting on a train that's running off the track. She starts to sob, little gasps at first, and then like a child that can't stop crying. She tries to tell Savannah what happened, but it comes out all garbled, with incoherent blubbering about a farmhand, and being Catholic, and how she thought she was just going for a walk, and..."

"Hush now," Savannah says. "Sounds like you need to go to confession, sis. I just have one piece of advice: you better let Wayne know and tell him before someone else spills the tea."

"I can't. He'll fire me for sure and then I don't know what I'll do. I don't have any place to go." Molly abruptly realizes how ridiculous it was to imagine that she could hide her expanding abdomen forever. What was she thinking?

"You are a total train wreck, my friend." Savannah is shaking her head back and forth in broad slow strokes. "God help you."

"Well, what would you do?"

"I wouldn't get pregnant," Savannah says.

Molly finds the smugness in her voice irritating. "But what if you did?"

Savannah shrugs, turning her head away, her eyes drifting to the floor. "I'd probably take care of it."

"Well, good for you, but I decided not to kill my baby." Molly is indignant, raising her voice unexpectedly in her own defense. "But I can tell you that I'm scared to death and I sure as hell don't know what's going to happen to me next."

"Well, what's going to happen next is you're going to tell Wayne about this secret pregnancy of yours," Savannah says in a voice meant to be calming. "And then you go on from there." She picks up a tissue from beside her bed and offers it to Molly. "You know Wayne now," she says. "He's a kind man. You can see it in his face."

Molly pictures his kind face and that makes her start crying and sobbing and trying to explain it all over again, until Savannah says, "I feel really bad for you, Molly, but I can't take care of you. Understand? I've got my research to complete."

Molly lets two days pass, trying to find the right time—more like trying to work up the courage—to tell Wayne. Before she can, he slips her a note asking her to come over to his house for a few words. Conferences with employees are always held in Wayne's office so for sure he knows about her now and he's going to fire her privately. She's heard a rumor that Wayne has a temper and although he seldom loses it, when he does, you need to keep your head down until it's over. She hopes she will be spared a dose of anger like what she got from her father, although Wayne has every right to be upset with her for failing to disclose her pregnancy when she applied for the job. No matter how scared she is, she has to show up.

Molly is surprised to see a log cabin structure so nicely decorated on the inside with beautiful oil paintings hanging on flat white walls and built-in book cases on either side of a moss rock fireplace, an unusual combination of rustic and elegant. He offers her a place to sit in an old oak rocking chair, and she sits there rocking, knowing that she can't conceal that noticeable bump protruding from her belly any longer. She stares blankly at his denim jacket and cowboy hat on the wood pegs next to the front door. So, this is where he hangs his hat, so to speak. Is he alone in this swanky house? She just rocks, waiting for him to say what he has to say, controlling her urge to whistle while she waits. She doesn't mean to make him uncomfortable; it can't be easy for him, firing some young woman about to have a baby. "It's okay," she says, hoping to help him begin. "I know what you have to do."

He shakes his head back and forth slowly at a loss for words. Then he asks, "Who's the father?"

"A farmhand," she blurts out. "Older. In his late twenties. A real talker. Full of promises I didn't want to hear."

"I've known plenty of those guys," he says "That's why I don't even like having them around."

Is this why he hires all women? No randy cowboys to get the women in trouble. She tells him, "He persuaded me to go on a long walk one morning. I trusted him. I guess that was my mistake."

"Did you love him?"

"Oh gosh, no, but he said he loved *me*."

"Were you raped?"

The word jolts her and instantly her memory is catapulted back to images and sounds and movements she hoped were forgotten. Raped? She has no idea how to answer this. "Well, I told him to stop, but he didn't." She remembers how she struggled and implored him and screamed. "I tried to resist. Yelled as loud as I could. I guess I shouldn't have gone on that walk." she says.

"You think it was your fault?" Wayne asks, frowning.

The picture of that disgusting farmhand on top of her, holding her down by her wrists just keeps coming back to her over and over, and for the first time she wonders, because of Wayne's question, how it could have been her fault, young as she was and saying *no* like that so many times and struggling and screaming, but she still answers Wayne as she had answered her father. "Partly," she says.

"How old were you then?"

"At the time? I hadn't turned eighteen yet."

Wayne shakes his head back and forth. "Where is he now?"

"I haven't a clue. My dad fired him straight off. Better than shootin' him, I guess, though sometimes I have to wonder."

Wayne cracks a guarded smile at that. "Your parents blamed you?"

"Not my mom so much, she listened, but my dad, oh yes, he raised a terrible furor. Called me a slut. A little whore. Made me feel ashamed. He told me to get the hell out and never come back."

Wayne's eyebrows rise and seem to stick in place. "That's what I told my daughter, same exact words." His gaze goes off into space as he rubs a hand slowly down the back of his neck. "I lost it."

"You had a daughter?"

"And as you might suspect, a wife, too."

"You told your daughter to leave?" Molly can't believe her ears. Surely Wayne wouldn't do that.

"Same circumstances as yours only she said he was her boyfriend. Speaking those harsh words turned out to be the stupidest thing I ever did in my whole entire life because I never saw her again, or the baby, and two months later my wife left me."

Oh, my God, a farmhand got *his* daughter pregnant? That explains so much: why he hires all these women to work on the ranch and no cowboys. Being so kind to them, trying to make up for what he did to his daughter. Finally, she stammers, "You're...you're not going to fire me?"

"You've already been sent away once, and we both know that doesn't fix anything." His voice has a gentle but solemn tone that makes her want to cry.

"But what am I supposed to do?" She wrinkles up her nose and puts one hand on her tummy. "I'm terrified."

"A lot of these women here have delivered firstborn calves from young heifers. Take Rainbow, for example. And Jersey. No big deal to them. I'm sure they'll provide expert assistance, and folks will be standing in line wanting to help."

"It's not a calf, it's a baby," she says, frowning, her voice a little louder than she intends.

"And that's why we're going to get you in to Doctor Archuleta in Alamosa this week to see if everything is developing okay."

"But the birth?" she asks.

"That's a natural process, and like I say, you'll have lots of help."

"But then what? Where will I go? What will I do?"

"Maybe take it one step at a time. Don't panic. We'll take care of you for a while."

"That's so nice of you," she says, her voice cracking, not feeling deserving of such kindness.

"Maybe I have a soft spot in my heart now. It was an awful thing I did to my daughter. Horrible." He goes back to shaking his head.

A single tear rolls down Molly's cheek, not for herself but for him, and she brushes it away quickly, hoping he won't see, won't think she's weak.

"I've noticed that none of the bison on this range are married," he continues, "at least not as I can observe, but they sure do take care of the herd. The little ones are the responsibility of the whole herd. No such thing as an orphaned bison. We'll take care of you and your baby. At least for a while."

"I don't know how to thank you," she says, too sad to smile, too confused to know what to say.

As she walks back to the cabin, she feels the warmth from the summer sun, and the distant mountains seem closer and friendlier, not so forbidding now. She even feels a little bit hopeful. Strange how a mountain can make a person feel hopeful, but maybe it is more because of Wayne, the way he treated her.

After dinner that night—Molly notices that she is eating non-stop like a grazing bison—she returns to the cabin and finds a note from Savannah: "Gone to Pepe's. Back late." So, Molly is home alone again, if this pine box can be called *home*. She paces back and forth and then around in circles. It is the only home she has for right now, but if she is truthful with herself, she has to admit that it is not home, and to think of the Horseshoe, as folks call it, as her home is simply a delusion. At best, it is a stop-gap place to live until her baby is born, not a paradise but better than the tin-roofed shack where Rainbow was born in that hippie commune. Wayne did not throw her out like her father did, but Wayne's kindness shouldn't be taken for a long-term solution to her problems. This is a temporary sanctuary. When this baby is born and the summer job is completed here, she will need to have work and a place to stay where she can raise her baby. Take responsibility, Molly, she tells herself. But how terrifying. Well, she will just have to figure something out.

She pulls up one of the pine chairs, opens a window for some fresh air, and sits down to think. That's another nice thing about the ranch: there's time to think. Her secret will be out now. No more deception and denial. When the women ask Wayne about her, he will tell them, and she's sure they will be kind enough not to ask about who the father is. The women here aren't like that. They don't gossip. They are tight-lipped, tough, and tenacious. They stick together and she is beginning to feel like one of them.

She's glad she didn't disclose her pregnancy—what a horrible word—when she arrived, because concealing it gave her time to prove herself as a worker and earn Wayne's respect. But she never had to tell such a long lie as this one and she was getting sick of trying to hide her lump. It's interesting how a secret turns into a lie. She didn't actually tell a lie; it was a lie because of what she didn't tell. Anyway, now she can be herself. But is this herself? A pregnant teenager? She reaches down and folds her hands around her belly. She thinks she feels a heartbeat, then some movement, maybe a leg or arm. Oh, my god, there's a little person down there. Now the cat's out of the bag, which for sure has been a lot easier than it will be to get this baby out of her body. She can't begin to imagine how that will happen.

The next day she's staining a fence, working alone again in solitary confinement with her thoughts although this time she is really stirred up. Wayne's comments have sent her head to spinning and she's asking herself what really happened with Tommy that day. Even though she had pledged to leave his worthless carcass buried, she starts to relive the whole episode over again. Going back over it makes her jumpy as a toad and she wants to twist her hair round and round or just yank out a big clump of it, but that won't be easy with the big stained work gloves she's wearing. She contents herself with whistling. How could she have been so stupid? But like Wayne suggested, maybe it wasn't her fault.

Tommy Dawson was handsome and well built, and she was attracted to him even though she knew he was not meant for her, being without any college or even any aspirations in that direction. Tommy never said where he was from; was it Oklahoma, Arkansas, Texas? No one knew, and that was part of the mystery about him, his unspoken past, although her mother was sure that he had one and was probably running from it. After school, she had certain chores to do around the farm and Tommy always popped up next to her to throw her a few smiles and watch her move around. Like the other girls her age—they talked about this at school—she liked having the eyes of a good-looking older guy on her even though it made her uncomfortable. What exactly was he thinking as he watched her so carefully?

Being beautiful was never a part of her self-concept, or even an aspiration. She was certainly no Miss Kansas, although in the beginning of her senior year she noticed how female classmates and teachers would comment on how attractive she looked on a fairly regular basis. She had a reputation as a matchmaker, fixing up this one with that one behind the scenes, but she never had a boyfriend of her own because the boys all seemed way too young and immature. So it was nice when Tommy, standing there amidst the racket of the mooing cows, the clatter of their stanchions, and the metallic clank of the milking machines, started calling her *beautiful* and giving her compliments. Said she had gorgeous red hair, that he liked her smile, that she looked sharp that day, even though it was the same tattered sweat shirt and torn jeans she wore to the barn all the time, just freshly laundered. She knew he was flirting with her, but she didn't see anything so wrong about that even though he was older and she knew she shouldn't be encouraging it. It made her feel like she had some kind of power over him that she could make him come around and pay attention to her, because maybe that meant that someday she'd be able to attract a guy she really liked.

She can't remember exactly how they started to speak, but it wasn't long until they were talking about almost anything, and he seemed to like showing her that they agreed about most things. Once he said, "Let me say, most respectfully, it ain't no picnic working for your dad." And she remembers replying, "Tell me about it. How would you like to be his daughter?" He got a funny look, so she said "son," and they both laughed. So, they had a topic of conversation now, completely inappropriate of course, but it gave them something in common, complaining together about her dad.

Once he said he dreamed about kissing her and she giggled and asked if he meant dreaming in his sleep or daydreaming while he was working, and he said both. Looking back now, that's where she should have drawn the line and said something stern like "of course that's out of the question, Tommy," but she was actually wondering in her teen-age mind what it would feel like to be kissed by Tommy Dawson. So maybe that's where her trouble started right there.

Molly carefully pours more stain from the gallon bucket into the roller tray. She rolls the stain onto the cedar fence boards and goes back over them with a wide brush to catch places that didn't absorb it from the rolling. It only takes half a brain for work like that, but she enjoys it.

One Saturday in February, her parents and her little brother Danny went into town to do some long-neglected shopping. The nice clear morning, unseasonably warm, without a threat of a winter storm, made it a perfect day for the trip to Colby, twenty miles each way. She was dressed in a skirt and leggings ready to go, but at the last minute she begged to stay home to finish a book report for school. She remembers her mother asking, "You'll be okay alone?" and she nodded because she really thought she would. Tommy worked sometimes on Saturday mornings, but he was always gone by noon, sometimes sooner if the boss wasn't around. Shortly after they left, Tommy came knocking on the back door, asking for a glass of water. He never did that, but she let him in and filled a plastic cup for him, and that's when he invited her to go on the walk. She said she had school work to do, but he flashed his smile and found her coat hanging on the rack in the hallway and held it out for her like a real gentleman. Whatever happened to the line she was going to draw?

He took her on the path along the creek that flowed next to a pasture frozen over with a white crust of snow, that little trail being one of the few places to walk without dodging cow pies every step of the way. And on that walk, he told her he loved her, that she was beautiful, that he had been saving his money to get a place, and that he had plans for him and her. He promised her he would marry her when he got ahead a little financially. She remembers being shocked that he would say brazen stuff like that, so she just giggled each time and then she said, "Oh, Tommy, don't be ridiculous. I couldn't ever do anything like that." Maybe the word *ridiculous* hurt his feelings, kind of set him off, but he didn't show it. They just kept walking along until they reached the old grove of tall maples about a half mile behind the house.

They took a few steps along the path into the secluded maple grove and before she knew what he was doing, he had grabbed her in his arms and started kissing her. She thought maybe one kiss would satisfy his curiosity as it surely had hers, but when he tried again, that's when she said no. She remembers now clearly saying, "Stop, Tommy, no, no more. Stop!"

It was quiet there in the grove, not a sound except for the gurgling of the little stream nearby and the chirping of a few birds returned early from the South. She actually thought he would stop. Then she heard the sharp *zip* of a zipper and his fumbling with the big brass buckle on his leather belt and she started screaming. She remembers screaming loud like never before in her life, screeching and wailing, begging for him to stop, but who would hear her with the next farmhouse, her uncle's, being two miles down the road?

The rest is kind of a gruesome blur. She remembers him throwing her down in the rotted leaves and her twisting and resisting, doing pretty good for a while, but withering under his superior strength, her screams turning to whimpers of pain, while she just waited under the weight of his body for the tornado to be over. Scratching him or biting his hand was something she considered, but she wanted to come out of this ordeal alive without getting smacked around. She doesn't know how she got back to the house—maybe she passed out—but the next thing she remembered was waking up on the couch, suddenly horrified, knowing her family had returned.

Molly has finished staining the fence, and she wonders why she is just standing there with the brush in her hand, looking for unstained spots, as if her life depended on having that fence perfect. But she doesn't move. Doesn't whistle. Just stands there. And her brain kicks up questions like a cross examination on one of those judge shows on TV. Was it her fault? Partly. Was it his fault? Mostly. Was she raped? She hadn't thought about it that way until Wayne asked her, but now it sure seems like she was actually raped. After all, he forced her. Would she be able to prove it in a court of law, as they say, beyond a reasonable doubt? Hardly. Her word against his? No third-party witnesses. The defendant being innocent until proven guilty. And does that make her guilty until proven innocent? And the worst part would be tracking down Tommy, the guy with no past, and she didn't want any part of looking for and finding him, coming face to face with him again. If she made accusations against him, she would be picked apart by his lawyer right there in front of the whole world.

The questions keep coming, but the fence is finished.

Molly freely admits her condition now. She has even told Carlos, but he keeps asking her out for milkshakes anyway. Says they're good for her. She is ready now to talk to Savannah without outbursts of crying, to tell her about how it happened and why it happened and share with her roommate the worries she has about her uncertain future, but Savannah seems to be more interested in the parturition of bison, as she calls it, than the birth of a human. Rainbow and Jersey smile at Molly fondly and stop to ask her how she's doing, eager to help, telling her that Wayne wants her to be cared for graciously. Jessica and Verónica are still her friends and they're extra nice to her, but they speak to her with a condescending tone as if she were sick or handicapped. Thelma and Jolene sometimes slip an extra apple or pear into her sack lunch.

Wayne takes her to Doctor Archuleta, the OB in Alamosa—he and the old doc seem to be longstanding friends—and she finds out that everything is fine and that it's going to be a girl. The women are full of suggestions for names, like they've started some kind of contest or something. Wayne says that of all the names he's heard suggested, he likes Norma Lou, but it's really up to her. When her belly begins sticking out there so that only the blind would miss it, they all start referring to Norma Lou by name and they want to see if they can feel her move. Molly is not abandoned; to the contrary, everyone wants to know everything about her, like she is a pregnant celebrity. She continues with her regular assignments and she's proud about still being able to do her job responsibly. She notices that she's not been given any work that involves riding horses, but other than that, she does what everyone else does. And fixes stuff.

But now she's getting totally worked up about her only source of help coming from those tough women who help calve the heifers. Will they really know what to do? The shame of getting pregnant and the torment of *being* pregnant have left her depressed. How did she get into such a mess? Now she's gone and mutilated her whole life, smashed her future into smithereens. She hasn't had time or inclination to ponder the miracle growing inside her each day. More like a time-bomb. It makes her sad as the hoot of an owl and she longs for a visit by someone from back home, especially her mom. Because her father kicked her out of the entire family—he made that clear—she doesn't phone home, not even when she goes into town. Her mother writes to her each week, probably in secret, and Molly answers back, but she doesn't tell her how scared and lonely she is because she doesn't want to be the cause of her mom's having a stroke or heart attack or something awful like that. In her mother's last letter, her brother Danny enclosed a note saying he hoped she would come back soon, and that made her bawl for the better part of that afternoon, being sure that neither parent had told Danny why she was gone.

Like the sun appearing from behind a Kansas cloud, Wayne shows up from time to time to ask how she's doing. As she goes about her work, she feels like Wayne is being especially attentive to her, but then she has to remind herself that his concern is not expressly for her because he's attentive to everyone. That's his way of caring. So, she goes back to being lonely and scared and trying to hide her feelings. Always hiding something. But there's no way to hide this baby when your belly is screaming to the whole world that some guy got you pregnant. It's totally embarrassing to her being single and so young, so that when she has spare time she prefers to stay in the cabin.

What's that smell? Bacon? The aroma of cooking bacon is drifting over from the lodge on the cool breeze of an early August morning, flowing toward the cabin's open windows, more effective than an alarm clock. Molly sits up slowly and lowers her legs over the edge of the bed, not quite ready to begin another day thinking of herself as the farmer's daughter who was raped. That smell of bacon sets off a sudden burst of homesickness that chokes her up. Every morning her father ate a stack of bacon, eggs fried in the bacon grease, and buttered Wonder Bread toast, washed down with several cups of coffee brewed in an old campfire-style blue pot on the gas stove. Naturally he stirred into the coffee ample quantities of fresh cream from his own dairy. She wonders what name Rainbow would give to this breakfast. Maybe the Dairyman's Death Diet?

Molly remembers these details clearly just as she recalls her antique maple study desk, the closet full of her skirts and jeans and jumpers, and the pennants and pom-poms from Colby High decorating the upstairs bedroom to which she escaped each night and woke up to each morning. Will she ever see that room again? Probably not. And that's what makes her so sad this morning. Now that she comprehends that she was raped, she finds that she is growing more resentful each day that she was kicked out of her own house—her own room—by a father so lacking in understanding, so driven by his own interpretation of the events, that he was unwilling to listen to her and believe her description of what actually took place. Nothing could change his view that she flirted with Tommy Dawson and brought this on herself.

Remembering her father's breakfast renews her dedication to keeping herself healthy through this pregnancy, so when she goes up to the lodge, she assembles a collation of granola, whole wheat toast, and fresh fruit, things that will be nourishing for her and Norma Lou. She overhears Thelma and Jolene disagreeing about which is better for her: orange juice or cranberry juice. She listens with detachment to the empty conversation of her co-workers Jessica and Verónica, buses her dishes, and heads outside to cut the grass and weed the new beds of annuals she has planted behind the wall near the lodge. Bending over the petunias and marigolds is not so easy anymore, but maybe being that close to the flowers will inspire Norma Lou to love gardening, like listening to Mozart in the womb is supposed to make a kid smarter or love classical music. She needs to ask Wayne if she can plant some tulips and daffodils in a few weeks. That is, if she can bend over at all by then.

Working around the lodge has become so routine now that it doesn't even require half of her brain—more like one-eighth. The nostalgia for home this morning, oddly set off by the smell of bacon, is producing an intense longing to see her mother, or at least to talk to her, to let her know that the baby is growing, that she is taking good care of her health, and...and that she is totally freaked out with the thought of giving birth to a baby. It's bad enough that her mother won't be there, but to deliver in that cabin with a cowhand for a mid-wife really has her dreading the birth.

Was her mother worried like this when Molly was born? Obviously being the oldest, she was the first. She's pretty sure she was born in a hospital. Did her mother have natural childbirth, an anesthetic, or maybe even a Caesarian? She never talked with her mom about such things, maybe because she never thought about what her mother may have gone through bringing her into this world.

She tries to picture her mother's face, but the image is starting to lose focus, blurring a little in her memory. That's disconcerting. She can't let that happen. She thinks of her all the time, but maybe she should consciously try to picture her more. But which mental snapshot can she recall best? Her mother never smiled much, mostly if something struck her funny while she was reading, but the rest of the time she hardly smiled at all. Her life was hard, keeping the house, doing laundry, fixing the meals, and taking care of two kids—three if you count Father. Totally frazzled. Maybe there wasn't much in her life to smile about, and that's why the image Molly remembers most clearly is a face of unrelieved stress, as if her mom was always wondering if she had done everything she was supposed to do and done it right, perpetually on guard for her husband's criticism for some trivial mistake or perceived omission.

It would be wonderful to sit down with mom and talk about all of the things they never talked about and compare notes on being pregnant.

As August begins to fly by and Norma Lou continues to grow, Molly gets more and more anxious about how this baby of hers is going to get born. She arranges her work schedule to be with Rainbow and Jersey in the corral for the next few days so that she can ask a few questions. Working side by side, there's time to talk without actually looking up at each other, which suits Molly fine because it gives her a chance to hide her embarrassment and slip in an indirect question. "Where did this natural childbirth idea come from?"

"You're asking me?" Rainbow says. "From what I understand from my mom, everything was supposed to be natural with the hippies: natural foods, natural hair, the natural look with no make-up."

"Going topless in the communes," Jersey adds, always ready with a taunting dig.

"Not topless, Jersey, so much as without a bra." She shakes her head like sometimes she's had enough of Jersey's annoying observations. "So natural childbirth was just one more natural thing at that time." She looks up at Molly for a moment and asks, "What is it you really want to know about childbirth?"

"I just want to know what I'm supposed to do," Molly says, stretching out the work gloves, palms up, at the end of her long arms.

Jersey laughs and says, "Push like hell and scream."

Jersey gets a frown from Rainbow. "We'll do some exercises to get you ready," Rainbow reassures her. "It's a natural process, like a cow giving birth to a calf."

There they go with the cows and calves again. That's never reassuring to Molly. And that word *natural*. "Wayne told me that you ladies..."

"Oh, please don't call us ladies," Jersey insists.

"Sorry." Molly's not sure what's wrong with being called a lady. "He said you were experts with calves, but this is a baby, so tell me, how did you have *your* children?"

"All three natural," Rainbow says, shrugging.

"I just have one, but same way," Jersey says.

"Okay so I guess you guys know what to do." She wonders if it was all right to call them guys. No one objects. "I'm just a little scared, that's all."

"Oh, honey," Rainbow says, giving her a little squeeze around the shoulders. "Try not to worry. We'll be right here for you."

They all concentrate on their work without speaking for a while and Molly gets lost in her thoughts. Natural childbirth still seems pretty vague to her, but what's the alternative? She has hardly any money, no insurance, and no way to pay for a doctor or hospital. Maybe natural is what you do when you're broke. She wonders if her dad realizes that he has turned her into a charity case, maybe even a welfare mom. He wouldn't be happy with that.

Molly doesn't sleep very well that night—couldn't get comfortable—and the next morning she has a new disquieting worry: What if Norma Lou is blind or deaf or physically handicapped? What if she is mentally challenged because Tommy Dawson is her father? Seriously, couldn't that happen? A baby as dumb as Tommy? She is nervous about raising a normal baby, so how could she possibly raise... She can't let her thoughts go there.

She chows down enough buckwheat griddle cakes and fruit for two, chug-a-lugs a tall glass of orange juice, and picks up her sack lunch before catching a ride out to the corral with Rainbow and Jersey in Rainbow's old truck. When they are working side by side again, Molly blurts out, "What if Norma Lou isn't normal?"

Jersey jumps right in with, "You mean like..."

Rainbow gives Jersey a stony look this time and cuts off what will be another predictably provoking remark. "We don't need to put any disturbing ideas into Molly's troubled mind just now, do we, Jersey?" Then she turns to Molly. "Every mother worries about that. It's natural. But the probability is very low at your age to begin with, and here on the ranch you are out in the fresh air and sunshine, eating good food and..."

"Working hard with nice people like us," Jersey adds, apparently getting the point. "Like Rainbow says, it's very unlikely."

"I just hope Norma Lou is okay." Molly says, "because I don't even know how to take care of a normal baby."

"Maybe we can start calling her Normal Lou," Jersey suggests.

4

SAVANNAH, WAYNE, AND THE MAJESTIC BEASTS

On Molly's day off in the third week of September, she has accepted an invitation from Carlos to see the leaves, but not without teasing him a little. "We have leaves in Kansas, Carlos."

"Oh, but in Colorado you need to see the aspen leaves."

"What's the big deal about these aspen leaves? What do we do? Watch them fall?"

"So, you really don't know about the quaking aspen turning bright gold, glowing in the sunshine, shimmering when the wind passes through them?"

"I guess not. Wow! You're such a poet."

"You need to go with me. I know just where to go."

She tightens up the muscles in her shoulders, remembering that other walk in a grove of trees, but she is pretty sure she can trust Carlos. Besides, he knows now that she is pregnant.

He stops by for her at the ranch in his SUV and she notices on the back that it's called a Nissan Pathfinder. Well, for sure she needs to find a path, so maybe Carlos can come up with some ideas. They turn right on Route 160, passing Pepe's Cantina, as they head west toward Monte Vista and Del Norte.

After they turn right on 129 toward Creede, Molly asks, "What's this gleaming clear river we're following here?"

"Headwaters of the Rio Grande. You know, part of the border with Mexico. It all starts here in the San Juan Range, the mountains you see on the other side of the Valley." Carlos is mostly quiet, but when he speaks, he has a deep resonant voice. She likes that deep voice. They follow the river for a few miles and then Carlos pulls onto a dirt road that climbs into the forest. He glances over at her and says, "I hope this won't be too bumpy for you."

"I'll just provide a little support." She laces her fingers together underneath the baby. "But thank you for thinking about Norma Lou." She grins and he smiles back. For some reason, she's not uneasy with Carlos. She trusts him. For sure he wouldn't take advantage of a pregnant woman. Maybe this baby will protect her from men for a while.

Part way up the mountain, Carlos finds a place to pull off the road, and the way he does it makes her think it's a spot familiar to him. There is a sweet little hewn wood picnic table set right there in the middle of an aspen grove, the trees all glowing like gold in the sun as he promised.

"You had this all planned, didn't you?"

"My parents brought us here as kids. It's a fantastic place to appreciate the aspen. Here, sit here. What do you think?"

What she thinks is that it is an incredibly romantic spot being wasted on someone incapable of being anyone's girlfriend. Carlos helps get her seated at the table and then goes to the Pathfinder and pulls out a basket full of everything needed for a fancy picnic, including a container of fried chicken and a bowl of rice with black beans. "Mother wanted you to sample her cooking. She's a pretty fantastic cook."

While they are eating, Molly says, "I've been assuming all along that you work at Pepe's. Is that true?"

"Oh, no, I just go to Pepe's once in a while for a beer and to see my friends. My only work there is that sometimes I have to help Pepe throw guys out when they are disrespectful to the young ladies."

"Like Sonny. But then what's your work?" she asks.

"I'm a potato farmer."

She doesn't know what to say next but eventually she comes up with, "What kinds of potatoes do you grow?"

"Mostly russets, you know the popular one for baking, like Centennial and Rio Grande. But then we raise some yellows as well, mostly Yukon Gold."

"I didn't know they raised potatoes around here."

"My family owns one of the largest potato farms in the San Luis Valley."

"Why do they call it *the Valley?*"

"It's a high plateau, around seven thousand, six hundred feet and runs about a hundred miles north and south clear into New Mexico. But it is a valley between the two big mountain ranges and it's filled with potato farmers like us, about a hundred and fifty families in all."

"So, is there something special about these potatoes?"

"Yeah, there is actually. Because the Valley was once an ancient lake bed, the soil is filled with minerals and the irrigation is from snow melt runoff. We are certified potato growers and we've won our share of awards at the annual potato festival in Monte Vista. We also raise a little barley to sell to the folks who make Coors Beer, but that's a sideline."

"And your family owns the potato farm."

"Yes, and I'm already part owner with my dad and brother. Someday my older brother and I will own it all."

"Just the two of you?"

"I have a little sister still in high school, but she says she doesn't want anything to do with potatoes. And there's *abuela*, too, my grandma."

"Has your family lived here a long time?" She sees Carlos grinning. "Why are you smiling? You're laughing at me."

"It's not you, it's the situation. My great, great grandfather left the Ute Reservation and married a Spanish woman."

"So, you're not Mexican?"

"I know you will think I am making this up, but our family name is Ouray, going all the way back to a chief of the Utes although we aren't direct descendants."

"So, the Utes were the Indians in this region before anyone else?"

"Only the Great Spirit was here before the Utes." Carlos grows quiet for a moment and then says with a half-smile, "So I am not one of those guys who work in a Mexican bar as a bouncer, if that's what you thought."

"Nope. You're more like a rich Indian prince."

"Well, I've never heard it put that way before." He laughs and shakes his head. "But that's just half the family history. Do you want to hear the rest?"

"Sure."

On my mother's side they are all old Spanish, people who came directly from Spain and settled here before the so-called pioneers came out from the East. The Valley is full of us."

"Really?"

There's a little town south of Alamosa called San Luis. It's the oldest non-native town in Colorado and it was settled by the Spanish. One member of *abuela's* family started a grocery store there in eighteen fifty-seven that still operates today."

"I didn't know any of that history."

"Few people do. It never got into the high school history books, that's for sure."

"We just learned the states, the capitals, and the presidents, over and over again each year because no one actually learned them from the previous year."

When they're finished eating and talking, Carlos packs the picnic back into the Pathfinder. They just sit at the picnic table awhile enjoying the breeze in the aspen grove. He rubs his hands together over and over like he's trying to get up the courage to ask her something personal. Finally, he says, "You've never told me how you got pregnant, only that you are."

Molly knew that this day would come but she still doesn't know how to explain it to Carlos. She leans forward with her elbows on the table and her face in her hands. "It's painful but I can tell you. Not all of the details, I can't stand to go over that." She sits up and looks at Carlos directly. "It was a farmhand named Tommy Dawson."

"Did you love him?"

"Oh, no. Nothing like that." She waves a hand in emphatic dismissal. "And after talking to Wayne—I had to tell him after I started showing—I've come to think...I was raped."

"Raped? My god, Molly, how awful."

They are both silent for a moment as she ponders her humiliation and wonders what he is thinking of her now. "My dad said it was my fault, blamed me, and threw me out of the family."

"Out of the family? That's why you are at the ranch?"

"I had to leave. Get a job somewhere."

"You must miss your home."

She nods, biting her lower lip. "Especially knowing that I can't go back."

Carlos looks stunned, like he's having trouble processing this startling story. "You say the guy's name was Tommy Dawson? He needs to be brought to justice."

Molly doesn't mention her reluctance to appear in court, so she just says, "Fat chance of that. He's long gone."

"That's terrible." Carlos looks away.

Molly presses both hands to her jaw as if to soothe a toothache. "That's why someone as dignified as you doesn't need to be burdened by a girlfriend with a baby, especially me, carrying a child whose father is an ignorant farmhand. It's left a terrible stain and I don't know how to wash it away." Now that Carlos knows this about her, he probably won't stop by anymore. She thought she could hold back the tears, but she starts to cry. Suddenly she realizes that she really likes Carlos, but knows she doesn't have a chance with him, nice as he is. He's a rich and handsome guy with plenty of opportunities for a decent life with a respectable woman. So why would he like her? She can't seem to stop crying.

Carlos puts an arm around her, comforts her, dries her tears, and finally when she calms down, he says, "You are carrying many heavy baskets. It's an expression we have for people with a lot of troubles."

Molly doesn't respond. She's looking down at the first layer of freshly fallen leaves on the ground. There's no pattern, no order, but it's beautiful.

They sit silently together for a moment until he suggests that they go for a little hike. They start to stroll up a hushed dirt road overhung with tall old aspen, their lustrous gray trunks and shimmering leaves of luminous gold standing out against the dark green spruce deep in the forest. The smell of the evergreens mixed with the scent of aspen is unlike anything Molly remembers. She takes a deep breath that revives her. Suddenly she asks, desperately wanting to change the subject and get out of the spotlight, "Did you go to college?"

"For three years, but then my father had heart surgery and I needed to stay home and help my brother harvest the potatoes. I never graduated."

"Did you like the university?" she asks, calculating that he must be in his early twenties now.

"Well, I studied agriculture, soil science and land management, but what I liked most was the courses I took for my general requirements and electives: a course on Impressionist painters, a survey of English literature, and an American poetry class where we studied Native-American writers and all the famous poets like Longfellow, Sandburg, Poe, Emily Dickinson, clear up to Robert Frost."

"So, you like to read? Me, too. I had a teacher this year, Mrs. Braxton, who taught me to enjoy reading novels." She throws him a faint smile. "Maybe you *are* a poet...hiding inside a potato skin." Then she says, "Geez, I'm sorry. I really had you all wrong. A bouncer at Pepe's?" He's strong and sensitive, the kind of guy she had hoped to meet someday. But now? In this condition?

When she blinks, she still feels the wet tears hanging on her eyelashes.

On the drive home, back along the river, across the abandoned railroad tracks, and through the small towns with their speed traps and traffic lights, Carlos is quiet. Maybe he's just watching the road, but he could be thinking about all that was said. At first Molly wants to know what he is thinking, but then she realizes that he may not be having very positive thoughts about her anymore. And if he is not, wouldn't it be best not to know what he is thinking? Does she even want him to be having nice thoughts about her, messed up as she is?

It's hard to stay awake on the passenger side with the engine humming and soft music playing on that satellite radio he has. She's not sure she's staying awake all the time and her thoughts appear to her as fleeting sensations that pass over her and then drift away like the pink clouds on the eastern side of the sunset. She tells herself that it really doesn't matter what Carlos thinks about her because she is in no position to respond to any feelings he might have for her anyway. She doesn't have the time or interest to be developing a romantic friendship. Besides, she knows she is completely incapable now of relating to a man even one as special as Carlos. So that finishes it. She's not ready for male friendship.

She must have drifted off because she awakens, glances out the window at the scenery to try to locate where she is, and suddenly feels beset with sadness and melancholy. She has the sensation that her life is completely over now as far as attracting any nice guy. No respectable man would ever want her now with a baby on her arm. How embarrassing it must be for a guy to have a girlfriend with a baby that's not his. Who wants a cow with a little calf branded "R" for rape? It's not a question of whether or when she's ready for male companionship. Forget that. The choice is not hers, it's his, and no man in his right mind would choose her in such a battered condition. At the tender age of eighteen, she is done!

Carlos looks like he is having deep thoughts, too, maybe second thoughts. He's probably trying to think of some graceful way to end their friendship now that he knows what he knows. Sometimes it's best to keep silent. He can't know her thoughts and she can't know his. That way at least he won't know what a shambles her life is. Our private thoughts are our last refuge from the world, the one impenetrable castle where we can hide. Who said that? Someone famous or was that Molly O'Reilly's gem of wisdom on an old book report?

The song playing on the radio sounds like something from those Lawrence Welk reruns her dad used to watch. Where is Carlos getting this music? Is there a WAARP channel?

She must have fallen asleep again, soundly this time, because the next thing she knows they have come to a stop in the parking lot of the lodge at the Horseshoe.

"Sorry for drifting off," she says, shaking her head to wake up.

"It's okay," he replies. "Maybe you're sleeping for two."

She twists around and struggles to step out. "Thank you for everything," she says. "I had a wonderful time." Is that all she can think of to say after all he did to make such a fantastic day? She sounds so juvenile. Then she asks, "Where is the potato farm? Is it far for you to get home?"

"About half an hour on the back roads. I don't go back through Alamosa." He walks her back to the cabin and she takes his arm to keep from tripping in the fading twilight. As he opens the door for her—it's never locked—he says, "I hope I can see you again soon. Get some rest. You're going to be okay. The Great Spirit is watching over you."

She is shocked that he wants to see her again, but his words, his blessing, make her feel better and she smiles at him. Why doesn't it bother Carlos that she has someone else's baby inside her growing bigger each day?

Molly has been mowing and trimming around the lodge today, maybe the last time for the season, and she finishes early, early enough to be in the cabin when Savannah comes home.

"Hey, what are you doing with my binoculars?" Savannah asks, entering the cabin without saying hello or asking how Molly is doing.

"I'm fixing the case. Nice aluminum case here, but a screw is missing from the hinge, and the top is going to fall off any minute unless it's fixed. I can stop if you have a problem with my touching your binoculars." She lifts her hands abruptly from the case held between her knees.

"No, that's okay. It's just that they're really expensive and I need them for my research."

"Which is why I thought the case deserved a little attention. It took me forever to find the right size screw replacement up at the shop, but I've got one now. I just like fixing stuff, as you may have noticed; like the towel racks aren't falling off anymore, the float in the toilet actually shuts off, and the window screens now keep out the flies. Which is what screens are supposed to do, you know."

"Yeah, well, thanks. I didn't know it was you doing all that stuff. That's really nice of you." Savannah throws down a clipboard and stack of papers onto her bed.

"How's the study coming along?" Molly asks without looking up from her work with the binocular case. She wishes she could fix the relationship with Savannah, too, hoping for her to be just a little friendlier and more understanding.

"Most of the births happened before I arrived. From what I can gather by talking to people, they all seem to give birth standing up. The bison, not the people."

For a fleeting moment Molly pictures a bison rearing up on its hind legs like a horse. Can they even do that? "Which for them is on all fours, right?"

"I guess that would be so." Savannah looks puzzled. "And the males are always absent."

"That figures. How big is your sample?"

"Sample?" Savannah registers surprise. "You know about research?"

"My pre-calculus course had some statistics—populations and samples;

mean, median, and mode; and standard deviations. Great teacher. Quiet. Rational. Hardly ever cracked a smile, except when she told a subtle joke like: Did you hear about the statistician who drowned in a river that averaged only six inches deep?" Molly checks to see if Savannah got the joke and she is pretty sure she didn't. "So how big is your sample?" she asks again.

"Well, uh, yeah, I mean, that's part of the problem. It's so hard to catch them actually giving birth."

"How many births have you seen?"

"Two. Right after I arrived."

"Two? To generalize to a population of two thousand from a sample of two? Maybe you ought to change the study to their procreation behavior. You might catch them at that more often."

"Bison fucking? Oh, yeah, I see that all the time now, but that's not what I came here to study."

"If you changed topics, what would your professor say?"

"My advisor? Oh, she'd probably go along. She should have known I was going to be too late for empirical observation."

"She? Well, hey, *she* might like the new topic. But you'd need to change the name of your study from 'Bison Birthing Behavior' to..."

"Yeah, to 'Bison Fucking Behavior.' Or maybe just 'The Fucking Bison Study' because really I'm so sick of that damn research now."

By then they are both laughing together and Molly thinks this is probably as close as she's going to get to a friendship with Savannah. "Here. Your case is fixed. You may need these binoculars more than ever."

One lovely afternoon in mid-October—why is it called Indian summer?—Molly has a little free time and decides to mosey out along the gravel trail in front of the lodge, a loop of more than a mile that winds through tall cottonwood trees and their fallen branches, everything kept natural. The trail is used mostly by guests, particularly older guests, for taking a stroll across relatively flat land, but today Molly wants to go off by herself for a little solitude and this is the closest place at hand. She remembers that Carlos told her that the town Alamosa means *under the cottonwoods*. There's no one out here today except for a few rabbits and prairie dogs.

Autumn has its own beauty and special colors here on the ranch. The yellow leaves from the cottonwoods are mostly down on the ground now, providing a bright carpet for the orange and red undergrowth dotted with sage and rabbit brush. Occasionally she spots an old farm implement, such as a plow or hay rake, that sits comfortably nestled in the landscape, adding its own rustic touch to the setting, as if it had naturally stopped functioning in that very place to trade in its usefulness for scenic decoration. Beyond the grove of cottonwoods, the Western wheat grass looks like it stretches clear across the horizon toward the other side of the Valley, its boundary marked by the distant San Juan Range, formed nineteen million years ago from igneous rock, she remembers from her tour-guide speech to guests.

Molly feels like a duck waddling down the trail between the grasses and sedges and she'd like to sit down and soak her swollen feet in a rushing stream, but there is no river on this ranch, only irrigation ditches filled with water for the cattle and bison. The pointed red leaves of an occasional oak still cling to their branches, defying the approach of winter. Absorbed in her worries and traipsing around all alone, she hears a rustling sound on the path behind her. Is she being followed? Perhaps a pronghorn antelope or a stray deer? When she twists around and fixes her eyes on the spot where the sound came from, she recognizes Wayne hurrying toward her, so she waits for him.

"Are you okay?" he asks as he catches up with her.

"Just trying to take a little walk."

"Excuse the intrusion. I saw you heading out this way from my office, and I began to worry. You've looked mighty sad the last few days. You're sure you are all right?"

"Everything's fine. Well, not really. Did I say fine? I admit I've been brooding a bit lately, but I can't drown myself without a river and there's no canyon to fall into on these grasslands. I just wish I could sit down for a while, soak my feet in a rushing stream, and talk to someone. As long as you're here, that someone might as well be you."

She sees him glancing around and the next thing she knows he has swept her up and put her on a big deadwood tree trunk a few steps off of the trail. My God, he is strong as a bison, steady and sure-footed, too. "You'll have to imagine the stream," he says, "but there's no reason why you can't take off those boots." She tries to bend over to remove her boots, but she can't quite reach, so he helps tug them off and as she flexes and stretches her feet, she makes believe she's dangling them in the cool water of a babbling brook. "Where are the rivers when you need them most?"

"Well, there's one over by the sand dunes, but it's dried up this time of year." He sits opposite her on a fallen log and they talk for a while.

She tells him she's been thinking about those questions he asked her about whether it was her fault or if she got raped. "I'm sure now that I was raped and I'm starting to get really angry and resentful about what has happened to me."

"That's natural," Wayne says, "once you see what really took place. It's a shame the jerk got off so easy."

"I've been thinking about that, too."

"Was it ever reported?"

"Not that I know of, but I really can't see myself in a courtroom facing his lawyers."

"Well, don't forget, he's not going to be too eager to be in that courtroom either. He's the one who broke the law and it's a serious offense, so he's probably on the run."

"Yeah, to find his next innocent victim."

"See, that's the problem. It just goes on and on."

Then she tells him how anxious she is about the delivery and fretful over the future. "I guess they call it depression, whole days of being sad and tearful. That's just not me." She looks up at him sheepishly and tries to smile.

"Seeing me now would you believe that I used to be a cheerleader?"

"Hey, you had a really horrible experience, but you're young and in good health. I'm sure everything will be fine with the birth of this baby. Women have been having babies..."

"Since Adam and Eve," she finishes his sentence.

"Oh, long before that," he says with a twinkle. "Thousands upon thousands of years. It's hard to imagine how, but the species did survive."

"Somehow."

And these cottonwoods," he says, looking up at them, "most of them are more than one hundred years old. They survived."

"Well, yeah, but look at all the dead trunks and branches and stumps on the ground here."

"I guess that's the difference between looking up and looking down." He smiles and runs a hand through his hair. "Heck, I would be pleased as punch to live a hundred years."

"You've got a point, I guess." There is a moment of silence as Molly collects her fears. "Okay, I know I will be nearly hysterical giving birth, but let's say this baby gets born and I survive that, how am I going to raise little Norma Lou? I don't know anything about how to raise a baby let alone earn a living at the same time. I'm going to be like one of those barn swallows up there," she says, motioning with her head to the sky, "zigzagging around. No plan, no future, just dipping and diving for the next meal."

"What the barn swallows know is that the future usually takes care of itself," he reminds her, "so you just need to be ready for the unexpected."

"Well, this whole dang thing was unexpected, so I guess I'm experienced now on expecting the unexpected." She's not sure that what she just said makes any sense at all, but it makes Wayne grin.

"Just be calm," he advises and changes the subject. He asks if the old timers have told her about the bison roundup, and she says she's heard plenty about it from Rainbow and Jersey and she's starting to get the picture.

"The roundup is the most important thing we do on this ranch," he says, "and potentially the most dangerous. Wild animals can be unpredictable. We use the most modern equipment and design, but I don't want anything to happen to you or Norma Lou. I'd like you to see it and participate, but let's give you a simple job where you can be safe."

"Count me in. I'll be careful," she promises.

During the first week of November, the whole staff is devoted to twelve-hour days for the bison roundup. When Molly gave tours to the guests, she showed them the buildings where the roundup took place, and she knew Savannah's speech by heart. "Growing this herd," she used to say, "to bring back a once-endangered species is an elevating mission, but there's no income to the ranch because we don't take them to market. They're just living off their endowment." She had described many times what happens in the roundup, but seeing it in real time live action is something else.

The first objective is to get the herd headed toward the holding area.

Wayne has discovered that the most effective way to do this is to use a low flying single-engine plane to get them moving and riders on dirt bikes to coax them in the right direction without causing a stampede. They are given cake, a compressed grain, as an enticement to keep them moving along. Next, they are forced into fenced areas and then into holding pens. It takes metal pipe fencing to hold them when they are being crowded together. Then gradually they're grouped in smaller pens before they enter the chute. My God, the women on this ranch who move the bison are as strong and brave as soldiers in an army.

The bison aren't really happy about being confined, so that's why they have a special chute system at the Horseshoe designed especially by Temple Grandin, an autistic woman who used her own fears of human contacts as intuitions about how to calm the bison and reduce the stress for them as much as possible. The chute curves, so they don't see much of each other, and the herders move in the opposite direction from the bison, instead of working behind them. Natural light pours through ceiling skylights to keep the setting as natural as possible. Hydraulic gates, controlled by one operator from the center of the barn, keep the bison moving through one at a time in a steady flow. Temple Grandin also designed the final portion of the chute using ideas from a safe compartment that she built for herself, to which she would retreat to restore calm after disturbing human encounters that exacerbated her autism. When the bison finally enter that yellow securing chute, feeling it clamp down on them gently no matter their size, they become calm and are quickly given a vaccination and pregnancy test. A tail sample is taken to see if they are pure bison or part beef. The goal at the Horseshoe is 99.6% bison. When they are released, they go back to the wild herd to nibble away on the shortgrass prairie.

Molly's job is to help Rainbow giving shots at the yellow chute. It's like being a veterinarian's assistant, making sure that supplies are ready and handing her things at the right time. "Routine work, but important," Wayne says, looking over her shoulder at each bison individually as it passes through. "This is where we get reacquainted with the herd each year. And of course, we've got people posted to count the number of females and males, the first-year calves, and the old bison that need to be culled. Our job is to keep the herd growing, but not too fast. Thank god we haven't had trouble with poachers or trophy hunters." A baby bison enters the line, nudged on lovingly by one of the grown-ups from the herd. Why are baby animals so cute? Will her baby be cute?

"Do you know how old each bison is?" Molly asks.

"Sure. From the first two numbers on their tag, but it's also possible to tell their age by examining the front leg hair, which never sheds."

"What do you do with that information?"

"It's good to know," Wayne says, shrugging, a little embarrassed that he doesn't know.

"Do you have a profile of the herd by age?"

"I'm not sure what that is exactly."

"By computing how much stock you have at each age level, you can construct an age pyramid and predict the trajectory of growth or decline. They do that routinely on dairy farms. You should be able to predict herd size for the next few years into the future."

He looks at her for a moment a little dumbfounded but truly impressed. "Can you help me do that when this is over?"

She grabs her bulging abdomen. "You mean after this is over? Sure, I'd be glad to do a little brain work for a change."

Molly is bedazzled by seeing this huge operation up close. These guys are really huge majestic beasts, five to six feet tall with that humped back and weighing as much as two thousand pounds. Massive oversized heads and big thick horns. Their dark eyes peer out with a warm glance, as if there is a being with feelings beneath all that muscle and fur. They stand there, impatient with their confinement, in an awesome embodiment of power and force, lumbering forward as the next gate opens before them, tossing their heads in a swagger of confidence, ready to use those horns.

At first, they scare her a little, but by the second day she's more relaxed. It's noisy, too, with all those bellowing bison and women hollering back and forth at each other to coordinate the flow of the animals inside and outside of the barn. For Molly, it helps keep her mind off of being so uncomfortable in what is supposed to be the last week of her pregnancy...until she sees another baby bison come through the line. It's hard not to have babies on the brain when her due date is so close.

5

UNNATURAL CHILDBIRTH AND SOLITARY MOTHERHOOD

At the beginning of the following week, with the roundup complete and the bison once more stretched out along the grassland's horizon grazing contentedly, the women usually begin to pack up. It's the end of the tourist season—the lodge closed at the end of October—and only a skeleton staff remains through the winter months, mostly the commuting old timers like Rainbow and Jersey. But this year, no one seems to be in a big hurry to leave. Maybe they're hanging around to meet Norma Lou. Even Savannah is staying through the next week to finish her fucking bison study before heading back to LSU.

On Wednesday, Molly wakes up feeling that this will be the day. A few minutes later she yells out to Savannah from the shower, "I think my water's broke."

"Hang on," Savannah replies, tossing her head. "I'll set things in motion. But then I'm outta here. I'm not exactly a fan of human births. Besides, with mating season over I need to write up the results of my new study." She grabs a stack of folders and shoots out the door seemingly propelled by an uncontrollable desire to escape. Molly doesn't know what Savannah means by "set things in motion" but she soon finds out. Women begin arriving with kettles for water and stacks of towels. Rainbow, taking command, comes over to her and reminds her that she will be the midwife and Jersey will be her birthing coach. One of the spare beds is set up as a makeshift birthing station. Thelma and Jolene carry in a handmade pine cradle. Jessica and Verónica are standing by outside ready to help, while some with nothing to do just pace back and forth in front of the cabin, as if substituting for the absent father.

"What's going on?" Molly asks. "How do you all know what to do? I just found out and here this whole team arrives totally prepared."

"They have their prearranged assignments," Jersey says.

"Assignments? Has the staff been given work assignments for the delivery of my baby?

"Let's just say that they care and know what to do," Rainbow clarifies.

The first contraction hits hard. It doubles her up and almost knocks her over. Rainbow walks her over to a chair.

"Sit tight," Jersey says, "They get worse."

When the pain eases momentarily enough for Molly to catch her breath, she says, "I don't know how I feel about everyone getting extra work assignments on my account."

"Months ago, Wayne looked hard at you, nodded, and told us to mind the herd," Rainbow says. "We knew what that meant. So here we are, setting up our version of a miniature ER. Surely you don't think this is the first time there's been an emergency at Horseshoe Ranch."

Jersey puts two hands on Molly's shoulders and looks her straight in the eye. "Now you can lie down over there, or squat, or swing from the rafters— whatever the hell it is you want to do—and we'll jiggle this squirming little Norma Lou out of you lickety-split."

Rainbow frowns at Jersey and tells Molly, "Maybe just lie down on this bed and try to remember the exercises I taught you, how to breathe, how to push. Right now, all you need to do is relax and breathe. Remember it's a natural process. You're in good hands. Come on, child, breathe!"

Actually, Molly feels like she *is* in good hands. These women exude such confidence and composure that she forgets to be afraid.

Norma Lou, it turns out, is a perfectly formed baby, healthy and vigorous, breathing well, and crying sweet little whimpers and coos. She has tiny hands and amazing little toenails on her doll's feet, which are freed at last to kick without running into mother's ribs. Bright red hair is matted against her beautifully shaped head, what Molly's father would have called *"hair-red-ity."* Molly is holding her close and as she looks down on her she is sure Norma Lou is the most beautiful baby in the world, totally unique like no other. She hasn't seen many babies and she doesn't remember anything about her brother as a baby, but she's sure that this one is completely special. Just look at her, so perfectly formed and already so beautiful. Hard to tell just yet, but it looks like there's not a sign of her father in her. Then it dawns on her, like the angel Gabriel has come down from heaven to whisper in her ear: look at the miracle in your arms, how this gorgeous baby, without fanfare, mysteriously grew all by herself while her mother has been mowing lawns and tending cattle and bison. "How does it happen?" Molly asks in wonder, not really expecting an answer.

Rainbow is standing at her side still, sharing Molly's euphoria. "Mighty amazing, isn't it?"

"To think that I produced this sweet little baby without even lifting a finger. I mean, I know I did it, but..."

"Well," Rainbow says, "it's even more amazing once you understand the process: how the sperm and egg come together, how the neutral stem cells are formed at first, and then how organ tissue begins to form for a tiny heart, a little brain."

"And it's all done in secret, like I didn't know anything that was going on, sort of behind my back."

"Actually, it's in front of your back," Jersey points out.

Rainbow rolls her eyes. "And you know what's even more amazing? Ontogeny recapitulates phylogeny."

"What the heck is that?" Molly asks. "You sound like Savannah."

"That phrase is about the only thing I remember from biology. It means that as the embryo grows and develops it goes through the stages of evolution, the lines of descent from a fish to a tadpole to a frog, and on to a human. It is one of the startling proofs of evolution."

"And it all just happens."

"One more natural process," Rainbow says, beaming down at Norma Lou, asking if she can hold her. Then in a moment she passes her to Jersey, who takes her to the front window to hold her up over her head to show her off. The folks standing outside peep through the window as if it was a hospital nursery and then come storming through the door with a whoop to get a look because they can't wait any longer to see that baby. Among them are Thelma and Jolene and the dining room staff, Jessica and Verónica and their friends, and some people that Molly hardly knows.

Later in the afternoon, Doctor Archuleta, the OB from Alamosa, stops by and asks to see Molly. He listens to the baby's heart and lungs and counts fingers and toes. He reviews the details of the birth process with Rainbow, whom he seems to know well, and presents some forms to be filled out and papers to sign. Realizing that he doesn't have anything else to do, he talks to Molly for a while, congratulates her on having produced such a little package of loveliness, and leaves. She is exhausted, but too pepped up to sleep. She tells herself to calm down.

Just as she begins to doze off, she is awakened by a soft knock on the door. Wayne asks if it would be disturbing anything for him to come in. He takes off his wide brim hat, holding it over his heart, and swipes his feet twice on the entryway doormat. "How did it go?" he asks.

"Perfect. Just like you said. Rainbow and Jersey were wonderful." Molly manages a full smile that doesn't seem to go away. "Would you like to hold her?"

"Well, it's been a while. I'm not sure..."

"She's right here in that sweet little cradle someone made for her."

"So, I see. Well, maybe just for a bit." He picks her up ever so gently, pulls up a straight chair, and snuggles her into his arms. "I forget how small the newborns are."

"Didn't seem so small to me. But isn't she adorable? Look at her fingers."

"The red hair is familiar. And the pale complexion. Yep. Definitely Molly O'Reilly's baby." He rocks her gently like an experienced father would and hums softly.

"Thank you so much for allowing me to stay and have my baby here at the ranch. And thank you for assigning that whole team of people to help out."

"Assigning? They volunteered."

"Where are Rainbow and Jersey? They must have slipped out while I slept."

"They're up at the lodge grabbing a bite to eat. Rainbow will be back. I told her I'd come over to see you so she could take her time."

For the moment Molly is not thinking about time, neither past nor future, just the joy of the here and now, watching Norma Lou snuggled in Wayne's arms.

That evening, Carlos stops by and he goes completely bonkers over the baby. "I've never seen a baby like this," he says. "Such light skin. Look at that. And red hair already? Not much, but you can see it's going to be red just like yours. Oh, wow, can't you picture her growing into a little girl? May I hold her?"

"Sure, of course." Molly is a little surprised at how excited Carlos seems to be about her baby. He's a little awkward with her, like he's lifting a sack of potatoes, but he looks down at her with love and at Molly with admiration.

"You made this baby, Molly. Aren't you proud of her? Don't you just love her?"

"I do love her. I don't know why exactly because she and I have just met, but she feels like she's definitely my child already, and I want to do the best for her that I can."

"I'm sure you will, but don't worry about that now." He looks down at the fragile infant in his arms. "Just enjoy her tonight." Carlos looks around at the spotless cabin, scrubbed up before everyone left. "Are you alone?" he asks.

"Not when you're here." She gives him a smile. "Rainbow said she'd be back later tonight to get me settled. They have families, you know."

"That's good. Rainbow coming back, I mean."

The word *family* reminds Molly of her own. It felt like her mom was right beside her all day long. She and Danny need to know about Norma Lou. "Could you do me a favor?" she asks. "When you leave—not now and please stay—but when you leave, could you call my mother and tell her that my baby was born, that her name is Norma Lou, and that everything is fine with both of us. I'll give you the number. Just tell her you are a friend."

As Carlos nods, Norma Lou begins to squirm and whimper.

"I think I need to feed her," Molly says.

"I better go." Carlos looks a little bashful.

"No, it's okay. Stay until someone else comes, so I'm not alone."

Carlos hands Norma Lou over to Molly and then walks around the room examining the furnishings. He takes out one of the notecards that he keeps in his shirt pocket and a little wooden pencil he carries with him. "You need some things," he suggests.

"Oh, I'll be okay. Don't fuss over me."

Just as Molly and Norma Lou get settled into a feeding, Savannah bursts through the door, no knock, no tip-toes, no excuse me. "What do we have here?" she asks, without a hello or how-did-it-go.

Molly says to Carlos, "You know Savannah, I'm sure."

"Oh, yes, a regular customer at Pepe's Cantina." He looks away as he smiles. "How's it going, Savannah?"

"Just celebrating this evening with my friends. I finished the bison study."

"Well, congratulations," Molly says, realizing Savannah hasn't said anything about her baby. Is Savannah a little drunk? She seems kind of tipsy as she lurches across the room to her bed, her books, her binoculars.

"It looks like I need to find a place to stay tonight. I'm leaving tomorrow morning, so if you don't mind, I'll just pack most of my stuff into the Cherokee tonight." Molly notices that Savannah still hasn't come around to take a good look at Norma Lou and it hurts her feelings. "Hey, Savannah, what do you think of my baby?" she asks loud and directly.

"Oh, yeah, that's right." Savannah stops what she is doing, as if she suddenly comprehends that Molly must have had her baby today and comes over to take a peek. "Well, that's one beautiful baby you've got there, sis. Pretty as a picture."

Molly, sure now that Savannah is drunk, has to be content with a trite and belated compliment. Norma Lou has fallen asleep in her arms.

"I assume everything went alright," Savannah says, going back to her packing.

"Just fine." Enlivened by Savannah's rudeness, Molly is emboldened to have a parting shot at her, and since it's the last night, what does she have to lose? "Yeah, Rainbow has this kind of trapeze apparatus that swings from the rafters and I tried that for a while, but I was getting queasy, so Rainbow tells me to get down on all fours like the bison do, and which you call standing up, but the baby was almost dragging on the floor. So, then I finally settled down on that bed over there—not your bed, the other one—and Norma Lou just came popping out."

Carlos has turned his back on this outlandish description and Molly is sure he is laughing on the inside and maybe all over his face, too.

Savannah looks up a little fuddled, scratching her head. Eventually she says in a mixed up Southern drunken drawl, "You're shittin' me, of course."

Molly's pretty sure Savannah is buying at least part of the story and that's good enough for her. "Well, not entirely. Rainbow really was a great help, you see, because she's seen a lot of baby bison born. By the way, did you ever talk to her?"

"I didn't know she knew anything about bison birthing."

"Well, there you were with an expert right in front of your nose. She's probably got a whole theory about natural bison birthing behavior. Oh, I forgot, you have another topic now."

"I guess I should have interviewed her in June."

Now Carlos is emboldened, up for a little tormenting. "Hey, Savannah, do you have a place to stay tonight? I heard that Sonny has an extra room available."

"Now I know you're shittin' me. No thanks. There's an empty space in the cabin next door. I need to get an early start in the morning. And sleep this off."

"I understand." Carlos nods, keeping a straight face while sneaking a glance at Molly.

"Well, Molly, in case I don't see you in the morning," Savannah says, "good luck with that baby and...and...thanks for screwing my binocular case."

"Here, let me carry some of those boxes for you," Carlos says as Savannah weaves across the room leaning on the handle of her fancy four-wheel suitcase. She accepts his offer and never comes back for a final good-bye for Molly.

When Carlos has Savannah all packed up, he comes back into the cabin and sits beside Molly. "What got into you?" he asks.

"I think it's more like what got outta me. Having this baby has given me some kind of strong natural high." She grins. "Why? Was I bad?"

"No, you were terrific. I've just never seen you so devilish."

They sit together in silence for a while and then Molly says, "See if you can put Norma Lou back in the cradle without waking her up. Oh, shoot, I probably need to change her. I need to start reminding myself about that. Here, let me take her for a second."

"Do you have diapers?"

"Oh, yes, at least I planned ahead for that." Molly struggles to get up out of bed. "Geez, this is the first I've been up. Not fun." But she notices a welcome lightness without that baby inside her.

Carlos rushes over to give her a steady hand. Just then there comes a soft knock on the door as Rainbow enters. "How is she doing here?" she asks Carlos. They seem to be well acquainted.

"I was thinking I need to change the diaper," Molly says.

"Only if it needs changing. Let me see." She examines the situation and concludes that Norma Lou could indeed profit from a diaper change. "Here, I'll just do it, and while I am here you can take a little trot around the room. Help her, Carlos. No galloping, just a few slow steps. You need to get moving, Molly."

In a few minutes, Carlos takes his leave, complimenting Molly again on her beautiful baby and promising to come back soon. Rainbow explains that she will stay most of the night.

"But what about your family?" Molly asks.

"I called them from the office phone. They're fine. They know the routine when I'm bringing new life into this world. My husband's a gem."

"That's so nice of them, and you."

"I want to make sure you're waking up when the baby awakens and that this nursing process is working okay."

"I just fed her."

"And how did that go?"

"Fine, I guess. I really don't know." Molly shrugs.

"Let's see if you can get some rest. It won't be long before you have to wake up again."

Molly eventually comes down from her natural high, slowly, gradually, like a hot air balloon descending to earth. She jerks and twitches a couple of times and drifts off.

Rainbow stays through the night, helping her off and on with the feedings and changings. Then around four o'clock she tells Molly that everything is going so well she thinks she can go on home. Molly encourages her to leave and thanks her many times for everything and drifts back to sleep.

At six o'clock Molly awakens to Norma Lou's cries and suddenly realizes that she is completely alone with her baby without any clear idea of how to take care of her. No instruction manual, no page with diagrams, no HELP button to press. Molly doesn't remember much about the weather yesterday, but it seemed sunny and nice. Now it is dark and blustery and she hears a wind moaning at the windows, like the first real storm of winter is on its way. As she shuffles across the room to pick up Norma Lou, she realizes that she is absolutely terrified.

The first few weeks, difficult for any new mother, are especially challenging for Molly because she is now all alone: no Savannah sharing the cabin, no Jessica and Verónica to provide idle conversation, and the kitchen is closed so Thelma and Jolene aren't around. Rainbow and Jersey, who continue their employment at the ranch during the winter months four days a week, stop in every now and then to see how Molly is doing, but more as a professional follow-up call than as a social visit, and they can't stay long because they have work to do. Wayne looks in daily, talks with Molly for a while, and holds Norma Lou, as if he is visiting his granddaughter. He never asks Molly about her plans or mentions her leaving.

So, Molly isn't abandoned, but on the other hand, she doesn't have the family network of mother, grandmother, or aunt to advise her on what to do as she cares for her new baby. Thank goodness Carlos drives over every other day to check on her. Why does he do that? He shops for her, picking up frozen foods, cereal, milk, orange juice, bread, and lunch meat for sandwiches, as well as food for the mind, novels to read when the baby sleeps. He fusses over Norma Lou and listens to Molly as she tells him how incompetent she is as a mother and how lonely it is here in this dreary cabin back under the leafless old cottonwoods.

The euphoria Molly experienced at the moment of Norma Lou's birth is long gone and now she is seeing how demanding this lovable little creature can be. Molly has no life of her own except for the brief periods when Norma Lou is asleep, giving her a chance to read, which provides her with life-saving intervals of escape. Everything seems to revolve around that baby, the absolute center of the circle—yes, that's it, a flabbergasted mother running in circles around this helpless baby. She knows that there is no choice but to do what needs to be done each day, each hour, but because she never really chose to have this baby, like most parents do, she begins to harbor a lot of anger and resentment. She feels trapped in a repetitive cycle of caregiving with no end in sight, and that has her worried. She wonders if she will crack under the pressure and she thinks she might be heading for what her mother would call a nervous breakdown.

Tonight, on Norma Lou's two-week birthday, she sits alone in the sparsely furnished cabin reading *Pride and Prejudice*, one of the books her mother threw in the back of the truck on the morning she left home. She is immersed in an eighteenth-century provincial English village, wondering which of the three daughters, Lydia, Jane, or Lizzy, will land the new resident, Mr. Bingley. Molly has grown a little drowsy, always a problem for her when reading at night, and she puts the book open and face down on her lap, rubs her eyes, and begins to think about Mrs. Braxton, her beloved Honors English teacher.

Mrs. Braxton, like the first-person narrator of a novel, would reveal herself gradually to her students by dropping a few key words and phrases here and there as hints: "a former nun," "my studies at the university in England," "marrying an ex-priest," "advocate of social justice," and "exploring matters of the heart." Her students, like dedicated readers, would chatter outside of class as virtual members of a spontaneous book club, wondering if their teacher's romance came during or after her religious vocation and whether she and her husband had been excommunicated, separately or together. They never received answers to those questions because no one dared to ask, certainly not Molly.

Molly remembers how Mrs. Braxton opened up for her the fascinating world of fiction: painful human dilemmas, strained and fractured relationships, and the contradictory behavior of attraction and avoidance in the same heroine. She said that Jane Austin's novels were about the economics of love, and that in those times the only way out for an impoverished young woman was to marry well. Have times actually changed?

Mrs. Braxton took a special interest in guiding Molly to discover the elements of plot and character that gave substance to an author's themes. On Molly's book reports, which usually earned her an A+, Mrs. Braxton wrote extensive comments, sometimes seeming to have written more in her own hand than Molly had typed in her ten-page paper. As an English teacher, Mrs. Braxton loved words and in addition to the twenty-word quizzes in vocabulary and spelling administered solemnly each Friday, she actually used the words of the assigned study lists in her everyday speech, so that Molly and her friends marveled at how their teacher could speak in such a natural manner using elegant words and perfect grammar. Molly would deny being Mrs. Braxton's pet, but she was aware of her undeniable personal interest in preparing her well for college. But of course, going to college is quite out of the question now with Norma Lou in hand, and tonight Molly even feels ashamed for having wasted Mrs. Braxton's precious time on her now pointless education.

She checks the time: almost ten o'clock. The owls are hooting a mournful chorus tonight and the wind is howling like there is another storm on the way. The windows make that whistling noise like the wind is sucking the heat right out of the cabin. She's exhausted but not sleepy enough to go to bed, and when she hears a sharp rap on the cabin door it sends a chill up her spine. But she quickly realizes it's the particular knock Carlos uses as a code so as not to scare her, and she unlocks the bolt she's installed on the door and invites him in.

"Sorry to be so late," he says, hurrying through the door and closing it quickly but quietly. She feels the cold air walking right in behind him. It must be below zero out there tonight.

"It's okay. I'm happy to see you." But she is so weary it is hard to show him that she really is.

Soon after Norma Lou's birth, Carlos had brought to her cabin a used crib and a portable table for changing diapers, a gift from his family he said. He has fastened onto the crib a feathery-looking thing he calls a dream catcher, supposedly to filter out bad dreams, assuming, that is, that babies dream. Seems a little superstitious to her. He also hauled in a rocker for nursing, an easy chair and a bright floor lamp, good for reading after Norma Lou settles in for the night—well, at least part of a night now. Molly notices Carlos looking around at everything, scrutinizing the new lock, checking to see how bad the windows are leaking, and spreading out his hands in front of the space heater. He has a quiet intensity that she likes, but she feels totally undeserving of his attention. Finally, he says, "It's cold in here."

"I don't fix heaters. I think it's just a little inadequate for the size of the room and the wind tonight."

"I'll bring a bigger one from home next time."

"That's nice." This time she doesn't say, oh, but you don't need to. "Wayne's trying hard to take care of me, you know, but really, he has no obligation, so it's hard for me to ask for things."

"You're asking on behalf of Norma Lou. Think of it that way."

"You've got a point." She gestures toward the rocker. "Here. Sit down."

"Thanks. Long day here. How's it going?" Carlos inquires as he rocks.

"Oh, just hunky-dory," she says sarcastically. "Really, Carlos, you don't want to know. She's sweet and I love her—don't get me wrong—but it's really lonely here with nothing to do but tend this baby. She doesn't even talk baby talk yet." Molly bites her lower lip and doesn't smile at her own humor.

"I think about you every day out here all alone. It must be miserable."

"Yeah, and if something happens to Norma Lou, I'm sure I wouldn't know the first thing to do for her."

"You call me, that's what you do first."

Molly stands and begins to pace. "I feel like I'm one of those prairie dogs you have around here, and this is my subterranean burrowing hole, everything underground, earth piled on top of me, and if I go outside, I'll have to squeeze through a tunnel first to wiggle my way up to the sunny surface." She holds her hands up in front of her chest, mimicking a prairie dog. "At least a prairie dog gets to stick its head up out of the hole once in a while for a look around." She continues the prairie dog mime, exposing teeth and bunching the contours of her face into a rodent-like expression while snapping her head left and right. "So here I am, buried in responsibility day in, day out, confined in this grim hole, all the weight of this illegitimate baby pressing down on me, and..."

"Stop."

"It's only a metaphor. I'm trying to tell you that I feel like I'm suffocating."

"And you are. Maybe starving, too, on those frozen dinners." He glances at her gaunt face and the empty boxes in the trash can.

"Sorry." She plops back down on one of the straight chairs and props her chin on her fists. "Sometimes my imagination goes a little wild, you know." She throws both hands in the air and lets them whack the top of her head, lacing her fingers together and crossing her feet at the end of her outstretched legs. "I'm just a little bothered and bewildered today."

"I can see."

"Sorry to be chattering like a squirrel. She sits forward, too nervous to relax. "Do prairie dogs chatter?"

"More like a bark. But how can I cheer you up, my gloomy friend?"

She shrugs. "Tell me about blue sky and puffy clouds and singing birds. I suppose it was nice out today before the wind came up, but I haven't actually been out for four days because it's too cold for Norma Lou." She glances over at Carlos. He's looking at the floor. "I haven't seen the bison since the roundup. They used to inspire me. They're strong." She pauses for a moment. "I used to be strong." She flips the pine chair around and sits in it backwards. "Let me see, what else could you tell me about to cheer me up? The mountains. I don't think I've actually looked up at them in a week. I'm always looking down at this baby in my arms. Are they still there?"

"The mountains have not moved."

"Maybe I lack faith. A priest told me that faith could move mountains."

"Only if there's a reason to move them, I guess. Better to have faith that they'll stay right where they are. That's what makes them sacred. They've been there for eons."

"You're right." She gets up and goes over to the crib to check on Norma Lou and finds her sleeping soundly. "Tell me about the potatoes," she says with a forced smile, not knowing how to get out of her narrow world and into his.

"Well...ah...there's not much to say about potatoes." He pauses, seeming to search for something interesting to tell her about potatoes. "The harvest was over long ago and it was a good one. They've been inspected. Some are in storage in the Coop. They go to various wholesale and retail markets."

"Maybe we could teach Norma Lou something like...this little potato went to market, this little potato stayed home." She crosses one leg over the other and pulls on the toes in her thick wool sock. "Or...one potato, two potato, three potato, four," counting on her toes.

Carlos ignores her and gets up to take a look at Norma Lou. "She's adorable now. My mother would love her."

"Everyone does." Molly says flatly, wondering whether or not she does.

Carlos starts to move around the cabin, gathering up stray baby rattles, pacifiers, and bibs thrown every which way. He busies himself with folding up an extra blanket, straightening up the stack of diapers, and eventually looking through the titles of books he had brought her. "Have you read any of these?"

"As a matter of fact, I've finished them all except for this one here that my mother sent with me. I'm still reading it. But I'd sure like some more sometime. I love those English classics. Anything to help me escape the four walls of this cabin."

"I have more in the Pathfinder already. Remind me when I leave and I'll bring them in."

"I love Jane Austin, the way she describes all those young women marrying the wrong guy for money, being mismatched for life. She makes her point, but she understands us—women, that is. How our fate just dangles there." Molly stretches out one arm and wiggles her hand back and forth, as if to play with a marionette. She is silent for a moment, thinking about her own particular form of dangling. She sits back down backwards in the pine chair again.

Carlos continues to pace around, looking like he is searching for the words he wants to use to tell her what he is thinking. "Look, Molly, I may not be the right guy for you, and you may not be ready, but it breaks my heart to see you out here, cold and lonely like this, when I know my family would give you a warm room and help you with caring for Norma Lou."

Molly looks at him and jerks back, not once, but twice, taken by surprise, dismayed at his surprising offer. A frown pinches her face. Of course, she's not ready for anything like that with Carlos. That would be downright lunacy.

"I'm only offering a room, you understand," he continues, noticing her reaction.

"That's very sweet of you, but I don't know your family. I hardly know you. I think I just have to work this out on my own." As she speaks her voice grows louder, but she doesn't mean for that to happen. She wonders if she is a little out of control tonight.

"But how will you do that?" Carlos asks her directly.

"Well, that's just it, isn't it?" she says, louder still. "I don't have a frickin' clue." She lowers her voice and says, sincerely puzzled, "Why do you keep pursuing me like this? I'll only be a problem for you—and with this baby?" She nods toward Norma Lou with the flick of her red ponytail. "Carlos, why would you want to be so generous to someone like me?"

"It's not someone like you, it's you. I've tried to tell you before how much I like you. I enjoy being around you. And...and...you are so good with mechanical things and so clever, but still so attractive. It's like you have the best qualities of both a man and a woman: a complete human being. I never met a person like you before."

She is overwhelmed by this barrage of odd compliments. "Well, it's very nice of you to say these things, Carlos, but they just go blowing right by me, because I don't know who you are talking about. Surely not me. I don't think of myself like that. Come on, I'm just the farmer's daughter who got..." Norma Lou whimpers and Molly jumps to her feet. She pulls the blanket up over her and adds another. A few gentle pats send the sighing baby back to sleep. "You see what a burden I'd be?"

"Not really." He paces nervously back and forth in front of her. "Maybe

I've fallen for the wrong person—maybe I need to accept that—but don't expect me to stop trying to help you. I can't let you starve to death out here." He picks up a stack of books and opens the door. "I'll be right back with some more." The wind howls as the door opens and closes and the blast of cold air makes Molly shiver.

When Carlos returns, he says, "Actually..."

Frowning, Molly asks, "Actually what?"

"You let your anger slip out a little tonight. It's a start. Once you deal with that anger, maybe you won't be so depressed." He is shifting his body from side to side with nothing more to say. "Looks like it's time for me to get out of here. My offer stands, even though I am aware that you just turned it down." He leaves abruptly, looking terribly rejected, without his usual tender glance at Molly. She hears the door of his SUV slam.

When Carlos is gone, the cabin feels cold and desolate again, without a sound except for that constant whistling of the wind. Not even a whimper from Norma Lou. To fight off the chill of the cabin, she slips on her fleece-lined jacket and zips it up. She keeps a tissue in the pocket to use on her dripping nose. When she has had time to reflect a little, Molly decides she has behaved very badly toward Carlos tonight. Why does she push him away and reject his kindness? He visits because he likes her, and even though she doesn't understand why, she has no reason to be so insensitive to the way he feels about her and Norma Lou.

Will she go through life like this always feeling so unsuitable for romance, making flippant remarks, hurting the very people who are trying to love her? Why won't she let herself like him? He says he's fallen for her. Maybe that's what is so terrifying. Another man attracted to her. She knows where that can lead. But Carlos would never take advantage of her even though he has every opportunity back here in these woods alone at night with these cabins all empty now. So why does she panic when he is just being nice to her? Because she was raped? Will she never get over her suspicion and distrust of men? Will these feelings just go on smoldering in her soul forever creating strained relations even with well-meaning guys like Carlos?

She checks on Norma Lou, putting her hand in front of the baby's nose, as she often does, to see if she is still breathing. A lot of Indian babies must have slept in tepees on cold winter nights like this, generations of Carlos's ancestors. Maybe that's why he is so strong. So why was she babbling on about the unbearable burden of this baby? Stuck in this cabin like a prairie dog? How did she come up with that one? A prairie dog? Sometimes she feels a little unbalanced, slightly deranged, like her mind is taking flight, making things up. Was she going a little mad tonight? She goes over to the door and slides the bolt shut. My god, maybe Carlos will never come back. No doubt she's really done it this time, broken their friendship permanently, beyond repair. Maybe she will never hear that coded knock on the door again.

Molly continues to inhabit the vacant cabin. By the second week of December, she realizes that she still has no plan for her future. She has not been asked to leave the ranch, nor has she left, because she has no idea about where to go. Now the holiday season is approaching. Carlos continues to come back to bring her groceries and to check on Norma Lou. He is keeping his distance, not making suggestions, and she is guarding what she says, trying not to sound crazy. They talk, but it's not the same. And she is as lonely as a barn owl in that cabin with just herself and the baby. She feeds her and changes her because that's what you do for a baby, in one end and out the other, and that dull routine continues to make her angry and depressed.

One morning, she and Norma Lou are invited over to Wayne's house for breakfast. As she walks over there through the silence with her little baby bundled up tight, she notices a small grey wisp of smoke coming up from the chimney and spreading out in the light wind against the leafless cottonwoods etched in gray against the snow-covered peaks. An icy white moon is still visible near the horizon. Such a beautiful spot for a home. As she looks around, she notices that it's quiet and peaceful here at the ranch now with the guests gone—even the birds are gone—and she appreciates the calm because it helps her forget how much tumult and chaos was created in her life by that horrible Tommy Dawson.

Wayne has prepared sausage patties and scrambled eggs along with fresh-squeezed orange juice and toasted English muffins. The hot breakfast tastes especially good on this chilly morning. After breakfast, Wayne pulls the rocking chair near the fire and asks to hold Norma Lou. He seems eager to get his big arms around that little baby.

Molly thanks him again for letting her stay on and for the comfort and attention he has provided, the help from the ranch personnel, and the medical care from Doctor Archuleta in Alamosa. She doesn't mean to sound so formal, but she knows she needs to leave the ranch soon and wants to make sure she thanks him properly before she goes even though she's still stymied about where she will go. He acknowledges her thanks with a gentle shrug, as if it were an employment benefit or a natural courtesy, nothing exceptional. Seeing his preoccupation with rocking her adorable Norma Lou, she stirs the fire and adds a log, then clears the dishes and pours him the rest of the orange juice and a second cup of coffee. She sets them on the end table next to the rocker.

Without looking up at Molly, his eyes fixed on that baby, totally absorbed, Wayne asks, "Why don't you move in here instead of staying in that drafty cabin? There's an extra room. It will be warm and comfortable."

Oh, my God, what is he asking? She panics and starts to twirl the curl in her pony tail. To live with him? To do the chores in exchange for room and board? Companionship? Something more? "I'm not sure..." is all she can say.

She floats over to the window and looks out, biting her thumbnail, not knowing how to reply. Her mind is a muddle. The breeze is blowing the fallen leaves into little whirlwinds now. Is this some kind of marriage proposal? She shouldn't be presumptuous. She goes back to the table and nervously flicks crumbs from the placemats and folds up the napkins just so. It would be nice to have regular meals and she surely knows how to fix them if she had the ingredients. The more her mind spins out possibilities, the more agitated she gets. For sure Norma Lou deserves to be warmer and more comfortable—Carlos was right about that—but through an arrangement like this? She hears the creak of the chair runners as Wayne rocks back and forth. Like a ticking clock. Maybe he's just offering to share the extra room where his daughter grew up. Maybe that's it. Nothing more.

She needs to say *something*. She can't just flit around here like a cloud of gnats, letting his gracious proposal go unacknowledged. She remembers watching the bubbling stream on their farm back in Kansas and her dad saying to her that the water in a river never comes by twice. Let's face it, she tells herself, you are desperate. You can't just sit in that cabin and sulk, and you certainly can't afford to refuse any more offers of help. "I'd like that," she says, not believing that she, Molly O'Reilly, the proper Kansas farm girl, her head filled with religious scruples, has spoken those words like a woman of the world. What has she done? It would be so wonderful living here on Horseshoe Ranch as Wayne's daughter, even a little romantic. Healing together. Is that what she has agreed to do? Or has she taken on an unexpressed obligation? She slips up behind the rocker to sneak a peek at her baby—the newborn child he never got to hold? The rocking has stopped. Grandpa has fallen asleep with Norma Lou snuggled in his arms, but she's still awake, twirling a conspicuous curl of red hair at the crown of her head.

When Molly returns to the cabin to pack up her scant belongings—Norma Lou seems to have more possessions than her mother now—she notices the crib, the changing table, and the easy chair and lamp given to her by Carlos. She begins to wonder what he will think of her latching onto this agreement to live with Wayne. Especially when Carlos so graciously offered the home and care of his family and she spurned his gallant invitation scornfully without discussion. Just turned him out into the cold. What if he comes to visit her, as he surely will, and she's not here? She will leave a note on the cabin door telling him to look for her at Wayne's house. For sure he won't like that. But will Carlos just disappear when he reads that note and figures out, she's with Wayne? She hopes that won't happen but knows it could. Oh, my, what is she doing? How disheartening this will be for such a kind soul as Carlos.

After two weeks, Molly is sure that she and Norma Lou are simply filling the place of Wayne's daughter and the grandchild he has never seen, and she feels completely safe and comfortable in this relationship, but she knows it can't last forever. For the moment she is glad to be out of that cold cabin, and this arrangement is working well enough to get her through the worst of the winter. She cares for Wayne in ways that a dutiful daughter would, helping with the cooking—making apple crisp like her mother's—and cleaning, dusting those beautiful oil paintings signed Emily, and taking out the trash. In the spare time she has, which isn't much, she works with the data collected on the bison to construct the age pyramid she had described to Wayne during the roundup. But none of that, not even the study of the herd, seems important to Wayne, who spends whatever free time he has doting on Norma Lou, crooning cowboy songs, rattling toys in front of her, and reading books she can't possibly understand. Surely, he too must know that this arrangement can't last and that he best not become too attached to this stand-in grandchild.

At least Molly has a comfortable if temporary home for Norma Lou now, that much is accomplished, but she still has only a vague idea about how to be a mother to her. She watches Wayne to see what he does and notices that he is very good with her in a fatherly sort of way. Being her mother, she suspects, should be different, but she's not quite sure how. She likes her baby and thinks she's cute, but she's not sure she loves her. Something stands in the way. Maybe her anger and resentment are getting the best of her. She has to remind herself continually that this is not Norma Lou's fault and that she's not angry at Norma Lou but with the torment this baby has come to represent in her life.

Then one day, just as she is getting a handle on being a better mom, Norma Lou wakes up crying and doesn't stop, no matter what Molly does for her. She changes her, tries to feed her, carries her around humming to her, rocks her—she even tries whistling—but nothing seems to comfort her. After about an hour of that, Wayne looks at the baby closely and notices that she keeps swiping her left ear. "She might have an ear infection," he suggests.

"Oh, my god, what do I do for that?"

"Let's bundle her up and take her in to Doctor Archuleta. Then we will know if she does or doesn't, and if she does, he may prescribe some remedy."

It sounds like a good plan to Molly, but the visit to the Doctor's office with Norma Lou screaming the whole way, is inconclusive, not about the ear, which appears to be fine, but about any other physical causes of the crying, so Wayne and Molly return home with a fussy baby who remains an annoying puzzle the rest of the day.

After Norma Lou is put in her crib for the night Molly usually sits by the fire with a novel supplied by Carlos. Yes, he found the note and still visits, still brings her novels. She can only wonder at his continuing devotion after she was so rude to him. When Norma Lou is no longer available for entertainment, Wayne tends to doze off, finally succumbing to the day's battering of wind, cold, sun, or storm, often in combination. The harsh climate combined with the stresses and strains of running this huge ranch short-handed during the winter months leaves him nearly exhausted at the end of the day. Although he is ready to hit the hay when Norma Lou does, he prefers to snooze through the evening by the fire, eventually rousing himself from his pre-sleep sleep to go off to his bedroom around ten o'clock for a more serious attempt at slumber.

But tonight, Norma Lou is having trouble going to sleep after her trip to the doctor and she gets into another crying jag when Molly puts her in her crib. Was it because she was put down from being held? Was it too early for bedtime, or was she overtired? Was it because she had to be taken away from Wayne or separated from her mother? Is she not getting enough milk, or does she need to dislodge a burp? Who knows? Maybe the problem is that she has an anxious mother. Rainbow says that being a mother is a natural process, mostly instinctual. But for Molly, it seems horribly complicated and full of unanswered questions.

She begins to pat Norma Lou on her back, soft little pats to soothe her, and when Norma Lou keeps crying, she just keeps patting. She doesn't want to pick her up again which could make it even worse when she has to put her down the next time. Finally, Norma Lou starts to calm down and the screams turn into intermittent whimpers. So, the pats on her back become softer and less frequent. It's working. Molly starts to tip-toe softly out of the room without a sound, like she is sneaking away, and then for no reason at all, Norma Lou starts her infuriating screaming again, even louder than before. Could she sense that her mother was surreptitiously abandoning her?

So, Molly starts patting her back again, only harder because she's losing her patience this time. Harder and harder. She is patting her in a way now that couldn't possibly be calming to Norma Lou. More like a spanking. Molly is not sure at what point her own anger and frustration take over, but at some precise moment, perhaps just in time, she realizes that what she is doing is out of control and that she could in fact hurt her baby if she doesn't get away from her, so she simply leaves the room.

Wayne, still very much wide awake, pacing in front of the fireplace, asks her what's going on, and she says she doesn't have a clue. So, Wayne offers to give it a shot, if that's okay, and in less than five minutes Norma Lou is sound asleep. When Wayne comes back into the living room, Molly gives him a look, like what did you do? Wayne shrugs. No words are exchanged for fear of awakening Norma Lou, who is fully in charge of the household now as the screaming princess.

Wayne goes to the couch and Molly slips quietly into the rocking chair by the fire. She picks up her book, as if to read, but she can't concentrate because she is too agitated about what just happened and her hands are trembling. She needs to examine what is going on with her emotions before she does something she regrets. What she knows is that she still feels trapped in this house the same way she felt trapped in the cabin. Same prairie dog, different holes. So, it's not the cabin or the house, it's the tedious, repetitive caring for Norma Lou that is wearing her down, day after day, without relief. No wonder she's starting to lose it. She wakes up each morning hoping to get something done on the study of the herd that day, but after a few hours, sometimes after a few minutes, she realizes that nothing will be accomplished. She is just a mommy robot. Nursing, breast pumps, bottles, pacifiers, rattles and diapers—both clean and dirty—are her endless preoccupation. She feels another rush of anger coming over her and she wants to scream. Yes, why shouldn't *she* be the one to scream all day long? What the hell, she never contracted for this. No, this whole damn thing was just thrust upon her like 'here take this screaming baby—whamo—it's yours, raise it.' She never agreed to this crushing responsibility.

Molly tries to read again, seeking solitude in escape, picking up where she left off, but she has to put her book down when she realizes that she has read the first sentence of the new paragraph over three times without comprehending a word. Let's just concentrate on Norma Lou and think this through. Maybe she could put Norma Lou up for adoption. If Molly had had the good fortune of being born to reasonable parents, adoption might have been given some consideration the moment her pregnancy was detected. Surely her father could have sent her to some nice cloister to have her baby where the nuns would also find a loving couple for her child. When she thinks about adoption, though, she wonders if she has the guts to do that. Poor Norma Lou, growing up knowing that her mother didn't want her, that she actually *gave her away.* How would she adjust to that when she found out?

Being raised Catholic, even if they seldom went to church, she knew that abortion was out of the question. She is glad she didn't do that to her baby, but if she had, why would those government politicians call her a murderer while the rapist goes free? Shouldn't she have at least had some choice in the matter instead of being sent out into the world empty-handed by her father to survive on her own. She remembers her social studies teacher explaining about Pro-Choice and Pro-Life, but what good is Pro-Choice if no one gives you any choices?

Wayne seems to have fallen asleep on the couch as quickly as Norma Lou fell asleep in her crib after he soothed her. Wayne is definitely a soother. Her mind goes back to what she did to Norma Lou a few minutes ago. Is she really capable of hurting her? For the baby's own safety, maybe she needs to get rid of her. She has heard that in Colorado you can take a baby to the police or the fire station and just leave it in a bundle on the steps, no questions asked, no crime committed. Could she do that? Probably not. Better to leave her with Wayne, that way she wouldn't be totally abandoned. She wonders if Carlos might adopt Norma Lou if she left her with Wayne. Why is Carlos so attached to Norma Lou?

Molly doesn't sleep well that night, as her distraught mind insists on bounding back and forth among the many choices, she has been considering but is reluctant to make. Norma Lou seems to be in a profound sleep that even a bison stampede would not disturb. Unlike Molly, her baby awakens the next morning refreshed, cheerful, and ready to go, as if she had no recollection of yesterday's bouts of crying that set off such dark thoughts in her mother. Recollection? Molly wonders when babies begin to remember things. Will Norma Lou remember if Molly hurts her?

On one of Carlos's visits to Molly at Wayne's place, in addition to bringing a new stack of novels with him, he brings his younger sister Selena. Molly wonders if he thinks she will be more comfortable if he has a chaperone. Or is it that he wants her to get acquainted with some of his family before he asks her again to move in. Does he think that Selena, being more her own age, will know how to cheer her up? Whatever. Selena is definitely a live wire and she and Molly hit it off immediately.

"How's Norma Lou?" Carlos asks.

"She'll be waking up in a few minutes." Molly stops to listen. "Actually, I think I hear her cooing in there now."

"Let's go pick her up," Carlos says. So, they all trek in to stand beside the crib, bending down to look through the bars like spectators at a zoo.

"Oh, my gosh, she's cute," Selena says.

"What did I tell you?" Carlos says as he lifts her up gingerly. "There's not another baby in the Valley like this one."

"I know she probably isn't old enough for this yet," Selena says, "but I brought Norma Lou a toy, actually a string of carved wooden beads to stretch across her crib. Something to look at while she's lying there. I mean, you know, it must be boring being a baby."

"Oh, wow, that's really nice of you. And the beads, they look special," Molly says.

"Well, you know Indians and beads," she jokes. "My dad carves little figures, drills a hole in them, and I string them on a leather thong." She hands them to Norma Lou who examines them closely but seems to be just as interested in Selena's small brown hands.

"Cool present." Molly admires Selena's shiny black hair drawn back in two pigtails as well as her square face with its shadow of resemblance to her brother. "You're still in high school?"

"Yeah, I'm a junior."

"Grade eleven like my younger brother," Molly says.

"Oh, you have a brother my age?"

"I really miss him." Her eyes look off and she finds it hard to speak of him, her head full of cherished memories of their companionship as kids.

"Selena runs track," Carlos tells her. "My dad started calling her Running Deer, and now everyone in the Valley is cheering for Running Deer."

"But my mother spells it D-E-A-R," she says with a sly grin, "which is a secret just between me and my mom."

"Well, not anymore," Molly says. "But tell me about your running. Are you fast?

"You mean because I'm so short? Well, I came close to a couple of state records this year, but that's not the point. The truth of it is I can't sit still. Twenty minutes or so, that's about the limit for me. Then my feet want to take off for somewhere. The school labels me hyperactive." She shrugs and then a smile comes over her face, like a bright idea has just landed on its feet in her brain. "Can we take her for a little walk?" Selena asks, pointing at Norma Lou. "I mean, I know she doesn't walk yet, but us guys, we could walk with her."

"Is it cold?" Molly asks.

"Not today. Unseasonably warm," Carlos reports. "But the forecasters are saying it will turn cold for Christmas. Do you have a little jacket for her?"

"Not really, but we can wrap her up in some blankets." As she searches for her favorite soft blanket—she remembers that Carlos brought it to her when she still lived in the cabin—she says, "Hey you guys, I have an idea. I'll bet Selena's never seen the bison up close."

"Do I want to?" Selena holds up her hands and pretends to look scared.

"Not that close," Molly assures her.

"Actually, she hasn't seen them up close," Carlos says. "And neither have I."

So, they all troop out the front door together, with Carlos snuggling Norma Lou in his strong arms.

"We can stop at Wayne's office to ask if it's okay," Molly suggests, "and pick up the keys to the Chevy Suburban. I miss driving it." She has a fleeting memory of good times at Horseshoe Ranch before Savannah confronted her about being pregnant.

Molly gets the keys—Wayne thought the bison viewing was a fine idea—and they pile into the old van used for the summer tours. Molly is about to start her speech from force of habit, then thinks better of it, but she does share with Selena a few choice facts about the bison. Molly has picked out a place where she hopes the bison will be grazing next to an irrigation canal. They bounce along the tire tracks of a seldom traveled road and sure enough, there are some bison just across the irrigation ditch, close enough to be seen clearly, but protected from the barrier. The bison seem to know this, because they glance up and over a few times, but continue their grazing unperturbed as everyone jumps out to take a look at them. Carlos is carrying the little bundle of blankets containing Norma Lou. Molly can see how Selena is itching to run in a wide-open space like this. She has a buoyancy about her as if she's just born to run and seems like such a happy, gregarious person, full of energy and spunk. Molly wonders if taking up running would make her happy like Selena. Even Norma Lou is making happy sounds today, gurgling and cooing.

"Watch where you step," Molly warns. "It's not a potato field."

"I can see they were here recently," Selena says. "My gosh, they are such big bruisers and we are so close."

"Yeah, we're a lot closer than where I used to take the tourists. They stand there in the Western wheat grass under a vast blue sky with scattered white clouds. The mountains are not just snow-capped today; because it is winter and they are full of snow clear down to the sand dunes.

"Are the bison fenced?" Selena asks.

"Against the road over there, but we're in their pasture right now, so there's just the ditch between us and them."

"And what's that road over there?" Selena asks.

"County Road Ten."

"Really?" Carlos says, speaking up for the first time as Molly and Selena are chatting away like old friends. "The road is that close?"

"They wander around some while they are grazing in here, but, yes, sometimes they're quite close to the road." Molly has been carrying a pair of field glasses she picked up from the van and hands them to Selena now. "Want to take a look?"

Carlos grins as he bounces Norma Lou. "I don't know, Selena, do you think you can stand still long enough to focus those things?"

"Oh, hush." She adjusts the glasses and a cluster of bison comes into view. "My gosh, they are so majestic looking. And the little ones are so cute."

"A little over six months old now. There are two thousand bison altogether, so you're just looking at part of the herd there," Molly tells her.

"Awesome. Really awesome." She hands the glasses back to Molly. "I'm sure you are asked this all the time, but how do you tell the males from the females?"

"By their horns. The horns of the female are more curved, like the letter C. The males have more of an L shape and are straighter. But the men aren't around today. They live in bachelor groups or go solo. They come into the herd in late summer to make a few more babies, and then they're on their way." Selena shakes her head and bugs her eyes as if to say *typical*. "Bison are matriarchal, so the calves live with their mothers."

The outing with Selena and Carlos was like a breath of fresh air, an oasis in the desert—every cliché imaginable to describe this spontaneous moment in Molly's dreary life. It was good to feel the sun shining through the scattered clouds and to be with good friends even if only for one afternoon. But then tomorrow it will be back to her distressing routine alone with Norma Lou.

As the holidays approach, Molly realizes that the comfort of Wayne's house is no substitute for being with her own family back in Kansas, and she gets a little more nervous each day, wondering how she is going to survive her first Christmas away from home. The wintry weather turned even colder as predicted—sub-zero lows—and when she goes into town to shop, carrying her bundled-up little baby, Molly sees her breath steaming in the frigid air and hears the packed snow crunching under her feet. She hears the joyous Christmas carols, but there is no joy for her, only the reminder that the good times together with her family—the time of year when her dad seemed to be almost cheerful—are a thing of the past. Now the carols sound like the saddest music in the world, and whenever she hears them, they keep her on the edge of tears for the rest of the day as they drum through her head.

She knows from her Catholic upbringing that the true purpose of Christmas is to celebrate the birth of Jesus and his love for mankind, but she doesn't find much to celebrate this year in *her* unexpected baby. The Virgin Mary is one thing, but the rape of a virgin? Who would want to celebrate that? Not exactly an immaculate conception with that filthy scuzz. Joy to the world? Where are you, world, that men like Tommy Dawson go unpunished? Where are the wise men? Then she feels guilty for having such a gloomy outlook in what is supposed to be the most joyous season of the year.

As she finishes her shopping and leaves the mall on the west end of Alamosa, she goes back to where she has parked her dad's old truck. She promises herself she will try to shake off her despair and have more cheerful thoughts, but she can't seem to find cheer in anything and starts to cry instead. At least the truck still runs even in the cold weather. Okay, good. That may not be a cheerful, but at least it's positive. She plops Norma Lou on the passenger side all wrapped up in her blankets, no car seat, just strapped in with the seat belt in the best way she can manage. Is this even legal? Probably not. But she got her shopping done for Wayne and Carlos—after shave for each one, but with different fragrances—that's another positive thing. She drives slowly back to the Horseshoe on snow-packed roads to resume the tedium of her life. How will her family be celebrating Christmas this year? Without her, that's for sure. Could the Christmas season bring a change of heart to her father?

On Christmas Eve, Molly sits by herself in the Kentucky Fried Chicken fast food restaurant in Alamosa—by herself literally, because the grim place is empty except for two servers. Is it because of an early closing time or the fact that everyone else has a family to be with tonight? She is a little uncertain how she actually got to this particular spot at this exact moment because she was so nervous when she left Wayne that she hardly remembers what happened. She just knows that she asked him if he would watch Norma Lou for a couple of hours while she went into town to call home. She had charged up her phone and when he told her to use his land line, she said it was okay because she needed to get away for a little while anyway. It must have sounded like a lame excuse, and when he asked her if she was okay, she said she would be if she could just talk to her mom. She remembers telling him that she was going to the Colonel Sanders. Wayne looked frightened, as if he thought she was losing it, cracking up. Maybe she is.

She had felt more and more despondent as the day wore on in spite of Wayne's sweet efforts to cheer her up. He had cooked a nice breakfast, put on a CD with Christmas music—that was a mistake—and he was wrapping Christmas presents with red Santa Claus paper for a six-week-old baby that had no clue about Christmas. Wayne was alone, too—she knew this—and they had shopped earlier in the week for the ingredients needed to make an old-fashioned Christmas dinner for tomorrow, but it seemed like the more they talked about that dinner, the more depressed they became, knowing that the missing ingredient for both of them would be the family members from whom they were estranged. No amount of magic in the kitchen could cook up enough culinary delights to dispel the ugly goblins spoiling their Christmas Day.

The sadness gnawed at her. Molly's depression became so severe that she told herself to leave before she said something nasty to Wayne or pinched Norma Lou to make her cry. Would she do that? Hurt Norma Lou? Could she do something even worse? She was afraid she could. She pictured herself snatching up her baby and holding her straight out in both hands and shaking her hard, over and over again, like a dog with a rag doll toy, and the ghastly fragmentary image of that violence, repeating, repeating, tormenting her mind, left her full of dread that she was actually capable of doing such a thing. That's why she had to get out of there. Immediately. But why did she pick this lonely spot for her morose brooding? To make herself even more miserable? Yumm! I'll have a bucketful of depression, sir. But the smell of the actual chicken, when she notices it, makes her nauseous.

She tries to call her mother, but there is no answer. Maybe they went to church; after all it is Christmas Eve and that's the time when they go. Slumping in her chair, she hardly notices when a vehicle pulls into the parking lot and some guy slams the door as he gets out. A little bell rings as a male customer enters. She looks up, in a moment of panic. Oh, my god, it's not a customer, it's Carlos. Holy crap, what's he doing here?

"Are you okay?" he asks in a wooden tone, and when she doesn't respond quickly enough, he repeats the question. "Are you okay?" He's kind of breathless and his dark eyes gaze at her intently.

"Yeah, I'm a little depressed tonight, but how did you know I was here?"

"Wayne called me. He said you left him with Norma Lou, and that you ran off mumbling something about going to Colonel Sanders to call your mom. But after a few minutes, he told me, his mind started spinning and he was afraid you had left him with Norma Lou permanently. He thought you weren't coming back and asked if I would go out looking for you."

"Now I've messed up your family's Christmas Eve, too. I'm sorry," she mumbles.

"Right now, you are a little more important than midnight mass," he says, serious and unsmiling.

"You didn't need to come searching after me like this."

"Oh, yes I did, for you and for the sake of Norma Lou and for Wayne's peace of mind. He sounded terrified, and Wayne doesn't scare easily. So, tell me, what's going on?"

"Well, first of all, I did come here to call my mother," she tries to sound convincing but can hear how badly she fails.

"Did you reach her?"

"No."

"Were you running away? Wayne was sure you were running away. Nice as he is to Norma Lou, you can't just leave her with him on some harum-scarum impulse. You wouldn't do that, would you?" He gives her a withering look.

"No, not permanently." She's never seen Carlos so intense. He seems really upset. "I just needed to get away from her for a while. She's been cranky and crying most of the day." She doesn't tell him that she was afraid she would hurt her, because once she got away, she could tell it was just a kind of delusion, or delirium, or something scary in her imagination. Her desperation is gone and she feels better now. In fact, she misses Norma Lou terribly all of a sudden and she is filled with remorse for harboring such sinister thoughts. She pictures her in Wayne's arms in the rocker by the fire and wants to be with her. How could they think she would abandon her?

"So, what's going on?"

"For crying out loud, Carlos, it's Christmas Eve. I was sad, for god's sake. I miss my family. I wanted to talk to my mother."

"But why here? KFC? Of all places."

"Maybe I wanted to be in a good place to be sad." With this the tears start to well up and she has to fight them back.

"To be even sadder you mean? Well, if you're feeling sorry for yourself, you picked a fine spot to celebrate doomsday."

"It's Christmas Eve. Don't you get it?" There she goes again, raising her voice when she doesn't mean to at all.

"Of course, I do. Here you are out West away from your family on the most important family night of the year. What could be sadder? So, you know what?"

"What?"

He sits down in the stamped plastic chair opposite her at the small table and begins to give her some blunt advice. "I think you need to do something about this mess with your father. Things need to be set right. Go back there. Try to straighten things out with him. Insist that he listen to your explanation. Tell him he has no right to banish you from your family, to prevent you from seeing your mother and little brother. If he doesn't want to see you, that's his problem. He can leave while you are there—take a long hike. And who knows, once he sees Norma Lou, maybe he will change his mind."

"But he hates me," she objects. There. She's said it. Her own father hates her.

"I doubt that, but if he hates you, show him you love him anyway."

Carlos seems to be full of Christmas kindheartedness tonight. If only it were that simple. "You just don't know my dad," she says.

The idea of straightening things out with her dad, as Carlos puts it, surfaces conflicting emotions for Molly. On the one hand, she wants nothing more than to have this whole mess with her father resolved. She wants to go back to her family, or at least have the choice to go see her mom and be with her brother. On the other hand, she's unsure how her father will respond. She's seen his anger once, and she doesn't need a second helping of that. She realizes that as much as she likes certain things about her father, his better qualities, deep down she is afraid of him—scared to death—and she knows that facing him will most definitely be torture.

As she is thinking about this, she slowly reaches out to Carlos and takes his hand and cups it in both of hers. She's never done this before, but suddenly she wants to hold his hand. "Thank you," she says. "Thanks for the encouragement."

They sit there composed like that for a moment in respectful silence and then Carlos says, "Why don't you try your mom again?"

She punches in the number and this time there is an answer. "Hello." Molly doesn't know what to say and she is afraid she will cry, so she hesitates.

"Say something," Carlos whispers, "or she'll hang up."

"Hi, Mom. It's Molly." And then she does cry. She can't hold it back any longer.

"Where are you?"

"Oh, I'm at the Colonel Sanders." Molly holds the phone so that Carlos can hear her mother's voice.

Now it is her mother's turn to cry. "Are you that desperate?" she asks.

"I'm not having any chicken, Mom. I'm just sitting here with a friend." Carlos smiles. "It's very sad for me at the holiday all alone here." She starts to cry again. "I knew it would be tough on us both for me to call, but I just wanted to let you know that I am safe and my baby is fine. She's growing. It's easier for her to do that now that she's born." Molly is sobbing so hard that she's not making any sense. "Her hair is still red."

"I know she is beautiful."

"Do you think she is beautiful enough for dad to love her? Do you think he would at least like to see her?"

There is silence on the line, longer than Molly wanted or expected, but finally her mother says, "You can always try, honey. We never know with your father, but maybe you need to make the first move. I'm dying to see that baby."

"Well, I guess I'll have to think about that and try to figure something out." Then Molly pauses, trying to gather up her courage to say "Merry Christmas." When she finally does, she adds, "I miss you and Danny a lot. I just wanted you to know that I'm thinking of you tonight." When she clicks her phone off, she stares through the Jack Frost patterns on the window out into the street. Hardly any cars tonight. Just one or two moving slowly between the banks of snow.

Carlos calls Wayne to tell him he's found Molly, and then he says to her, "Come on, I'm going to follow you back to the Horseshoe. I want to make sure you get there, but first, I have a little present for you. I was going to bring it over to you tomorrow." He reaches in the big pocket of his parka and pulls out a small box neatly wrapped in paper with bells and snowmen on it. "Open it. I want to see if you like it."

"I have a present for you, too, but I didn't expect to see you tonight." When she opens it, she finds a silver clip with turquoise stones, something for her hair.

"I noticed you're wearing your hair long now," he says, looking a little bashful commenting on her appearance.

She wipes her tears with the back of one hand. "Well, I haven't had time to cut it and I don't even know where to go for that out here. But, yes, it is longer now." Molly takes the clip out of the box to examine it.

"It's a Navajo piece. Fine stones. They are still the best at jewelry."

"Look, I can clip my hair together right by my neck and just let it flow down my back. Oh, Carlos, this is very beautiful. Thank you, but really you shouldn't."

"I shouldn't try to make you happy on the saddest night of your life?"

Better to remain silent than to say something foolish and ruin this beautiful moment. How kind he his, tracking her down, being with her while she called home, and now bringing her such a beautiful gift.

This time he takes her hands and just holds them. She feels calm and doesn't resist. It's like there's some special power flowing through him into her arms. Finally, she says, "I think that's a good idea about going back home to straighten things out, but it frightens me."

"I know it's scary but you can do it. You may not think you are strong, but I know you will find the strength. You may not know where that strength comes from, but it will be there when you need it."

6

A GOURMET PICNIC AT THE DUNES

Somehow, by the grace of God and with a lot of encouragement from Wayne and Carlos, Molly survives the holidays, including the beginning of a new year, which she hopes will be better than the last even though she still has no clear picture of what it will hold for her and Norma Lou. She agrees with Carlos that it would be a good idea to go back to Kansas, but she can't just walk in and say "I'm here. Let's all forgive each other." She has been going over in her mind how to approach her father and what to say, but she can't quite picture it yet. The idea of talking to him is definitely frightening. She needs a strategy, a convincing argument.

In many ways, her situation and Wayne's are parallel, because they both involve fathers and daughters, perceived sexual impropriety by the daughters, angry dismissals by the fathers, and the consequence of broken families living apart. In Wayne's case, Molly knows that he has had second thoughts about what he said and did, but he doesn't know whether his wife and daughter would forgive him enough to return. In her case, she is willing to return, but doesn't know how she will be received. Returning to Kansas might be a dangerous gamble, but she makes it her primary New Year's resolution.

Wayne doesn't talk to Molly much about his wife and daughter and he never mentions them by name. He's a quiet cowboy, that guy. She knows that he feels bad about what was said to his daughter and wishes he could take back the words spoken in anger. He's told Molly that much. This gives her a glimmer of hope that maybe her father might also be willing to take back the ugly things he said to her. The door may be open at least part way already if he had a change of heart over Christmas. Wayne seems to be prepared to forgive and forget, but are his wife and daughter likely to forgive him? One evening she musters the courage to ask him that and he says, "I don't know because I don't even know where they are."

"Would you like to see them?" she asks.

A long silence fills the room before he speaks again, as if he had to hack his way through an underbrush of painful memories to find the words to continue. When he finally responds, Molly can see he is embarrassed.

"We all made a bad scene when my daughter left, hurling insults at each other and saying inexcusable things we shouldn't have said. You know how that goes."

"I certainly do." She doesn't remember doing any hurling, just being the target.

"And that makes it difficult to repair the damage. Kind of a Humpty-Dumpty situation that no one knows how to put back together again, if you know what I mean."

"I can understand that. But tell me, do you still love her?"

His face brightens and he nods his head. "Oh, yes, no doubt about that."

Molly finds that encouraging. If she could find Wayne's wife, maybe she could help bring his family back together. She needs to do something for this man to repay him for all his kindness toward her. Besides, having a project like this might pick up her spirits a bit so that she can stop feeling so sorry for herself.

The next day Jersey is babysitting for a few hours while Molly helps her good friend Rainbow check the watering tanks for the cattle. Each pasture has a tank, and the pasture has a name, such as North Highway, or Purebred, or Big Southwest. The tanks are fed by artesian wells and they have a name, too, such as Clearwater or Sweetwater. So, the task is to ride out to the various pastures and check the plumbing around the tanks to make sure that everything is flowing and the water level in the tanks is adjusted right. It is nice work for an unusually warm winter day and it feels good to be useful and to ride a horse again. Wayne has encouraged Molly to work a couple of afternoons each week while another employee babysits, the closest the Horseshoe has to a child-care benefit. While they are busy with the Sweetwater tank, Molly asks Rainbow, softly, in a tentative voice, without looking up, "Whatever happened to Wayne's wife?"

"Emily?"

So, she is the one who painted the pictures. Wow! "Did you know her?"

"Oh, yes, dear, quite well."

"Doesn't anyone know where she went? And the daughter. What happened to them?"

"Emily and Heather? Skipped town, I guess. Nobody seems to know."

"Well, didn't anyone try to find out? Isn't there someone around town who might at least have a clue?"

Rainbow makes a face and shrugs. "Most people don't consider it to be any of their business."

"Why don't you ask around? At least see if anyone has some ideas," Molly says, with enthusiasm in her voice. "Come on, use some imagination. Where would a woman like that be likely to go?"

"You might be stepping into some trouble, young lady. Are you sure you want to go meddling like that?"

"You can't walk the range without stepping into a little something, you know that, and besides, there may be some good to come of it, not just trouble.

Wayne and Emily can make up their own minds about what to do if he finds her," Molly insists. "I think he'd like to have her back." She can't stand to think of his being all alone by himself in that lovely cabin once she heads back to Kansas, constantly reminded of his bad mistake by Emily's beautiful paintings.

"Wouldn't that be a little awkward for you, her coming home?"

"If she'd come back, obviously I would leave, but that's just the way it goes."

Rainbow looks up at her, looking like she's ready to hear more. "Where would you go?"

Molly clears her throat. "I'm thinking of going back home. I don't have a real plan just yet or a date. I need to work up my courage to face my dad. I just know that I can't stay here being a substitute for his daughter and granddaughter the rest of my life." She pauses, then starts again. "Do me a favor, Rainbow. Ask around. Don't ask people where Emily is, ask where a woman like that would go."

It takes Rainbow a full week of asking, but eventually she reports back with a promising lead. Molly meets her in the empty bison barn, completely deserted at this time of year, cold and metallic, but private. Molly has Norma Lou over her shoulder all wrapped up in warm blankets.

"Hey, that baby of yours is getting big. And cuter every day."

"Thanks. We're getting used to each other now. But tell me, what did you find out?

"Well, I talked to the painting teacher in the art department at the college. For a few years Emily taught painting there part time."

"And..." Molly asks.

"This art professor, an old friend of my husband's, said that he had heard that she had left with her daughter, but he didn't know where she had gone. Then when I asked him your question, where a person like that might go, he didn't hesitate for a split second. He just said, "Santa Fe."

"Why Santa Fe?"

"Because it's not just the capitol of New Mexico, it's a big artist colony with lots of galleries and museums, the home of Georgia O'Keefe, that woman that paints flowers that look like vaginas." She grins and shrugs. "Oh, sorry, I guess you didn't need that part."

"So Santa Fe is a good lead, but maybe a long shot."

"But not so long, sweetie, because the professor at the college said Emily used to sell some of her work through a gallery there, and that in fact she knew a lot of people in Santa Fe."

"Well, hey, let's go," Molly says. "Will you take me?"

"Well, it could be a wild goose chase," Rainbow says with doubt spread across her tilted face. She scratches her forehead. "But why not?"

"If you can get Jersey to come over and help Wayne babysit Norma Lou for a day, I'll tell him it's something urgent—a family matter."

"Which is true. Only it's his family, right?" Rainbow winks.

So, Rainbow and Molly go on a day trip to Santa Fe, turning right in Walsenburg onto Interstate 25 South. As they cruise along, Molly peppers Rainbow with every question she can think of about raising Norma Lou because she wants to know what she should be doing for her baby and how to be more relaxed as a mother.

"Well, it's a natural process," Rainbow begins. "The little critters go through their stages as they grow, just like they do in the womb: fish to frog to monkey. Right now, she's just all floppy like a jellyfish, but already, if you notice her when she's on her tummy, she can hold her head up off the floor and look around like a little snake."

"What a terrible comparison." Molly frowns.

"No, I mean like a snake does. And pretty soon you can try to sit her up and cross her legs in front of her."

"Like she's doing yoga?"

"Only you'll have to support her. She can't support herself at first with that."

"So that comes later."

"Supported sitting at three months, steady on her own at five. And later on, they creep, crawl, and pull themselves up to stand. But you don't need to do anything about any of that because..."

"It's a natural process."

"An amazing process, and that's why you can relax. If your baby is normal, which she is, you don't have to actually teach her to do any of those things." Rainbow flicks the fingers of one hand, as if to show Molly how unnecessary it is to teach what comes naturally.

"But right now, she screams a lot."

"Some of them have an underdeveloped digestive system and it takes them a month or two to catch up."

"*Now* you tell me."

"Well, hey, it's better than staying in the womb for a couple more months so that mother can finish the job."

"I'll go along with that for sure, but meanwhile she just screams."

"That's what they do when they have a belly ache."

"Endless screaming?" Molly thinks it would make a good title for a novel where all of the characters are babies.

"They drive you a little crazy for the first three months, don't they, but it gets better, believe me. Pretty soon she'll smile and recognize you. Then she turns into a little charmer. I'm sure my mother didn't know any of what I was just telling you now, but look at me, raised in a shack, passed from one hippy to the next, the communal baby adored by everyone. That's what mom told me anyway."

Rainbow smiles and looks over at Molly. She's pretty good at keeping her eyes on the road while she's talking, so Molly decides to ask a few more questions. "Your kids. How old are they?"

"Ten, eight, and six."

"And do they eat brown rice and bean sprouts?"

"Not together, but they eat pretty well, actually. No sodas. Limited sweets. Nothing from bags or cans. Mostly natural. They're strong and healthy."

"I'm still pretty nervous around Norma Lou because I don't know what I'm doing."

"There's no one best way to raise a child. You have options. Pick one. Try it out. If it works, stick with it. Don't beat yourself up about doing the wrong thing. Talk to her, sing to her, and read together. Surround her with interesting toys and then let her do her own thing."

Molly can't help but think that this is exactly what Wayne does. How does he know all of this? "Was Wayne raised by hippy parents?" she asks, spontaneously, leaving Rainbow looking puzzled over the abrupt change of subject.

"Like me? No, I think he grew up on a ranch in Wyoming. But we have a similar philosophy, if you can call it that."

They both hear a siren. Rainbow's hands grab and release the steering wheel nervously as she checks the rearview mirror and slows down. Luckily the ambulance is coming toward them in the other lane. That's a relief. They pass a few miles in silence before Molly says, "You have a Spanish last name."

"That's my husband. Gallegos. His parents came to California as migrants, but he's a citizen, a Spanish professor at the college. I met him when I first came here after graduate school."

"You went to college?"

"And grad school. Agronomy. That's soil science but I studied the basics of farm management, too. I like being outdoors. I got the job at the Horseshoe before my husband moved here to teach twenty years ago, and I've been having a good time following my own interest out there ever since. Like that old Cole Porter song says: *Don't fence me in.*"

"It makes you wonder," Molly says, "How the bison feel about being fenced in."

"You've got a point, honey."

They park a little distance from the plaza where native people in small booths tend displays featuring hand-loomed rugs and turquoise jewelry. They browse a bit and then ask where to find all the art galleries. The main place for the galleries is Canyon Road they are told.

"You'd recognize her?" Molly asks.

"Oh, hell, yes. Knew Emily well and the daughter Heather, too, from the time she was a young girl. It was a terrible thing that happened to that family. I even knew Miguel."

"Who's that?"

Rainbow puts a knuckle in her mouth. "Ah...sorry. I didn't mean to spill the beans, but, well, he's the father of Heather's baby."

So, Molly and Rainbow trudge up Canyon Road, prowling in and out of galleries, looking like two lost rancheros fixing to buy an elegant abstract painting, not having any idea what they are looking at, but certain of who they are looking for. They have sauntered up one side of the street, and now they are working their way down the other, systematically, shop by shop, when they stumble into Emily in the New Concept Gallery talking to a customer. Rainbow spots her immediately and mumbles to Molly, "Oh, my god, now what do I say? She's already recognized me."

"Leave it to me," Molly says, not quite sure she can identify the source of her newfound confidence. She's nervous, too, though, so she thrusts her fists into her pockets to keep from twirling her ponytail. On the far wall is a Western scene with mountains and aspen trees, like the one hanging in the entrance to the lodge. She watches Emily closely by sneaking glances at her, sizing her up as she thinks about what she is going to say to her.

This woman is not just a talented artist; she is also a picture of loveliness. Her naturally blond hair with its few streaks of white is cut short and brushed back over her ears framing the delicate features of her face. Her pale skin is smooth and radiant and her eyes sparkling and searching. She and Wayne must have been the perfect match, a gorgeous couple when they were young and would be even now if they were back together. Molly and Rainbow hang around pretending to look at the art with the semblance of shoppers, and when Emily gets free, she comes up and says, "What a coincidence to see you here, Rainbow. It's been a while."

"Likewise." They embrace with the hug of old friends. "Oh, this is Molly. She worked at the ranch this summer and...and...I got to know her really well."

Molly knows the ball has been passed to her and that she needs to relay her message, but she doesn't know quite what to say first, certainly not that she is living with Wayne in Heather's bedroom, so she just blurts out, "We were hoping to find you here today, ma'am. I know your story, what happened, and I have a message for you. Wayne has been unburdening himself to me and I can tell you he is really sorry about those things he said. He's a different man now and wants to be forgiven."

"Who *is* this young woman?" Emily asks, peering at Rainbow with a frown, indignation creeping into her voice.

"She's..."

When Rainbow hesitates, Molly continues, "I'm just a messenger, ma'am, an unauthorized one at that. And pardon me for sticking my nose into your business, but I know Wayne would like to see you." For a moment, Molly admits to herself that this is only a hunch and that she's never heard Wayne say that for sure. But she continues on anyway. "I'd like to go back and tell him where you are so he can come down here and find you because he's suffered a lot and he still loves you." That much she knows is true.

There is a long silence as Emily sighs and shuffles her feet, facing first one way and then the other, hands on her hips, seemingly puzzled about where to look or what to say. Molly hopes she won't tell them to leave, but finally Emily says, "Well, inasmuch as you've gone to the trouble to come down here, you can tell him you've found me and that I don't plan on moving anywhere." She throws her head to one side, maintaining her pride.

"Good. That's what I wanted to hear," Molly says. "That means you will be right here." She points with a forefinger to the floor. But then she wonders if Emily was implying that she wouldn't move back to the ranch.

Rainbow pulls close to Emily and asks in a low voice, "What happened to Heather?"

"Oh, she had her baby. Cute little fellow now. Then Miguel came back for her and their son and they moved to Mexico."

Molly is listening closely. It seems that Emily, like Wayne, doesn't get to see her daughter and grandbaby either. How sad.

"To Mexico?" Rainbow sounds surprised. "She's a U.S. citizen. She could bring him back."

"I suppose, if she was willing and Miguel felt welcome. Some rather harsh things were said, as I'm sure you know." There is a firm brittleness in her voice.

"Excuse me, but sometimes people regret their harsh words later," Molly says. "But we might be getting ahead of ourselves here. I'm just going to tell Wayne where to find you if that's okay. The rest is up to you guys."

"Well, thank you for your...audacity, I guess. We'll just have to see." She shrugs, but she is also looking off into the distance and Molly can't read her expression. Emily seems a little distant and evasive, not as thrilled to hear the news about Wayne as Molly had expected her to be.

Turning to Molly, Rainbow says, "We better ramble on back."

Molly peers at Emily one more time to fix her features in her memory and says, "Don't forget that he still loves you." She hopes she hasn't made a mess of things by coming to find Emily.

The next morning at breakfast, while Norma Lou is napping, Molly tells Wayne exactly how to find Emily: the address on Canyon Road, the name of the gallery, and which side of the street it is on. He is surprised, he tells her, when the story unfolds, that she'd be so bold in tracking Emily down like that and representing herself as his messenger, but he's not angry. In fact, he's so delighted he can't stop smiling, and he reassures her that the message she delivered was spot on. "There you go again, trying to fix everything that's broken," Wayne teases, finishing the last of his scrambled eggs. They start to clear the table together.

"I hadn't thought of it as fixing, but I guess you're right. I just think you guys need to get back together."

"But I'm a bit uneasy, Molly," he says, with a mixture of enthusiasm and trepidation in his voice, "because I'm not sure whether she will welcome me."

"Well, of course you and Emily will both be on edge when you first meet, but you need to give it a shot and see how it goes. Just be your better self, the one you are to everyone around here all the time."

"Aw, that's nice of you, but if I go to Santa Fe looking for her, she could just tell me to buzz off." While they rinse off the dishes, he asks, "What about you? I mean if she comes back. What will you do?"

"Oh, I can't stay here forever, you know that. I'll have to go."

"That's very considerate of you, but where?"

"Home. Kansas. Back to the dairy farm."

"Well, yes, but..."

"Knowing you has made me think that my dad may have changed his mind like you did. He may be sorry about those things he said about me."

"And of course, you'll take Norma Lou?"

"She's my secret weapon, my way back into dad's heart. Three generations of red hair, you know. He'll like that. And I'm going to tell him about how kind you were to me."

"I'll miss her like crazy. And you, too, of course. My god, you've become like a daughter to me."

"I know. That's why I've got to go." He wipes his hands on a towel, reaches out to her, and wraps her in a big bear hug. She throws her freckled arms around his neck, clinging to him, and lets the tears roll. When he finally releases her, she sees that his eyes are teary and red.

Molly pours Wayne a second cup of coffee and sets it on the side table next to the rocker. She settles on the couch as Wayne sits down beside his coffee. "What about Carlos?" he asks.

Molly sighs and looks down at her hands fidgeting in her lap. "I don't know what to say to him."

"We talk sometimes when he stops by to check on you. He's a fine guy." Wayne stirs his coffee and blows on it before taking a sip.

"But right now, he's only a good friend," Molly assures him. "He says he just wants to understand me and make sure I'm okay."

"That's pretty close to a definition of love, I'd say." Wayne shrugs and throws open one hand. "You'll just leave him?"

"For now. I can't go back to Kansas with a Norma Lou on one arm and a Carlos on the other." She lifts her elbows as if to offer an arm to each one.

"Maybe you'll invite him to visit?"

"At my dad's farm? Are you crazy?"

"Well, then you can come out here to visit Carlos. I think he really loves you. He wishes you'd give him a chance."

Molly nods her head up and down several times and then switches to back and forth. "Not right now. I've got to get this thing straightened out with my father. I'm not ready yet. I'd like to have a future. Maybe go to college. Travel."

"So, what do I tell Carlos when he tries to track you down? I know he'll ask."

"He knows where I'm going and why I'm doing it. I mean, heck, it was his idea."

"Really?" Wayne gets up to go get his coat from the hook by the door. "But you will come back out here to visit me, won't you?

"Of course. I know my mom will want to meet the person who took me in when I had no place to turn. Besides, I want to meet Heather, Miguel, and your grandson someday."

Wayne stops in his tracks and whirls around. "Did you say grandson? A boy?"

Molly knows she should tell him they are in Mexico, not New Mexico, but for today she thinks she's said enough.

The next morning after breakfast when the dishes are done and Wayne has gone off to his chores outdoors, Molly decides to sit down on the floor with Norma Lou to observe her more closely to see what she can do. She puts her baby face-down on a blanket spread over the sheepskin rug in front of the fireplace. It isn't but a few seconds before Norma Lou lifts up her head, looking every bit like a snake just as Rainbow said. Molly hasn't really noticed that she was doing that. And now she sees her baby looking around like she's observing things. Obviously, she can see, but she looks like she's intentionally examining the yellow block that Molly has placed in front of her. She kicks her legs like she is doing the breast stroke, seeming to be excited about that simple little block that's in her view and making gurgling noises to accompany the dance she is doing with her legs. Oh, my, that's so cute.

Molly lets her enjoy her tummy time until she starts to fuss a little, but instead of picking her up, she gently helps her roll over onto her back. More kicking—this time the resting backstroke frog kick. When she's comfortable, Molly gives her the yellow block, but she can't quite hold it yet so it keeps rolling off of her tummy. Then Molly remembers Rainbow telling her to talk to her, but how the heck do you talk to a two-month-old baby? She starts by telling her she's cute. Cute as a button. She knows people say that about babies, but doesn't remember seeing any cute buttons. Her baby babbles back with random noises. Then it happens. Molly runs an index finger across her soft cheek a few times and Norma Lou smiles. Not gas, nothing intestinal, but an intentional smile. Oh, my, gosh, look at that beautiful smile. Molly feels a warm sensation all over her body and she can't remember the last time she was this happy. Her baby can smile. Is this the first time or has she been smiling at Wayne? Surely, he would have told her. Does Norma Lou recognize her mother now like Rainbow said she would? So, Molly talks to her baby some more and sure enough there comes that smile again. This is just so exciting! How could she ever have thought of harming her? So, Molly plays with Norma Lou like that until it is time for her next feeding.

Molly slips into the rocking chair and while she is nursing her, she starts thinking about what Carlos said about why she should go back to Kansas. It's a good idea. She needs to set a specific date. Surely her father will like Norma Lou, cute as she is now. Wait till she throws grandpa one of those smiles. How can he resist that? How? Quite easily. She can drive all the way to Kansas and before she can get out of the truck he could say, "What are you doing here? I told you to leave. You can just turn around and take yourself back to Colorado." That would be just like him, saying stuff like that before she's even had a chance to show him Norma Lou. What she hopes is that if she can just introduce him to her baby, and little Norma Lou smiles at him with that smile like she did just now, maybe his heart will melt. Maybe he will fall in love with his granddaughter and forget all about those mean things he said. It could be really easy. She looks down at the baby in her arms and enjoys for a moment that vision of a satisfying return to Kansas.

On the other hand, what if he sees her but the sight of the actual baby ignites his anger? What if an argument ensues all over again about what really happened? She will have to tell him flat out that she was raped and stick to her guns. She's talked to Wayne and to Carlos about it and heard their perspective, so that now she's convinced of what happened. She has no experience in contradicting her father, but if he starts blaming her again for flirting with Tommy Dawson and giving in to his amorous ways, she will have to tell her father that it simply didn't happen like that. It wasn't her fault; it was Tommy's fault. He raped her.

She touches her forehead with the back of her hand and notices that she is damp with perspiration. There she goes again getting herself all worked up. Maybe she shouldn't go back to Kansas after all. Maybe she hasn't thought through this dream of hers. The sweaty forehead is giving her cold feet.

For a few days, Molly goes back and forth on her plan to return to Kansas. She was hoping that Wayne would announce one day that he was leaving for Santa Fe, because that would force her to vacate the bedroom and depart, but so far, he hasn't said anything about going.

One morning Molly shares with Wayne her ambivalence about returning to Kansas. He says he's having the same problem: can't make up his dang mind about going to Santa Fe.

"I thought you would head off the next day once I located Emily for you," she says.

"It's not that easy. Like I told you we had words. I don't know how she'll receive me, like a lovable lamb or a wounded mountain lion."

"Don't you want to see her?" Molly asks, trying to test his eagerness.

"Oh, of course I do. I'm just..."

"Scared?" The word slips out and she wishes she could retrieve it.

"Well, I hate to admit it, but I guess that's true. Yes, I want to see her, but no, I don't."

"Same with me and my dad." Then she remembers something funny and she breaks into a laugh.

"It's no laughing matter."

"No, I'm not laughing at you. I'm remembering a cow we had that loved the green grass on the other side of the electric fence. She'd stick her neck through to snatch some of that grass and of course she'd get shocked. After a few shocks she learned about the fence, but you could tell she hated to give up that patch of grass. So, she would mosey up to the fence, getting as close as she could, her head bobbing up and down, but then she'd turn away. In no time at all she would be approaching the fence again. We used to call her Dilly-Dally."

"And you're thinking I'm like that cow."

"Not just you, but both of us. Willy-Nilly and Dilly-Dally. That's us,"

Molly says smiling a broad smile. "Quite a pair." Wayne is smiling, too. He's not taking it the wrong way, so she can continue. "So, here's what we need to do. We set a date and we both go on the same day, you to Santa Fe, me to Kansas. We'll follow each other and there won't be any turning back."

Wayne grins. "Molly, you are something else. But you know what? You are exactly right."

"How about the first Monday of March? That's a couple of weeks away, so we have time to pack and say our goodbyes."

Wayne is still grinning as he nods. "We'll ride off into the sunrise together."

"So, it's agreed?"

Wayne looks happy now, knowing he's going to see Emily. "You've got a deal."

Now she needs to say good-bye to Carlos—Molly knows that—but she is not looking forward to it, suspecting that he will shower her with kindness that will make her want to bawl. She's already sad about leaving him. They've become such good friends again, and he has been really kind to her and Norma Lou. She tells herself that this idea about going back to Kansas really came from Carlos. He has urged her to do it, but that won't make saying goodbye easier for either one of them. She hopes he will call today to set a time for a few moments together before she leaves. She can't just drive away. But he doesn't call.

On the Wednesday morning of the week before she and Wayne are scheduled to leave, she hears the slam of a car door in the driveway. She recognizes that sound now and when he raps on the front door, she invites him in, but she's flustered, not having had time to prepare what she is going to tell him. Is she just going to say goodbye to him standing in Wayne's living room like this? It looks like he has a present for her under his arm all wrapped up in fancy paper and ribbon.

"Did you see what a beautiful day this is?" Carlos asks her, full of energy. "Have you been outside?"

"No, I haven't had a chance. I'm trying to get Norma Lou's things organized for the trip."

"Oh, yes. The trip. You told me you will leave Monday. Is that still the plan?"

"Yes, Monday."

"Oh, man, that's soon." He shifts from one foot to the other. "Well, maybe we can do something today that you will never forget."

She feels her whole-body tense up. Please not that. They don't even kiss. She knows he is staring at her and she goes to the window, trying to appear as if she's looking outside, but actually to try to get her panic under control.

"I'm sorry," Carlos says. "I could have been more specific. The chinook winds are blowing across the Valley today, and I thought we could take advantage of the warm weather and go to the Great Sand Dunes National Park. It's spectacular and I'm guessing you've never been."

"You're guessing right." She blows out a big breath that puffs out her cheeks, feeling relieved and a little foolish. "Here I am with the park right next door, and I never find time to go over there." Feeling more relaxed she turns to him from the window and smiles. "But what about Norma Lou? It's still winter."

"We'll bundle her up and take her along. I have to say goodbye to her, too, you know. I wouldn't want to leave her behind today." He takes the present from under his arm and hands it to Molly. "I was hoping you would say yes so that we could use this today. Go ahead, open it."

Molly had been thinking it was something for her and she didn't want still another present from Carlos, but it turns out that this is for Norma Lou. It's a winter jacket with a fur-trimmed hood. When she discovers what it is, she says, "Oh, my gosh, Carlos, it's beautiful."

"My mom stitched the rabbit fur around the hood, but look, there's more."

Pants, mittens, a knitted hat, too. "A matching outfit."

"We'll need to put a little sunscreen on that fair skin because it's really bright out today." He holds up a small tube. "And I brought her this, too." He pulls out another present, this one unwrapped, from one of the big pockets in his parka. "They call it a front pack carrier. The baby faces forward. You can put her inside your jacket and leave it unzipped a little so that she can take in the scenery, too."

"Carlos, you are so thoughtful. Of course, we can go. Just let me leave a note for Wayne so he won't think I ran off."

Molly goes to the bedroom to change her clothes and gather up Norma Lou who has just awakened from a mid-morning nap. She hopes the little dickens will smile for Carlos.

"Be sure to wear boots, not sneakers. There's a little river and we'll need to do some climbing around, too," Carlos yells in to her.

So, they slide into the Pathfinder and in no time at all they are passing through the Entrance Station at the park. Molly can't tell whether Carlos has some year-round pass or just a familiar smile, but the ranger waves him through and nods at her. Carlos parks in the visitor parking lot and they get their stuff together for their hike.

"In the summer time this place is packed with visitors from all over the world. But today I think we have it almost to ourselves," he says.

"What's this river?" Molly asks. "There doesn't seem to be much to it."

"It's called Médano Creek, accent on the first syllable, a Spanish word meaning *sand dune*. From July through April, it carries only a few inches of water, if any at all, but when the mountain runoff comes from the snowmelt of the Sangre de Cristo Range up there, in late May and early June, you can look for a flood, because it turns into a real river then." He nods his head several times. "I think I'm like this river, Molly. Sometimes I'm real quiet like my dad. A stranger could think there's not much to me, you know, kind of shallow. Then at other times I have a lot of words and they just come flowing."

"And then you're deep." She likes the deep side. Then she says, "I think we all have different sides to our personality and sometimes one comes out and then another."

"Right here," Carlos points the way across the river, "we can just kind of tip-toe through on the dry spots today."

When they are across, she looks up. "Holy cow crap, look at these dunes. I didn't know they were so huge, seeing them from so far away like I usually do."

"Seven hundred and fifty feet in some places. The highest dunes in North America and a long way from any ocean."

They start to climb a little but the sand slips away and Molly loses her footing, falling to one knee. "Here, let me take Norma Lou," Carlos says.

"I'm okay."

"No, seriously. I forgot how difficult climbing in the sand is for a first-timer, and I want to make sure you can go up a little higher for the view. Here. I've got her." Norma Lou is transferred to Carlos and he snuggles her into her new pack facing out, so that all that Molly can see of her is her little nose and big eyes looking out from under her furry hood, a strand of red hair showing. An Irish papoose.

They climb until they are winded, then they rest and climb some more. When they reach a spot high enough for a good vista, Molly says, "Look at how they twist and turn, looking all sculpted by the sun and shade. They seem to be connected together and they just go on and on for miles. I've never seen so much sand. Where did it all come from without an ocean?"

"Well, thousands of years ago the San Luis Valley was a huge lake, with the Sangre de Cristo Mountains behind us here heaved up on one side of the valley and the San Juan Range on the other side of the valley coming from volcanic activity. Well, the lake in the middle, which drained into the upper Rio Grande, gradually flowed away leaving behind its sandy bottom. That sand out there," he gestures with a sweeping arm, "blows toward the three mountain passes up here, and it lands in a little curve in the Sangre de Cristo Range right there, which serves as a natural pocket—the original sand trap."

"Wow! That's so interesting."

"And sometimes the wind blows back toward the valley again and that's how the dunes get piled up so high. Sand is still blowing in from the valley floor and back from the mountains adding to the height of these dunes all the time."

So, are they constantly changing shape?"

"Good question. Yes and no. The top layers are dry enough to be called desert, and in July the surface can be as much as one hundred and fifty degrees, so they blow around some. But underneath, believe it or not, the sand is moist, so the base pretty much stays in place." He points to a flat space carved out like a little bench. "Here, we can sit down for a minute and enjoy the sun. I think Norma Lou is asleep again." He shades her eyes with his big brown hand. "So, to answer your question, the surface shape is constantly changing, but the base remains."

"Like me. That's the way I've felt this year. Really blown around so that sometimes I hardly knew what shape I was."

"Well, you were in a lot of different shapes this year, that's true." He grins.

She recalls those shapes and how uncomfortable she was at the end. She looks down and congratulates herself for having her trim look back. "I want to believe that there's an old Molly underneath here somewhere if I can just find her."

"I guess that's why you have to go home, to see if you can find that old Molly again." He smiles at her but the smile quickly disappears. "It makes me really sad to think about your leaving, but I know it's important for you to go back and try to patch things up with your dad. And I'm sad to say that I was the one who suggested it." They are both quiet for a moment, and then he says, "I sure hate to think of never seeing you again." He has to look away.

Molly starts to say that she will visit, but she knows that's not what he means. He's talking about losing her, and suggesting a visit would be an insult to him, the way she knows he loves her. And by the time she visits he will for sure have another girlfriend. He's certainly handsome enough to have his pick. Finally, after an awkward silence, she says, "Well, I don't know how things will work out back there. My dad's pretty stubborn, you know. I mean, what if he just sends me away again?"

"You'll always have a place here."

Molly lets that pass and says, "And you know what? I doubt I'll find the old Molly back there in Kansas. Too much has happened. Besides, I'm not so sure there was much of an old Molly to begin with, just a confused high school kid blowing around in the wind. Maybe I'm just loose sand waiting for the next breeze to shape me into something I can't even imagine."

He makes a low humming sound before he says, "I like that. Beautiful. I went through some windswept years like that, and I guess I'm still going through it some, but now I have a better sense of what I want out of life."

"And what is that?" Molly asks, truly curious about how he will answer.

"Someone to love. A person to take care of and protect, to make happy. Something more than potatoes. Heck, I can make a good living off of potatoes with one arm tied behind my back. I want to read books and be able to talk to someone about what I read. Maybe read the same things sometimes. Listen to music together. I'd like to bring a little justice into this world. Right a few wrongs. That's my vision and I will pursue it as the eagle seeks the deepest blue of the sky."

They sit there together in the sand, the three of them, quiet, enjoying the warm sun and the cooling wind. It is a sad goodbye, and now she's not sure she really wants to leave. She wants to shake off the sadness before she starts to cry, so she tries a new subject. "Were the Utes here, too?" she asks.

"They say the earliest inhabitants were called the Clovis or Folsom people and came eleven thousand years ago, hunter-gatherers who lived off of the mammoth and prehistoric bison. But after that, you bet, the Utes were here."

Molly looks up and gives him a sly smile. "Those Utes were everywhere, weren't they?"

"Yes, and it's pretty amazing to think that they came walking, because horses didn't exist in North America before the Spanish arrived. So, they couldn't just pick up one morning and say 'Let's go to the dunes.' Their travels often took generations.

With the sun casting shadows of his sharp features on the sand and the breeze blowing his black hair, Carlos looks quite Indian to Molly at that moment, the kind son of Ute ancestors she will never know. Lately, though, she hasn't thought of him as Indian or Spanish or anything in particular, just as her handsome friend Carlos. And he is handsome. What is she doing leaving him?

Suddenly, Carlos stands up, takes a quick peek at Norma Lou, and says, "Let's go to the Preserve."

"The what?" The word brings to mind strawberry jam for Molly.

"The Preserve is the other part of the park, a sanctuary for hundreds of species of animals in that forest land that stretches up the side of the mountains over there. A lot of people don't even know it's here. We won't go far because it's an old dirt road meant for a Jeep, but come on, we can go in a little way and I'll show you some of it." He takes Molly's hand and they run, walk, slide, scream, and giggle their way down the dune like a couple of kids.

"Don't drop my baby," she yells.

"Now why would I want to do that?" he asks, with a serious countenance as he wraps his other arm tight around Norma Lou. When they get to the bottom, he peeks at Norma Lou in the front pack and she gives him a big smile. "Oh, wow, look at that smile. She must have liked that little adventure."

Molly is smiling, too, and she turns back for a moment to glance at where they walked down the dune. She notices how the breeze quickly wipes out their footprints in the sand. In a moment, no one will even know they were there and the smooth surface of the dune will be restored. Nothing left but a memory. Is that how it's going to be with Carlos?

Back in the Pathfinder, they leave the parking lot and head up to the deserted campground on the main road back into the Preserve.

"The bumpy part is up ahead," Carlos says.

"Isn't it always," Molly observes.

"There are two picnic areas along this road, but you need to hike into them, and I've got the cooler here." He motions to the back of the SUV with his head.

"Another picnic? In the winter? You planned this all out, didn't you?"

"My grandmother, *abuela*, wanted you to taste her tamales."

"But what if I had said no?"

"The hot tamales wouldn't be so hot eaten cold tonight."

"They're in the cooler?"

"Keeping warm. Wrapped up tighter than Norma Lou."

Carlos pulls into the campground and they find a picnic table. Norma Lou starts fussing—actual, outright crying, like she's hungry—so Molly sets herself up to nurse her. "I hope you don't mind."

"Mind? I'm sure that's what our ancestors did. No, I'm getting accustomed, so you go right ahead and I'll just set stuff out here." He has a picnic basket and a thermos besides the cooler and spreads out a tablecloth which he holds in place with silverware that looks like his family's best. Pottery mugs for the hot cider hold down the corners.

"Carlos, I can't believe this. Another gourmet picnics."

"Something else you will never forget. And not just the tamales, either. Look at how much she sent. What a wonderful mother!"

"And grandmother, too. But the food. Won't it attract the wild animals? Don't we need to be careful? We're in the Preserve, right?" She starts to fidget. "What animals do they have here?"

"Mostly mule deer, but also some pronghorns and elk. Big horn sheep, but they're higher up."

"Bears?"

"Oh, yeah, but this time of year you'd have to wake them up. Remember?"

"Rattlesnakes?"

"Heavens, no." He looks at her and furrows his brow. "Geez, Molly why are you getting so nervous out here when Mother Nature, Saint Anthony, and the Great Spirit are all standing by to take care of you? Not to mention me."

"I'm sorry. I never used to be this way. I'm just jumpy. Afraid of everything. I'm working on it."

"Think of something peaceful. My father says that if we listen, we can hear the voice of the Great Spirit in the winds. That breath gives life to the entire world. There's nothing to fear."

"Sorry. I know." She lowers her eyelids, a little embarrassed.

"Look up there almost to the tree line, before the mountain becomes all rock. Do you see those crooked trees up there all twisted and stunted in their growth? We call them *Krummholz* meaning *crooked wood* in German. They are battered by the winter winds and the snow and ice. They have a short growing season. Shallow soil. Well, there are people like that, too, that seem to have a lot of misfortunes and terrible things that happen to them. And they get all twisted up and find it hard to grow. I'm not blaming them, you understand, I'm just saying it happens. *Krummholz* people, like that twisted wood. God bless them." He shakes his head and looks over at Molly, who is listening intently wondering where this scraggly tree comparison is going. "But the difference between a tree and a person," Carlos continues, his usual reticence displaced by a flow of words, "is that the tree is just rooted there and has to take whatever hits it. A person can get up and walk away, change the environment, start over. I believe you can do this, Molly, and much as I hate to see you go, you need to leave here." His eyes have no tears but there is a cracking sound in his voice that tells her he might be crying on the inside. He swallows hard and continues. "There's one thing more."

"What's that?" she asks, not sure what more there could be to add to her nervousness about this trip back home.

"I want you and your father, once you get back together, to go to the county sheriff's office and tell them exactly what Tommy Dawson did to you. A full report. The police need to have it on record."

"I'm not sure I could do that."

"I know you don't want to be in a courtroom with Tommy, but look at it this way: how many more young women is Tommy Dawson going to rape if he goes free?"

"Just report the crime? Then I can choose what to do if they catch him?"

"Exactly. You need to meet with your father, get him to see it your way, and go to the courthouse together." Carlos is firm in what he is telling her, and she can see that he really wants Tommy brought to justice. "Then," he continues, "you need to go back to the place where that terrible thing happened. Get rid of the fears that make you panic. Start working it through." Molly frowns at this frightening suggestion. "As I told you before, you will find the courage to be strong. I believe you can eventually throw off that horrible experience—not that you'll ever forget it completely—but you will get free of it somehow, free enough to live your life."

Molly finishes nursing and doesn't say anything more. She just nods her head, wondering how Carlos can keep believing in her the way he does, always wanting what's best for her. She knows he wants her to stay, but even so he urges her to go home and do what she needs to do. Wow! That's pretty amazing. But she doesn't reply because she is so wrought up with emotion.

"Are you mad at me for saying these things?"

"Oh, no, not at all. Actually, I like it when you talk to me like this. I feel like you are pulling for me, that you're on my side. The way you care about me makes me feel like I can do it." But the thought of doing it, the pain of it, is still terrifying. This trip back home is getting really complicated.

"Are you ready for some tamales?"

"For sure."

They eat the tamales and Spanish rice and beans in silence, maybe because they are both so hungry and a little tired of the serious conversation. Finally, Molly says, "Do you have something I can write on?"

"Well, you know me, how I carry around a few note cards in my shirt pocket, but I've got to find my pencil." He looks through his pants pockets and jacket until he finds the stub of a yellow pencil. "What's this for? A sudden inspiration for a poem?"

"No, I just remembered that I haven't said goody-bye to Selena. If I write her a note, will you give it to her?"

"Of course. She told me she would miss you."

Molly takes the card and writes:

Dear Running Deer,

I'm sorry to leave without a personal good-bye. We really hit it off great,and I'm sure we could become friends if I didn't have to go back to Kansas. Something in my heart tells me that I will see you again. Good luck with your running, dear.

    Fondly,
    Molly

"May I read it?" Carlos asks.

"Sure, why not?"

As he reads, a broad smile creeps across his face and he nods his head, yes, several times. "I surely hope so," he says, looking up at Molly, the smile still in place.

7

THE MUTE CORPSE AND THE TALKING CURE

Wayne helps Molly pack up her few belongings and all of the picture books and toys and dolls he has given to Norma Lou. He buys her an infant car seat for the trip back and installs it. He services the rickety old truck: puts new tires on it, gets a new rear-view mirror, and changes out the battery. Does everything he can think to do, and then makes sure the gas tank is full.

On Monday morning, as agreed, Molly and Wayne start out together before dawn with the fog lifting slowly, he following her down to Route 160 and then up over La Veta Pass. Scattered patches of melting snow on the shoulders of the road are signaling spring in the Valley, but the drifts are still piled high on the pass. Her body seems half asleep, but her mind is running fast and deep. Why are people never what they appear to be? She worried that Wayne was some kind of sex sultan or religious nut. Then she thought Savannah would be her friend but she never really was. Rainbow, her midwife, turns out to be a hippy's kid with a degree in agronomy. And Carlos, well, she had him completely wrong. She already misses him a lot, and even that is different from what she expected.

She drives along with Wayne following her east into the pink and gray sunrise to Walsenburg, where she will go north on Route 10 and then take 50 on east back to the family farm in Kansas. Hard to say how she will be received—for sure she's been back and forth on that one—but she can't imagine, now that she's actually on her way back, that her father will throw her out a second time, not if she can show him Norma Lou. She realizes that she's proud of her baby. Molly smiles fondly at Norma Lou and checks to make sure she's still sleeping. Then she glances in the new rear-view mirror to watch Wayne signaling to turn onto Interstate 25 South heading toward Santa Fe.

Molly drives on through that desolate stretch of Route 10, mostly grassland and sagebrush, and turns onto Highway 50 in La Junta where she fills the tank at the same station she used on the way out. For sure, that seems like a long time ago. She stretches, snacks, and pushes on, and on and on. She has just crossed the state line into Kansas when she hears the ringtone on her phone, which she recharged for the trip just in case of an emergency. Now that's a surprise. Who could that be? Not Wayne. He should be with Emily by now. She answers and pulls over on the shoulder like her mother told her to do, and it's a good thing she does because the news is not good. It's her brother Danny.

"Hey, little brother, what's up?" She listens intently, panic and disbelief bubbling up together. "I'm on my way now. Seriously! I'm already in Kansas on Route Fifty. It was supposed to be a surprise." Danny says to go straight to the ER at the hospital in Colby because that's where the ambulance is taking their father. She clenches her teeth and puts the truck in gear. "I'll get there as fast as I can." Throwing a glance at Norma Lou, she pulls back onto the highway and speeds along with the engine roaring. Come on, old clunker, don't let me down now.

She tries to control the agitation from her swirling emotions as she wonders how bad this heart attack is. She had a friend at school whose father had a heart attack, but the first responders knew exactly what to do for him and when he got to the hospital the doctor put in some stents. No big deal. She needs to think on the positive side. She glances back at Norma Lou, who seems to be wide awake now, and she talks some baby talk to her. Sure enough, there comes that smile. "Keep practicing that smile, honey," she tells her.

She should have told Danny not to tell their father that she was on her way home. Let her dad recover a little in the hospital first and then meet Norma Lou when he's feeling better; he doesn't need to be upset with any surprises right now. But she *does* want him to meet her and she *does* want to be reconciled to her father because that's the whole point of her coming back home. So, should she stop at the farm and wait for him to recover enough to come home, or go straight to the ER? As she drives along her mind is going in circles while the straight tube of highway and gray dishwater sky seem endless. She is still a long way from home.

She has decided to go straight to the hospital in Colby, even though it adds another half hour onto the already long trip. Her family will be expecting her. Norma Lou went back to sleep again, thank heavens. Now she will just bundle her up, put her in that lovely fur-trimmed jacket, and take her inside to meet her grandfather. She hopes seeing them both won't give him a second heart attack or, god forbid, a stroke.

She knows where the hospital is because the cheerleaders sometimes went there to visit the injured football players with their broken legs and collarbones. She finds a spot in the parking lot, checks her appearance in the new rearview mirror, and grabs up Norma Lou. With her baby on one arm, she marches toward the ER entrance, anxious about what condition her father is in and wondering what this encounter will produce. She certainly doesn't want to say anything that will affect his well-being or make things worse between them. Her trip home is not going as planned.

As she enters the ER entrance and looks around, she finds signs to a waiting room at the end of a corridor, and sure enough, her mother and brother are sitting there waiting for her. Her mother jumps up to greet her immediately, but instead of fussing over Norma Lou as Molly had expected, she just clings to her without letting go. As Molly looks over her mother's shoulder at her brother standing behind her, he breaks the news with a solemn face. "He didn't make it."

"What?" Molly pulls back shocked, wiggling from her mother's grasp.

"Dad didn't survive the heart attack," Danny explains. "He died a few hours after we got here. Actually, just a little while ago.

"They did everything they could, but they lost him," her mother sobs. "He's gone, Molly He's gone."

Molly is stunned. She shifts Norma Lou into a more comfortable position and jiggles her nervously. "When did this heart attack start?" she asks. "Tell me what happened."

"When dad woke up this morning, he was having chest pains," Danny says, "but he insisted it was nothing. Said he'd had them before."

"Oh, my gosh. I can't believe what I'm hearing." Her face feels frozen, stiff and expressionless with shock.

"Well, it's true," her mother says, "but before we say another word about your father, please, I need to be introduced to this little bundle in your arms."

"This is Norma Lou," Molly says with a proud smile, but barely able to choke out the name. "What do you think?"

"Oh, she's adorable, Molly. Just look at her," Molly's mother says.

"She's Irish all right," Danny says. "A redhead like the rest of us."

"She's just learning to smile. You can tease one out if you talk to her just right."

So as Molly's mother gives her some real professional down home Kansas baby talk, Danny puts a forefinger under her chin, and sure enough, on comes the smile like someone just plugged in a Christmas tree.

"Look at that," Molly's mother says. "If only your father could have seen that," she says and then mother and daughter both start weeping while Danny hides behind a stone face. The crying goes on like that for a while until Molly's mother says, "Would you like to see him?"

Molly is puzzled. "Who?"

"Your father. He's still here. We asked the undertaker not to come and get him yet."

Molly is petrified. She doesn't remember seeing another dead person unless maybe it was her grandmother in her casket. But this is different. Her father? Still in the ER?

Before she can answer, her mother speaks. "Take Norma Lou with you. I'm sure you meant to show him your baby. It's a shame he can't see her now, but you can see him."

It sounds like this is something her mother expects her to do, but for sure this would not be her preference if she had any choice in the matter. See her father dead? After she's been driving all day to see him alive? No thanks.

"Go ahead, honey. Stand by his side and tell him what you have to say."

Just as Molly has almost convinced herself to go take a peek, now she's supposed to talk to him, too? This is really getting creepy.

Molly notices that Danny has been watching her, observing her reaction, and he must know how uncomfortable she is. So, it surprises her when Danny says, "It's not as bad as you think. You may regret it if you don't tell him good-bye. Come on, show him Norma Lou. I'll take you back."

They weave through the maze of beds and curtains and equipment, trying not to disturb the living. A nurse asks if she can help them find something and as Molly nods, her brother makes the request. "Yes, Mr. O'Reilly, please." Danny turns to leave. "She'll show you where he is and leave you alone with him. I've already said my good-byes. I'm a little ashamed. I kind of gave him an earful."

Soon Molly finds herself standing before the lifeless body of her father, the nurse having pulled the sheet from over his face halfway down his body. He's wearing a hospital gown. His brown hair mixed with gray still has a strong reddish tinge, the family signature. His expression is generally peaceful, but he has that same stern look of determination. Always right, even dead. His arms are muscular from all of that physical labor on the farm and his sturdy chest is broad, containing the heart that let him down so young. He seems young to Molly, even though she has only known him these years as her father. She can't resist an urge to lay her free hand on his arm but pulls back quickly as she finds it hard and cold to the touch. She switches Norma Lou over to her other arm, as if to position her better for her father to see her. She tries to touch him again, this time resting a hand on the gown covering his shoulder.

She has rehearsed several speeches she would have made to her father, always anticipating the worst, but she never imagined meeting with him would be like this. She feels her heart beating and it reminds her that his has stopped. Suddenly she realizes that she can say whatever she pleases and he won't talk back, which is what she had always wanted, but not like this, not because he's dead. She draws a deep breath and begins softly. "I was coming back to surprise you, Dad. I wanted to show you my baby here. Her name is Norma Lou. If you could, you would see that she has red hair. I'm sure that's the first thing you would notice about her, that red hair we have in this family."

Molly doesn't know what to say next and she feels self-conscious standing here talking to her dead father. Mainly, she would like to have this over with, but as long as she is here, she decides she may as well tell him the rest. "I came back to tell you one more time my version of what happened with Tommy. I was overpowered and raped, dad. I screamed and fought back, but it didn't do any good. And I was going to ask you to go to the county courthouse with me this week and report the crime." She pauses to adjust Norma Lou in her arms and take another deep breath. "The hardest thing about this whole mess, Dad, was being sent away—banished from our family. I was returning to ask you to take us back, Norma Lou and me, so that we could be together again as a family. I guess that's not going to happen now." Barely controlling her crying, silently holding it inside, she pauses to maintain her composure before she says, "You always taught me to be on time. Well, I'm afraid I was late for the most important moment of my life." What else does she want to mention? "I never got to tell you how much I appreciate all the things you taught me to do. I know you were trying to bring me up to be a good person." Norma Lou starts to fuss and that makes a wonderful excuse to exit. She has said all she has to say anyway, and can't see what good it's doing trying to have a conversation with a dead person who doesn't hear, understand, or reply. Sort of like when he was alive.

Danny tells the nurse she can call the funeral home now. They find their mom and go out to the parking lot together. It seems the family has a new sedan, an actual car, maybe to replace the missing vehicle she drove to Colorado. She stands by the truck for a moment looking back at the hospital, trying to convince herself that the calamity she witnessed in there wasn't a dream. She puts Norma Lou back in her car seat, and they all drive off together, Danny and her mother in the lead in the sedan and she following close behind in the truck. They travel the road that the school bus always took carrying her and Danny back and forth to Colby High, and eventually they turn onto the long dirt road that leads straight back to the barns, the maple grove, and the house that was once home. It has been a long day, and in the new rearview mirror she sees the sun, partially obscured by grey clouds, finally setting in the west. Who knows what tomorrow will bring and the day after that? No doubt a lot of unconventional grieving full of mixed emotions. How ironic: the bearer of the surprise was the one to be most surprised. Why is life like that?

The next few days are tough for Molly because nothing at home seems like home anymore: a house that feels too large and quiet without her father, a barn full of noisy mooing cows apparently upset by the perceived neglect by their owner, and a flat gray landscape without snow-capped mountains or blue sky. All winter long she was longing for her home, and when she finally worked up her courage to return, look what she finds. Her father's death has turned everything upside down so that it's no longer home, but this is where she is right now and where she needs to be.

Her mom is a sight to behold, completely lost, wandering around the house trying to find things to do, not sure how to proceed without the man who each morning gave her a list of things to accomplish that day. She falls into a dither when she comes upon something of his: a discarded jacket, an old pair of boots, seldom used reading glasses. Molly wonders if her mother has mixed feelings about her loss, as she and Danny do. It's not easy grieving for the husband and father whose unachievable high standards left everyone in his wake diminished. So, for the first few days back home, Molly cries uncontrollably and because the crying is so frequent and intense, seemingly out of proportion, it has her worried. Why is she crying like this for the father who threw her out?

Molly becomes inconsolable as the day of the funeral approaches.

Should she go? After all, her father kicked her out of the family and didn't live long enough to welcome her back. Would he have wanted her present at his funeral? Sometimes she thinks he would, but at other times she is sure he would not. Certainly, it would be presumptuous of her to go, thinking that he would have wanted that when there is an equally good chance, he wouldn't have welcomed her presence at all. If it were a birthday party for him, for example, surely, he would not want her there. But it's his funeral. It's his *funeral,* Molly repeats to herself for at least the hundredth time, and then she starts to cry again. Molly's turmoil seems to be picked up by Norma Lou, who cries more than usual and fusses when she is not out and out screaming.

When the day of the funeral arrives, Molly is still undecided, but when she shares her indecision with her mother, she is advised to stop trying to guess her father's wishes and follow her own heart. At least, she learns, her presence will provide some comfort to her mother.

So, Molly and Danny and their mother and Norma Lou drive to the cemetery in Oakdale—why Oakdale?—where they meet the long black hearse. They join her Uncle Russ and Aunt Doreen and the other mourners in a brief graveside memorial service before the comital. Molly worries about how Norma Lou will behave, but who can fault a baby for crying at a funeral?

After they greet the solemn-faced mourners, mostly other farmers from the dairy co-op where they sold their milk, people gather around the casket, which has been carried in and laid on the straps and bars that hold it above the opened hole dug for the grave. Molly is so uncomfortable being there, with one side of her still sure that her father wouldn't want her around, that she drifts to the back of the crowd away from the designated space for family, out of the public eye, where she can cry in relative privacy.

The rest of the funeral is literally a blur for Molly because her crying continues unceasing and the tears obscure her vision. She doesn't hear much of what is being said and understands even less, knowing only that nice things are being expressed about her father. It's hard to believe that this funeral is actually real and is for her own father. At this moment everything seems to be swaying—the people standing at graveside, the tall leafless oaks—and then she realizes that she is the one who is swaying, trying to soothe Norma Lou into a temporary slumber that will last at least until the end of the funeral. When the service finally ends, she heads straight for the car. She can't bear the idea of having to talk to people who will be judging her as the daughter who let a farmhand seduce her. Let them talk among themselves if that's what they want to do.

What saves Molly in the next few days after the funeral are the moments she can spend again with Danny. He's still in school, of course, finishing out his junior year, but when he gets home in the late afternoon, he glues onto her and they try to talk and joke together like old times. She tells her story to him in fragments, incident upon incident, character by character, and gradually over several afternoons she gives a clear picture of Horseshoe Ranch and what happened to her there, how beautiful it is, and how kind the people were to her. He says he'd like to work there, but then remembers it's mostly for women. No cowboys.

Molly continues her routine with Norma Lou, feeding her, changing her, always the responsible mother, but with the exception of her few enjoyable moments with Danny, she is depressed, moving around the house under a cloud of gloom that makes her cry a lot. She knows that it's normal to cry for a while after people die, but her crying seems to be more than the normal grief. Why should she be crying so much for a father that treated her so badly? She hadn't been around him for almost a year, so why is she suffering his loss so much? Is something else inspiring these tears?

One evening after she's put Norma Lou down for the night, Molly sits in the rocker by the fireplace without a book, just sitting there, crying in an endless outpouring of tears. She can't seem to get control of herself even when Danny comes down the stairs, homework finished, to be with her.

"What's wrong?" he asks softly. She doesn't respond, so he asks again, "Is it dad or something more?" There is no reply, only a shake of the head. "Bad news from Colorado?" Still no response. So, he sits down with her and waits.

Finally, she says, "I came home to see dad, to get permission to return to the family." She dries her face with a fresh tissue, the last of that box, and drops it on the floor to join the accumulation of crumpled ones at her feet. "And I wanted to make sure he understood what really happened, even if it meant another argument."

"It would have," Danny says in a flat, matter-of-fact voice.

"I would have shown him Norma Lou and she would have smiled at him." She suffers a new attack of crying and sobbing. "You've seen her smile."

"Well, yeah, she's really cute. But I'm not so sure..."

"And now I'll never know. It's just so unfair his dying like this."

"Well, it wasn't on purpose, but I know what you mean."

Even now, with Danny's understanding, she can't seem to stop her crying. Danny seems concerned. "Look," he says. "I have an idea. It's going to sound weird coming from me, but, well, there's this girl at school and her father was killed in a car accident this year."

"Who?"

"You wouldn't know her. Anyway, she went to this counselor to talk about it and she said it really helped."

"I have a little money saved."

"I'm sure mom would pay."

"For sure I can't go on like this." She rocks for a while and then she asks Danny to get her the name of the counselor and the phone number.

A week later, the soonest they can get an appointment, Molly finds herself seated in the modest office of the counselor in Colby, the one recommended by her brother's friend. She hopes it helps because she's still crying, day after day and every night. Can't sleep. Has no appetite. She's worried about herself but also about Norma Lou, resurfacing that old fear that she's not fit to take care of her.

Molly finds it hard to believe that she is telling her whole story to a perfect stranger, a licensed psychologist, young and casually dressed, not what you would expect. The woman has that kind look on her face like Wayne always did and seems to understand her from the way she nods and comments every now and then on what Molly must have been feeling while she was going through all of that. When Molly finishes her story—everything in order and compressed this time—she looks up at the counselor for some advice, some instructions, or maybe just some comforting words of encouragement to make her feel better, but the counselor just says, "Some things go unresolved."

"Unresolved?" Molly hears herself repeating the word, her eyes blinking.

"Yes, unresolved," the counselor continues in a firm but tender voice. "We can't always fix everything. Time runs out. We don't get to say what we meant to say. Loved ones die unexpectedly. Death has its own calendar and our feelings are left confused, in disarray."

"But what should I do?" Molly pleads.

"It may bring you some consolation in the weeks ahead to know that there is nothing you are supposed to do. There is nothing to fix because it can't be fixed now."

Molly's tears, which had nearly dried up, start to flow bitterly. "So, everything is left hanging, my life completely shattered, and I'm just supposed to go on?"

"Yes, in the best way you can. Build the life you want to live as an adult. You are an adult now. I'm sure you sense that."

"If this is what being an adult is, it really sucks," she sobs. "I'm just so completely disappointed that my father never got to see his granddaughter." Her voice rises with her anger. "It's so unfair." Now she's crying uncontrollably, and the counselor just lets her go like an off-leash dog. She offers tissues and nods vigorously, showing her support for Molly's right to cry unabated.

Then the counselor says, "Your good intentions were never realized. It feels like you were cheated, right? And you were. That feeling of being cheated, of the unrelenting unfairness of life, may come back to you a lot in the days ahead. So, cry it out, that's okay, but then stop and try not to dwell too much on what didn't happen with your father and will never happen now. Think about the attention shown to you by Wayne and those amazing women at that ranch without cowboys. Let their strength and kindness be your guide."

Molly uses a tissue to wipe her cheeks and nose, trying to regain her composure, wondering if she will ever be strong like Rainbow and Jersey.

"And be sure to enjoy that precious third-generation redhead."

"Her name is Norma Lou." Saying her name again brings a lump to her throat, but she pulls herself together quickly this time and says proudly, "Norma Lou O'Reilly." She swallows hard and fights back the tears that want to flow from her mentioning the last name of a family that isn't a family anymore. Then Molly glances around and wonders if her appointment is over, if she should stand up to leave. What is she doing in this strange office?

"You will come back to see me, won't you?" the counselor asks, rolling her chair forward and placing a hand gently on Molly's forearm. "We need to talk about your plans."

"Plans? I can't make any plans for myself. I need to take care of my baby," Molly replies.

"Not forever, and not all alone. People will want to help you."

"Everyone really likes Norma Lou," Molly says.

"And what about your friend that you told me about, the potato farmer? What's his name?"

"Carlos Ouray." Molly smiles through her tears, a big broad smile. She pictures his sharp features against the blue sky at the sand dunes.

"It sounds like he treats you with dignity and I'll bet he's waiting for you."

"If he is, we need to talk about why I'm so dang scared of him." She stands up to leave and notices that she feels taller and lighter than when she came in. But what she notices most is that the image of Carlos at the dunes stays in her head.

8

MOM'S SECRET AND DANNY'S MISTAKE

Molly's mother is wonderful in the way she helps with Norma Lou: slipping her just the right toy, slinging her over one shoulder to pat out a burp, and rocking her before a nap.

"Mom, how do you remember the way to do all of this stuff?"

"You don't forget what's mostly instinct anyway," her mother says. "I just do what comes naturally."

There's that word *natural* again. She just treats her cooing little granddaughter as Molly's baby, which is what she calls her when she doesn't think to say Norma Lou. She doesn't seem to mind that this baby's father is that abominable Tommy Dawson, whom she knew and disliked intensely. Is her mother forgetting about him?

Norma Lou seems to fill an empty spot for her mother, one generation replacing the other, but Molly continues to wonder about the balance of loss and relief in her mother's grief, knowing that living with her father was not only difficult for his children, but even more so for his wife. Molly admits she probably wouldn't have thought about something like that a year ago, but now with her father gone, she's beginning to see her mother more clearly as Ida, a woman in her own right.

Molly and her mother are in the kitchen making dinner together tonight, an old routine that Molly enjoys now, a way of being reunited with her mom again. She notices that her mother is wearing slacks and she recalls that when she was out West, she always remembered her mother in a house dress. Did her father not permit pants? "Mom, do we really need so many potatoes?" she asks, and of course the mention of potatoes reminds her of Carlos. "It's just the two of us and Danny now, and I know he's still a growing young man, but really."

"I just keep making everything the way I did when your dad was still here. I need to cut down a little, I guess."

"Yes, smaller portions and fewer dishes. Like we don't really need dinner rolls or dessert."

"You've got a point." Ida wrings her hands and bites her lower lip.

"There are just so many adjustments I need to make."

"And *can* make now," Molly suggests, hoping her mother will ponder her new freedom. She and her mother are teaming up to fry chicken filets breaded with cracker and egg, one dipping the chicken in the beaten egg, the other in the ground up cracker. Quite spontaneously Molly says, "I'm wondering if you can tell me a little bit more about how my father came to die from this heart attack. Being as shocked as I was that day, maybe a lot of the details didn't register with me. So, tell me more, mom, about what happened leading up to that morning."

"More?" Her mother looks up at her as if to question why they need to be talking about this subject, but then she begins, "Well, he'd been accumulating symptoms over several months, right after you left. It didn't take him long to realize that he had done a terrible thing by sending you away, but you know how stubborn he was. He couldn't admit that he had broken his own heart."

Broken his own heart? Molly is touched by her mother's description. It sounds like he may have had second thoughts. "That's what happened to Wayne, too, the manager of the ranch. He sent his daughter away and then really regretted it. But these symptoms that dad had, did he go to the doctor?"

"Well, that's another thing he was stubborn about. He kept saying the chest pains were indigestion and would go away, when in fact they were getting worse."

"He used to tell us kids that hard work never killed anybody. I'm sure he felt it was impossible for a big brawny guy like himself to get sick."

"And not to get well all on his own. He used to brag that anything he had could be cured with Vitamin C, Neosporin, or Sloan's Liniment. He said that if he got really bad off, he'd have to break down and use some Udder Balm."

"On what?" The question slips from Molly's lips.

"Well, I don't know." Ida scratches her head. "On his udder, I suppose."

They exchange sly glances, holding back closed-mouth smiles, and Molly resists the temptation to make a joke about "udder nonsense."

Then her mom turns serious. "I'm sure a doctor could have done something for him if he had gone to one."

So, he could have been treated. He didn't have to die of this heart attack. He might have met Norma Lou. "Is it possible to say that he died of stubbornness?"

"You know, Molly, sometimes you have a way of saying things that goes right to the point."

"What about his last days?" Molly asks.

"Or last weeks. He was hobbling around here for quite a while trying to do the usual chores, denying that there was anything wrong with him at all. Danny noticed it and said something to him, but your father about bit his head off, so Danny never brought it up again."

"Poor Danny." Molly wonders what Danny must be feeling about losing his father. She's been so enveloped in her own grief that she hasn't asked her brother very much about his.

"Well, then he had what I'm sure was a full-blown heart attack with all the pain symptoms in the neck and arm, so that's when I called nine-one-one that morning you were driving home here to surprise him." She stands motionless and looks off into space like she is reliving the whole ordeal. "But you know how far out we live and the distance into Colby to the Citizens Medical Center. That's when Danny called you, when your father was on his way there. Naturally Danny and I trailed along after the ambulance in the sedan and raced into the hospital when we arrived to tell him you were already on Route Fifty. He wasn't able to speak much when we got to see him and it was hard to hear him, but he just kept saying he was sorry."

Molly feels a surge of hope. "Do you suppose that could have been meant for me?"

"Let's hope so, honey. He wasn't specific. But..." Her mother's voice trails off. "Yes, probably," she tacks on.

Probably? To Molly that means that she still doesn't know for sure if her father forgave her or not. The words of her counselor come back: "Some things go unresolved." Will she ever know? It doesn't look like she will. "But tell me, Mom, did you guys ever talk about what happened to me? I mean, I told you the facts before I left for Colorado."

"The facts, yes, I told him the same facts you told me, but his interpretation, well, that's another matter." She wipes her hands on her apron. "When I tried to talk to him about it, he just sat there across the kitchen table from me twisting and turning and rolling his eyes. But who ever knew what was in his mind? Not me."

Molly can picture her dad from her mother's description, disagreeing like that, stubbornly silent. "So, he continued to blame me."

"Yes, but even so he could have forgiven you, too, in his heart, you know, on his death bed."

It sounds to Molly more like her mother's wish than what her dad actually did. "So, we don't really know whether he continued to blame me or not." Molly notices that her desire to know what her dad thought has become an obsession; she's like a dog with a bone. She needs to let go. Drop it. She checks the chicken to see if it is getting brown and turns over a few pieces that are. "But what about you, Mom, did you blame me?"

Molly's mother doesn't need to think that over before she answers. "No. Of course not. I kind of blamed you a little for flirting with the jerk, but no I couldn't possibly blame you, not after the terrible things you told me."

What exactly has Molly learned from this conversation? That her father didn't need to die but he did. That he might have forgiven her but never said so. That she needs to stop wondering what he thought about her and let it go. Accept that it is unresolved. At least her mother is talking like she never did before.

Molly didn't notice much of anything about her counselor's office the first time she visited. She just had a street and a number and the name of the counselor, Bonnie Bradford. On this visit, now that she is less nervous, she notes the plaque at the entrance that reads *Heartland Help,* and that two social workers share this brightly painted old Victorian home for their offices. Oh, my gosh, one is named Braxton. Related to her teacher somehow?

Bonnie sits in an office chair on wheels, and she rolls forward and back as she listens intently, zooming in occasionally for a close encounter as she asks a challenging question. The client—that is what she is, Molly has been told, not a patient—gets to sit in a big easy chair with a view out the side window of a maple tree with leafless branches soaring into the gray sky. Isn't spring about due?

The counselor asks her to call her Bonnie, but that's out of the question for Molly, and because none of the diplomas hanging framed on her wall says *Doctor,* she just calls her ma'am. Molly slips off her loafers and curls her feet up under her lanky legs, covered up today in green tights and a plaid skirt. She notices that her counselor is wearing the same sweatshirt as last time. It says Fort Hays State. Bonnie is reviewing the notes she took in a small notebook. She goes over a few things to make sure she has them correct, including the names, and then she asks Molly how she's doing. Molly says that she has much better control over the crying and isn't so depressed.

"Good," Bonnie says. "That's progress."

"I couldn't figure out why I was crying so much about my father."

"Perhaps it was only partly about your father. You lost your father, but you also lost the opportunity to settle up with him, to win back his support and affection. That was a huge loss."

"Maybe bigger than the loss of my father?"

"We don't need to weigh the comparison, but yes, it was a big loss for you to have that go unresolved, a terrible disappointment. A double loss."

"And to know that I can't do anything about it helps me recover?" Molly asks, hoping to discover how.

"Helps you give it up. Let's you move on."

That gives Molly a sense of relief from her obsession to know what can't be known. Then she tells her counselor that what she really wants to know is how to make sure nothing like this ever happens to her again.

Bonnie pauses and rolls back in her chair as if to give Molly plenty of space to consider her next suggestion. "Perhaps it would be helpful to you if we explored in a little more detail your relationship with Tommy Dawson before the day when he took advantage of your being alone."

"Well, I would hardly call it a relationship." The thought of a relationship with Tommy Dawson really turns her stomach, and she feels indignant about the suggestion. "He just worked for my dad."

"Okay, then let me ask, "Did you have boyfriends over here at the Colby High School?"

"Not really. I had many friends who happened to be boys, but those guys seemed really immature, not yet grown to their full size, you know." She recalls some of them and it makes her smile. But the question causes her to ask herself why she never had an actual boyfriend. "Maybe because I was a little taller than most of the guys, they were too shy to approach me. But I knew the game by ninth grade: they did the asking and it was the girl that needed to do the attracting."

"What do you think you were doing with Tommy looking back on it now?"

That's a tough one. "Maybe just sharpening my skills a little by seeing if I could attract a guy?"

"Just hoping to attract his attention?"

"I guess I would admit to that. For me, that's all I was doing, but for Tommy it must have meant something else." She wonders now why she had anything to do with Tommy at all.

"Or Tommy, being older and more experienced, or perhaps just a sinister character, hoped to turn it into something else."

Molly fastens on the words *sinister character*. That's what he was. She knows that now, but she totally missed it at the time. "Looking back now, I think he planned all along what he was going to do to me. He played the schemer's game with the farmer's daughter, just waiting for the right opportunity. I was the stupid one."

"Or maybe we should say, speaking without self-recrimination, that you were somewhat over your head in this flirtation game with Tommy."

Flirting with him? That makes her a little annoyed. *Flirting* was her father's word. She surely didn't think of it that way. "I really wasn't flirting. I only wanted his attention to make sure that I could get guys to look at me and talk to me and pay me compliments. I never wanted *him*."

"Good point. But isn't that a perfectly normal thing for a high school girl to want to do, to test out her powers a little? Wasn't that something that the other girls were doing, too?"

"For sure, but with the other high school guys. My mistake was to try to attract a guy like Tommy."

"Your mistake? Hold on." Bonnie draws her chair in close and gazes intensely at Molly. "Tommy took advantage of his position and his superior strength as a male to overwhelm you. He raped you. That's the bottom line and don't ever forget it." Bonnie pauses for her words to sink in and then speaks more softly. "Did Tommy make any advances toward you before that morning in the grove?"

"Never. I was taken completely by surprise."

"That's important to note. He tricked you, deceived you. Do you see that? What would you do differently now?"

That's what she's asking: how to keep this from happening again. Couldn't Bonnie just give her a little advice once in a while instead of asking so many questions? It looks to her like she will have to come up with the plan. "Rule One. I would never get myself into that situation where I'm all alone far away from everything where no one could even hear me scream. Rule Two. I'd never be so trusting with someone I don't actually know."

"Good. Be aware of your surroundings. Be conscious of who you are with and how well acquainted you are. But tell me, did you and your mother never talk about things like this?"

"Tommy? Ha! Or anything else. Birth control? Never. Being sexually active—which I was not—heavens no, we didn't discuss such things in the O'Reilly household." Molly notices that she has raised her voice. She sounds really resentful.

"Have you ever wondered why you have never talked more openly about these things?" She rolls her chair away, leans back, and folds her hands behind her neck. "Okay, here's your homework assignment. Without being too bold, try to explore with your mother what it was like for her as a teen-age girl. She was a young woman once, you know. An interesting way into that might be with a few questions. 'Did you have dates in high school, Mom? How did you meet dad? What made you want to get married?' It's just a hunch, but you may discover some reason why she has never talked with you about 'these things' as we have been calling them."

"Well, I can guarantee you right now that I don't know the answers to any of those questions because as a teen, I never had those conversations with Ida O'Reilly. She was just my mother, and she took good care of me, but we never talked person to person about stuff like that." There she goes with that loud voice again. It looks like they have touched on something important without her realizing just how important it was. She doesn't want to blame her mother, but she suspects there was definitely something missing in her mom's mothering.

In Kansas, March is the mixed-up month that doesn't know whether it is supposed to be winter or spring, one day warm and clear, the next cold and blustery. Molly's father called it the farmer's month of certain uncertainty. As fresh green shoots are pushing through the soil, a heavy snow covers their fragile structure. The day you are ready to plow, the fields are drifted with what is supposed to be winter's last storm. The tornadoes come later.

This particular night in March, Molly and her mother are sitting in the living room in the antique rocking chairs that face the fireplace. They rest on an oval hooked rug in shades of tan and gray, a precious family heirloom although no one can remember who actually made the rug. Molly has been down on that rug earlier in the evening so that her now four-month-old baby can practice sitting independently. Norma Lou fits neatly into a perfect little spot for sitting up when Molly folds her own legs into a yoga position and then puts her baby in there and folds her legs the same way, like a Buddha within a Buddha. Norma Lou almost has it, holding herself upright with a straight back for several seconds before collapsing to one side or crashing to the other. She's sleeping soundly upstairs in her crib now apparently exhausted from her strenuous workout.

Danny is up in his room watching the Final Four basketball playoffs, a common pastime for Kansas fans during March Madness. The wind whistles audibly in the fireplace chimney and the floor feels draughty on the feet. When Molly was a kid, she had often begged to have a fire in the fireplace, but her father always had a stack of objections as to why they couldn't: we're almost out of firewood, it makes such a mess, it upsets the thermostat and makes the rest of the house cold—all of which were true, but in Molly's mind insufficient reasons for not making a beautiful warm fire.

"Hey, Mom, what about my making a fire tonight? I'll build it, and you can just sit there with your crocheting."

Molly remembers her mom on most nights after the dishes were done sitting by the fireless fireplace reading a novel, escaping off to some distant land, while her father sat in the recliner at the far end of the room and snored. If her mom wasn't reading, she was crocheting on some baby blanket that she never seemed to finish. Because she and her brother were nearly grown, why was her mother still making this stupid blanket anyway? Who was it for? No one asked. Tonight, she has pulled out that old baby blanket and is working away on it intently. Is it because she has a reason now? Finally, she says, "Do we have enough wood?"

"Plenty. Nice and dry, too, Aged for three years." Molly tries not to sound sarcastic.

"Has it been so long?"

"Except for a year ago at Christmas."

So, Molly slips on a heavy plaid flannel shirt, heads out to the shed near the equipment barn and comes back momentarily with an armload of split pine and some ash logs, as she dangles a hatchet from a free forefinger. She chops one piece of pine into kindling and in no time at all has a crackling fire blazing. When it burns down a little, she sets on the hardwood logs and the room fills with the slight scent of smoke and the cozy warmth she wants for the "homework" conversation she is planning to have with her mom tonight. She rocks and her mom works with her crochet hook.

"Tell me what it was like for you growing up, Mom, like when you were my age."

"Why would you want to know about that?" Her mother frowns, but a faint smile curves her lips, suggesting she may cooperate.

"Just tell me, like, what you did."

"Oh, I hate to bother you with ancient history. The only thing worse would be to have to hear about the Greeks and the Romans."

Molly rocks a little to give her mother time to relax and bring up her memories.

Ida begins with an outburst: "Babies, babies, babies! That's all I remember. I was the oldest and then there was a gap, maybe for a miscarriage no one mentioned, and after that this onslaught of babies one after the other, some boys, some girls, but all of them screamers."

"How many of them were there?"

"Six, counting me. Because I was the oldest, I had to help take care of them. It was not a choice, it was something I was expected to do, a duty." She puts her work down for a moment and gazes into the fire, as if she were searching for the rest of her story in the flickering of the flames. "I just remember kids crying all the time. It was like an infant jazz band, when one stopped tooting the next one took it up, one after the other, so that it seemed like there was no ending to the blues, no quiet ever in that house."

"What did you do to soothe them?"

"Well, first you had to figure out if there was a legitimate reason for them to be crying. Were they hungry? Were they thirsty? Was a diaper pin sticking in 'em?"

Molly isn't too sure about what a diaper pin is. The disposables for Norma Lou have snaps. "And you had the responsibility for them just because you were the oldest? That doesn't seem fair."

"When you are poor and there are no options, *fair* doesn't come into it. You just do what you are told to do." Ida sounds matter-of-fact, but Molly thinks she hears resentment in her voice.

"Wow! Sounds like you had it kind of rough."

"I did what I could because mom was cooking or cleaning or scrubbing or ironing, so she expected me to see to it that the brothers and the sisters were cared for and safe. My job was to keep them alive." Ida grows more and more agitated. "Sometimes, of course, there was nothing wrong and they were just bellerin' or fighting or throwing a tantrum over something they couldn't have. There is nothing like the word *no* to make a little whining two-year-old explode into a screamer."

"So, you had no normal teen-age years," Molly observes, hoping her mother will continue without having to ask her too many questions.

"That's right. I went to school, of course, and I was pretty good in school. Let's say I found it interesting compared to home. But I had to come right home afterward to tend the little lambs."

"Maybe that's why you're so good with Norma Lou now. I'm amazed at the bag of tricks you have for getting her to settle down."

"I have an impressive resumé for being a mother, but not much else."

Molly wonders what else she wished she might have added. "Did you go on dates or have boyfriends?"

"Now there's an interesting question. Why would you be asking that?" Molly assumes she doesn't need to provide an answer. "Basically, I would say no. I didn't have much idea what men were like except for my father and little brothers which left me almost nothing to go on at all. I think you could say I was totally ignorant about men my age."

"And your mom wasn't much help in telling you about men?" Molly thinks she is beginning to see a pattern.

"She had too much on her mind and wasn't very talkative about such things. Close mouthed. Never told me what to watch out for or avoid."

"But eventually you met someone. How did you meet dad?"

"You're just full of questions tonight, aren't you?" Molly's mother pulls up more yarn for her crocheting and starts working her hook furiously as if to signal that the conversation is over.

Molly gets up to adjust the logs so they will burn a little brighter. She remembers her father saying, on those rare evenings when he built a fire that a good fire results from the right balance of fuel and air. Too little air and there's smoke; too much air and the wood burns up too fast. Everything had to be just right for her father. For him, there was no room for a fire that burns too fast or too slow. Molly hopes that while she adjusts the logs, her mother will find the courage to answer her question. Is it so difficult? Duh. How did you meet dad?

Ida puts down her crocheting and stares into the fire again. It looks like she might be coming up with some words. "My father ran the general store in Rexford, inherited on his father's side from his parents. He made a living but they weren't rich, that's for sure, especially not with all of those kids. Anyway, one night there was a traveling carnival that came to Colby. You don't see them much anymore, the closest thing being those little carnivals they bring to the county fairs. I was just dying to go to that carnival and to get away from those squalling kids for one night before I went stark raving mad. So, I got a friend from school who drove and she took me to town. I met your dad there at the carnival."

Her mom is overcome by an attack of wheezing and sneezing, so Molly has to run and get a box of tissues, and she is afraid that the story has come to an end for tonight. When her mom gets settled, Molly says, "And?"

"And? Oh, yes, he took me on the Ferris wheel and carousel and won me a Teddy bear at the shooting gallery. We met secretly after that—I guess it was a secret because my parents didn't know—but we had a good time doing things together."

"And?" Molly asks again, hoping to recover more relics from her mother's past.

"And what?" Ida frowns, looking like she's shutting down.

Molly decides she will need to push a little. "Most kids, I'm beginning to find out, at least know how their parents met and married. Is there some reason I don't know?" Now Molly is growing suspicious. Maybe there is a reason for her mother's silence.

Ida goes back to her crocheting in earnest, and Molly is afraid that she's been prying or rude or something and won't hear the end of the story. She fixes the fire again, sits back down in the rocker and rocks, waiting out her mother's silence.

Eventually, looking up from her work, Ida says, "Your father never wanted you kids to know anything about this. That's why I've never told you."

"I don't mean to be disrespectful to my father, Mom, but he *has* passed away and you are free now—free in a lot of ways actually—but free at least to tell your own children whatever you want to tell them." Molly wonders where she found such a strong voice, but now she really wants to know what happened.

Ida opens her mouth as if to speak but hesitates. She picks up her crocheting again and then drops it as if she is having trouble summoning the will to tell something of such importance. Finally, she says, "Well, we had ourselves quite a little romance, or at least we thought we did, him driving over to Dexter on the weekends and always taking me somewhere for hamburgers and milkshakes. In my eyes he was rich because he was already working the prosperous dairy farm that he and your Uncle Russ would inherit. I was surrounded by screaming little urchins and I wanted out in the worst way. So one night, necking in his truck, our affections got a little out of hand, and..."

"You got pregnant and that's me," Molly blurts out. My god, do out-of-wedlock babies run in this family? Is it an inheritable trait? She wants in the worst way to say 'that son-of-a-bitch,' but she knows that if she does, she will never hear another peep from her mother. So, she literally clamps her two lips together with her first finger and thumb, and waits. But she doesn't have to wait long.

"No, not you." Ida waves a forefinger in front of herself to suggest to Molly that she's got it wrong. "There's more to the story than that, but it's very painful for me, Molly. Neither I nor your father told anyone, not even your Uncle Russ or his dear wife."

"Aunt Doreen? It's okay, Mom, you can tell me, and I really think I need to know."

"Your father's solution to our problem was to get married, to do the honorable and respectable thing. Young as we were, we thought we were in love, or at least he was sure he was in love with me, but the truth is we hardly knew each other. We were just pals drinking milkshakes and kissing." She rubs the knuckles of one hand with the fingers of the other.

"But wait. You're saying this baby is not me?"

"Hold on, I'm getting to that part, but it's not easy. So, this was kind of an unloaded shotgun marriage, the shotgun being your father's Irish Catholic conscience." Her eyes water and she looks as if she is going to cry.

"Just a second, Mom, take your time." The fire has burned down and is giving the room a soft glow, just enough darkness for revealing secrets. Molly goes over and gives her mother an awkward hug around one shoulder and a kiss on the top of her head. "I'm thinking I was conceived out of... Oh, just go on. Please." She pulls her chair closer to her mother and rests her elbows on her knees, her face in her hands.

"So, I did everything a conscientious pregnant woman does: I ate right, went to the doctor, and drank lots of whole milk. I even went to the hospital to have that baby delivered properly, but..." She breaks into deep uncontrollable sobs.

Molly's eyes are bathed in tears that cling without falling. She sits up abruptly. "It's okay, Mom. The baby. What happened?"

"The baby was stillborn."

"Born dead? Oh, my god, Mom, how awful! I worried about that with Norma Lou."

"Every mother does. But this actually happened." She continues to sob.

"Oh, jeez, Mom, I feel so bad for you. I can hardly absorb all of this. Wait a minute." Molly's brain is hurtling ahead to the implications. "So, you were left with no baby and a husband who thought he had to marry you. And you've lived all these years not sure if he really loved you or just felt responsible? Not knowing if you were really meant for each other or for someone else?"

"Over the years, honey, I've just tried not to think about that part and I've never told a soul." She stares down into the flickering shadows. "I don't know if I would have gone to college. Would I have married him or someone else? But the story has a happy ending." She lifts her head and brushes the tears from her cheeks with the corner of the blanket she is crocheting. "I was hysterical for a few short months, but eventually I got pregnant again and had a normal baby."

"That was me?"

"That was you, honey."

Normal? Molly is thankful in a new way that she was at least born normal, not having given it much thought before she had Norma Lou. But to be born dead? Not even to have had a chance at life? This is something else to put on her list of things that make life completely unfair: stillborn babies.

"I need to take Danny to the counselor with me," Molly says at breakfast the next morning. "I have to tell Danny what you told me because I don't want to put you through telling that whole story again. He needs to know, but I don't want to be alone when I tell him because he'll just run upstairs and lock himself in his room and stew about it forever. I'm sure Danny is just as confused about his father's death as I am. And now this."

"If you're asking whether I can afford to pay the counselor for Danny, too, the answer is yes."

"Danny needs to talk to someone about what happened to you and to understand what happened to me, too. And we can be sure our father never talked to him."

"Not unless it was tractors or cows." Ida gets up and wanders back and forth across the kitchen, then stops suddenly, as if she's wondering what she got up for in the first place.

"My hope for Danny," Molly says, "is that he will be kind and respectful to women."

"Actually, your father was never disrespectful." She casts her eyes toward Molly, a little defensive.

"At a certain level, Mom, that's true. He never spoke crudely to you, but look at what he expected of you, pouring him his second cup of coffee before he had to ask for it. He treated you almost like his slave."

"Was it that bad?"

"Just let yourself think about that a little."

Bonnie Bradford pulls in another chair for Danny to sit on, and after he is introduced and encouraged to call her Bonnie, Molly begins to report on her homework assignment. "You just listen to what I'm saying, Danny, and when I finish, we'll all talk about it together. But I swear to God, I'm not making this up." So, Molly tells her counselor a mini-version of what she learned from her mother as Danny fidgets and squirms, looking out at the leafless maple tree, but now and then glancing back at Molly to frown and register his astonishment.

At first the counselor focuses on Molly, as if Danny weren't there. "And what did you conclude from this conversation with your mother?"

"That there were a lot of things we should have been talking about, stuff I should have been learning about men that my mother wasn't able to speak about because of her own traumatic experiences."

"And because my dad shut her up," Danny says. "He told her she couldn't tell."

"Did you know about any of this?" the counselor asks turning toward Danny.

"Of course not. But I'm not surprised. I always wondered if they were happily married, and how she ended up with *him*."

"Maybe he just felt trapped," Molly says, "knowing he had to marry her."

"Well, yeah," Danny continues, "but he set the trap and stepped right into it."

"Do you think your mother felt trapped, too?" the counselor asks Molly.

"She didn't say so, but I think it was implied in the way she told the story. She seems more inclined just to accept her fate."

"As women often do, blaming themselves," Bonnie says. "You know how that goes, right Molly?"

"For sure."

"What do you think about all of this, Danny?" Her chair rolls toward Danny. "Kind of a lot to take in?"

"What I think is that our family didn't communicate very well. For example, when Molly left, no one told me why. Dad said she wanted to go out West for a summer job and I thought that was cool. I never knew she got kicked out. Nobody told me that she got pregnant, that she was off on that ranch having a baby all by herself. One of the guys at school told me that he had heard that my sister was pregnant. I started to get into a fight with him until friends separated us."

"How did it make you feel when you found out the truth?"

"Really stupid and left out, like my parents thought I was too young to handle it. Like they thought I was a little boy. Or that things like that are just for women and need to be kept secret."

"So, it's hard to know how to be a man if they treat you like a boy, and if no one talks to you about serious things," Bonnie says.

"Then when I found out she had actually been raped by Tommy Dawson," Danny can barely control his anger, "I wanted to kill the asshole."

"I'm glad you didn't, but I understand your anger. It's natural to wish to defend your sister."

"I hope they catch him someday and string him up."

"Well, that's another matter, isn't it, bringing guys like this to justice," the counselor says. Then she asks Danny, "What kind of a man would you like to be?"

"Besides not a dairy farmer? Well, I don't plan to go around getting women pregnant, not after what happened to my sister and my mother."

"Do you think you'll be like your father?" the counselor asks.

"I hope not, but I have to admit he had some good qualities, too. He knew a lot about farming and machinery and he wanted to teach us what he knew. But everything had to be perfect, and heck, we were just kids. Mol and I both had to put up with his browbeating. But a son doesn't have to grow up to be just like his father. I can choose not to be like him."

The counselor nods and says, "That's a very mature response, Danny."

Danny looks surprised at first, then smiles. "Thank you. No one has ever said I was mature before, certainly not my father."

"How would you say his death has affected you?"

He glances at Molly. "I would say it's been a lot worse for my sister here, but I had my cry and now—geez, I hate to say this—but I'm kind of relieved."

"Sounds like he was pretty strict with you. Are you angry at him?"

"Still? I've spent a lot of time in my room this year. He'd lambaste me about something and I'd be pissed at the moment, but then I'd get over it." He blows out a deep breath that puffs his cheeks.

"You're sure you haven't accumulated all of that anger?" Bonnie looks at him directly, her head tilted to the side.

"I'm not one to carry stuff around. Now that he's gone, I figure I won't have to deal with it anymore." He shrugs.

Bonnie pushes her chair back and says, "Okay, Danny, I can see that you are on the right track." Then she turns to Molly. "But we still have some unfinished business. We need to help you get over this horrible experience you had, restore your self-confidence, and make sure you develop positive attitudes about men and love and sex. It's meant to be a good thing, you know. A wonderful thing actually. We can't let you spend the rest of your life being afraid of men." Bonnie pushes her chair away, leans back, and folds her fingers together behind her neck. But this time she doesn't have another homework assignment. Instead, she sits there looking puzzled, as if she is thumbing through a mental textbook of therapy options for such a challenging goal.

After a moment of silence Molly says, "Carlos told me that I should return to the spot where Tommy Dawson threw me down." She squirms in her chair, hesitating, "But I'm not sure I can do that."

"And I'm not sure I would recommend that," Bonnie says, leaning forward. "I don't want you to relive the whole episode. We don't need to go back over that. You can go there if you wish, but keep in mind that the point of such a visit would be to triumph over your feelings, to take charge of your fears. Master your panic. Tell yourself that you are in charge of what comes into your mind. You are the gatekeeper of unwanted feelings." Then she scoots back in her chair as if to ponder her own recommendation. She seems to be warming to the idea.

Molly sits there bug-eyed, only partly convinced, wondering why Carlos suggested this.

"Do you have anyone who could go with you?" Bonnie asks, glancing over at Danny.

"Me? Why me?" he asks.

"For some support."

"Well, I suppose I could, but..."

Molly cuts her brother off. "Hold on. I have an idea. I'll go with O'Grady."

"Who's O'Grady?" Bonnie asks.

"Her horse," Danny says, looking relieved. "I think O'Grady might give her the courage she needs for this. Better than I could."

"It sounds challenging," Molly admits, "but if it would help me get over my panic around men, O'Grady and I will give it a try."

A few days later Danny says to Molly, "Let's go fishing."

"Fishing?" Molly squints. "What brought that on?"

"The fields are thawing out and the streams are flowing into the lake. I'll bet the fish are waking up hungry after the long winter."

"Hungry for worms?" she jokes. "To tell you the truth, the only thing I liked about fishing with you and dad was not being left out."

"Just wanted to be one of the guys, eh? Sometimes I still hear dad's voice, like he was right here with us. *Children, like everything else, there's a right way to fish and a wrong way to fish, and you're going to learn the right way.*"

Oh, my, god, Danny has dad's voice and he's mastered perfectly his way of speaking. "Cut it out, Danny. That's really creepy how you sound so much like him." She shudders. "Well, hey, at least we learned to fish."

"So, are we going fishing or not?"

"Well, there's Norma Lou to think about. I can't just..."

"We can leave right after you put her down for her nap, and mom takes care of her when she wakes up. How's that? Just for the afternoon. We might even catch one or two for dinner. Besides, there's something I want to tell you."

"Now you've got me curious."

Molly makes the arrangements with her mother while Danny assembles the fishing gear, makes a couple of bologna sandwiches with mustard and red onion, and grabs up some chips and cherry Cokes. He asks if they can take her truck because he wants to drive it. Well, why not? So, they go down to Lake Scott for the afternoon. As they drive along together, Molly on the passenger side for a change, she says, "I'm really enjoying talking to mom lately. It's like starting our relationship all over again."

"Yeah, I've noticed you guys. You're good at getting her to talk."

"And it's more adult to adult now. I know it's odd because I'm so young and still her kid, but it's like we have this new bond now over motherhood." Molly looks out the side window at the vacant fields drifting by and has trouble believing she is actually a mother. What happened to her life?

"That was a pretty shocking story mom told you about that first baby."

"It was, but because she told me that, I feel like we could talk about anything now."

Danny glances over at his sister. "Yeah, I even feel closer, too. I can say more what I think and tease her a little bit. She's changing, that's for sure."

"And having a real mom now makes me more comfortable as a mother, like I can ask her for help and advice."

"She's all we've got now." Danny stares straight ahead as the truck bounces along. It dawns on Molly that the death of a father might be a little different for a son than for a daughter. She's sure that Danny must have some ambivalence about losing his dad, some remembrance of good times with him as well as relief from his high expectations. Right now, Danny sounds like he's missing him. Maybe that's why he wanted her to go fishing with him.

Danny pulls onto the narrow dirt road that takes them to the back side of the lake to their dad's favorite fishing spot, a deep inlet with a strip of sandy beach. In no time Danny has two lines baited and cast in, their bobbers appearing red and white on the surface. Molly is amazed at the memories this spot brings back. Danny pulls out the lunch, sets out two paper plates on a blanket, and they sit there on the shore, eating and talking.

"What's this thing you wanted to tell me?" Molly asks.

"Oh, no big deal. I just wanted to talk to you more about what happened to you."

"I'm sorry no one told you. I figured that was the case when I got your note. It really upset me."

"Yeah, it was hard learning the way I did." He washes down a mouthful of sandwich with the Coke.

"Who told you?"

"A guy at school named Gil. His older brother was in a bar in Colby and overheard Tommy Dawson a little drunk bragging about what he had done to that O'Reilly girl. The older brother told Gil and Gil asked me if it was true. Of course, I got pissed at the accusation. I told him that all that I knew was that my sister had gone to work on a bison ranch in Colorado for the summer."

Molly reaches out and clasps his forearm. "Oh, my god, Danny, that was probably not the best thing to say."

"I know that now, and that's why I'm telling you. I've worried all winter that if that information got back to Tommy through Gil's brother, he could track you down because there probably aren't that many bison ranches in Colorado."

Molly panics, short of breath, her heart racing. She certainly doesn't need to add Tommy Dawson to her worry list. She's always assumed that he was gone out of her life forever. But could he have tracked her down in Colorado to attack her again? What a hideous thought. And where is he now?

"I'm sorry," Danny says. He finishes his sandwich and offers Molly the other half of hers, which she refuses with the wave of a trembling hand. "Are you okay?" he asks, frowning.

"Ever since it happened, I get these panic attacks and I'm having one now. It's not your fault. It'll go away." She stands and crosses the sand to the water's edge, gazing out at the calm lake to get herself under control. Hardly a ripple, the trees on the opposite shore reflected down into the glassy surface.

"The chances of his finding you again are pretty slim," Danny calls after her. "I thought you should know."

She turns back to him and nods her head several times. "You're right about that, so thank you for telling me." But it's not exactly what she wanted to know.

Danny sees one of the bobbers on the fishing line bouncing so he jumps up to check it out. He finds he's hooked a nice size bass. "Look at this," he shouts. "We got him."

Feeling better, Molly congratulates Danny on his catch, and as she does, she wonders if Tommy Dawson will ever be caught. Maybe just a catch and release if there are no charges filed against him. Carlos is right. She needs to turn him in. "What about your other line?" she asks. She holds the net with the bass while Danny checks.

"Just a little perch," he says. "We'll let him go."

Molly comes up to her brother and says, "Danny, could you put an arm around my shoulder?"

"What this?" he asks, but stops what he is doing to embrace his sister.

"Mom and I need to go to the courthouse this week. I'm ready to file charges about what happened to me. I'm not afraid anymore, but I'll need some support. If it came down to it, do you think Gil's brother would testify?"

"I'm sure he would. And so, would I." Danny nods and presses his lips together. "I'd love to do that." He releases the hug and clenches his fist, as if ready to go that very moment.

"Then I'll do it."

It's a short stay by the lake and they only caught one fish, but she is anxious to go home even though she knows Norma Lou is in her mother's experienced hands. The mention of Tommy Dawson has left her feeling uneasy.

They pile everything back into the truck, including the fresh fish for supper, and Danny starts commenting on the truck. "New mirror. New tires. Starts like a charm. It seems to run good. How'd you get all this stuff?"

"Wayne fixed it up for my trip back."

"Sounds like a really nice guy."

She decides it's too hard to explain how she ended up in his daughter's bedroom for the winter, so she just says, "You wouldn't believe how nice." The word *nice* brings to mind Carlos and their trip to the sand dunes and she realizes that she misses him. "Not to change the subject, little brother, but how's school this year?"

"It's been a good year except for being without you."

"Aw, that's sweet. I missed you, too."

"I have honors math and it's tough but I'm getting it. And let's see, oh yeah, I'm in the choir."

"The choir?" Molly tries not to sound too surprised.

"Yeah, when my voice stopped cracking, it turned out to be a good steady second bass. The director thinks I might be able to make All State Choir next year."

"Go for it. That's better than second base on the baseball team."

"You have a weird sense of humor." He smiles but doesn't laugh. "But the really fun thing this year is social studies. We have this really cool new teacher, a kind of a weirdo for around here—long hair, beard, tattoos—and he's always getting us into discussions."

"About what?"

"Free college tuition, immigration, universal health care, the environment. But the class loves to get off on all the problems between men and women. He just lets us be free to talk about anything as long as we don't shout at each other or interrupt. And sometimes he gets into the discussion, too."

"And what does he say?" Molly asks, curious about this teacher she missed.

"Uhm...well, he says that the problems women have with men can't be solved by women alone. They have to be addressed by men. And first off, we have to get control of our toxic masculinity. We just don't need any more high-testosterone cowboys around the global ranch. He actually talks like that. He says that the biggest myth out there is that a horny guy can't control himself. It's just not so. It's only an excuse for aggression. So, then what we do is we put the blame on women and give them a bunch of rules. Don't be out late. Don't walk home alone. Don't wear sexy clothes. Don't get men aroused. Like all of this male aggression is *their* responsibility?"

"And what do the women in the class think about this?" Molly asks.

"They don't speak up a whole lot, which is true in other classes, too, but you can tell they agree with him the way they nod their heads. The guys love those discussions and they disagree a lot with each other and with him sometimes, too."

Molly can't help smiling through Danny's enthusiastic description of the discussions and then she says, "Maybe you guys are going to be the new generation of men we need."

"Well, there are still some guys that talk smack about women, but not my friends. We are serious and we discuss things. Everybody says guys don't talk seriously, but *we* do."

Then Danny himself turns serious and begins to scowl, so much so that Molly notices. "What's wrong, Danny? What are you thinking?"

He shakes his head a few times, as if he's trying to speak without becoming too emotional. Finally, he says, "But here's the thing. We're having these laid-back discussions in class, but it's all on a different level than where I'm at. The women are talking about unwanted physical advances or being touched inappropriately, and I know it is important stuff, I get that, but I'm sitting there thinking: my sister was just raped. Where does that fit into the discussion? This isn't just about being touched." His voice is filled with emotion and grows louder with each comment. "The repulsive scumbag raped her. He plotted the whole thing out and then he raped my sister, who was only seventeen. Left her with a baby. Ruined her life. When do we talk about that?"

9

THE HORSEPOWER OF O'GRADY

They fried the fresh fish and it was tasty, but two nights later Molly's mother is standing in the kitchen looking a little haggard and confused, turning this way and that, like she doesn't know quite what to fix for dinner. "Are you hungry for anything in particular?" she asks Molly.

"Let's go to a restaurant tonight," Molly suggests.

"In Colby?" her mother asks as if it were an all-day trip to Wyoming. "And with Norma Lou?"

"I've got that car seat that Wayne installed in the old truck."

Danny seems to have heard the word *restaurant* and comes bounding down the stairs from his room. "Which one? Where?"

Molly recalls that they almost never went out to eat. Was that also because of her father? "Why not, mom?" she asks.

"Well, I just never think to go out to a restaurant. Your father really liked home cooking."

"But since he's not here..." Danny begins, thinks twice, and shifts gears. "Don't you think you deserve a break, mom? What about that Mexican restaurant?"

Molly knows the Colby restaurants—not that there are so many of them—from going to high school there. Do you mean *El Oasis Sobre Mesa?*" She surprises herself with such good pronunciation.

"I don't think I've ever had real Mexican food at a restaurant," Danny says, "just those tasteless tacos they serve at the school cafeteria. Yuk!"

"Your father didn't like Mexican food, Danny," his mother reminds him.

"I don't think he liked Mexicans either. He used to say, 'Thank god there aren't too many of them around here.'"

"Danny, that will be enough impertinence. We have other ways of remembering your father," his mother tells him in a sharp voice that Molly seldom hears from her, followed by a flinty look she rarely sees.

Molly smiles at Danny's blunt talk and wonders how much of her father's views she herself has absorbed. Was that why she felt uncomfortable at first in Pepe's Cantina? No one at school thought much about who was what, maybe because ninety-five percent were white and the rest just had to blend in somehow. But Danny's remark makes her wonder if she has a little prejudice under that freckled white skin of hers. Is that holding her back from liking Carlos more? She ponders that for a moment and concludes that this is not really the problem. Besides, he's not Mexican. He is Spanish and Indian, she reassures herself, then realizes that her father would not have thought that to be one whit better. Could her mother accept Carlos, even if her father wouldn't have?

"Let's go," Danny says. "Get an early start."

"Well, okay," their mother agrees, "as soon as Norma Lou wakes up."

"I'll go pinch her," Danny says. "Just kidding."

While they are waiting for Norma Lou to awaken, Molly's mother gets a hairbrush from the downstairs bathroom and flops down in her favorite rocker by the fireplace. She motions to Molly and says, "Come over here and I'll braid that lovely long hair of yours."

"Like when I was a little girl? I'm not sure I want that look anymore."

"Well, just for tonight, for old time's sake. You can always brush it out in the morning."

So, Molly sits on the floor with her legs folded under her as her mother brushes her hair into long strands and braids one long pigtail. She's not so sure about how it will look, but the feeling of being her mother's daughter again with the love that's going into the brushing and braiding makes her happy. She recognizes that happiness comes to her in little packages now, spontaneous moments, but she's still not sure what it will take for her to live a happy life. She needs to figure that out.

As they're driving into Colby, Molly's mother points out, "This Ford was one of the first of those crew cab short bed trucks to come out with two sets of seats. Very elegant in those days. Your father gave it to me one Christmas although he ended up driving it a lot."

"Wait a minute," Danny says, "are you telling us that dad gave you a truck for a Christmas present?"

"It was the thought behind it, Danny." Ida smiles. "Actually, it was a great gift. He knew I wanted one and they were very expensive at the time."

"But didn't he give you necklaces and rings and stuff like that?" Danny continues.

"Just this diamond here when we got married." She holds it up on display proudly.

"After he knew he had to."

"Danny," Molly says with a slight reprimand in her voice, "it was hard for Mom to tell us about her marriage, and she'll never tell us any more if it gets thrown back at her like that."

"There's more?" Danny asks.

"Oh, yes," his mother says in a teasing voice. "I'm just full of deep dark secrets."

"Like what? Did you ever have affairs?"

"Danny, stop it, that's rude," Molly shouts at him, but admitting to herself that she's curious about what the answer would be to a question like that.

"Just one," Molly's mother says, seeming to be quite unperturbed by Danny's inquisitive intrusion.

Molly's jaw drops, speechless. Holy crap! Is she putting them on or is she about to make another big revelation? Certainly, she would never joke about such a serious thing. But neither would she have an affair. What is going on here?

"Well, let's hear it," Danny begs, in a voice rippling with delight.

"Some other time."

"No, Mom, you can't torment us like that and leave us hanging." Danny waits expectantly.

"Well, it was years ago, with a photographer. He drove up the drive to our house to ask for directions to the covered bridge. I went with him to the bridge and afterwards I invited him in and we talked. He took photos of covered bridges on assignment for National Geographic. Your father was traveling. So, I invited him to stay for dinner. He stayed and that night..."

"Mom. Cut the malarkey! I've read *The Bridges of Madison County*. I know the book and the movie, too. You're putting us on."

"But wasn't that a delightful affair that Francesca had? I've always fantasized about an affair like that."

Danny and Molly look straight into each other's eyes for a flash before Danny says, "But, Mom, fantasy is one thing. It's in your head."

"Ah, yes, those must be the unclean thoughts the priest used to talk about," his mother reminds him.

"Oh, give me a break," Danny says. "Those priests just want to make you believe that anything having to do with sex is bad, just because they can't have any. Don't get me started on those hypocritical molesters."

Does he sound a little like his father? Molly never dreamed that she and her little brother would be bantering like this together with their mother. Things *are* changing. After Danny's last comment, no one says anything as they drive toward Colby, but the silence is comfortable.

Molly's thoughts drift back to the priest who led the Bible study when she was in 10th grade. Even though her parents were not active in church, they made sure she learned her catechism and took the classes that were to prepare her for her first communion when she was a little girl although she can't remember whether she ever took first communion or not. She does remember that priest from Bible study, though, an older gentleman with white hair, not much flesh on his bones at all, leading interesting discussions, but avoiding any mention of sexuality, the topic at the top of the list for most of the participants. Even without discussion she came away knowing that abortion and birth control were sins. How did they get that pumped into her brain? She remembers his saying that Christianity could be boiled down to the words *love one another* and his insisting that the world's religions were very different from Catholic Christianity and from each other, but that they also had words like *love one another* and *do unto others* buried in their own beliefs and scriptures.

Those words *love one another* keep bouncing through Molly's head as they drive into Colby, bringing to mind all of the loving things Wayne did for her, and the love shown for her by Rainbow and Jersey. She's sure there is a similar sentiment behind *mind the herd* and *love one another*, and she remembers watching the bison caring for the little ones as they came through the barn in the roundup. And then there is Carlos, who tried so hard to show his love for her in so many ways even as she kept rejecting his offers and trampling on his feelings. She wonders if she will ever get a second chance to allow Carlos to love her.

El Oasis Sobre Mesa is bigger on the inside than it looks from the exterior, but its rows of small tables, dark paneled walls, and a low acoustic ceiling give it a tidy and cozy feeling. The few people there are speaking softly, full of small-town politeness. The owners are Mexicans, but the customers are white, sunburnt Kansans, which figures because there probably aren't enough Mexicans in Thomas County to fill a restaurant this big. Molly sets Norma Lou in her car seat up on a chair next to her. They all get their menus and Molly starts to consider the choices—fajitas or rellenos or enchiladas or tamales—and she wonders what Carlos might be eating for dinner tonight. "What are you looking for, Danny?" Molly asks, noticing that Danny is searching intensely for something on his phone.

"Mexican foods," he says, not looking up.

Danny seems much more into his phone these days. Reception still breaks up on the road back into the farm, so using the phone is pretty much restricted to Colby and its closest towns.

"Tired of tacos?" Molly asks.

"Yeah, I need to branch out."

After being without service at the Horseshoe all those months, she hardly thinks to look up something on her phone. She used to just ask Rainbow. She leans over to Danny to suggest, "Why don't you try the combo? That way you get to sample a lot of things."

Danny nods. "Good idea." But now he seems to be searching for something else.

The waiter arrives with chips, guacamole, and salsa. Molly lets Norma Lou try a little guacamole but most of it gets pushed back out with her little tongue and spread all over her face. While they wait, Danny looks up from his phone and says, "Breaking news, this just in. Our Irish ancestors with red hair and blue eyes are thought to be the very first European stock, the original peoples of northern Europe before all those Anglos and Saxons invaded. That's us, right?"

"What about the freckles?" Molly asks.

"It doesn't say anything about freckles."

Molly looks up and sees a familiar face coming toward them as they wait for their food. Oh, my gosh, it's her Honors English teacher, Mrs. Braxton, still dressed from class, neatly and with simple good taste, as she always was.

There is a constant incandescence about that woman, a glow that is never extinguished. Molly leaps to her feet as Mrs. Braxton envelops her in a big hug. "Oh, it's so good to see you. You remember my mother, Ida, and you must know my brother Danny." Molly is a little embarrassed with her braided hair.

"Oh, yes, Danny has quite a wonderful reputation at Colby High already. I believe you will be my student next year. Is that not so?"

Danny, raised as a gentleman by both parents, is on his feet to reply, "I'm looking forward to it, Mrs. Braxton."

"And who is this?" she asks, bending toward Norma Lou, who now manages to hold onto her rattle when she isn't throwing it on the floor.

Molly picks up her baby to show her off. "This is the cute little dickens who threw my life into total chaos, but we're learning to be good friends now."

"She's adorable and with a strong resemblance to her mother I must say, whom I remember as very attractive in addition to being an A student."

Molly blushes at the compliments. "I have to tell you, Mrs. Braxton, that reading novels has saved my life this year during many a dreary day and dark night."

"They give us a destination, a place to go when we need it, don't they, dear? I'm glad I could help facilitate that journey for you."

"And how are things at school?" Molly asks.

"Tolerably well, but they've made me the chair of a committee to investigate some harassment charges."

"Mr. Gooding?" Danny asks.

Mrs. Braxton is somewhat taken aback. "Do students know about this?"

"No, but they know about Mr. Gooding," Danny says.

Mrs. Braxton glances at Molly, searching her face with a questioning look.

"Everyone always knew they had to put up with Gooding, an arm around your shoulder, hugs that last too long." Molly explains this to Mrs. Braxton although she suspects that a teacher as astute as she is must already know much more than this.

"He was advisor to the cheerleaders, so you must have encountered him that way."

"Looking back from where I am now, after what I've been through, I'm sorry we put up with him like that."

"It must have been terribly uncomfortable for all of you. I'm sorry you had to deal with that." Mrs. Braxton shakes her head and hesitates before she asks, "Might you be willing to contribute some documentation to my report?"

"You can count on me."

The food arrives and Mrs. Braxton takes that cue to make her departure with another hug for Molly and a soft touch on the cheek of Norma Lou, eliciting a smile. "Bless you," she says, smiling back and making a small sign of the cross with her thumb on the baby's forehead. And turning to Ida and Danny she says, "Bless you all. I'm sorry for your loss, but look what you have gained."

They settle back into their places as Mrs. Braxton leaves and they begin eating.

After a few bites of his smothered burrito, Danny takes the conversation in a new direction. "Mom, did you love dad?"

"My, my, such a question, son." He continues to gaze at her, waiting for an answer, so she says. "I think overall with a little explaining I would say yes."

"What explaining?"

"Well, I was so young that I don't know if I could have loved anyone else or someone differently. You need to keep in mind that I don't know a whole lot about love. Although you kids saw a side of him that was rigid and demanding for you and for me, don't forget that he did make me feel secure and took good care of me. I loved him for that." She takes a big gulp of ice water to calm the heat of the green chilies, waving a hand in front of her mouth.

"You see, Danny, women sometimes trade off love for security," Molly says. "You'll learn about that by reading novels in Mrs. Braxton's class next year."

"But our father," Danny begins respectfully, "really expected a lot in return for the security. I mean, it was his way or the highway."

"Well, he just expected us to fit into his way of seeing things, how things should be done," his mother clarifies. "I don't think he thought he was being unreasonable."

"He was such a perfectionist," Molly says, "and I think he just wanted to teach us the right way to do everything."

"Yeah, *his* way," Danny insists.

"But I learned to appreciate his way while I was working on the ranch last summer. I found out how many things I could do and learn to do because dad taught me how."

"Maybe I'll appreciate that someday," Danny says. "Somehow I could never please him."

"Forget about pleasing him," Molly says. "Sadly, he's gone now and he will never know how hard you tried to please him, Danny." Something else unresolved, she notices. "Just think about pleasing yourself now when you do good work. The thing to remember is that he taught us how to work."

Danny looks like he wants to respond to that but he stops himself. Finally, he says, "It's going to take a while for me to get over how he treated you and mom. I hate to say it, but he was kind of a bully."

His mother starts to open her mouth to defend her deceased husband, but Molly intervenes. "I think Danny's going to grow up to be a kind and caring man, Mom. You would have been proud of him at how he spoke with the counselor this week. He's going to be like Wayne and Carlos."

"Who's Carlos?" Danny asks. "I keep hearing that name."

On the drive back to the farm after the early dinner, Molly's mother says she'd like to stop in Oakley to visit the cemetery. "I haven't been there since the service because I wasn't up to it, but I'm ready now. It's a good night to visit the cemetery."

Even though she would prefer not, Molly knows it's important to her mother, so she replies, "Sure, Mom, we can do that. There's daylight savings time now." Danny is messing with his phone again in the crew seat and probably has not heard his mother's request; otherwise, Molly is sure, he would be voicing an objection. "You just tell me where to turn in, Mom."

As Molly drives along old Route 40 toward Oakley, she begins to wonder once again why her father is buried in Oakley. Why not Colby? Come to think of it, she doesn't know where her grandparents on his side are buried. Is it here? In this family, the only thing discussed less than sex is death. How odd it is that he is buried in Oakley because the church her parents used to attend is in Colby. Well, that's true, but she remembers something about a feud her father had with the priest in Colby over a baptism fee. Was that for her baptism? Oh, my god, maybe it was for the baptism of the stillborn baby. If her father was nursing a grudge against the priest in Colby, maybe that's why his burial is in Oakley. But her family never had any reason to stop in Oakley, no business, no friends to speak of, so why Oakley? She notices that the question has turned into a major obsession and she knows she needs to quit dwelling on it before she swerves into the ditch. Maybe she will find out why he is buried in Oakley when they get there.

Following her mother's guidance—turn right here, now left, just past the next stop sign on the right—Molly finds the entrance to the cemetery, a lovely open gate marked by stone pillars. Huge old oak trees are scattered among the tombstones. Well, it is Oakley, after all. She drives the old truck over the gravel paths as her mother directs because she remembers almost nothing from the day of the funeral. "Right over here, Molly. You can park here and we can walk across right there."

"Where are we?" Danny asks, finally looking up from his phone.

"At your father's grave," his mother replies.

"Oh, geez." Danny says under his breath.

Molly picks up Norma Lou from the car seat as her mother starts toward the grave. "No, Danny, you can't stay in the car. Come on." As she starts to follow in the path of her mother, she notices an odd smell. What is that smell? She hadn't noticed it at the funeral. It starts to make her nervous, even a little nauseous. Is it from the graves? She hears the sound of her feet kicking through dead leaves. What *is* that stench? And then it dawns on her that the smell is of rotted leaves and it is a bad smell to her because of her association with having been thrown down and raped on a bed of rotted leaves. Rotted leaves, rotted leaves, the smell persists in her nose. When will those horrible memories go away? She follows her mother toward the grave as Danny tags along reluctantly, still fooling with his phone. "What are you listening to so seriously on that phone?" she asks Danny, grabbing him gently on the arm.

He takes out one earplug. "What?"

"What are you listening to?"

"Spotify. Beethoven. Some choral music."

Her little brother is listening to choral music by Beethoven?

Molly doesn't know exactly what she is supposed to feel when she arrives at the gray granite stone with dates of her father's birth and death, but she is surprised at how much she actually misses him. Knowing he is close, at least his body, she feels like she ought to be able to try once more to talk to him, but she's pretty sure that he—his soul, his spirit, whatever might be left of him—is somewhere else. She would still like one more shot at setting him straight about what happened in that maple grove, and if he were here, she would tell him how rude it was of him to throw her out of the family to whom she now feels closer than ever. She's glad he's no longer standing in her way. In fact, sending her away seems rather hypocritical now that she has learned that he had to marry her mother. Was he still angry with himself for getting his girlfriend pregnant and taking it out years later on his own daughter? There's a great question for Bonnie Bradford.

She watches her mother and wonders what she is thinking, what she might be trying to say to her deceased husband. Then her mother moves over to the next grave stone, kneels down in the leaves, and crosses herself, as if to pray. Molly jiggles Norma Lou and moves to where she can read the stone, not sure who's grave it marks. 'Angela O'Reilly' the stone says, and the date of birth and death are exactly the same. Molly glances at the next stone over and notices her mother's name, Ida, and it shocks her at first until she notices that the stone in engraved with only the birth date and a dash. Oh, my god, they have arranged to be buried on either side of their firstborn who never lived, the baby that brought them together to marry. Whose idea was this? Her father's? Her mother's? She can't ask her mom something like that, but it must have been an arrangement made a long time ago. It is a beautiful gesture if it's what they both wanted, setting up these graves like this.

Danny, having abandoned his music, slides up next to his sister and whispers, "What about us? Where will we be?"

"God only knows," Molly whispers, "but let's hope it's not here." She sees her mother rise and come toward them. "The sun is setting," she says. "I think we better be getting on home."

Molly is just now noticing the beautiful sunset of pink on gray clouds with small patches of blue in the background. The twigs of the old oak trees make dark silhouettes against the colorful sky. In a few weeks the leaves will come back at just the right time, and the cemetery will be filled with flowering shrubs. Kansas has its scenic spots and beautiful days, but not like the dramatic landscapes she remembers in Colorado. It will be better to visit the cemetery later in the spring, but she has to admit that she doesn't have much interest in staying in Kansas permanently, certainly not to endure the mugginess in the summer months. Each day it becomes more difficult for her to picture herself living the rest of her life here.

Molly missed her horse while she was at Horseshoe Ranch. Not that there weren't plenty of horses around to ride, because there were, but none of them was quite the same as her childhood horse, O'Grady, a dapple-gray gelding full of spirit but gentle and protective. Her father bought the horse for the children—one horse was less expensive than two and learning to share would be good for them—but the horse became more attached to Molly, so that Danny never enjoyed O'Grady as much as she did. While she was gone, Danny told her, he and O'Grady became pretty good friends again, but he doesn't like having all the responsibility for her. Since she has been home, Molly has begun once more to take an interest in O'Grady, who is a little older and wiser now, but still spirited. He seems to have grown into his gray color, made into a permanent pun in the Irish name they gave him years ago. Molly helps Norma Lou reach out with her little hand to touch his long nose.

Naturally, the horse was also provided by their father to teach responsibility, so Molly and Danny had to make sure that they divided up the brushing and feeding as well as the mucking of the manure from the stall so that they wouldn't get yelled at by their father. "Are you neglecting that horse?" she can still hear him ask, even though they never did. Most of the regular exercise routine fell to Molly, and that's how she became such a good rider. And she was the one who trained him. When she and Danny were younger and smaller, they both rode O'Grady bareback, seated together— there is a framed picture on the mantel in the living room—but they are way too big and lanky for riding like that now. O'Grady was gentle with them as children, but as Molly grew older, she discovered that her horse had a spunky side, too.

Today, while Norma Lou is napping, Molly decides to go for a little ride, and because this partly-sunny April day is much warmer than yesterday, it is a good afternoon for a little gallop across the barren fields and down the familiar paths through the meadows. She hasn't lost her touch and O'Grady seems pleased to have his favorite jockey back in the saddle again. As she crosses the creek, she realizes she is not far from the maple grove and it reminds her of her pledge in front of Bonnie Bradford to revisit the horrid spot where Tommy Dawson threw her to the ground in the rotted leaves. If she ever sees Carlos again, she wants to be able to tell him that she had the guts to do it. She has been procrastinating, so this is the day to go out there.

But first Molly wants to see if O'Grady remembers some of the special moves they used to perform together. She never had dressage lessons—that was too hoity-toity for her father—but she learned a lot about riding during free time in study halls at school by downloading videos and blogs on the internet. She taught O'Grady marvelous tricks with a handful of oats or chunks of rock candy for a reward. At the end of the meadow there is a section of even ground where she used to train him to prance like the horses she had seen in the Fourth of July parade in Colby. So, she rides him down to the familiar clearing and starts putting him through his paces: a little lateral work—shoulder in, haunches in—and then a piaffe, slow trotting in place like a proud little dance.

"Good, boy, O'Grady." She leans forward and pats his neck, and he seems perfectly happy to be performing his old tricks for only a hug. She rides out on a path across the meadow and checks out his gait transitions from trot to canter to gallop. It looks like he hasn't forgotten a thing. Nor has she.

Then Molly remembers a fallen maple branch they used to jump. It isn't a real jump, but the branch has a prominent arch to it and sticks up in a way to make a good open field jump. It's a little dangerous without a helmet, but she is sure O'Grady won't balk. So, they trot over to the old branch and give it a run. No problem. She taps her heels and over he goes, effortlessly in a fluid motion that makes her feel like she's a supple extension of her horse, at one with his strength and power.

"Wow, O'Grady. You haven't lost a thing from this year of neglect." She doesn't know whether or not Danny has been working with their horse on these things while she has been gone. She never told her parents about O'Grady's training, especially not the jumping, because her mom would worry about her safety and her dad would lecture her about things that girls should and shouldn't do. Danny could be trusted so she always told and showed him everything, but otherwise these were secrets that she and O'Grady kept to themselves.

She circles O'Grady back for another run at the jump, faster this time. Up and over with ease. O'Grady seems so strong and confident today. Does a horse have fears? Did O'Grady have to conquer his fears? What strength he has, she feels it transferring to her so that now she has the courage to ride back to the maple grove. She has to remind herself why she is doing this. To master her panic. To control the invasion of bad memories. She turns O'Grady in the direction of the grove, keeping on the path near the gurgling brook. The memories *do* come back: the terror, the fear of being beaten, the humiliation and anger all over again. But there's a difference this time. Even though she wants to head for the barn, she knows that the goal is to master those feelings and she believes she can. So, she pushes on to the exact spot.

Then, quite unexpectedly, she feels that surge of strength that Carlos told her would arrive. And even though Carlos said she might not know where the strength would come from, she has no doubt about the channel. O'Grady has given her all the strength and confidence she needs. "Let's go, boy," she tells him.

When they get there, she dismounts and walks straightway toward the spot, holding tight the reins to her old friend's bridle. O'Grady nickers, a little edgy, swishing his gray tail and glancing around, as if sensing danger. She soothes him and lets him drop his head to nibble what stubble of dried grass he can find on a spring day in Kansas. Is she afraid? Not really. She edges a few steps closer to the exact spot, covered over with another season of fallen leaves. There is no panic.

It was a horrible thing, she tells herself, but it is now past. She will have memories and feelings, but they won't overwhelm her. She will live her life with courage, not fear, as a person with a source of strength she can draw on when she needs it. You wrecked my life, Tommy Dawson, but you didn't change me into some battered being living with unmanageable panic. Not anymore. I'm free to have a future. As for your future, I only hope that someday you'll get what's coming to you.

O'Grady looks like he wants to linger here, but a brisk wind has come up. She picks up his bridle and tells him, "Come on, O'Grady. There's nothing nourishing in this barren place, so let's go." Besides, Norma Lou is probably awakening from her nap and Molly wants to see her smile. "Let's go back to the barn and see if we can find some treats."

She mounts her horse and turns him toward home, but then she pulls him suddenly to a stop. "I just remembered one more trick, O'Grady. Can you still do it?" She sits up straight, leaning forward slightly, pushes her knees into his shoulders, and pulls back on the reins. He knows the command. "Yahoo!" Up he goes, rearing back on his hind legs like a true bronco, holding it for a breathtaking moment, and then coming back gently to all fours.

With a whoop from Molly and a shake of the tail from O'Grady they gallop off with the wind at breakneck speed toward home, cutting a reckless path through the sodden, winter-drenched pasture, leaving her fears behind.

Bonnie Bradford is dressed up today, as if she is going somewhere after Molly's appointment. Molly notices that she is wearing a skirt and blouse, she has done something to her hair, and she is using a little blush, all of which make her look like a different person from the casual counselor who rolls forward and back in her desk chair helping people to make a new go of it. Molly can think of her now as Bonnie Bradford, but she still can't call her that.

"You look nice today, ma'am, like you might be having a date."

"Oh, there's an alumni meeting over at Fort Hays State where I did my master's degree. It's only about ninety miles east and a familiar commute. And it's a nice chance to see some of my old friends."

"Maybe some old boyfriends," Molly teases.

"Ouch! You put your finger right on the sore spot. I had a failed romance while I was a graduate student there, but chances are good that *he* won't show up."

Molly can't hide her surprise at this disclosure. "You look like you might still be feeling sad from it," Molly says, as if she were the counselor. She knows it's not her place to counsel her counselor, but it is good to know that Bonnie has feelings and failures, too.

"Certain feelings linger and we have to learn to manage them," Bonnie says, "and my notes tell me that we are here to talk about that today. Did you visit the maple grove?"

"I did. I rode my horse O'Grady right out to the very spot."

"How did it go?"

Molly tells Bonnie the whole story, not being sure that her counselor gets the connection between the things she did with O'Grady and the sudden welling up of power and confidence that came to her from riding her horse, but it's the result that Bonnie seems to care about most.

"So, you have a new sense of mastery over your feelings. You're acknowledging them, but they aren't going to throw you into a panic."

"Exactly. I'm still working at it, of course, but I feel much stronger now after riding out there with O'Grady."

Bonnie nods. "Okay. That's real progress." She slides her chair back a bit. "You're not so panicky, but what about the anger? You have a lot to be angry about. You don't want to bottle it all up inside, but you don't want to displace it on people who don't deserve it."

"I do that once in a while with Carlos. Sometimes when I'm angry, I push him away, and it's really nothing he has done at all. I just get standoffish and can't explain why."

"And what does he do?" Bonnie asks, pushing her chair forward again.

"He just keeps coming back," Molly says, marveling at how Carlos still came to visit her even after she moved in with Wayne.

"Does he love you?"

"Yes, that's the problem."

"Problem?" Bonnie raises her eyebrows. "Do you love him?"

Molly has to ponder that. "I think so, but I'm not very good at expressing it. I hold him at arm's length. After being raped—I actually said it, didn't I?— I'm really hung up about sex, so I won't let myself fall in love because that's where it leads."

Bonnie rocks an outstretched hand back and forth. "Well, eventually, if that's what you both want." Her eyes examine Molly as if to discern whether that *is* what she wants, but Molly only appears more frightened and confused. "Okay, so how do we get you past the experience of being raped so you can enjoy a sexual relationship?"

"I wish I knew, but that's exactly my problem. I don't want to be like this the rest of my life."

"It could take weeks and months, but hopefully not a lifetime. You can shorten the time by working at it in small steps with an understanding friend. It's called desensitization."

"Like getting an untamed horse used to a saddle?"

"That's maybe not the best comparison, but, yes, the process is the same."

"What do I do?" she asks, growing interested.

"A lot of touching. Take his hand and hold it. Let him hold your hand. I know it sounds embarrassingly silly, but that's where to begin."

"Like a ninth-grade dance at school?" Molly gives her a hint of a smile.

"If that's what it reminds you of, why not? You're starting over, remember?" Bonnie puts her two hands together, interlocking the fingers, and pressing the palms together. "Okay, so you have his hand. Think calm thoughts. Work on your head. Tell yourself it's okay."

"What else?" Molly asks, wondering how to move on from holding hands.

"Let him put an arm around you."

"Ah, like the movies in tenth grade." Molly giggles.

"Why not? But don't freak out when he does it. Be calm."

"Next?" Molly is growing interested in the progression.

"Let him come up behind you and wrap his arms around you. Be cool. Rock from side to side with him. Keep working with your feelings, telling yourself it's a nice thing to do and won't hurt you."

He does sway like that, but he hasn't tried to hold her. "What if he wants to kiss me?"

"When you are ready, go for it. Tell yourself that you are in charge. You permit it and you stop it." Bonnie holds her hands up as if to indicate a small wall.

"What if he doesn't want to stop?"

"Well, hey, it takes two to kiss, and if you stop, just tell him that's enough for now. You'll get there eventually."

Molly is enjoying this, picturing herself kissing Carlos and liking it. "What if he takes the kissing as a sign that I want to, you know, do it?"

"Tell him that he's reading the sign wrong, that it's a stop sign and you are still down the block in the kissing stage."

Is it really all this reasonable? Molly wonders. "What if I never get beyond it, I mean kissing?"

"What's your fear? That you won't be responsive, that you'll freeze up?"

"No, that I'll actually like it and get pregnant again." Molly smiles and then frowns.

"Well, once you master your desensitization shtick, you'll need to get some birth control. I mean, in your case it's really justified, don't you think?"

"Okay, we got to it, my real hang up: getting pregnant." She squirms around in her chair. "I just don't want another baby next year at nineteen years old."

"Who could blame you for that?" Bonnie pushes herself back in her chair and glances at her watch. "I've got to get on the road, but before I do I want to ask about Norma Lou. How is she doing?"

"She's doing fine. Healthy. Not so demanding. My mom helps out a lot. And you know what? I don't see a single trace of Tommy Dawson in my baby's face. I guess I got lucky for once."

One night at dinner, Danny asks bluntly, "What's going to happen to the farm?"

"Well, now that's a good question, Danny," his mother says. "I've been thinking about that."

"Are you going to sell it?

Without answering his question directly, Ida says, "I should remind you, Danny, that our property and Uncle Russ's property were all one farm until your grandpa died. Then it was split evenly between the two boys, Russel and your dad."

"One farm?" Danny frowns. Maybe that comment got something moving in his head.

"Before we do anything, I think we better invite Uncle Russ over here to see what he thinks about our situation," Ida says.

"And soon, too," Danny says, "because those cows keep pumping out milk and they don't shut off. Dad was right about that."

That week, Molly and Norma Lou and her mother go together to register the death certificate at the Thomas County Court House, to straighten out the bank accounts, and put the truck in Molly's name, not exactly the vehicle of her dreams. While they are there, they also stop at the sheriff's office to report the crime of rape against Tommy Dawson. This is not as complicated as Molly thought it might be, just filling out some forms, giving fingerprints, and swearing under oath that what she has written and said is true to the best of her knowledge. If Tommy is apprehended for some crime or another rape, the officer assured her that he would be arrested and charged for this crime as well. Meanwhile, they would be looking for him. It was a good day for Molly and her mom to finish up unfinished business.

But the looming business problem of the family right now is what to do about the farm. So they invite Uncle Russ over, as Ida suggested, to join them at the kitchen table while they put their heads together to figure out what to do next.

"Luckily we have a good man in Joe right now," Ida begins, "but he was hired on as temporary and I don't know how long he will stay."

Molly wonders if this is the new replacement for Tommy Dawson. She tells herself that Joe is not Tommy and to calm down. It works.

"Well, Joe's a diligent worker but there's a lot more to running a dairy farm these days than just milking," Russel says.

"I'd like to do my part," Danny pipes up, "but I don't think I really want to be a dairy farmer."

"Right now," his mother reassures him, "your main job is to do well in school."

"What I tell my own kids" Uncle Russel says, "is that you could grow up to do a lot of things, but farming is only one of them."

"I think my dad was raising me to take over this farm someday. Looks like I'm going to disappoint him again."

"First you need to find out more about what's out there in the world," Molly tells him. Like Uncle Russ is suggesting. As for me, I don't really see myself here on this farm the rest of my life." Molly checks to see if her mother looks hurt, but surprisingly, she's nodding in the affirmative. But then Molly can't quite see herself anywhere yet. She just knows that if she had plans, this dairy farm would not be a part of them.

"And you, Ida," Russ asks, "do you have plans?"

Molly notices how gently Uncle Russ speaks in that same respectful voice like Wayne did. She always liked Uncle Russ and sometimes she wondered if he and her dad really were brothers because they were so different.

"You know, Russ," Ida says, "I think this may be the first time in my life since I was a high school girl that anyone asked me about my plans. Kevin made all the plans. He always checked with me to see what I thought, but I never had any plans of my own. So, I don't know much about making plans. Let me admit this, though, I don't know enough about this farm to run it."

Uncle Russ nods, hesitates, and says softly, somewhat apologetically, "I don't know quite how to say this, but I need to be honest. Running this farm isn't just about continuing to do what's always been done here. Technology is coming to small farms like it is to everything else. It probably won't surprise you if I tell you that Kevin wasn't much interested in change."

Danny doesn't look surprised by that at all, but he does look a little more interested. "Technology? Like what?"

"Robotics. They have automatic feeding systems now. Even robotic milking machines. The udder is washed with rotating brushes and the machine fastens on the pumping devices by itself. Finishes up in about six minutes."

"The technology increases efficiency, which dad always valued," Molly says, but she wonders what the cows feel about being milked by a robot.

"Well, yeah," Danny says "and devices like that eliminate a lot of hard labor. But dad always resisted improvements he didn't understand. So, are you saying, Uncle Russ, that our farm has fallen behind?

I'm just saying that it needs a lot of modernization. That will take some investment, but it will eventually increase yields and cut costs."

"I see what you're saying," Ida agrees with a nod. "So, without this stuff, it's pretty hard to compete and stay in business."

"And the other thing," Russ adds, "is that even a small farm has to diversify. Grow hay, for sure, but other crops, too. Soybeans. Grains. Feed corn, but maybe some sweet corn, too, to sell in Denver. I even keep my own bees."

"I agree," Danny says. "We can't get by on a hodge-podge of hay fields and some tired old cows. We need a plan and some better equipment."

There is a long silence before Molly asks Uncle Russ, "What should we do?"

"Well, you could sell it as is. I could probably supervise both farms for a while until you find a buyer." He pauses and then with sincere modesty says, "I could even buy you out, but it would mean a lot of debt. Either way, you'll have steady income, Ida."

"Maybe you could sell out and move to Colby, Mom. Get a job as a teacher's aide," Molly suggests. "You're good with kids." Ida doesn't respond.

It's not the kind of problem to be resolved in one swoop. The possibilities need to be mulled over; options explored. They thank Uncle Russ and agree to meet again.

The discussion of selling the family farm, the last stable thing in Molly's life, the only home she has ever known, has her upset. She came back to Kansas to have a home for herself and Norma Lou. Her goal was to have her father welcome her back, but now, because of his death, the home she has returned to is breaking up, crumbling, like an old barn in a twister. It would have been fine to live here for a while enjoying her mother and brother again, even though she was discovering that she was not all that enamored with Kansas anymore. But now here she is with even that hope shattered and the distinct possibility of being homeless again like she was at the Horseshoe. Is it really too much to hope for a home? Even the robins returning after a winter away know where to build a nest for their young. She had some sense that her mom couldn't go on with the farm, but the explicit talk about selling it, either to

Uncle Russ or someone else, and everyone moving away is really disturbing. And what's the alternative, to live together in a little bungalow in Colby? She realizes now that things are never going to be the same ever again. Things are falling apart, and she's right back to square one.

Just as Norma Lou is reliably sleeping through the nights, Molly finds *herself* sleepless, worrying about what will happen to her, especially if her mom and brother move to Colby. She takes these worries to therapy, but when she starts listing out options, like moving in with her mother or getting a place of her own, she realizes the list is pretty short and nothing on it sounds very promising let alone realistic. All she knows is that she has Norma Lou to raise. But how? Where? She thinks she has made a lot of progress in getting over her trauma, as the counselor calls it, but she still has no concrete idea of what is to become of her.

After an even worse night of tossing and turning, while little Norma Lou is sleeping like a sawed-off log, Molly is awakened the next morning by her mother calling up the stairs to her that she has a phone call on the landline.

"How's Norma Lou," Wayne asks right off the bat. "I'm missing her like crazy."

"She's doing fine. Turning over. Sitting up. Sleeping through the night. Smiling a lot."

"And what about you?"

"Oh, no, I'm not smiling and actually I'm not sleeping through the night either." She hears Wayne's gentle chuckle and feels better. "Full of restless brooding and without plans as usual."

"And how did it go with your dad?' he asks gently.

So she has to tell him how her father died before she could get back home and show him Norma Lou. She finishes up the story by telling him that the mess with her dad is unresolved and she's pretty lost right now because her mom might sell the farm. "But what about you?" she asks. "How did it go with Emily?"

"She came back. She's living right here with me in our home again." There's an unnatural pause and Molly wonders why he doesn't sound more delighted. Is there still some strain between the two of them, as if the damage really was irreparable? Then Wayne says, "Emily wants to meet Norma Lou."

"You told her about my baby?"

"Everything except the part about your sleeping in Heather's bedroom. She'd probably leave me again if she knew that. But, yeah, all the rest."

"And your daughter Heather and husband Miguel?" Molly remembers they're in Mexico.

"We're working on it. That's not going to be easy, but they know they are welcome to visit."

"That's good. I never got to find out if I was welcome back here before my dad died." Molly recalls the word *unresolved* and wonders if Wayne's situation is still a little unresolved, too.

"But the reason I'm calling is on behalf of Carlos Ouray," Wayne continues. "He stops by every week to ask about you and I don't have any news for him. He says he is missing you terribly and is desperate to see you."

"Really? He doesn't have another girlfriend? I thought he would at least have an actual girlfriend by now." She is surprised at how strongly she hopes he doesn't.

"I think he really cares for you and he's waiting for you to return. But there is another matter just now that he's working on, and he says he really needs your help."

"My help?" Molly wonders what this could be. "Why didn't he call? He has my number."

"He said he respects your privacy."

"Well, for sure he can call." Especially if he needs her help. "What's this all about, Wayne?"

"Actually, he is right here standing beside me now. Would you like to talk to him?"

"Sure, I'd love to talk to Carlos." She knows she's smiling a big smile. "But after we all finish this call, tell him about my dad for me. I don't want to cry."

After a brief silence, Carlos says, "Hello, Molly, it's me, Carlos."

"Yes, I know." It's good to hear his deep voice again, but he sounds nervous. "Is everything okay?"

"For me, yes. But something has come up and I need your help."

"I don't know how much help I would be here in Kansas."

"That's why I need you here."

"What's that? You want me to come to Colorado?"

"Yes, as soon as possible."

"Really?" What's going on? Why so mysterious?

"Tomorrow if you can."

"Tomorrow? Something that urgent?" But there is no reluctance in her voice, only enthusiasm. That surprises her.

"Yes, I have a great opportunity here and I don't want it to slip away."

"Can you tell me about it?"

"I could, but I'm afraid that if I tell you, you won't come."

Molly is silent for a moment trying to figure out what this could possibly be. If he doesn't want to tell her something that would upset her, maybe she should stop asking questions. The surprise invitation from Carlos is so exciting that the secret surrounding it hardly matters. "Well, it's really short notice for me, Carlos, but let's leave it like this: if you don't hear from me later today, I'll start out with the sun early tomorrow morning." It's the least she can do for him after he was so nice to her. "Make arrangements for me to stay with Wayne and Emily tomorrow night. Tell him I'm bringing Norma Lou."

"He'll love that. And me, too, of course. I want to see how much she has grown."

"Well, she's not running races yet, but she's perfected her smile." Molly takes a deep breath. "Okay, Carlos, this is crazy, absolutely crazy, but I know you wouldn't call me like this if it wasn't important."

"You're right about that. Trust me. It's very important."

Molly had no plans to return to Horseshoe Ranch, at least not so soon, but then, she admits, she doesn't have plans about anything, surely none that would interfere with a few days visit to see Wayne, Emily, and Carlos. She talks it over with her mother to make sure she will be okay alone. "Go, honey, we all need to move on from this terrible thing that happened," is what she says. "Besides, I'm not alone, I have Danny." Her mom offers to keep Norma Lou, but Molly knows she wants to take her baby and besides she wants to show off her sitting up and her smile to Wayne and Carlos. She dreads the long drive, which will be even longer with stops for Norma Lou, but at least she knows the way.

Molly is eager to see everyone again and is a little surprised at how excited she has become so quickly. She phones her counselor who tells her, "I'm sure this will be good for you. Be open to anything. Don't panic. Remember your desensitization plan." Molly is pretty sure that her therapist thinks there's no future for her here in Kansas, and Molly can't see much future for herself anywhere. She's sick of her life in limbo, so why not venture out West again? And if she can help Carlos in some way after he's been so nice to her and Norma Lou, that's a good enough reason for going right there. He needs her and maybe she can help fix the problem whatever it is. The ten-day forecast shows a window of high pressure and clear skies without the threat of storms or tornadoes. It should be clear sailing tomorrow. In her heart, she has to admit that she's missing Carlos. Yep, after hearing his voice, she realizes she's been missing Carlos a lot.

10

HANGING TOMMY FROM A TREE

Molly finds the mail boxes and negotiates the bumps and potholes back into the lodge. She has forgotten how beautiful this remote storybook setting is back here with the log lodge sitting cozy under the big old cottonwoods, and the Sangre de Christo Mountains standing tall in the background, still full of snow and stretching out for miles. As soon as she steps out of the truck, she notices how quiet it is. She stretches and looks around. The daffodils she planted last fall, bending over with that baby in her belly, are already in bloom inside the stone fence around the lodge, and the tulips are nearly ready to open. Soon it will be summer and the leaves will be out and the birds will be twittering. It was almost a year ago when she first arrived, shy, scared, hiding her secret. Apparently, Wayne has been looking out the window for her—hasn't he always been looking out for her?—because he comes toward her now hand in hand with Emily. She unfastens Norma Lou from her car seat and hands her over to him, and that baby snuggles right into his arms as if she senses that this is her old soother Wayne, her grandpa by love.

"She's adorable," Emily says, and with a little baby talk has Norma Lou flashing smiles on and off like the lights at a railroad crossing. She looks up at Wayne and says, "So this is the young woman you allowed to stay in the staff cabin to have her baby."

The remark has an unwelcoming tone to Molly, but she can understand how Emily might be upset that Wayne had rejected his own daughter and then made room for a pregnant stranger.

"Yes, indeed, and she's the one, don't you remember, who tracked you down in Santa Fe?"

"Oh, yes, I had no idea of the full story at the time, and I believe I insulted her by thanking her for her audacity." She laughs and Molly can't tell whether Emily is apologizing or bragging.

"Your husband was very kind to me," Molly says, "and I just wanted to bring you two back together. We can all laugh about my boldness now, I guess, but I didn't want to miss my opportunity to be a match maker, or rematch maker, or whatever that would be."

Wayne's log home is as cozy as ever but seems to have a different feel to it with Emily back: tidy and a bit more formal, not quite the same. Molly examines her lovely paintings more closely. A fire is crackling in the fireplace. A casserole is warming in the oven. As she looks around, Molly finds it hard to imagine that she actually stayed there those weeks pretending to be Wayne's daughter.

They pass a cordial evening together, talking, playing with Norma Lou, relaxed like old friends, but Molly senses the tension in the air and wonders if Emily really appreciates what a good man her husband is. Finally, when it is way past time to put Norma Lou down, Molly asks, "Where shall we sleep?"

Wayne answers, motioning with his head, "Well, right here in the guest room." He's nodding at Heather's old bedroom, which of course had been Molly's old bedroom, too. And Emily doesn't know that she stayed here. Emily shows her the new crib they have installed in anticipation of a visit from Heather and Miguel someday. Tonight, it is for Norma Lou. That's the story at least. To her it looks like Norma Lou's old crib. Molly feels awkward being in this house again and hopes Carlos might invite her to stay at his place for a few nights.

"Oh, I almost forgot," Wayne says. "Carlos called to see if you arrived and said he wants to see you first thing in the morning."

"What's this all about anyway? Did he tell you?"

"Not much. He says that there has been a visitor at Pepe's Cantina and a suspicious situation that he needs to address before it's too late. He wouldn't elaborate, but says he'll pick you up here at the main lodge at eight o'clock sharp." Wayne shrugs as Molly's eyebrows knit together in a frown. "Sorry. That's all I know," he says apologetically.

Now what could this be? But it doesn't disrupt her first good night's sleep in several days.

Wayne suggests that he and Emily keep Norma Lou for the morning while Molly meets Carlos. Wayne wants to introduce the little precious to the Elmo paraphernalia he's bought. Molly meets Carlos in the parking lot by the lodge as scheduled and they drive away.

"Sorry to hear about your father," Carlos begins, as they cruise along in his Pathfinder.

"It's been tough. I'll tell you all about it. But right now, I'm curious about this situation you mentioned to Wayne. What's going on?"

"Well, here's the thing. You remember how I go to Pepe's Cantina some nights to stave off my loneliness and be with my friends?"

"Yes, and to help people out the front door as needed. How could I forget how you saved me from that Sonny creep?"

"Well, for the last three nights there's been this stranger in the bar."

"Yeah, well, you do get some strange ones at Pepe's, but what's the reason for calling me back to Colorado?" she asks, still lacking a concrete clue but with deepening suspicion.

"His name is Tommy."

Molly freezes like a rabbit trying to hide in plain sight and she notices that Carlos is looking hard at her to gauge her reaction. "That's the name of..."

"I remembered that name, Tommy Dawson, when you told me your story. Put it in my hard drive memory right back here in my noggin." He points to the back of his head.

"I figured this had something to do with Tommy as I was driving out here. That's why you wouldn't tell me."

"Let me finish. This fellow comes in and after a few drinks we ask him if we can help in any way since he seems to be new to these parts. He says he's looking for a redhead he's heard is working at a bison ranch around here."

"Oh, no, Carlos. That's horrible. So, you get on the phone and call me out here to identify if he's Tommy Dawson? But you know I don't want to see him."

"But all you have to do is look at some pictures. Then confirm in person that we have the right guy. Carlos pulls over on the shoulder of the road and takes out his phone. "While the newcomer was talking to the amigos, I was able to take a few photos."

"I can't stand to see that face." She covers her eyes.

"I know this is uncomfortable for you, but I just need you to tell me. Look here. Is this the same Tommy?"

He flips through five good, clear photos quickly as Molly's hands drop from her eyes to cover her mouth. "Yes, that's Tommy Dawson all right."

"I was sure it was. That's why I had to have you come back here immediately. Please don't be upset with me. We've been stringing him on, telling him this is where you hang out. Looks like we got him." Carlos looks more excited than she's ever seen him.

"I can't believe he would actually come out here to find me. My parents never explained to my little brother what happened, so he just told his friends that his sister was working on a bison ranch in Colorado."

Carlos puts his phone away. "There aren't many bison ranches in Colorado, you know, and Horseshoe is the best known. It wouldn't be hard to track you down."

"Danny knows that saying such a thing was a mistake now." She doesn't want to blame Danny.

"Maybe not a mistake at all if our plan works." He grins.

"Plan? Oh, god, Carlos, be careful. Tommy could be dangerous and I know what he wants with me."

"I'm glad to see you're getting over your innocence."

"But I'm completely..." She prevents herself from saying the word *terrified*, remembering her promise to herself to control her panic. She starts biting her thumbnail. "Do you really think he's after me?"

"You or some other young lady to his liking."

"You won't believe this, Carlos, but my mother and I went to the county sheriff to report the crime, just like you told me to do."

"Sounds like you're getting over some of your shyness, too. And don't worry about going to trial. There are other ways." He nods vigorously in the affirmative with his lips pressed together. "Such a crime should not go so long unpunished." Carlos spins the tires as he pulls back on the road and speeds toward town.

"Where are we going, Carlos? I don't want you or your friends to get involved in this. I don't want revenge."

"Revenge, no, but justice, yes. Listen to this. We've already been to the Alamosa County Sheriff, in a general way, not with your name or anything, but we gave them a pretty good description. It turns out that Tommy, alias Thomas, alias Tom, is wanted for rape in three states besides Kansas. We know a lot about Tommy now."

"I still hate to think of being in court with him, but I would do that if I had to. I'm changing my mind about a lot of things now."

"You wouldn't have to go to trial if we had a signed confession from him." Carlos looks over and grins.

"Oh, he'd never confess." Molly shakes her head back and forth. "Not Tommy."

"Want to bet? The amigos are standing by. You need to come with us now because there's no time to waste. He's sure to skip town soon. Just be with us to kind of verify things."

"Are you going to torture him? I don't believe in torture."

"Really?" Carlos cuts his eyes over at her. "Rape isn't torture? No, don't you worry, we're just going to persuade him a little."

"Jeez, Carlos, I'm really getting nervous about this."

"But are you in? This involves three other cases of innocent women. Do you want him running around hither and yon raping young girls? Tell me, are you in?"

If all she has to do is identify him, then why not? "Of course, I'm in, but don't kill him and don't get yourself or me in trouble. I'm a mother. I can't go to jail. I have to think of Norma Lou."

"This is *for* Norma Lou and all the other children like her."

Carlos stops briefly at Pepe's Cantina where the amigos are waiting with their pickup trucks. They rev their engines and start off in unison when they see him, driving together to a dingy old motel on the edge of town where they pull in as quietly as possible outside of Room 124.

"He's in there?"

"You just watch and tell me if we have the right guy, the Tommy Dawson in our photos. That's why you're here."

The friends knock on the door and when he answers they enter quickly. In a few seconds out comes Tommy bound up like a calf in a rodeo. Her stomach starts churning. "Yes, that's Tommy. Oh, the sight of him makes me sick."

"Hang in there. You haven't seen anything yet. And don't puke in my van."

They drive away together in a line like a funeral procession, but without the motorcycle cops.

"Where are you taking him?"

"Somewhere secluded that he won't remember. I'd best not say."

They drive on together for a few miles and turn off onto a dirt road, then onto another and another, each one getting smaller, bumpier, and dustier than the last, several miles in all. The trucks pull up together behind a parked Dodge Ram with a horse trailer. There's nothing out there but a few chipmunks scurrying around chasing each other in circles. Another amigo is already waiting there at a prearranged spot with an old palomino that he transported in the trailer.

"You aren't going to drag him with that horse, are you?" Molly asks.

"No, but it's a good idea. Drag it out of him, so to speak. You have a good imagination and you're starting to think like us."

"Don't hurt him."

"Not nearly as much as he hurt you. But we may need to humiliate him a little to gain his cooperation. That's okay, right? Humiliation?" The Pathfinder bounces as it crosses a short stretch of open terrain. "I'll pull up close to the tree right here. You can watch from the window, and when the time comes you can join us if you'd like." Carlos picks up a clipboard and a couple of pens. "The college boy here is going to write out Tommy's confession." He lowers her window so she can hear as well as see, turns off the engine, and shuts his door with an unintended slam as he leaves the Pathfinder.

His friends have taken Tommy, still bound up tight, and seated him on the horse. A rough rope noose, dangling from the strong branch of an old cottonwood is slipped around Tommy's neck. One of the friends holds the bridle of the aged brown and white beast to keep him still. Another friend stands behind the horse with a whip. Carlos explains the arrangement to Tommy and he seems to catch on pretty quick.

Carlos begins in his deep, clear voice, "I will write down your confessions and we can be done with this in no time if you cooperate."

"I didn't do whatever it is you think I did. You've got the wrong man. Some other Tommy," he whines with an unfaltering veneer of confidence.

"Now don't make this difficult," Carlos says. "I really don't like having to beat an old horse." The amigos laugh out loud and chatter in Spanish: ¡Es una lástima. Patético caballo!

"What do you want me to say?" Tommy asks.

"I'm here to write it down for you," Carlos says. "You're just going to sign on the bottom line. First," he writes as he speaks, "I raped Molly O'Reilly in February of this last year on her father's farm near Colby, Kansas."

"I didn't do it. I don't know no Molly O'Reilly," he says in a tone of deliberate indifference.

"Think before you speak. I'd sure hate to have to whip this horse and just leave you hanging here blowing back and forth in this nice breeze. Take a look over there at my van on the passenger side. Who is that red haired woman in there?"

"I don't know." But his eyes bug out in recognition. "I don't know no Molly."

"Oh, oh, that horse is getting mighty jittery standing there so long. I sure hope she won't run off." While Carlos is tormenting Tommy, Molly slips out of the SUV and strides over to face Tommy directly her hands on her hips. She's feeling a little feisty all of a sudden. Tommy looks a little disheveled, his hair tousled and unkempt, the strain beginning to show on his ashen face. "Tell me now, who is that beautiful young woman standing next to me here?"

"Oh, my god. It looks like Molly O'Reilly." His jaw drops and she can see his confidence beginning to crumble.

"Don't gawk. Eyes to the ground." Carlos says. "That's much better. Let's not make a big to-do of this. You just need to fess up. Now if you can give me the names of the three others you raped and where they are from, we can finish this up quickly before that horse gets fidgety."

Tommy remains silent for a moment in a test of wills. What's Carlos going to do to squeeze it out of him? Just then Molly startles as she hears a gunshot ring out. Oh, my god, did they shoot him? No, he's still sitting there on the horse. She looks around and sees one of the amigos holding a handgun aimed at the sky, but it looks more like a starting pistol used at a track meet. A warning shot to gain a little more cooperation. But what's this? A dark wet spot? Oh, no, it looks like Tommy has peed his pants.

"Oh, my," Carlos says, in a voice of shocked mockery, "I thought that was supposed to happen *after* the hanging." The amigos are pointing and laughing hysterically. "Maybe we don't need the hanging now, just the confessions. So, give me slowly and accurately the information I need for all three of the other young ladies."

Tommy complies.

Carlos nods to his friends and they take Tommy down from the horse, carefully releasing his head from the noose first, and once he's down, positioning his arm with a pen so that he can sign his own confession. "Your actual full name in nice cursive writing, the signature you use at the bank. And then your name printed with a steady hand. Got it?"

When Carlos and Molly return to the truck, she says, "Wow! That was gutsy."

"Seven on one? Not really." They get in and sit side by side.

"No, the idea. Where did you come up with that?"

"I saw it in an old Western a few years back." Molly smiles and then begins to laugh. "What's the matter? You think Indians don't watch cowboy movies? A person can find a lot of creative ideas in those Westerns." He grins.

"What happens next?"

"The boys will take him, still tied up of course, back to the sheriff's office and the FBI will be standing by. I'm sure that they will contact you and they might even take a deposition, but you can refuse to appear in court," he reassures her.

"What if some smart lawyer says the confession was obtained through torture?"

"Well, there is not a mark on him and who would be a witness to torture? Not you, certainly."

"Nope. Not me," Molly agrees, with a broad smile. "I didn't see any torture. Maybe a little mental cruelty, but certainly not torture." They exchange grins. Molly likes the way Carlos assumed command today. She can tell that his friends respect him. And what an act of love this was to capture Tommy and get his confession. Wow! She smiles at him overjoyed to have Tommy on his way to the police. She nods her head up and down as she says, "I liked what I saw here today, but there's just one thing."

"What's that?"

"I need to tell you that the noose you made to go around Tommy's neck probably wouldn't hold him. My dad taught me a thing or two about knots and I'm pretty sure that this one wouldn't work."

"That's what the amigos kept saying, too. It would come undone with that much weight, and I said that was fine because I never really had the intent of hanging him anyway. Just so Tommy wouldn't notice, that was the key thing."

"My dad tried to teach him knots, too, but I don't think he could have learned knots if his life depended on it."

"Like it did today?" Carlos throws her a grin.

Shaking her head from side to side, Molly says, "You just never know when you're going to need something you didn't learn." Oh, my god, she sounds like her dad.

Carlos glances at his watch. "Everything done before high noon. Now we need to get you back to your Norma Lou."

"Thank you, Carlos. I can't thank you enough for getting Tommy Dawson out of my life."

"Tomorrow I'd like you to have lunch with my family. Can you do that?"

"I'd love to," she says, realizing that what she just said is one hundred percent true. She bites her lip and wonders how to express what she wants to say next. "Actually," she begins, "I'm not completely comfortable staying with Wayne and Emily. It's a little awkward, as you might guess. So, after all of these months, I'm ready to accept your invitation to stay with your family, if that offer is still open."

"You mean to stay at our house?"

"Yeah, if that's okay."

Carlos is grinning. "Wow! Everything in its own season. He starts swaying from side to side, caught off guard by the turn of events. "Let's see now. In the morning I could come by for you and you could follow me over in your dad's truck. Oops. Sorry."

"No problem. That's what we always called it. It's actually my truck now." She thinks for a moment about the arrangements Carlos is suggesting. "I'd prefer to ride with you for the first time so you can point everything out and describe things for me. Maybe give me a crash course on potato farming so I don't say something stupid at lunch."

"You don't need to worry about that, but I like your idea. We can go pick up your truck in a day or two. How does that sound?"

The next morning when Carlos arrives at Wayne's, Molly packs up her stuff and moves Norma Lou's car seat to the Pathfinder for the drive over to the farm.

"We'll go on the back roads."

"The way you came to visit me when I was staying in the cabin?"

He nods as they turn north on the highway to catch an improved road called Lane 6. They drive west for a few miles through the sagebrush, content with their own thoughts. They have so much to say to each other, but neither one begins. When they come to State Route 17 just north of Hooper, they turn south. After they pass through Mosca on 17 Carlos tells her, "We turn west on Stanley Road up here and then it's the second right, the dirt road that leads back into our place." Molly wants to tell him about her mom's story, and fishing with her brother, and Bonnie Bradford, and her ride with O'Grady, but if she starts in on that stuff, it will take a lot of time, so maybe she'll save it for later. She watches the scenery in the Valley with Carlos and simply enjoys being with him.

They cruise along the dirt road that leads back into the potato farm and Molly checks to see if Norma Lou is sleeping. Instead, she's wide awake, her big eyes taking in the view of the passing scenery, apparently enjoying the soft hum of the tires on the gravel road.

"It may seem like a long driveway," Carlos says, "but it's not so far now."

"These fields seem barren," Molly observes.

"They've just been prepared for planting so you don't notice anything right now. During the summer, you just see miles and miles of potato plants."

"Oh, my gosh, so this is your potato farm."

"The family's potato farm." He smiles. "I never get tired of driving this road. Between the open land of the cultivated field there and the road, things just grow wild on the berm. It's early yet, but by mid-summer the blue penstemon thrive in the ditch and bright yellow prairie sunflowers—small like little daisies—survive in the gravel shoulder next to the road. So, we call this the golden road to potato paradise, in Spanish: *camino de oro hacía el paraíso de patata.*"

Of course, he speaks Spanish. He and his family and the amigos all speak Spanish. She always wondered why she took two years of it in high school. Would she dare to say something to him in Spanish? She wonders if he speaks *Ute,* too, if there even is a *Ute.*

"Actually," he continues, "it's a tough business, potato farming, because it requires water. All through these acres there are flowing wells, pumped wells, canals, rivers, creeks, streams, ditches, and of course the irrigation rigs. It's all about getting water rights, but our family has them and makes a good living at it because of the volume—acres of potatoes as far as you can see. And those plants have beautiful blossoms that hover like a white cloud over the dark green leaves in late July."

Molly smiles at his poetic description and the care he takes to describe everything so clearly. Now he's on his turf and back in one of his talkative moods. But then she wonders where he is he taking her. Where does this *camino* lead? It's odd how that old anxiety still comes rolling over her against all reason, but she knows how to control it now. Carlos is not Tommy, and Tommy is in jail. Be strong and be calm. They drive on in silence for a quarter mile, until Molly says, "Look at all of these houses back in here. Does one of these belong to your family?"

"Actually, all of them. The one up ahead there is the old homestead where my parents live. There's a great view of the Sangre de Cristo Range from their back porch."

"So, we must be going east."

"Good for you. You're getting yourself oriented." He grips the wheel tighter so that he can point everything out with his other hand. "On the left here, you are looking at the equipment barns. We have a lot of heavy equipment— deep chisels, cultivators, harrows, harvesters—and of course tractors and trucks. That building behind the others is a storage bin for the seed potatoes. Over here on the right is my brother Diego's house. He's traveling just now. And this one here," he leans to the side and points across Molly's shoulder to a small single-story house with its own drive and parking area, "is where I live."

"You have your own house?" She can't hide her surprise.

"I rattle around in there alone, but it's quiet when I want to study. This way we're still a family, but we all have the privacy of our own teepee." He smiles and gestures proudly at the houses.

"May I see your house?"

"Sure, sometime. Right now, we are due for dinner with father and mother and Selena. Our main meal is at noon."

"She's here? Running Deer?"

"You bet. She wants to see you. And you will meet *abuela*, my mom's mother."

The house of his parents is big, having the look of a well-kept old two-story farmhouse with tall gables, decorative trim, and a brand-new shiny copper roof. A fitting residence for a prosperous potato farmer. Carlos tells her, "I've told my parents about you and they are eager to meet you."

Surprised, Molly asks, "You've told them everything and they still want to meet me?"

"Nearly everything. I haven't had time to tell them about yesterday yet, but they will be proud of me." He grins. "I need to tell them before it comes out in the *Valley Currier*." Carlos pulls up and parks in a gravel space meant for visitors. When they step out of the SUV, they are greeted by a bouncy golden retriever with a silky red coat, his tail wagging furiously, hardly able to contain his excitement about seeing Carlos again, as if he had been gone for two weeks when it has only been two hours. "Down, stay down." Carlos takes his paws in his hands and shakes him and pats him on the head. "You be good."

"I didn't know you had a dog."

"I never take him with me. He likes it here on the farm. Besides, he's supposed to be our guard dog for my parents since we're so far out in the country."

"He's awfully friendly for a guard dog," Molly says, letting him sniff the back of her hand as she reaches down to pet him. "What's his name?"

"*Perro Rojo.*"

Molly smiles and tilts her head to the side. "Might that be Red Dog?"

"Yeah, Selena calls him Red Dog, but he answers to either one, Red Dog or *Perro Rojo.*"

"So, you have a bilingual dog?"

"Well, I never thought of it just that way, but I guess you're right."

They unload Norma Lou and all the baby stuff that goes with her now. Molly notices beside the house what looks like a small above-ground cemetery overgrown with wildflowers and weeds. White butterflies are hovering over the graves.

"You have your own private cemetery?" she blurts out. From the look she sees on Carlos's face, she realizes immediately that she may have blundered.

"It's our custom to bury our own on the land. As I said, we have been on this land for many generations."

"Did I say the wrong thing? I'm a little nervous to meet your parents."

"Don't be. They are lovely people. Okay, I admit it's going to be a little new for you, especially the food, but you'll do fine. It's not a test."

As they step up onto the small front porch and enter through the double front door, Molly notices what must be hand-loomed rugs everywhere: in the entry way, under the enormous oak dining table, hanging from the walls. She sees a lot of pottery, traditional pieces with red clay on the top and black and white geometric designs below. Lots of shiny hand carved wooden animals. His parents appear.

"This is Molly." No handshakes here; they embrace her immediately with hugs. His father is short and strong looking, built like a potato. He is introduced to her as Standing Elk. His mother is not as short, so Carlos grew taller, it seems, favoring his mother's side. She wears an ankle length straight patterned dress in muted shades of maroon and purple. A silver cross hangs on a fine chain around her neck. She is a model of simplicity and composure. She says to call her Carmencita. Her skin is light, her hair is brown, and her eyes are green. In facial features and manner Carlos resembles his father, who has black hair in two braids hanging in front of his shoulders, deep dark eyes, and a strong profile of the Native American heritage.

"Where's Running Deer?" Molly asks.

"Hang on," a voice shouts down from upstairs. "I'm changing."

"And this must be little Norma Lou that we've been hearing so much about," Carmencita says, reaching out both arms. Norma Lou leans forward to go to Carlos's mother immediately, with no shyness, no hesitation, as she seems to sense loving arms. So, everyone fusses over Norma Lou for a while, her red hair, her light blue eyes, her exploding smile, definitely a conversation piece in this family.

"I have a little present for her," Carmencita tells Molly. She reaches into her pocket and pulls out a handmade cloth doll.

"Oh, how sweet," Molly says, accepting the doll and trying to show Norma Lou, who seems much more interested in the "new grandmother's" earrings. Molly thanks her and adds, "So soft and lovable. Thank you."

Selena bounces down the stairs lickety-split, descending two at time, her feet barely landing on the treads, making her presence known as she enters the circle gathered around Norma Lou. "Look at how she's grown. She's like a baby supermodel."

Carlos frowns at her.

"Well, like you've told us," Selena says, "there aren't many babies in the Valley that look like this."

"Selena," Carlos calls her by name in a gentle reprimand.

"I was just trying to say I think she's really cute. I mean, she could be in one of those baby food ads."

Just then *abuela* enters from her downstairs bedroom, hobbling over to join the family, dragging her aluminum walker along, careening to the left and then to the right as she makes steady progress crossing the room, no one in the family daring to offer her help. "*¿Qué esto?*" she asks.

"This is Norma Lou, Molly's baby," Carlos says. Remember? The young woman over at Horseshoe Ranch we've been telling you about?"

"*Finalmente* I get to meet this baby. *Bueno.*"

"And the mother, too," Carlos reminds her. "Molly O'Reilly." He seems perfectly comfortable with what might be awkward moments in another family. But just then, *abuela* steps forward and hands Molly a feather that she has been grasping in her wrinkled hand. "A welcome gift for you."

Molly has never had anyone give her a feather before and doesn't know how to hold it or what to do with it, but surely, she has been raised with the manners to say, "Thank you." It is a very beautiful feather, and she is sure it must symbolize something.

Carlos turns to his father. "And what about you, dad? Don't you have a present?" he asks.

His father goes to a display case with glass doors near the entry and brings forth a tiny wood carving of a wolf, all sanded smooth and polished with wax. He hands it to Norma Lou who turns it over and over in her little hands and then looks up and grins.

"Such a beautiful smile," Carmencita says, as she hands Norma Lou to Carlos. She heads off to the kitchen and returns in a few minutes to say, "If you are ready, we can come to the table." Carlos resurrects an old wood high chair for Norma Lou, and Molly pulls out her bib and plastic dishes. When *abuela* is seated and the others are in their places, there is a moment of silence and then Standing Elk says the blessing: "Let us walk softly on the earth with all living things great and small, remembering as we go that one God kind and wise created all."

Carmencita serves a corn and bean soup in pottery bowls. Venison steaks have been thawed for the occasion, cut into short strips, and cooked with various peppers, onion, and lime. Roasted chicken breasts are covered with a brown sauce that tastes like peppers and chocolate. Round pieces of Navajo frybread are passed around and served with prickly pear cactus jelly. Molly is savoring every bite as she whispers to Carlos, "The food may be different, but it is delicious." Then she asks with a sly grin, "Where are the potatoes?"

"We got sick of them," is his hushed reply. "Mashed, baked, boiled, fried, creamed, in potato salad and potato soup. One day my father said, 'I think that's enough potatoes,' and everyone was relieved. You don't have to eat potatoes to grow them."

After dinner, Carlos shows Molly around the house while his parents put Norma Lou on a blanket on the floor with her toys placed just far enough away to give her a little incentive to creep. Red Dog stretches out alongside her, as if he is proud to have another human to guard. On the tour of the house, Molly stops to look at all of the furnishings, the knickknacks, the pictures, and the woven baskets fastened on the walls. One side table is filled with family photos and over it hangs a posed photo of the ancestors that must be as old as photography itself.

"There is a lot of symbolism in our tribal lore," Carlos says. "For example, the dinner today included favorite dishes of my deceased grandparents on both sides. Serving those dishes is like having them with us in spirit to meet you."

"Tell me about the doll."

"The little doll is a Hopi kachina and brings us good spirits from a sacred mountain range in Arizona. And the wooden wolf that Standing Elk gave to Norma Lou is like a guardian angel. We all have a special animal like that to watch over us."

"Besides Red Dog?" Molly asks. "And tell me about the feather."

"It is a sign of respect and honor. *Abuela* knows what you have been through and admires your courage."

They wander along through the house together and Molly is wide-eyed curious about everything, deep into a world she has never seen before, things she would only expect to find in a museum.

"What's this?" Molly asks.

"An old pump organ from *abuela's* family. No one plays it anymore. The pedals are loose."

Molly spots a beautiful old guitar leaning against the organ. "And this?" she asks. "Who plays this?"

"My mother knows some old Spanish love songs, but she hasn't played recently."

"Maybe she needs some inspiration," Molly says with that same sly grin.

When they are finished with the tour of the house, Carlos leads Molly out onto the back porch where they can be alone for a little while. He points out the view of the mountains in the background behind the long stretch of potato fields. Such a beautiful view from a simple back porch.

Then Carlos fidgets and clears his throat as if he wants to tell her something, but doesn't know what to say. "I don't know how long you plan to stay. Maybe just a few days. But I think it will take some time for us to get reacquainted again. Here, sit down." He points to an old loveseat with wood slats painted white. "It's a swing. My parents like to sit here in the cool of the evening to enjoy the view of the mountains. It swings," he says nervously. "I mean, you can swing it." She sits and tries it out. It squeaks.

"It's really smooth," she says.

"You can't imagine how much I've been missing you. I'm sorry to sound so formal. I guess you can tell I'm a little nervous." He is pacing in front of the loveseat glider.

Why is he so ill at ease? Maybe it's because he thinks he is talking to the old Molly who rejected him. He doesn't know she has changed because they haven't talked yet. "I know you want us to become friends again," Molly says, "and I'm ready to listen to you now."

"Okay then, just let me say the speech I've been rehearsing over and over to myself during these lonely weeks."

He leans against the back porch railing, a little more comfortable now, and folds his arms across his chest. "I don't want to rush things even though I've already been waiting several weeks to see you." He pauses, as if to remember his speech. "Well, here's my offer. I want to give you as much space and time as you need. You can come here and see what life is like with this family. Like a visit at a guest ranch. Stay in this house or mine as long as you wish. We will help you take care of Norma Lou while you are here. If you want to explore going to college in town later on, we will watch her while you go to class and study. If you want your mother to visit while you are here, there are lovely rooms in this house where she can stay. If your little brother Danny wants to work here in the summer, he can."

Molly is wide-eyed, trying to take it all in. It feels like she is holding her breath waiting for the rest of his speech. What more could there be?

"I don't know whether you can learn to love me, or any man for that matter, after what happened to you. I know it will take time for you to learn to be comfortable around me, but I'm a very patient guy. And if you fall in love with me one day, I would be the happiest man in the world. But I know we need to go very, very slowly. If you want to leave permanently, we can part at any time without explanation. Although it will break my heart, that must be part of the agreement. If someday you want to get married—to me, that is—you will need to tell me when and how. I know this is an unusual offer, and it might sound strange or premature, but I think I know you and understand what you need. We will walk the path of life together for a while, and I will try to put your aching heart to rest."

Molly is stunned by his beautiful words and the thought that has gone into his offer, and she doesn't know what to say. For sure it's not a marriage proposal. It sounds more like a treaty drafted by the ancient chiefs, but she thinks she hears in it a gentleman's invitation simply to get better acquainted. "You're so nice to me, Carlos."

His nervousness is gone. He's smiling through his seriousness, pleased that she is showing interest and not turning him down flat like she did before. Then he surprises her with, "The red-plumed bird must learn to fly free while the Great Spirit watches over her."

"You are such a poet." She's not sure what the red bird thing means exactly, so she lets it pass. "Here, Carlos, sit down with me." She motions to him. Then she takes a deep breath and says, "I want you to know that even though I am still a little jumpy about men, I'm making progress. I had a very good counselor back home. I mean, I really have a lot of stuff to tell you about how I'm changing." Then she takes his hand in both of hers and says, "I need to talk to my mom, but it would be stupid of me not to try out some kind of life with you and your family with your being so kind and caring the way you all are."

"It's okay. Take your time. Someday I can drive you back to Kansas, meet your mom and little brother, and pick up your stuff if you'd like. I'm sorry. There I go jumping ahead."

Molly and Carlos start to swing together gently on the loveseat glider and the rocking motion sets her to thinking. She notices that she is still holding his hand and realizes that she doesn't have that hesitation about Carlos anymore. In fact, right now she can't think of anything she doesn't like about him. Why did she give him such a hard time at first? Well, she was preoccupied then with keeping her secret. But after Norma Lou was born and she was alone in that cabin, oh, my god, she was positively rude to him. Then she went to live with Wayne. Another slap in the face. He must really love her to make such an offer after all of her rejections.

Can she picture fitting in here with these potato farmers and their generations of sacred objects and venerable traditions? Sure. There's a place for her and she is certain she would thrive. Like everywhere, there are things to fix: the mailboxes out by the main road need a coat of paint, the family cemetery needs weeding and replanting, and this squeaky glider definitely needs some WD-40. Is she making choices now about how she will live and who she will be—a dairy farmer's daughter who found the *camino de oro*—just by saying yes to an offer from Carlos to stay? Really, what would be her reason to say no? She notices that Carlos doesn't seem to mind sitting here with her for a few minutes silently swinging back and forth on the squeaky swing, while she is lost in her private thoughts. Maybe it is because she is still holding his hand.

She thinks she hears Norma Lou fussing and they both stand up together at the same instant like mother and father. They notice that and it makes them exchange bashful smiles. She says, "We need to relieve your parents."

As they go to attend to Norma Lou, Molly picks her up from the blanket on the floor, and with a little patting settles her into a fragile nap. Molly notices that she is the focus of the loving gaze of Carlos and the affectionate attention of his parents, *abuela,* and Selena, with all eyes on the baby wrapped in her arms. Even *Perro Rojo* raises his head from his paws to stare. She is not self-conscious or ashamed about her baby anymore, but proud and hopeful, knowing that there might be a place for her and Norma Lou in this loving family and a chance to bring a little happiness to these welcoming people who, like Carlos, are only hoping she will love them in return. She looks up at Carlos and smiles. He comes over to gaze at Norma Lou up close and Molly whispers to him, "I'll stay. Okay?"

"More than okay. I'll do my best to make you happy here."

Molly has to tell somebody so she phones Wayne that evening to let him know that she's staying with Carlos's family for a while. He's glad and not surprised. Carlos lives in the new single story ranch house that he pointed out to Molly on the way in. He and his brother Diego built it during the winter of the year that Carlos stayed home from the university to help harvest the potatoes. Carlos's father, unable to contribute much in the way of physical labor due to his surgery, surely made up for his being sidelined by supplying the capital needed for the lumber and materials for construction. Now both sons have their houses.

One of the two bedrooms at the east end of the house is where Carlos sleeps, the other being kind of an office for the farm with a set up for current and used computers, stacks of reports and manuals, and textbooks from his studies at the university. Molly speculates that Carlos is becoming the brains behind the farm now that Standing Elk is growing old although she reminds herself that she hasn't met Diego yet.

At the west end of the house, quite apart from the other two bedrooms, is a sizable but unoccupied guest room. Between the sleeping rooms stands a modern kitchen with new appliances and a small dinette with a round table. The living room is sparsely furnished with a big recliner looking out a north-facing picture window, a CD player and speakers, and a rocking chair that sits by a fireplace framed with bookcases on either side. So, this is where he had been borrowing books for her: from his own personal library, a collection from his days as a student.

"I see that the old crib and changing table that you brought to me in the cabin are in the guest room," Molly observes. Has Carlos been so confident of her reply that he has installed them here for her, or is this just where he stores his dreams and spare baby furniture?

"Yeah, and my parents have an old playpen and a small crib left over from us kids that they can use at their place while they are watching Lulu during the day," he says, ignoring Molly's implied suspicion about how the crib from the cabin found its way into the guest room of his house.

"Lulu? When did we start calling her Lulu?" she asks, letting the question about the crib slide.

"Just tonight. My father will formally assign the wolf to protect her and then we can call her 'Lulu Lobo.'" Carlos shoots her a sly smile to let her know that he is at least partly teasing, but then he appears to be serious, too.

So they put Lulu Lobo to bed and then sit down opposite each other at the round table in the dinette to enjoy some tea while piano music—Chopin waltzes, Carlos tells her—plays softly in the living room. "I need to call my mom tomorrow morning to tell her about what you did to Tommy Dawson." A smile creeps across her face. "She'll love it."

"What *we* did. You stepped up when the time came."

"And I need to tell her that I'm staying with your family."

"Will she understand?"

"Since my father died, my mom and I have become much closer. She's told me all kinds of things about her past that I never knew before. I understand her better now, and she understands me."

"What will Danny think?"

"Oh, he'll be really happy for me." She reaches over and touches Carlos on the forearm. "But I need something to do here. I can't just sit around. I should earn my keep."

"Well, you don't need to, but I'm sure we can find something."

"No, not just find something, Carlos. I've already found it. I see a lot of things that need to be fixed around here. I need some projects, little ones to start with but some big ones, too. But here's the thing: I don't want to offend your family, you know, by implying that things are run down."

"Offend? My parents aren't like that. They'll be delighted. On a farm like this, you have to tend to the farm first, so a lot of things around the houses and the yard have to slide until you get time. Then when you get time, you're too tired to face those chores, so they slide some more."

"Well, if you'll get their permission, I'd like to start to work tomorrow morning, first off fixing that squeaky swing."

"No permission needed. And just go ahead with anything else that catches your eye. Wayne said you have a talent for fixing things."

The next morning, Molly sets to fixing with fervor. The first thing she does is to attack that squeaky swing on the back porch with WD-40. Once she gets that spray can in her hand, she goes after squeaky door hinges all through the house, then the sliding patio door leading onto the back porch to make it close smoother, upstairs windows that get stuck half way up, and kitchen cupboard doors. It's good to have her lanky body back, bending and twisting, and some work to do. She uses the front pack that Carlos gave her so she can carry Lulu Lobo with her while she's working. She's growing to like the new name. The more difficult jobs she will undertake while the baby is napping or when the grandparents beg to watch her.

One afternoon she attacks the slow drains with Liquid Plumr and adjusts the toilet floats and seats in all three houses. She organizes the office in Carlos's house and asks him if it is okay to straighten up all the tools and spare hardware in the main barn. She paints the mailboxes out by the driveway entrance. She aligns the pedals on the antique organ and tightens them up— no big deal. When people compliment her on her work and ask her where she learned how to do things like that, she says it's from her dad who taught her how to fix things while she was growing up on the dairy farm in Kansas. It makes her feel good to remember that side of her father.

One day she asks Carlos, "May I fix up the cemetery? I know it is a sacred place, but it doesn't need to look all rundown and abandoned."

"What do you plan on doing?" he asks with a little frown.

"Pull the weeds and plant some flowers. I did the gardening at the lodge, you know."

"Just don't move any markers."

"Oh, I wouldn't do anything like that." So, she puts Lulu in the front-pack and gets a hoe and trowel to dig out the weeds. She hauls in five wheelbarrows of fertile soil from a nearby field and drives her truck into town to a nursery for some bedding plants, the reliable old favorites: geraniums, petunias, marigolds, and alyssum. The butterflies will like that. When it's all done, everyone is commenting on how Molly brought new life to the old graveyard. "Actually," Carlos tells them, "Molly brings new life wherever she goes."

Molly explains her plan to Carlos for renewing the parking area next to the main house with fresh gravel. He is doing paperwork in his office and she hopes she is not interrupting.

"While you're at it," he says without looking up, "you might as well put some on the driveways and parking spots for the other two houses as well."

"For you and Diego, too? Good. I figure eight to ten yards. Can you afford that?"

He finally looks up at her. "Money's not the problem around here; the problem is time. That's how stuff gets so deteriorated. Nobody has time to do what you're doing."

"So, order me ten yards then." And she adds, "For sure I've got the time."

"You said ten yards?" He looks puzzled. "How are you going to move all that gravel around—certainly not with a wheelbarrow."

"I've had my eye on that Bobcat." She nods toward the barn and throws him a grin.

"You know how to drive a loader like that?"

"You just watch me."

So, when the dump truck load of gravel arrives, Molly leaves it to the grandparents to listen for Lulu when she wakes up from her nap and heads out for an afternoon of distributing gravel. First, she gives the driveways and parking areas a little scraping to make sure everything is level. Then she scoops up the gravel with the Bobcat, distributes it around, dumps it, and smooths it out. She discovers that it's going to take more than one afternoon.

Carlos has been playing CDs of classical music and the sounds of Vivaldi and Mozart and Beethoven resonate through the house. His teacher for a course in music appreciation at the university, an enthusiastic young woman named Professor Sung, made classical music come alive for him, just as Mrs. Braxton made novels live for Molly. Patiently, he shows Molly what to listen for, repeating what his professor told him, so that Molly begins to hear how a melody repeats itself—a *theme* he calls it—or how the theme gets developed—a *variation*, he calls it—and how to listen for which instruments are playing what notes, high or low, string or wind. And he tells her to be aware of how music makes her feel, sometimes so sad it makes you want to cry, or so joyous it makes you want to dance.

This afternoon as Molly heads out to continue her distribution of the gravel with the Bobcat, Carlos hands her a fancy headset with earphones and a wire leading to a player that he slips into the pocket of her jeans.

"What's this?" she asks.

"Beethoven's Fifth," he says slipping the headphone gently over her ears.

"Oh, my god," she says, speaking louder than she needs to over the crashing music. "This is fantastic." Pointing to a space nearly a foot over the top of her head, she yells, "The orchestra's up here somewhere." She smiles. "Hey, that's your secret knock."

Carlos takes her by the hand and when they get to the Bobcat, he helps her on. In a flash, the little loader is running and Molly is driving it back and forth, spreading the gravel around with new exuberance to the accompaniment of Beethoven.

On the third afternoon, when she finishes the whole project, Carlos tells her it looks great. Selena, a little jealous for attention, wants some instruction on using the Bobcat, so she and Molly share the seat and Molly shows her how to go forward and back, lift and dump. Naturally they are bouncing and jerking all over the place and laughing their heads off as Selena is learning, not all that quickly. When the lesson is over, Molly drives the Bobcat back to its place in the barn with the planters and harvesters, and they both jump down as the engine dies. Molly says to Selena, "You could learn to run these machines, you know, and then maybe you'd discover that you like potato farming."

"I hate it. I have no interest in potatoes whatsoever."

"But it's your family's farm."

"Hey, do you see these legs?" Molly glances down and notices not for the first time the rippling muscles bulging in those short legs. "Well, these legs are going to run me to college, hopefully on a scholarship."

"In track?"

"For sure not basketball," Selena says with a big grin. "And then these legs are going to run me through college. And when I run across the stage with that diploma in my hand, they're going to run me around the world, far, far from potatoes."

"But don't you have a stake in the family business?"

"Not interested. But Carlos—by now you know how nice he is—says I need never go hungry. I'll have income. And I tell him that's not fair if I don't contribute. And then he says something funny. He says, "We take care of the herd," like I'm a baby bison or something."

11

LOWERING JIMMY JOE INTO A WELL

After three weeks, Molly is beginning to feel like she is blending right in with her new family, enjoying the kindness of Carmencita and the quiet support of Standing Elk. *Abuela has* become *her* grandmother, too, and Selena is a lively companion although she is still busy during the week finishing up the last days of the school year. Molly and Carlos have talked on and on about what happened to her while she was visiting back in Kansas, and he has been as patient and understanding as ever. In fact, he is excited about the progress she has made in building the new Molly. She never thought she could be this happy, and when she thinks back on how depressed she was the first few weeks after Norma Lou was born, she realizes how far she has come in the happiness department. Only a few weeks ago she was huddled with Bonnie Bradford feeling quite hopeless about her future. Now everything is nearly perfect, including a new level of comfort with Carlos. She hugs him like he's a big teddy bear. What could possibly go wrong?

Tonight, she is sleeping soundly in the guest bedroom on the west end of Carlos's house when she hears a familiar rap on her bedroom door, the beat of the opening of Beethoven's Fifth.

"It's me, Carlos. Sorry to awaken you, but I need to tell you something and get your advice." She glances at the luminous digital clock showing 4:30 A.M. Holy cow! What could this be? She checks Norma Lou and slips on the new robe Carlos bought her. He motions her to the dinette where she sits as he paces back and forth.

"What's up at this ungodly hour," she asks, "besides us?"

Carlos looks shaken. He slips into the opposite chair and speaks softly, almost in a whisper, as if to conceal what could be gossip. "Selena hasn't come home tonight. I don't think my parents know that yet. Two of the amigos from Pepe's Cantina drove all the way out here to tell me."

"What's happened to her?"

"That's just it; we don't know."

She's never seen Carlos look scared. Now she's scared, too. "What did your friends say?"

"It's Friday night so of course she was at Pepe's with her girlfriends from high school. Early in the evening, before sunset, she tells them she is going to show this guy the way out to Horseshoe Ranch."

"What guy? Someone she knew?" She feels a twinge of panic.

"No, just some guy who showed up and sat down next to her at the bar. The girlfriends were on the other side of her, so they couldn't catch everything he was saying, but apparently he was from Texas and said, in what they explained was an unmistakable Texas drawl, that he was looking for directions to Horseshoe Ranch, that he was really excited about seeing some bison."

"What did he look like?"

"They said he wasn't all that attractive, actually a little effeminate, bone-white skin and oversized ears, and he was dressed like a rich guy: designer jeans, Western type shirt with button pockets and a yoke across the shoulders, pointy polished cowboy boots, and a big white hat. They said he stuck out like a sore thumb in Pepe's with that outlandish outfit."

"At least they picked up on the details of his appearance. Sounds like a wealthy dude from Texas." She's beginning to picture him and it makes her nervous. "Driving what?"

"They weren't too sure what to call it but from their description, I'm sure it was a Hummer. Do you know what that is?"

Molly nods. "Yeah, it looks like a military vehicle, big wide tires, and enclosed space in the back. What color?"

"Her friends thought maybe orange or bright yellow."

Molly gestures with open hands. "Couldn't she just give him directions to the ranch?"

"That's what she tried to do, but he said he kept getting confused and wanted to make sure that he got to the part of the ranch where he could see a buffalo or two, so if she could just show him the way..."

"Oh, oh, and she wanted to be helpful..."

"...then he would drive her right back and be there no later than eleven so she could meet her friends." Carlos pauses to get control of himself. "So, she asked the friends to wait for her, and that's what they did—eleven, twelve, one, even after closing time, and she never came back. They haven't seen her since." His voice is cracking. "Diego is out driving around the perimeter of the Horseshoe, but we haven't heard from him." Carlos stands and resumes his pacing.

Molly has tried to get acquainted with Diego, but it seems like he's always running errands somewhere. Is he up to this task of searching for Selena? "This is awful, Carlos. Poor Selena. Do you think she has been kidnapped?"

"Abducted? I hate to think so, but...well...yes, I do. And I'm really worried about her safety now." He keeps shaking his head back and forth. "Here's where I need your advice. We haven't told any of the family up at the main house. I know we need to, but I'm wondering if we need to wake everyone up just yet."

"Do you think she could still show up this morning?"

"Not really." He buries his eyes in his hands. "I can't stop imagining terrible things happening to her."

"Yeah, and in cases like this we can't afford to waste a minute." She rubs a hand across her forehead. "Okay. Let's call Wayne at five—he's usually up by then—and we can alert him to what has happened. We'll tell him we're coming over. At six we'll put your parents in charge of Lulu, and you and I can go out to the Horseshoe together and start figuring this thing out. We can talk to Wayne. See if he has noticed anything suspicious."

"I just hope this guy hasn't hurt her. I hope she's still alive."

"Should we call the police?"

"I'd rather not because we'll look kind of silly if she shows up in the next hour or two."

At five they call Wayne. After grabbing some toast and coffee together, Molly leaves Lulu Lobo with Carmencita and Standing Elk and takes off with Carlos to search for Selena. Diego was looking for his sister most of the night, so he'll stay behind to supervise the day's work on the farm and try to catch up on lost sleep. Molly and Carlos take the back road over to the ranch. They check in with Wayne and for once he is actually in his office.

"Terrible news you gave me about Selena." Wayne's eyebrows shoot up. "She never came home?" When Molly and Carlos nod with solemn faces, Wayne says, "How can I help?"

Molly responds, "Well, like I told you on the phone, Wayne, Selena went missing last night while she was showing a total stranger the way out here to Horseshoe Ranch. So, my first question is: did you or anyone on the ranch notice anything unusual last night around sunset?"

"Sunset? Come to think of it, Emily was reading as I was dozing in the rocker, and she woke me up all frightened to say she heard shots. I asked her if she was sure it was shots and she said there was no doubt about it. So, I asked her how many and she said three. And then I realized I'd heard them, too. You know how it is when you're half asleep. He removes his hat to scratch his head.

"Is Rainbow here?" Molly asks.

"Yes, she was going to be mending fences today, but..."

"I need her," Molly interrupts. "I have a hunch about those shots. If that guy wanted to see bison, Selena knew right where to take him."

"Oh, good god, that's true," Carlos says.

They find Rainbow over by the supply barn for the cattle operations. Carlos and Rainbow need no introductions, so Molly quickly explains to Rainbow what has happened and tells her she needs her to join them. Molly asks Wayne if they can borrow some horses to ride out to the site she has in mind.

"No problem," Wayne says. "Do you mind if I ride along?"

"As you wish." Hey, it's his ranch. As they saddle up, she notices a funny look on Carlos's face. "What's the matter? You don't ride horses?" She can't imagine an Indian that doesn't ride a horse. There goes another stereotype.

"Mostly I ride tractors. But I'll be okay. I'm just a little slow."

He mounts the horse they've brought and as Molly watches him trying to get settled, she spots the need for some training and can't resist. "Don't put your feet so far into the stirrups. On the ball of your foot. There. That's better. Sit up." Carlos straightens up abruptly and picks up the reins with both hands. "One hand. Neck rein. Let the rein rest on the horse's neck and pull against it for a turn. That's better. Now you're looking like a real cowboy. Oops! Sorry."

"¡*Vámonos!* We need to find my sister."

About a half mile away near the county road that borders the ranch, they find the spot where Molly had taken Selena and Carlos sightseeing in the Chevy Suburban back in January. Except for the sage and a few patches of early-blooming groundcover, the site is dry and desolate, and they ride only a short distance inside the fence before they come upon what is left of the carcass of a bison. Rainbow looks down from her mount and points. "Oh, no! Look at this. An abomination if there ever was one."

Molly is horrified. Her mind flashes back to the time of the roundup in November, when the bison were counted and received their shots. Was this poor creature among them? Had to be as one of the herd. They all dismount and approach the dead bison cautiously and respectfully.

"The head is missing." Rainbow points. "And some of the hide, too."

"Souvenirs? In this day and age? How revolting." Wayne nods his head back and forth. "I thought we were well beyond poachers and rustlers."

"One would think so," Carlos adds, "but apparently there are still people like that, all hell-bent on a trophy. The dude sure fits the bill."

"You have a suspect?" Wayne asks, surprised.

"Selena's friends have provided a description of the guy who coaxed her out here. That's all we have to go on." Carlos looks down at the remains. "I'm sorry she had to witness such a slaughter because she would never have any part of a travesty like this." He clenches his teeth. "So, her captor has guns. Now I'm even more worried."

Molly is looking around the scene. "He clipped a big hole in the fence and dragged the head through right about here. And on over here it looks like tire tracks. Look, right here," she says, pointing. "What would you say, Wayne?"

"A Dodge Ram or even bigger. There's a wide distance between those tracks. Maybe a Hummer."

Molly and Carlos exchange knowing glances. "What's this?" Molly asks. "From the carcass over here to the tire tracks, I see a trail of seeds, like pumpkin seeds."

"Oh, wow! Selena loved pumpkin seeds. She always had them with her," Carlos says, excited to see them.

"But look at this. She didn't just drop a pile of them by mistake. She's consciously scattering them to leave a trail. But where would the bison killer go?"

"To a taxidermist," Rainbow says firmly and without hesitation. "He probably wanted to mount that head like they used to do. You know, hang it on the great room wall in his family's private ranch and make believe it's been there for generations."

"What taxidermist would do that these days?" Molly asks.

"Especially since it's against the law," Wayne adds. "What do you think, Rainbow? You know these parts better than any of us. Who would take on a job like this?"

"Well, there's a couple of places in Alamosa, but those guys are all above board. I've heard my husband talk about a guy over in Del Norte, not so shady himself, but not above making a referral to his friend."

"If you can give me directions, we'll go looking for him right now," Molly says. Rainbow gives the directions to Carlos, who seems to be familiar with every turn and landmark she mentions.

"I'll call the police," Wayne says. "It's required."

"You do that," Carlos tells him, "but don't expect me to rely on the police to find my sister."

"I understand."

"Thanks, Rainbow. Thanks, Wayne." Molly hugs them both, mounts her horse, and starts off at a gallop. Then she remembers Carlos, looks around, and sees him galloping at full speed right behind her, hanging on for dear life.

Molly and Carlos drive down to Route 160 and follow it west through Alamosa toward Monte Vista to Del Norte. Just outside of town they find the county road and the markers that Rainbow gave them—an old railroad siding and a gift shop—and they pull into the gravel parking lot. As they walk up to the weather-beaten shop with the TAXIDERMY sign in the window, Molly takes Carlos by the arm and whispers, "Don't be really obvious, but just look down and tell me what you see as we approach the steps here."

"Holy smoke! A trail of pumpkin seeds." A smile lights up on Carlos's face. "Good going, we got it right on the very first try." He stoops to pick up a few seeds. "You're pretty good at this, Detective O'Reilly."

"Thanks. Only remember, this is not likely to be the guy," Molly warns. "It's his buddy who does the illegal stuff, and we've got to pull it out of this dude as to where to find him."

They climb the wood steps, amble across the board porch, and enter. The place is crammed with every imaginable stuffed and mounted animal. A fox, two squirrels, and a beaver hit the eye first. A twelve-point buck head hangs up high on the back wall gazing down on the patrons. Birds are perched everywhere, cute little finches and bluebirds, an owl, and a big tan and gray hawk with vicious looking claws. For someone who likes animals as Molly does, this place is definitely creepy. But she reminds herself of the mission. A pudgy older man with thick glasses comes from the back room to greet them amidst his menagerie of fine work, no doubt his pride and joy. "How can I help you?" he asks.

"I'm looking for my sister," Carlos states without hesitation and in few words. "We believe that she was in here with an odd-looking dude from Texas."

"I don't really recall anyone like that," the taxidermist says, looking down and away.

"It's important to remember if you can. My sister is missing." The taxidermist looks surprised but just shakes his head. "I just don't recall any young girl in here."

"We didn't say she was young," Molly tells him. "She could have been older. But let me refresh your memory about the man. It would be hard not to recall a wealthy Texan attired in designer jeans, a Western shirt, polished cowboy boots, and a big white hat along with a girl not yet seventeen. She has dark copper skin like her brother here, and black hair done in two braids. I believe you would call her an Indian."

"She's usually munching on some pumpkin seeds, like these we found by your steps outside." Carlos holds out the palm of his hand with the seeds he picked up.

"The look on your face and that twitch on your cheek," Molly says, "tell me that you are beginning to remember."

"Look, folks, I don't want to get mixed up in nothing."

"We understand that," Carlos tells him, "so we want to keep you out of this and we promise to do just that, but we need to get directions to the guy you referred him to. It's no crime to give directions, either to us or the Texan who kidnapped my sister." Carlos looks directly at the taxidermist, as if to stare him down. "We don't care so much about the bison head he wanted to mount because the poor bison is dead now and gone, but I care very much about my sister and I hope she's still alive."

"Are you cops?"

"I'm her brother, we told you."

"But the young lady here, is she a cop?"

"Nope. Although she's smart as hell at figuring stuff out. But here's the thing, mister. If you can give us the directions to the guy who is mounting the bison head, we can keep you completely out of this. No blabbing."

"But your obstruction of the search for a kidnapper," Molly says, "well, that's a different story and could be serious."

The taxidermist takes a moment to think it over, massaging his clean shaven pudgy little chin. Then he goes to the back room and returns with a copy of a set of directions and a hand drawn map. "This is the place." And then running his fingers through his thinning hair, he says, "I'm sorry about your sister. I had no idea."

Carlos nods in silence.

"Thank you, sir," Molly says, taking the page of directions and folding it up to stuff in her pocket. "You don't mention us, we don't mention you."

As they start to leave, the taxidermist says, "It takes about a week to do a good mounting job. You might catch up with him when he goes to pick it up."

That night the only one who sleeps well is Norma Lou, snuggled into her old crib. Apparently, she had a busy day, being run here and there meeting neighbors and friends of the family with her grandparents. Molly is restless trying to figure out how and when they might descend on the guy from Texas, and Carlos is worried sick about Selena, wondering if she's even alive. Molly and Carlos meet at the round table in the dinette during their nocturnal wanderings, and they decide to make a list of what they know so far.

The key to the case, they conclude, is capturing the kidnaper by surprise when he returns to pick up his mounted trophy, but then they have to get him to confess where he's hiding Selena. Molly says he has no motive to harm her, but Carlos reminds her that Selena is a witness to his crime. Carlos asks some of the amigos to find the illegal taxidermist's shop and stake it out during the day, just to keep an eye on the comings and goings. If the Texan appears, they can call Carlos for advice, but they don't really expect him to show up again for a week. Carlos wants to keep looking for Selena, but he has no inkling of where to look. The waiting is nerve-wracking and Carlos is losing sleep.

Two days later shortly before noon, Carlos gets a phone call. "Where are you?" he asks and pushes the button for speaker phone.

"In Aspen at the Hickory House Ribs restaurant," Selena says. "I escaped. The owner of the restaurant says he'll feed me in the kitchen and hide me at the Hotel Aspen as long as necessary."

"Where were they holding you?"

"I don't know exactly, locked up in a small cabin part way up the valley of the Conundrum Creek. They say there's a ghost town out beyond there called Ashcroft, but I didn't see any ghosts, nothing but the four walls of the little cabin where they were holding me and it was driving me nuts being confined like that."

" When did you escape?"

"Early this morning I flew past the person bringing me breakfast and followed the creek down the valley like a good Indian girl. You know me and running. Then I saw signs at the roundabout for Aspen and this restaurant was the first place I found."

"Good for you, Running Deer. But tell me..."

"I haven't got time to tell you much, but listen close to this. Jimmy Joe, the guy who was holding me, is heading back to Del Norte to pick up a mounted bison head from a sketchy taxidermist who does illegal stuff."

"Thanks to your pumpkin seeds we've already tracked him down and we have a map to his place." Molly smiles at Carlos.

"Oh, you saw the seeds I was dropping? That's so cool."

"But we need to know when your captor—you call him Jimmy Joe?— will be there so we can intercept him."

"Friday. His appointment is for one o'clock. I know it's crazy that JJ would tell me that, but I made him think I was his friend. Speaking of friends, be sure to have the amigos help you get a confession like you did with that Tommy guy. And tell mom and dad and Diego and my girlfriends that I'm okay. Tell Wayne I'm really sorry. I had no idea he would do that. Don't tell *abuela* anything about this. She already thinks I'm scatterbrained."

"No problem. Hey, what's this Jimmy Joe like?"

"Pretty quirky guy. My friends would call him flaming gay. Talks a lot about his daddy. He wanted to get a trophy for the living room of his daddy's big ranch over in the Roaring Fork Valley."

"Tell me, what's he afraid of? Do you know?" Carlos asks.

"Almost everything. That's why he has so many guns. So be careful. He hates spiders and their webs, and, oh yes, he has lepidopteran phobia."

"What's that?" Carlos looks puzzled.

Molly blurts out, "Fear of butterflies."

"Is that you, Molly?" Selena asks.

"She's helping me find you," Carlos says.

"Well, consider me found. I just need you to come and get me."

"I'll send Diego for you right now. That's the first priority: get you home safe. It's a long drive but he should get there in the early evening. Sit tight at the Hotel Aspen."

"Can I go with you guys on Friday?"

"Probably, but I don't want you getting hurt. Which reminds me, I forgot to ask if he hurt you. Are you okay?"

"Not a scratch. Like I say, he's not too interested in women. In fact, don't be too rough on him. He's kind of fragile. He really needs help."

"Selena. He kidnapped you. We'll do what we need to do," Carlos tells her.

"Molly, I'm missing you," Selena says, and that brings a broad smile to Molly's face.

"We're just glad you are okay, Selena," Molly says. "Trust Carlos to do what's right."

Carlos and Molly grab up Lulu and run next door to tell Diego the good news and send him on his way to Aspen. When they fill him in on the plans to capture Jimmy Joe and wring a confession out of him, he says, "Count me in, little brother. Selena and I wouldn't want to miss this." Molly observes how different Diego is from Carlos: rough and tumble, more fun-loving, outgoing, not so serious. More like she would expect a potato farmer to be. There's no poet inside this potato skin.

The next stop is at the main house to tell the parents how Selena escaped. Standing Elk nods, looking proud. "I knew she would run away," he says with a sly smile. Carmencita hugs Molly as she hands off Norma Lou. While Carlos tracks down the amigos to lay plans for Friday and give instructions, Molly spends the rest of the afternoon enjoying Norma Lou with the grandparents. She notices how gentle they are with Lulu, and that her baby seems to adore them. Molly sits on the floor opposite Lulu watching her sit straight unassisted while she shakes and rattles her toys, things that Wayne gave her months ago that she's just now learning to use.

Molly, Carlos, Selena, and Diego start out early on Friday morning for Del Norte to intercept Jimmy Joe. Carlos has agreed to let Selena come along if she will stay in the Pathfinder and keep herself hidden. They meet two truckloads of the amigos at the intersection of Stanley Road and route 17. Molly has made copies of the map, and Carlos goes over the plan with his friends one more time before they continue on Route 160 to Del Norte. The amigos are dressed in camo although none of them hunts wildlife, just outlaws.

When they arrive at their destination, they park on a side road in an inconspicuous clump of three-leaf sumac beneath two huge cottonwoods full of new leaves. Then they slink like bobcats up to the grungy old house that serves as the taxidermist's secret shop and conceal themselves in the surrounding junipers and grasses. Diego is hiding close by, crouching as still as a stone behind a scraggly fir tree, so that when the right moment comes, he can ambush Jimmy Joe. Sure enough, JJ arrives right at one o'clock, parks his orange Hummer out front, and enters the shop quickly looking excited. He definitely looks like the dandified dude they expect.

It takes a while for him to come out, and the wait seems longer than it is, but eventually he reemerges with the owner, and together they carry the tightly wrapped trophy and place it in the back of the Hummer. When the taxidermist returns to his clandestine shop, but before Jimmy Joe can get back into the Hummer, the amigos pounce on him silently and shove a towel in his mouth. Diego catches him with a lasso around the shoulders and tightens it, while the others search him for weapons and bind him up, just like they did with Tommy Dawson. They carry him off to one of the trucks like he was on a stretcher in a straightjacket heading to an asylum. Diego throws the keys to the Hummer to Carlos, who nods for Molly to get in. "Wow!" she says, "I never thought I would ride in one of these." Selena follows along in the Pathfinder, driving at a safe distance so as not to be recognized.

They follow the amigos in their trucks down several back roads to what looks like an abandoned property with the falling down ruins of a shabby old house. Driving alongside it on a path nearly overgrown with scrub oak, they arrive together at what used to be a backyard. Selena pulls into a place where she can see but remain hidden, and she opens her window so she can hear.

"How do you guys know about these forlorn places," Molly asks, "out here miles away from everything?"

"The amigos know every corner of the Valley," Carlos says, "even better than Diego and I do."

At the back of the ramshackle old house, the amigos lead Jimmy Joe over to an abandoned water well. They remove the boulder that holds down the cover, a weathered sheet of plywood that fits loosely over the circular brick opening of the well.

As soon as they remove the towel from Jimmy Joe's mouth, he starts to speak like a talking doll. "You've got the wrong guy." Jimmy Joe says, sneering, standing close enough to the well that he can look down into it. "I don't have no drugs. I didn't do nothing."

"I can see we've got another fun-packed afternoon coming up," Molly whispers to Carlos. He nods silently and moves forward, taking charge.

"Don't hurt me," Jimmy Joe whines. "My health is not good. And for God's sake don't put me in that cruddy well." He struggles a little to step away from it, but his captors only tighten their grip.

"You say you're the wrong guy?" Carlos asks Jimmy Joe. "Don't be playing dumb with me. What about your trophy, that grotesque bison head, right there in the Hummer?"

"We watched you load it in there," Molly says, standing with the amigos, not much aware that she is the only woman on the team.

Carlos shakes a finger at him. "Maybe you should have gone to one of those exotic game ranches you've got down there in Texas."

"I tried. They don't have bison."

"But at least it's legal in those animal massacre camps. Up here, you are in big trouble with the law. Do you know that?"

"Are you cops?" Jimmy Joe asks.

"Worse than that, man," Carlos says, "so we urge you to cooperate. "Here's the deal." Molly joins Carlos as he steps closer to Jimmy Joe, holding out a pad of legal paper to make sure he has his attention. "We're going to write out your confession right here, so start cooperating. Let me see here, how shall it begin? I, Jimmy Joe..."

"How do you know my name?" he asks, inadvertently revealing that he is indeed Jimmy Joe.

"Thank you for identifying yourself," Molly says, nodding her head vigorously.

"But now I need your last name, JJ." Carlos tells him.

"JJ? I'm not giving you my last name. Leave my family out of this."

"Looks like we're going to have to use the well, amigos. Diego, make sure he's tied securely because we don't want to have him go plummeting to the bottom." Carlos gestures toward the well and JJ starts stomping his feet like a two-year-old in a tantrum.

"Gadzooks! Don't put me in that dreadful well!" JJ is scowling.

"There's no water," Carlos assures him. "Actually, no food either." The amigos laugh. "*¡Sin agua, sin comida. Qué lástima!*"

"Such a pity!" Molly says, surprised at how much she understands when the amigos speak.

"Are there spiders?" JJ asks, a look of terror on his face as he tries to peer down the well.

"My guess," Carlos continues, "is that large, hideous spiders are the owners of that well now, fully in charge, ready to say *bienvenido*. Let's continue here. Last name?"

"Richardson." He turns away from the well with a pained grimace.

"That's better. So, let's see. How about 'I, Jimmy Joe Richardson, do hereby confess to shooting and killing a bison at the Horseshoe Ranch on the evening of May twentieth just before sunset.'"

"Look, I'm sure we can work this out," Jimmy Joe suggests with the wily confidence of a rich guy. "I've got a considerable sum of cash locked up in the glove compartment of the Hummer." He nods toward his vehicle.

"Yes, but I've got the keys," Carlos says, dangling them in front of Jimmy Joe's ski jump nose.

"And I've already looked in there," Molly adds, "and I don't want to quibble, but I wouldn't call five hundred bucks a considerable amount of cash. But I did find Selena's cell phone."

"Do I understand that you are trying to bribe us by offering cash?" Diego asks.

"Is anyone here interested in cash?" Carlos shouts.

"¿Dinero?" The amigos solemnly shake their heads no.

"Let's go on," Carlos lifts the pad of paper and holds the pen ready to write. "I, Jimmy Joe Richardson, also confess to kidnapping on that same night Selena Ouray and holding her captive in...Now we need the place you are holding her." He turns to Molly and winks.

Molly glances toward the Pathfinder and thinks she sees Selena's eyes peeking up above the dashboard, but there's no need to worry with JJ completely preoccupied with his defense.

"Please don't use the word *kidnapping*. It was an accident. She took me to the right spot and the bison only happened to be standing there by the fence when we drove by that night, and I just got so excited..."

"We've noticed that you are excitable," Carlos says.

"I stopped the Hummer..."

"We saw the tracks," Molly notes.

"...and I told myself I'd never get another shot like this, point blank, on the side, you know, bam, bam, bam, so as not to spoil the head."

"Okay, so you admit you shot the bison," Diego says. "And you wanted the head for a trophy."

"But don't you see, I didn't mean for Selena to be right there when I fired, but she knew everything that I'd done. So, I'd gotten myself into a kind of predicament and I couldn't take her back to the bar like I promised or let her loose, because I knew she'd go running straight to the cops. So, I had to keep her for a little while until things blew over and I could clear out with my trophy, but I did not kidnap that woman. I was planning to release her today. I promise you. I told her that. She knew it!"

"Today?" Carlos smiles and glances at the Pathfinder.

"Did not *kidnap* her?" Molly asks, with raised eyebrows. "Please, I don't want to mince words here, but perhaps you could explain to her father and mother and two brothers that you were just holding her in safe keeping, while they were going through hell not knowing whether she'd been raped or was even alive."

"I didn't rape her, hell no, not me."

While the amigos are laughing, Carlos says, "I'm writing in the word *kidnapping*, but just to be sure we get your signature here, tip JJ upside down, amigos, and lower him slowly into the well a little bit at a time so he can get a good view of the real estate down there just in case he wants to make it his permanent home."

"Oh, no, don't do that. You don't need to do this." His voice is muffled and echoes in the well as they lower him down.

"Hold his legs tight, amigos. He's no good to us splattered all over the bottom of that well. We need him alive to sign this confession," Carlos says. But they lower him with a jerkiness that makes him feel like he's being dropped.

"Let me go," Jimmy Joe whines, and then when his words echo back, distorted in sound but clear in meaning, he realizes what he has just said. "No, no, no, don't let me go! I meant pull me out! In the blessed name of Jesus, just pull me up out of here!" Has he undergone a conversion? A dry baptism? Maybe now he will be a little more forthcoming.

He is sobbing heavily as they pull him out of the well and prop him up on a big boulder next to the well still tied up in his straightjacket. Molly pulls a big red bandanna out of Carlos's hip pocket and wipes the spider webs from JJ's pale face and then dries his tears. She suddenly feels genuine empathy for him. She suspects that he's trying to gain his father's love with this disgusting bison-head trophy. JJ is crying hysterically now.

Molly tells him, "You need to control that wailing."

He coughs and wheezes as he tries to pull himself together. "Please don't put me down there again," he splutters. "That's cruel."

"But not all that unusual in this part of the Valley," Carlos says. "What we need now is the exact location of where you have been holding my sister."

"She's your sister? Oh, my god, I'm so sorry. She's in a cabin near Aspen. My daddy has a lovely second home on a ranch on the Roaring Fork River on the way into Aspen. In fact, I'm supposed to be there this evening to help him put up my trophy. He would be so pleased."

"Well, there's been a change of plans," Molly points out. "Try not to get distracted, JJ. Focus. We are asking you about Selena's location. Where is she?"

"What are you going to do with me?"

"Turn you over to the police," Carlos says. "It's up to them to decide what to do with you when they read your confession."

"Well, look, if I tell you where she is, will you and her promise not to turn me over to the police? In exchange for your promises not to turn me in, I'll help you locate your sister."

"Such a shrewd deal that is," Molly has to suppress the laughter that wants to come bursting out. "We've had enough of your shenanigans, JJ. We need to know where she is. Carlos, could you get that jar of butterflies for me, please?"

"What butterflies?" Jimmy Joe jumps up from the boulder where he is sitting but nearly topples on his face being tied up so tight. They catch him just in time before he crashes and set him back down. He starts to twitch and tremble inside his straightjacket.

"That's right. Just start imagining them all over you," Molly says, delighted with the effect of the mere mention of butterflies. "Can't you just feel those little wings brushing against your face, Jimmy Joe? Tickling your ear? Picture a monarch getting caught in your shirt collar and flapping its way down your back or tickling your chest." She watches him squirm at her taunts. "I just love phylum lepidoptera," she says in a fitting imitation of the Southern drawl of her old bunkmate Savannah.

"Please, no butterflies," Jimmy Joe pleads, sitting there on his rock-hard seat. "They scare the bejesus out of me." He looks a little woozy, like he might puke.

"Okay," Molly says, "no butterflies in exchange for the address of the cabin. That's a much better deal."

Without further objection, Jimmy Joe gives them the address of the cabin: number 1424 Conundrum Creek Road. "Now are you satisfied?" he asks.

"Not quite yet," Carlos says, stretching out each word. "We'd like your father's Aspen address, too." Carlos says. "I guess you call him daddy."

"Not daddy's address." He seems truly aghast. "You leave my daddy out of this. He's a prominent citizen back home in Midland, a prosperous oilman. This here would be detrimental to his reputation." Molly can't help laughing outright at his bad grammar and school vocab list diction. "I was going to surprise him with this wonderful trophy. I was hoping that then he would accept me as his son." He starts to sob again, his joyful hopes turning to despair. "He's never been able to...to accept me. I just wanted to do something really masculine to please him."

"Oh, like plundering an innocent bison at the roadside with a high-powered rifle is really masculine?" Carlos asks in a stern voice, glowering at him.

Molly goes over to Jimmy Joe, sits beside him on the boulder, and offers him a tissue for his tears. He's really a sorry sight now. She speaks from experience when she commiserates with him. "Sometimes fathers can be very difficult." She nods her head several times. "Some things just go unresolved, Jimmy Joe. You need to understand that your father may never accept you. And because things are so bad with you and your father, we promise we won't contact your daddy." She looks to Carlos to obtain a nod of agreement. JJ is unresponsive, as if in a trance.

"But for you to get out of this mess," Carlos says, "you may need to contact your daddy yourself and explain it all to him as best you can because he's going to need to hire a real smart team of lawyers for you."

"As for Selena," Molly says, "we don't really need the address of the cabin because she escaped." She peers at JJ to see how he is going to react to this news.

"She what? You're jesting." He tries to stand, to gesture, to protest, but he is bound too tight. "Escaped? Those incompetent idiots."

"She called us," Molly continues, "to tell us that she escaped from your guards. Would you like to see her?"

"See her? Where is she?" He glances around, jerking his head every which way, like he's looking in the forest for a rare bird.

"Right over there in that Nissan." Molly whispers to Carlos and he nods. She takes a few steps toward the Pathfinder and hollers, "You can come out now, Selena."

The car door opens and slams and Selena comes running over. "I was getting the jitters all cooped up in there."

"Running Water." JJ greets her. "What are you doing here?"

And everyone exclaims in unison. "Running Water?"

"Certainly, you don't think I'd tell him my real name," Selena says proudly.

"*Agua Corriente,*" the amigos say one after the other and begin to laugh. Carlos and Molly exchange grins.

Then Selena comes up to JJ and says, "It looks like we've pretty much ruined your day, Jimmy Joe. I'm sorry about that."

"And it's only going to get worse as the day goes on," Carlos tells him, "because you're going to be taken to the police and charged with kidnapping, trespassing on a sanctuary ranch, and killing bison."

"One bison. Only one."

"I guess you can see," Selena tells him, "that it was a big mistake sitting down next to me at Pepe's Cantina that night. I thought I was being a friendly guide to a curious sightseer. But you tried to trick me, JJ. Big mistake!"

"I'm sure that your daddy has some real good lawyers," Diego says.

"Maybe not good enough," Jimmy Joe whimpers and starts sobbing again, holding his face in his limp hands, sulking. "I don't want to go to jail. Please." Molly hands him some more tissues.

"Just sign here," Carlos says, looking eager to finish up his work. "Your full name and signature." Then he calls out to the amigos, "Does anyone want a share of that money that was offered us?"

Jimmy Joe makes one final attempt to twist out of his rope straightjacket. "That deal's off now," he whimpers. "We're not going to haggle over money after the way you tortured me."

"Torture?" Molly says. "There's not a mark on you. Did anyone here see any torture?" The amigos all shake their heads and grin.

"Besides there never was a deal," Carlos says. "Men seeking justice never take a bribe."

"And for your enlightenment, JJ, there never were any butterflies." Molly makes an empty-handed gesture and shrugs. "You tortured yourself fretting about those butterflies. I never had a jar of butterflies. I just helped you imagine them. Isn't the imagination a wonderful thing?"

12

THE TRUTH COMES OUT AT A BACKYARD BARBEQUE

"Let's have a party. We've got a lot of things to celebrate," Molly suggests to Carlos.

"You mean a party here on the farm?" Carlos asks.

"In the backyard. A barbeque. A picnic. I know you like picnics."

"Who would we invite?" Carlos asks, looking like he's almost convinced that it's a good idea.

"Everyone. Wayne and Emily from the Horseshoe. Selena's friends from high school. Our amigos from Pepe's Cantina. Rainbow and Jersey from the ranch, Doctor Archuleta."

"It's a start. Sounds like a *fiesta auténtica*. Actually, I think my parents would like this idea. They'll invite some of the neighbors."

"You have neighbors?" She shades her eyes with one hand feigning a vain search across the broad fields of potatoes to find a neighbor. "Just kidding."

When were you thinking of having this party?" Carlos asks, stroking his chin.

"I'd say three or four weeks out."

"Sounds like you're planning to stay for a while." He grins.

"At least through the party." She throws him a teasing smile. "It will give me time to fix a few more things around here that need fixing and to do some painting."

"Painting?"

"I love to paint. The back porch needs paint, Carlos."

Molly shows Carlos how the paint is chipping off of the railings and spindles and asks him to get permission from his parents for her to paint out there. They insist she doesn't have to do things like that, but if she wants to, it would be okay as long as they get to watch Norma Lou. So, Molly scrapes, sands, and paints, and as always, the work occupies only half of her brain, so she has time to think.

It is strange, she notes, how she is more like her dad than her mom, while it was her mom, she felt closest to in her childhood years, and it was her dad she feared. Scared to death of that man. But as she looks back on it now, she remembers her dad taking time to show her how to do things, and even though he was gruff and grumpy, he did teach her how to fix stuff. He didn't just say to do this or do that, he taught her to study how things work, how to solve problems, and how to reframe problems. She remembers the way he went on and on bragging about how he took a low spot in a field and instead of calling it a drainage problem and filling it in, he turned it into a distribution problem and built a small pond to hold water for the irrigation of an adjacent field. "That's reframing the problem, Mol"—he used to call her Mol. His voice has been very close and persistent while she has been working on the houses and yards at the potato farm.

She has to decide how to paint the spindles, either one whole spindle at a time, or three surfaces of each one from the same side, while holding all the back side surfaces for last. If she can prevent having to walk around each time for each spindle, it will be a lot more efficient. "Efficiency matters, Mol," she remembers her dad saying. "There is no place for lollygagging on a farm. Time is money. If you're sawing boards, move the whole stack to where you are sawing.

Never move just one board at a time because it wastes precious minutes. If you're loading trash, put the trash barrel where the trash is; don't carry separate loads over to the barrel." So that's how she became such a good worker, by listening for the farmer's wisdom buried within her dad's harsh voice. An image of him lying there dead at the ER flashes into her mind, unexpectedly, involuntarily. How sad that he never got to meet Lulu Lobo.

The railings are a lot easier than the spindles. She has already scraped and sanded them, so now she just needs to apply the white paint with a four-inch brush in long smooth strokes without spattering and being careful not to leave any brush marks. She loves that challenge. Everything smooth with scrupulous attention to detail. She got that meticulousness from her dad, too. After two coats, it looks great. Tomorrow and the day after she will tackle the floor and steps, maybe a light gray. How about a bright blue for the molding around the sliding patio door?

She is surprised at how satisfying it is to find so much solace in work and is impressed by the healing power that comes through being useful. The more she fixes, the more praise she receives from the family members, one by one noticing what she has done, and this constant remarking about her contributions to the household makes her feel proud to be Molly O'Reilly again, as if there is some direct connection between work and worth.

After she has finished all of the painting on the back porch, she finds herself alone there one afternoon with Standing Elk and Carmencita. Lulu has been taking her afternoon nap in the main house regularly while Molly works on her projects.

"Here, sit a spell with us, my dear," Carmencita says, the silver bracelets on her wrist rattling as she gestures. "You are always working so hard." They are sitting on the swing that used to squeak and Standing Elk gets up to pull over a chair for her. For a moment, *Perro Rojo* rouses, then returns to *his* afternoon nap as Standing Elk is seated again.

"The work clears my mind and makes me feel good, like I'm contributing something."

"You don't need to worry about that," Standing Elk says. "We just enjoy having you around and we will never forget how you turned into a detective to help find Selena's kidnapper. Carlos told us all about it."

"It was my pleasure," Molly says, wondering if she has a talent for solving crimes.

"Carlos says that you ride a horse like Zorro," Standing Elk says with a little grin. "Did you have horses on the farm back in Kansas?"

"Just one. My brother and I had to share a dapple-gray gelding named O'Grady."

"Do you miss him?" Carmencita asks.

"My brother?" Molly asks, then laughs. "Oh, you mean the horse. Well, yes, sometimes I do, but Danny is taking good care of him, I'm sure."

"Would Danny miss him if we brought him out here?" Standing Elk asks.

"Actually, I think he would be relieved not having to care for him, but you don't need to go to all that trouble." She says the polite thing, but then her imagination goes nuts as she pictures O'Grady prancing around this farm, having his choice of unpaved roads for a good gallop, providing her strength when she needs it. Then she ponders the horrible prospect of O'Grady being sold along with the dairy farm. "Although it would be nice to have him here," she adds wistfully.

"We can just send someone out with the F-One-Fifty and a horse trailer," Standing Elk says, nodding thoughtfully. "I'll ask Diego to look into that." Nothing else is said.

Because there is a brief silence with no new topic of conversation, Molly perceives that this might be a good opportunity to learn a little more about Carlos. "Could you tell me what Carlos was like as a child, if you don't mind."

"Mind?" Carmencita says. "We're proud of Carlos."

"It has been easy to be proud of Carlos," his father says, rubbing his hands together in anticipation of being able to brag about him a little to Molly.

"Well, let me see," Carmencita begins, as if she is sorting through a scrapbook to find what Molly would most like to know. "He was always a good student, even as a child. He liked all of the subjects and brought home good grades. His older brother Diego was not so interested in school and poor Selena can hardly sit down long enough to do five minutes of homework."

"But there is no one who can beat her at running," Standing Elk says proudly.

"Although we don't know where she will run *to*," her mother says. "But Carlos has always had goals, and he pursues them persistently and patiently."

"Yes, I've noticed that," Molly says, controlling a smile, knowing that she has been his main goal for some time now.

"I am sorry he had to stay home from the university that last year when I was ill," Standing Elk says, "because, as you know, he never graduated."

"I think he will finish that up someday," his mother says. "He still reads a lot, as if he is studying for some exam."

"The daily exam of life," Molly says. "He thinks about things deeply. Sometimes I tell him he is a poet. And he is so *simpático*." Molly finds herself using a Spanish word quite naturally, but she hopes his parents won't think that she speaks Spanish.

"Yes, and *afectuoso*," his mother says.

Molly resets her hair in the clip Carlos gave her for Christmas.

Standing Elk speaks up in a kind voice. "He is *mucho paciente*. He's been waiting for you."

Molly smiles, a little embarrassed. His parents must know that Carlos has loved her for a long time and has been waiting patiently for her. But how much do they know about her situation, her trauma? Although Molly has never told them directly, she's sure that they know in a general way what happened to her. She's noticed that there is a lot of silence in this family, but somehow everyone seems to know what they need to know.

Molly catches a glimpse of Carmencita's guitar leaning against the porch railing. Has she been practicing? Molly glances at it, looks into Carmencita's eyes, and says, "I would be so honored to hear you play for me one of the old Spanish love songs that Carlos tells me you know."

"But I'm so rusty, dear," she complains.

"I don't have enough acquaintance with a guitar to notice mistakes, and besides, who cares? I'm sure you sing beautifully in Spanish."

Hesitating, Carmencita picks up her guitar, tunes it a bit, and begins to strum. She removes her bracelets and settles into the straight chair Molly has offered her. After the first song, she overcomes her shyness about playing and continues on, reassured and with poise, recalling quite naturally the words and captivating melodies from several old songs that she once played. From time to time, *Perro Rojo* flaps his tail against the porch floor as if to applaud. Does he really know Spanish?

Molly feels completely comfortable sitting here with Standing Elk and Carmencita, listening to these tender songs and looking out across the backyard grass and over the potato fields toward the outline of the mountains. Now that she has Carmencita playing her guitar, her next challenge is to get *abuela* to play the organ. Hey, it's fixed now. Maybe if she sits beside her on the bench and pumps, *abuela* will touch those keys and bring to life the old songs she once played. There's music in this family. Harmony.

Carlos seems surprised but delighted with the vibrant new Molly he is discovering each day, and she has to admit that she is enjoying being that new Molly, too, not having to go around all sad-faced and depressed. Wow! She was so young, so naïve, so scared last summer. She can't picture leaving this place anytime soon, not the way they have accepted her and made her part of the family. And her mom tells her that negotiations are underway with Uncle Russ to buy the farm, so where would she go? Besides, things are really going great with Carlos.

Carlos has been joining Molly occasionally in the guest bedroom. Some nights they start out that way; on other nights when he is working late on business associated with the farm, he comes quietly down the hall and crawls into bed with her at two or three in the morning, and she snuggles around him, often not waking up, but being pleasantly surprised to find him there the next morning in her arms.

At first, they just enjoy the company, the hugging and occasional kisses, but gradually they explore something more, ways of bringing each other intimate pleasures without actually having what everyone calls *intercourse*— another horrible word—in the usual manner. In a very informal way, and without thinking about it or discussing it, Molly has been following Bonnie Bradford's desensitization plan, and little by little she has lost her fears and learned how to have an enjoyable physical relationship with Carlos, which was not all that difficult once she discovered his gorgeous body. He is as gentle with her as the breeze blowing in through the bedroom window at night and he touches her as if he is holding a bouquet of wild flowers. She finds their restrained love-making really sexy—sometimes they go to his bedroom, too— and he seems to enjoy the alternatives they have invented without feeling deprived. It has been amazing to discover what gentle hands and loving lips can do.

But the real reason she still avoids doing it, she knows, is that she is terrified of getting pregnant and having another baby. Not terrified of sex— she's over that now—but of getting pregnant again. When she was growing up, she was schooled in the evils of birth control, but she's not going to let that stop her now. Come to think of it, her mom must have used birth control; otherwise, there would be a whole slew of little O'Reilly's running around that Kansas farmhouse. She realizes that the moment has come for her to go see Doctor Archuleta, and she promises herself that when this party is over, she will go talk to him about an IUD.

One evening while she is fixing her mother's recipe of cracker and egg chicken filets for dinner, she says to Carlos, "I thought of someone else I want to invite to the fiesta."

"Who might that be?" Carlos asks, with a look that tells her he's having trouble thinking of the name of someone they've omitted.

"My mother and my little brother Danny."

"Really? You mean you want us to drive back to Kansas and bring them out?" Carlos folds his arms and leans against the kitchen cupboards next to the stove.

"Yes, and my books, my clothes, and" —she looks up and gives him that sly grin—"my stuffed animals."

"You have some like the ones at the taxidermist?" he teases. "Like what? Birds? Squirrels?"

"No, silly, from my childhood, like Raggedy Ann, Elmo, and my Teddy Bear." Carlos rolls his eyes, so she says, "For Lulu, of course."

"To bring back your stuff. Wow! That's great! When should we go?"

"A couple of days before the party. I want my mom and Danny to meet everyone. I'll call to invite them if that's okay. I think they would like that."

"I know *I* would like that," Carlos says. "Does this mean you want to stay?"

"Hey, at least it means I don't want to leave."

Seeing that the chicken has been turned to its second side, Carlos sets out the plates and the silverware. He can't seem to stop smiling.

Molly's mother says she wouldn't miss the picnic, and Danny tells her that he thinks it would be awesome to go to a real barbecue out West, so Carlos drives Molly and Norma Lou in the Pathfinder to Kansas to pick up her family, along with Molly's stuff, in order to bring everyone to the Ouray Potato Farm LLP two days before the party. Her stuff now includes O'Grady, who has already been picked up and is enjoying the unfenced spaces of his new home in Colorado. She gallops him a little every day on the paths along the ditches and on the dirt road down to the mailboxes.

On the ride out to Colorado her mom tells Molly that Uncle Russ has made a reasonable offer on the farm that includes Ida's staying in the house, if that's what she wants, and a provision for Danny to work his way into a management partnership if he ever gets a yen for high tech farming. Danny says he'll think about it. The first step is to get early admission at Kansas State in the fall. Right now, he's getting more interested in music.

Ida and Danny are lodged comfortably in two extra rooms in the main house, and of course Carlos's parents welcome them as if they were already members of the family, lavishing praise on Molly for her skill in fixing things and for her detective work in helping to locate Selena. At dinner the next night, Carlos gets in a talkative mood and tells in humorous detail the stories of capturing Tommy and JJ. There is a lot of laughing around that table, but Ida and Danny look confused, like they don't know whether to believe him or not, until Molly tells them it's all true. Every word.

Because the preparations for this stupendous party are pressing—there are now a good fifty guests expected—the trip over to meet Wayne and Emily will have to wait, but Molly assures her mother that she will have plenty of time to talk with them at the fiesta. Danny quickly makes friends with Diego, who puts him to work the very next day riding with him in the air-conditioned cab of the huge tractor that pulls the cultivators. At the local butcher, Carlos orders a whole hog for slow roasting pork over a pit especially dug out for the occasion by Molly with the Bobcat. The wives of neighboring families, now formally invited, have been busy making covered dishes of Spanish rice, refried beans, and coleslaw. Bicolor corn has been shucked and is standing ready for boiling. Naturally, Navajo fry bread is on hand with prickly pear cactus jelly.

Carlos has purchased an electric ice cream maker for Molly and she has been turning out batches of ice cream, holding it in the freezers of all three houses to serve toward the end of the fiesta with a drizzle of chocolate sauce. Her mother has baked several sheets full of Molly's chocolate chip favorites. Five tables have been brought in from the church along with a pickup truckload of folding chairs. Two big narrow-leaf cottonwoods along the drainage ditch at the corner of the backyard provide ample shade and a good spot for setting up the tables and chairs. A keg of Corona beer sits beside one of the tables with coolers of soft drinks.

Guests start drifting in after one o'clock under a cloudless blue sky and the fiesta begins. A cool breeze blows and the familiar outline of mountains is seen off in the distance. The grass has been fertilized, watered, and mowed so it's green as a golf course, and Molly has planted a few pots with red geraniums and purple petunias to put by the steps leading up to the back porch. The yard extends clear back to the first of several potato fields covered now with strong green plants. Red Dog seems unsettled as the guests arrive, charging back and forth across the lawn, apparently confused about who is friend and foe, whom to bark at or give a friendly lick. Carlos makes sure that everyone has been introduced and is finding enough food to fill their plates. Danny has discovered Selena and they seem to be having a good time playing a game with rackets that is new to Molly. Actually, many things are still new for her, but that's okay; she expects new things now and even looks forward to them.

Molly asks Carlos, "Shouldn't you give a toast or say some words of welcome to everyone. Something like that?"

"Hey, that's a good idea. We always want people to feel welcome here."

Carlos runs up the steps, across the porch, and into the kitchen and comes out with an old cast iron frying pan and bangs on it with a metal spoon. When everyone quiets down, he's a little embarrassed, shifting from foot to foot for an uncomfortable moment, because he hasn't thought about what to say. So, he begins, "We have a lot to celebrate in this family. My wonderful parents and grandmother. My brother Diego. My sister Selena. Her friends begin cheering and whistling, showing that they know what there is to celebrate about Selena. "Be sure to meet my friend Molly," he says without giving any explanation of who Molly is. "And her mother and brother from Kansas." He looks out into the crowd and noticing the attentive faces, he continues, "Welcome to all you folks from over at the Horseshoe, and, oh, I almost forgot, Molly's baby Norma Lou. Be sure to get her to smile for you." He scratches his head, as if to wonder what he might have left out. "*Bienvenidos, todos*. We have plenty to eat and drink and, in a few minutes, we will be serving homemade ice cream and cookies so stick around."

Carlos comes down from the porch and finds Molly. "Perfect," she says.

Coming around the corner of the house is a group of five musicians. "Oh, good," Carlos says, "my surprise has arrived." They have guitars and violins and one guy carries a trumpet. Clothed in white shirts and pants with bright sashes, each has his own distinctive sombrero.

"Wow! You hired a mariachi band?"

"Not really hired. They play at the cantina on Saturday nights, and when they heard about the fiesta, they asked if they could stop by. Actually, they were playing there the first night that you and I met. They'll just wander around serenading people. It will be okay?"

"Okay? It's wonderful." Molly is beaming. "Do you think we could start serving the ice cream now?"

Diego does the scooping and Carlos dribbles on the chocolate sauce. Molly carries plastic bowls on a tray to the guests, and this gives her time to listen in on the conversations and greet everyone. Danny follows behind her with plates of cookies.

Selena's high school friends are seated together on brightly colored blankets in the shade. They keep asking for more details about how she escaped from Jimmy Joe. She tells them that when the person who was guarding her came to bring breakfast, she just bolted by him, shot out the cabin door, and started running like a deer. She spotted the creek and knew instinctively to follow it down, assuming she would come to a little town or something at the bottom of the valley. After all, wasn't she called Running Deer? She sure hated to pass up that good breakfast they were bringing her, but the guy at the restaurant fed her biscuits and sausage gravy. Her father told her later that the Conundrum Creek Valley was one of the favorite campgrounds of the Utes before the miners came to Ashcroft, which is now nothing but a ghost town.

Her friends couldn't get enough of her descriptions of poor wishy-washy, namby-pamby, Jimmy Joe. One of her amigas had heard a rumor that his lawyers had already got him declared unfit for trial and that he's in a rehab center in Texas, but they don't know what he is rehabbing from if he doesn't do drugs. Maybe his butterfly phobia? Or his fear of spiders? Or his daddy fixation? There is a chorus of giggles each time someone takes the joking to the next level. But as Molly listens, she can't help feeling a sad little pang of sympathy for poor Jimmy Joe, remembering his tears and how he longed to be accepted by his father. And then she thinks of the female bison that lost her life as JJ's intended gift to his daddy.

She picks up another tray filled with bowls of ice cream and takes it to the amigos from Pepe's Cantina. They are sitting in the folding chairs under the cottonwoods leaning forward, drinking beer, and recounting the fake hanging of Tommy Dawson. They are hoping that this is the end of their vigilante efforts to bring crude justice, as they call it, to the Valley. It seems like there are always creepy characters lurking around, though, and plenty of places are left to take them if necessary, to pull out a confession. How about the old railroad sidings where no trains come any more, a good place for tying them to the tracks to squeeze it out of them? Or maybe the old bridge over the Rio Grande where they can dangle a captive over the edge. Nothing like hanging a man upside down to get him to cough up the truth. There are endless ways to inflict mental torture without hurting people. Devising these methods is their innocent pastime.

The big surprise of the afternoon is that Wayne and Emily's daughter Heather, her husband Miguel, and their little boy have come back from

Mexico to visit this week, so Wayne has brought them along to the party. The daughter seems to have Emily's looks and Wayne's manner. Molly is really happy to meet them and take them ice cream. She is glad she had a hand in bringing that beautiful family back together. Molly's mother has been chatting with Wayne, trying to thank him for all he did for her daughter, and she agrees with Molly now in a low whisper that he is the gentlest and handsomest man she's ever met. Well, next to Carlos.

"What's this we are reading about the ranch in the *Valley Currier?*" Molly asks Wayne as she hands him some ice cream.

"I don't know much except that the National Park Service wants to make the bison ranch part of the Great Sand Dunes National Park."

"What will that do to you?"

"Probably not much. The bison ranch still needs a manager, but I don't know as I want to work for the Park Service."

"But that's probably years away, dear," Emily says. "I'm telling him he needs to retire so we can go live in Mexico."

Heather and Miguel are standing there proudly with Wayne's three-year-old grandson Angelito. He is pulling on his mother's arm and pointing to the ice cream, and as he looks up at Molly with sad brown eyes, she notices an overturned bowl in the grass. Uh oh! She signals Danny to bring another. Everyone deserves a second chance.

"Guess what?" Miguel says with enthusiasm. "Diego is trying to get me to stay on and work here at the potato farm through harvest."

"So, you know Diego and Carlos?" Molly asks Miguel.

"Oh, yeah, we've been friends for years."

"Well, dear," Emily says to Wayne, "there go your retirement plans. If they stay, we stay."

Molly carries a tray of ice cream up the steps between the potted geraniums onto the freshly-painted back porch where Lulu Lobo's "grandparents," *abuela,* and neighbors are sitting, along with Red Dog, who has finally stopped bounding around and come to rest at their feet, apparently having discovered that what you do at a party is listen to the music, enjoy the scent of the foods, and watch the people. She hears O'Grady nicker from the barn, like he senses that he's missing out on something. As soon as Molly arrives on the back porch, she notices that everyone stops talking. Nothing can be heard but the soft tapping of feet to the music of the mariachi band drifting in from under the cottonwoods. "If you are talking about me, I hope it's good," she says, teasing and with a confident smile.

"We didn't want you to get all puffed up," Standing Elk says, "because we've been bragging about all the work you've done around here."

"I was telling them," Carmencita says, "that you will fix anything that can be fixed. Now he's afraid the neighbors will try to hire you out and pay you a better wage."

"Better than room and board with this lovely Ouray family?" Molly asks them. "Hey, that's hard to find, and I wouldn't want to move." She smiles, and then looking around, frowns. "Where's Lulu Lobo?"

"Oh, we've just been passing her around. She loves everybody. Over there." Carmencita points toward the women from the ranch.

So, Molly picks up another tray of ice cream and goes over to visit with Rainbow and Jersey. "How do you like my little calf?" she asks Rainbow, who is holding Norma Lou and has her mesmerized with a smooth back and forth rocking motion.

Jersey jumps in with, "A grand prize winner considering how terrified the mother was."

"She's a cutie, this one," Rainbow says. And meet my husband Francisco."

He's cute, too, don't you think?" Jersey asks.

Molly ignores the remark about Francisco. "Yes, Rainbow, I remember your mentioning him, the Spanish professor at the university. I've been wanting to meet you."

"Well, yes. *Buenas tardes.* After hearing so much about you, I finally get to meet you and this charming Miss Norma Lou," Francisco says. He seems a bit stiff and formal, not the person Molly had imagined as Rainbow's husband.

"I've been thinking about starting college sometime, Professor Gallegos, but I don't know if I can handle it. I could only do a course or two at a time."

"A lot of people do it that way now. Some students take online courses and study from home." He seems bent on recruiting her, but she hadn't thought about enrolling so soon. "What do you think you might want to study?"

She's given that even less thought. "Something about solving crimes?" Molly's voice rises with uncertainty at the end of the sentence because she doesn't know if courses like that are even offered at a university.

"There is a criminology emphasis within the sociology major. You might like that."

"Really? That sounds interesting. But so, does psychology or English literature." Does she have to know what she wants to study? What about just taking a couple of courses?

"Get in touch with me. I'm a first-year academic advisor and we could put a course plan together for you in nothing flat."

But now Molly is distracted and whispers to Rainbow, "Is that doctor Archuleta over there? My OB?"

"Yes, in the flowered maroon shirt and tan pants," Jersey says. "His wife died shortly after you had the baby."

"Oh, no. I didn't know that. How sad. Let me take Norma Lou from you, Rainbow. I want him to see her." Molly signals to Danny to fetch another dish of ice cream and hurries over to the kind doctor, with Norma Lou bouncing along on one hip. As she walks up to greet him, she notices that his hair has turned completely white. He wears one of those thong ties fastened with a turquoise stone embedded in silver work. "Hello, Doctor Archuleta. Remember me, Molly O'Reilly? And this is my baby, Norma Lou."

"I remember you very well. Such a perfect baby you produced out at the Horseshoe."

"I had a lot of help out there, believe me. But look at her now." Still no trace of the paternal genes, Molly thinks, but doesn't say. "See how she's growing?"

"Yes, it's probably past time for her shots and a visit to the pediatrician. Come in sometime and see my wonderful partner. And I'd be happy to see you, too, of course." He smiles at her fondly, but in a professional way.

"Actually, I've been thinking about coming to visit you. I need something like a night before, during, and morning after pill."

"You mean fool proof birth control."

"I need to build an impregnable castle." She can't believe she is bantering like this with Doctor Archuleta over such a serious matter.

"At least you have the right adjective there."

"Yes, impregnable. I just can't think of having another baby right now. Molly glances down at Lulu Lobo slung over one shoulder. "I barely survived this one."

"There are many options for preventing pregnancy now. It is really none of my business, but because I have been your doctor, might this mean..." He seems to leave the sentence unfinished deliberately.

"Me and Carlos?" Molly is flustered, in a complete dither. She shakes her head, first up and down, and then back and forth. "Well, not really, but sort of. Oh, heck, let's just say I've overcome my fears of men now. Not men, but Carlos. She scratches her forehead and squints. "And Carlos and I..."

"You don't need to explain anything," Doctor Archuleta says. "Carlos is one of the nicest men in the whole Valley. And such a fine family, too. I helped all three of those children come into this world."

"Really?" Molly looks surprised. "Tell me about them, but don't let your ice cream melt there." Danny cruises in with cookies, offers them, and disappears.

"Well, Diego was born at home and I got there at the very end. He was just fine. Selena had a problem with her left leg. She had a wonderfully skillful repair by an orthopedic surgeon at the Children's Hospital in Denver. Then she began to walk normally, and when she could walk better, she started to run. It seemed like she just had to run everywhere she went. So, they started calling her Running Deer and the name stuck. I guess you know that she runs track in high school now but you may not know that next year she's probably going to be a state champion in something. It's quite a medical success story, a famous case."

Hearing this about Selena makes her ask, "What about Carlos? Was he okay?"

"Carlos was born premature at home, so we had to rush him to the hospital immediately. He almost died on the way."

"Oh, don't tell me that. I can't stand to think about a world without Carlos." She puts her free hand over her eyes. "Dying in the first hours of life, almost like stillborn."

"They saved him, but he had to have two surgeries afterward to rebuild his colon."

"He's okay?" Molly asks, frowning. Why hasn't he told her about his colon?

"Well, this is a private matter, and we have those HIPPA regulations now." He hesitates, as if he is pondering whether to tell her something confidential. "But it is rather important for you to know...if you don't know already...and it sounds like you don't..."

"Tell me, Doctor Archuleta, what is it? Just tell me."

"The surgeries fixed his digestive track perfectly but left him sterile as a steer. He told me that he had it confirmed last year at a fertility clinic and medical science tells us that there is nothing to be done for a condition that occurred in infancy. So, if you are looking for someone with built in birth control, Carlos might be your man." His eyes twinkle.

Molly's eyes stand wide open in complete shock. Carlos can't make a baby? Is this why he didn't mind having a girlfriend with a baby? Is Lulu Lobo the baby he will never have? It's as if the last piece of the jigsaw puzzle has fallen into place so that now she can see the whole picture. But does she? Her mind skips to the unthinkable: Because he has a reason to be attracted to a woman with a baby does that mean he loves her and Lulu any less? He does love her, doesn't he? She can't go through life always wondering, like her mother, whether she is really loved.

Doctor Archuleta jolts her out of her reverie. "I suspected that you didn't know. I'm sorry to break the news."

"Oh, no it's quite good news in some ways, but...well, some bad news, too. Why did he never tell me?" she asks, dumbfounded.

"For men in the Valley there is a fine line between *macho* and *simpático*. Sometimes he needs to be strong and silent."

"Yes, and that's okay, Doctor Archuleta." But Molly is reminded that at other times Carlos speaks like a babbling brook. So why hasn't he told her? She gives Lulu Lobo an extra hug and a rain of kisses. "Thank you for telling me now." She nods enthusiastically over and over.

"I thought you needed to know. At times it is my inclination to bend the privacy rules to create a better understanding among people who find it difficult to express themselves. As you may have discovered, Carlos is sometimes one of those people."

"Now I understand a lot of things," she says with a big smile on her face, then retreating inward again trying to answer her own question. Of course, Carlos wouldn't tell her about his condition because she might think that he didn't love her for herself but only for her baby. So he had to prove it to her on his own without telling her—slowly, patiently, convincing her by perseverance—that he loves *her*. And that's what he did. No, if there is one thing, she is certain about in this confusing world, it is that Carlos loves her. If anyone deserves to have doubts, it would be Carlos after the way she treated him. "I'm sorry for the lapses, Doctor Aguilera. My mind is whirling and this is a lot for me to grasp all at once." She smiles at him and studies him more carefully, as if he were one of those angel messengers that had suddenly taken

James R. Davis   181

on human form. She never thought of the doctor as handsome before, but now with that white hair and looking so sharp today in his flowered shirt, she asks, "Did you meet my mother?"

"Ida? Yes. A lovely woman."

"My father just passed away."

"We talked about that."

"She's lonely." Oh, my god is she matchmaking for her own mother?

"Well, Molly, I need to go home and catch a nap. Now that I'm older I'm not so good at delivering babies in the middle of the night and going through the whole day with no sleep. You have a very beautiful child here. Take care of her." He reaches out and Lulu Lobo clasps his forefinger.

Molly is still reeling from what she has learned about Carlos. Of course, it would be a relief not to have to worry about birth control, but *never* to be able to have a baby with Carlos? For sure she hadn't considered that possibility. One more thing unexpected. If they want to have another child in a few years, maybe they could adopt a cute little boy from the Ute Reservation. But really, no kids of their own? After she's worked so hard to get over her hang ups? Well, not to worry. Now she just needs to be thankful that she and Lulu are healthy and that the man she loves is even alive.

She adjusts Lulu to a more comfortable position in one arm, and with a jaunty gait, stepping in beat with the mariachi band, her long red hair resplendent in the sun, she strides over to meet Carlos. *Perro Rojo* bounds after her. Three redheads.

"You're walking different," he says, not giving her a chance to comment on what she has just learned.

"Something wrong?" she asks.

"Nothing's wrong at all. I've been watching you all afternoon— naturally I'm always watching you—but you walk with such confidence and pride, straight and tall like a soldier, and I'm remembering how shy you were when I first met you."

"Well, I was scared to death of men then—totally freaked out—and I was busy keeping my embarrassing secret from the whole world."

"And there's something captivating in your eyes, too."

"Maybe I'm in love," she says with an alluring smile, eyelids fluttering and a flirtatious lilt in her voice.

"Wow! You don't know how long I've been waiting to hear that. But you said *maybe*?"

"I didn't mean *maybe*. Forget the *maybe*." Lulu Lobo is reaching out to him so Molly hands her over and smiles as the baby snuggles against Carlos's shoulder. Then she says, "I just heard some shocking news. We need to talk."

"About what?"

"Birth control. How there's no need for it with us."

"Well...ah...yeah. That's so." Lulu seems to enjoy his shifting from one foot to the other. "I was going to tell you...but..."

"We can talk about that later." She takes his free arm. "I just told you I'm in love. What about you? She's convinced herself that he loves her, but she just needs to hear him say it. "What if I didn't have Norma Lou? Would you..."

"Would I still love you? Come on, Molly, you know how crazy I've been about you from the first night I met you, back when Norma Lou was still a secret without a name. Don't you remember all the milkshakes I bought just to be with you? Of course, I love you. *You* with or without Norma Lou, if that's what you are asking."

Carlos, who sometimes doesn't look directly at people, is concentrating intensely on her eyes as he tells her this, and she feels a melting sensation of happiness all over her body as she hears these words.

He holds Lulu Lobo under her arms and raises her up over his head. It makes her giggle so he does it again...and again. "Come on, I want to show her off to *mis amigos*."

"That's right, they don't know her; they only know that miserable wretch sitting on the Palomino with a noose around his neck. You can be sure I will never call him her father."

Molly looks up at Carlos and wraps her arms around his neck. She runs her fingers through his hair and smothers him in rapturous kisses on his tawny cheek, his forehead, and then on an ear.

"What's this?" he asks, delighted but a little bewildered. "Such a public display of affection?"

"Isn't that what lovers do when they want the whole world to know?"

His smile is his only answer. "Come on, let's go talk to the amigos," he says. "By the way, they love you, too. They say I'm the luckiest guy in the world."

"Tell them that it wasn't luck, not the way you had to work like a draft horse to drag me to my senses. I'm really sorry I was so messed up, Carlos."

Lulu Lobo wants to play some more, so Carlos throws her up over his head again, this time letting go for an instant, so she's suspended in mid-air. She catches her breath and starts to giggle again.

Hand in hand Molly and Carlos stroll across the freshly-mown grass with Lulu, floating along with the soft breeze as if in slow motion, passing through the thinning crowd of well-wishers to the circle of chairs where the amigos have gathered under the shimmering old cottonwoods to drink beer and tell tall tales. The band has stopped playing and the yard is suddenly hushed except for the robins warbling for rain. A few swallows are dipping and diving for an afternoon snack. The Sangre de Cristo Range is there in the east—nobody has moved those mountains—and the sun continues its southern arc toward the San Juan Mountains in the west. Carlos calls the Valley a permanently sacred place, full of peace and beauty in the four directions.

A smile is fixed on Molly's face as she glances around. Of course, she will stay here to live with Carlos and his family in her new home. How could she think of leaving? She is so thankful for a home, that it makes her want to cry, but not those old tears of sadness, only pure joy. It took O'Grady, mysteriously blessed with universal energy, to give her the courage needed, but now she is finally becoming the person she wants to be. Molly *auténtica*.

An immense expanse of blue sky stretches between the mountain ranges, and the ground beneath her feet extends past miles and miles of verdant farms over to Horseshoe Ranch and the Great Sand Dunes Park. The breeze continues unceasing, caressing the land—maybe the ineffable presence of the Great Spirit, wise and kind, connecting everything at the right time. How wonderful it is that Carlos loves her...and Lulu Lobo. But no more babies? Never ever?

LATER

THE WOMAN THAT MOLLY BECAME

Carlos and Molly got married, but the calendar of events was completely upside down and backwards. Part of Molly's informal contract with Carlos was the stipulation that she must ask him to marry her when she is ready; so that's the woman asking the man, which in itself is a little backwards. Then after a fantastic year-long honeymoon, they throw another backyard barbeque in July that serves as the reception for the September wedding, a family-only event held in the secluded aspen grove where Carlos had taken Molly on their first picnic. Roughly, the inverted sequence is: baby, honeymoon, proposal, reception, and wedding. But then, nothing had ever gone as expected in Molly's life, so why should this be different?

After four more summers, many things have happened, some expected, but others quite surprising. Carlos adopted Norma Lou Ouray soon after the wedding. Molly had already begun college in September after the first barbeque, attending the regional state university in Alamosa, where Rainbow's husband was her advisor. She started out slowly, a little unsure of herself, but when she regained her confidence, recognizing how well Mrs. Braxton had prepared her, she accelerated her program with a full schedule of campus courses supplemented by courses online and graduated in three years. When Lulu Lobo was old enough, she was enrolled in the university pre-school, and while Molly was finishing her major in psychology with a clinical emphasis, Lulu began to learn her colors, shapes, numbers, and letters.

Standing Elk introduced Lulu to his collection of carved wood animal figures and taught her the words for *wolf, deer, elk,* and *bunny.* When she spotted a rabbit running across the back yard, she would chase after it and scream with excitement, *"Bun, bun, bun."* Carmencita surrounded Lulu with books, and long before Lulu could read or even speak a full sentence, she would sit beside her grandmother turning the pages while Carmencita read to her and pointed out the antics of the characters in the colorful illustrations. Lulu learned to hold a pencil correctly—something some children never learn—and could be found frequently flat on her tummy, her pencil poised and working furiously on a fresh sheet of paper.

Sometimes Diego took Lulu along with him on one of the John Deere tractors, a short ride going a long way to entertain her. Uncle Diego bought her toy tractors and cars, pails and shovels, trains, trucks, and other toys more traditionally for boys so that she would appreciate what boys get to play with even though she didn't have a little brother. She liked all of her toys and mixed them together, sometimes placing a Barbie Doll on the seat of a toy tractor.

Perro Rojo and Lulu became good friends and when Lulu grew old enough to understand the game of fetch, she would pick up one of the dog's toys—naturally Red Dog had his own toys—and sling it across the room. He would run scrambling and slipping and sliding, claws clicking across the wood floor, undaunted by crashes into furniture and walls, until he had the toy grasped firmly in his mouth to retrieve it. Lapping up her attention, he was reluctant to put the toy down, and Lulu would try to wrestle it away from him while he growled playfully, until Carlos taught her to say "leave it" or "*déjalo.*" Red Dog quickly learned the command in both languages.

Abuela spoke to Lulu only in Spanish. Molly was concerned that this might confuse her, but Carlos assured her that it was a perfectly normal process for a child (or a dog) to learn more than one language, preferably beginning both together. In no time at all, Lulu Lobo was referring to Carlos's grandmother as *abuela*, listening intently to her as if she understood every word, and sometimes answering with "*sí*" or "*non*" or "*mañana.*"

Once Standing Elk said, commenting on her cute behavior without thinking about what he was saying, "Ah, there will never be another Lulu Lobo," and the room became suddenly hushed as everyone realized that truly there would never be another child for Carlos and Molly.

In the winter that followed the September wedding, Diego got seriously depressed and withdrew from the life of the family to live mostly in his own house. Carlos became concerned and asked him, "Are you jealous of me? Is Lulu Lobo getting too much attention? Is it something about Molly?"

Diego said, "No, none of that. I'm getting old and I don't have a wife. It's got me worried."

Diego was not yet thirty, but it was plain that his bachelor state was bothering him. Carlos suggested that he go to the Bear Dance Festival over at the Southern Ute Reservation.

"What's a Bear Dance?" Molly asked.

Carlos replied, "A dance to celebrate the new life and awakening in springtime at the end of the bear's hibernation."

Molly wondered, but didn't ask, if this was some kind of Ute Easter. Was Diego hibernating?

Even though the tribal leaders had moved the spring dance to Memorial Day Weekend, it retained the dress and old customs of the Bear Dance, one of which was that the women got to choose who they want to dance with by flinging their shawl toward a prospective partner who had no choice but to dance with her. With a lot of encouragement from Carlos, Diego went off to the Bear Dance Festival at Ignacio and was chosen to dance by an attractive

Ute woman about his own age named Chipeta. They danced and ate together for three days straight. Later, he went back to visit her several times and soon it turned into a serious romance. Carlos told Molly that Chipeta has the name of old Chief Ouray's beloved wife, but everyone calls Diego's Chipeta by her nickname, Peta. So, they married and Chipeta became a new addition to the family, ready to teach Molly how to cook some traditional native dishes.

Selena had free tuition at the college over in Durango. The family thought it would be a nice place for Selena to run track not too far from home and get an education if she could. She started taking courses in Environmental Studies and liked the subject a lot, but her grades weren't very good. Sitting in classes all morning and studying in the library in the evening were still a problem for her: too much sitting. Carlos kept trying to explain to her that she needed to take the right courses in the proper sequence, but she just kept taking what interested her: Ethnobotany of the Southwest, Weather and Climate, Political Ecology and Food, and Ecological Agriculture. Carlos would drive over to visit her and help her do some planning, but as he did, he began to sense that Selena would never lift her low grade-point average enough to graduate and needed a graceful way out. Naturally she was running track and discovered lacrosse in her second year, but the sports were always more interesting and rewarding than the studies. On one of his visits Carlos brought Selena a surprising offer to consider.

One of the properties adjacent to the family farm had gone up for sale and Standing Elk was ready to buy it if Running Deer would come back to manage the operations. She had sworn that she had cut all ties with potatoes, but when Carlos told her she could turn the property into pure organics, she became interested. "And maybe not just organic potatoes," Carlos told her. "Why not organic pumpkin seeds?" Then when Carlos told her that he and Diego would build her a house, she started to cry. Of course, she would come home. So, the purchase of the land was completed and Selena rejoined the family she never really left except for two years at college and her brief kidnapping by Jimmy Joe.

When Running Deer went off to college, she got rid of her Indian braids and cut her hair short, almost like a man's cut. No one was sure who she would bring to live with her in her new home, but Molly was fairly sure it would not be a man. For the time being, Running Deer seems unclear about what kind of woman she is and doesn't have much to say about either men or women, focused as she is on organic potatoes.

Once Norma Lou had developed a functioning digestive system and stopped that horrible fussing that nearly drove Molly out of her mind, she became a relatively easy child to raise, especially with all of the help Molly had from the family. Lulu went through a difficult period, though, as a two-year-old, but Rainbow told Molly on the day she called her to ask if this behavior was normal, that there was a stage called "terrible twos," and even though it was a natural phase, most mothers get extremely frustrated at that time with the continuous battling they have to do to civilize their children.

It may have been a natural stage, but Lulu Lobo became a little monster as a two-year-old, her friendly smile replaced with a hostile frown, her placid disposition interrupted by frequent temper tantrums. The biggest problem was that she had started biting other children and Molly began to wonder if the wolf that was supposed to protect her had started to inhabit her.

As predicted, Lulu outgrew her terrible twos, but a year later some new problems developed, primarily in her "social relations" at pre-school. At the end of her first year, she received a report card—not exactly a report card with A's and B's but a set of comments about her behavior—and during the parent-teacher conference it came out that Norma Lou needs improvement in "sharing," "respecting the property of others," and "playing well with other children." Recently she had become rather bossy, telling her classmates what to do and acting upset when they didn't follow her orders.

Carlos laughed, calling these problems the flaws of a normal child, but Molly was devastated, feeling responsible for her daughter's behavior or at least her tendencies. Then it occurred to her that she could blame it on Tommy Dawson. "When Lulu does good things," she told Carlos, "you and I will take the credit, and when she's bad, we've always got Tommy Dawson to blame."

Carlos laughed at that, but then he turned serious and said, "What she needs is a little brother or sister, but we both know that we can't deliver on that." It was on that day that their first earnest discussions about adoption began. Otherwise, they never discussed Tommy Dawson.

As the weeks and months went by, Molly became acquainted with the acres and acres of the family farm and saw how the potatoes were planted, grown, and harvested. For Molly the seasons of the year had become more sharply defined by the seasonal tasks of the potato farm. In spring, around the end of April, tractors drag the deep chisel—not a plow, but a curved hook-like tool—through the soil to loosen it up. Beginning around the first of May, when the soil is prepared, the planting begins. Molly thinks the planter is one of the cleverest machines she has ever seen and naturally she wants to know exactly how it works. Small metal cups attached to a five-inch belt hold the seed potatoes, and as the belt rotates around it drops a potato out of the cup and into a hole in the ground prepared by a wedge that goes along ahead of the belt. Small discs push the soil back over the potato, covering it up. How cool!

By mid-June the potatoes are up and the rows are clearly defined so that the cultivation of weeds can begin. The potato plants start blooming by the end of July on into early August, according to the variety, so summer is when the fields become really beautiful. The fall harvest comes at the end of September and the first of October, preferably after a hard frost at the surface of the ground to weaken the vines. The harvester—another amazing machine—digs four to six rows at a time, separates the potatoes from the vines and loads the potatoes on a truck driven along closely beside the tractor and harvester. Molly loved to drive that truck.

Although Molly never ran out of satisfying work to do, she was not destined to become a full-time potato farmer. She worked at it, liked it, and contributed her fair share to the family enterprise as needed at the busy seasons, but her main occupation was elsewhere.

As part of her requirements for her major in psychology, she was expected to do an internship in a local agency. Molly was placed in the Social Services Center, and it was there that she began to combine what she had learned in psychology with her personal life experience. She worked mostly in the treatment of battered women. Housed in a storefront facility in the town's main mall, the county agency delivered a broad array of services, including help for abused and neglected children, but the supervisor noticed that Molly seemed to be a natural in relating to the women who came through the doors seeking help and shelter—women who had been raped by strangers, abused by husbands, or had drifted from poverty to prostitution. Young girls told her about abuse by step-fathers, unwanted advances from teachers, and being already trapped in abusive relationships with boyfriends.

It was tough on Molly at first, and as she listened to these stories, dark memories of her own past bounced around in her psyche. Sometimes at the end of the day, she burst into tears. It was then that the kindly supervisor sat down with her, shared her own past, and taught Molly how to handle her disturbing feelings while being a sensitive listener and effective problem-solver. The next day, Molly would talk with her favorite psychology professor back on campus, who also provided support and guidance on how to handle her past while using it to enhance her empathy with her clients. At times, she also applied what she had learned as an alert client, remembering how her own counselor, Bonnie Bradford, had worked with her.

Molly was very good at what she did, and the women she worked with were helped and wanted more sessions with her. Some new clients even came in the front door asking the receptionist for her by name. At the end of her internship a position opened, and she was asked to work three days a week at the Social Services Center. She was assigned a slightly larger, but still small, office and given a file cabinet. It was a good job for her and she soon built a reputation in the community. She was asked to serve on the board of the Valley Safe House. She joined a women's advocacy group, and found there many of her teachers from the university, clerks from stores where she shopped, and community leaders she was pleased to meet. She soon realized she was not alone in what had happened to her, and understood why they called it "Me, Too."

Molly maintained contact with Wayne by driving over to Horseshoe Ranch every now and then to sit outside on the deck under the cottonwoods and have a cup of coffee with him. But Emily never accepted her, retaining some unresolved suspicion and jealousy of her, so Molly and Carlos never socialized with them as a couple. Sometimes, during the visits, Rainbow appeared on her horse and would wave or dismount to say hello and learn about Norma Lou. Jersey had apparently moved on to greener pastures at another ranch.

Ida and Danny came to visit Molly once after her mom sold the farm to Uncle Russ. Dany finished his degree in music education and took a job as choral director in a Kansas City high school. His mother struck up a friendship with the professional photographer hired to cover the wedding of Russ's daughter, and soon after, she moved to Wichita to live with him. The home where Molly grew up housed the new manager and his family, employed to run the dairy business, so Molly had no place to visit, not that she actually wanted to go back to that property. As for her father, Molly still remembers trying to talk with him when he was dead, and she is surprised that she misses him more, not less, as her life goes on. She would love to chat with him, not to settle anything—that's definitely over—but to get his advice when she's fixing things.

Some of the happiest times for Molly in the Ouray household were on the sub-zero winter nights when she was asked to build a log fire in the living room of the main house, and the family would huddle around to keep off the chill, while the wind whistled at the windows. Some nights it reminded her of that first winter in the cabin before she moved in with Wayne, but she tried not to remember much of that. Lulu Lobo would soon fall asleep snuggled in Carmencita's arms as she read to her. *Abuela* would slip away for an early bedtime under layers of quilts. *Perro Rojo,* who sprawled out on his favorite deerskin, his head settled on his paws, would appear unsure whether or not listening to the voices of humans was worth the effort of fighting off sleep. Those left for serious conversation were Standing Elk and Carlos, neither one known to be a great talker. But Molly learned that if she could bring the conversation around to something about the Utes, she could animate them.

One night while Molly was darning socks—one of her mother's favorite evening occupations—Carlos and Standing Elk were talking about how the ancient ones wandered into Southern Utah and Colorado from somewhere around the present border of California and Nevada. It hadn't dawned on Molly that Utah derived its name from the Utes, and it bothered her that she had to be told something so obvious. Carlos said that they came around 1300. He had the dates and Standing Elk had the lore.

In one of her anthropology courses, Molly had read about how each culture has its own creation myth, so one night she asked if the Utes had a story like that. Standing Elk, who is sitting most of the time as he grows older, jumped to his feet and paced back and forth as he told the story of Senawahu, the Ute creator of land, food, and animals, and eventually the Ute people themselves. One day Senawahu was going on a trip to the north to explore new lands, so he made a sack to carry firewood with him. His brother, Coyote, got curious about what was in the sack and cut a hole in it. Once he saw it was just sticks, he walked away. As Senawahu rambled along on his journey, he noticed the bag getting lighter, but not before many of the sticks had fallen from the sack and rolled down the hill. When they hit the land below, they turned into people: the Ute people. Standing Elk told the story with a deep dramatic voice and accompanying gestures, making it as credible as possible, but Molly couldn't help thinking that by this account, even the creation of human beings is a random act: sticks accidentally falling out of a bag. That's us? Not only mankind as a whole but individuals? Like Lulu Lobo?

In her spare moments, which weren't many, Molly had enjoyed getting to know *abuela*. Every now and then *abuela* would ask Molly to help her play the antique organ. By this she meant for Molly to get her situated on the bench and then sit next to her to pump the pedals, providing the necessary air to produce the sound, as *abuela* would pick out the melody to an old tune she had been taught as a child. Molly enjoyed these special moments together when neither had to speak, but she also wanted to learn more about what secrets were stored in this woman's heart, particularly her past. Sometimes Molly used Carlos to translate, but as her Spanish became more fluent, she ventured into conversations with her alone. Although *abuela* relied even more now on her walker to get around the house, her mind was still keen and her memory full of details although her eyesight was failing. Each day she appeared more worn down by the strains of aging, but it usually took only one or two questions to get her to talk.

As Carlos had told Molly when they were first getting acquainted, his grandmother was part of the Romero family that owned the historic store in the town of San Luis. "It's the oldest town in Colorado," *abuela* said, "founded in 1851 by the original Spanish settlers. The store is the oldest continuous business in the state of Colorado."

Carmencita is *abuela's* only child. "We were all Spanish until Carmencita married Standing Elk," she said, hinting at some loss in the purity of the Hispano blood line. When Molly asked her if it was unusual for a Spanish woman to marry a Ute, she said that initially she and her family were not happy about it, but later she read in the newspaper that a new study showed that descendants of the original Spanish settlers have twenty-five percent Native American DNA. "Maybe she and her daughter were already part Ute before Carmencita married Standing Elk," she said with a shrug that she held so long it threw her into a coughing spell.

Some mornings Molly wakes up abruptly, startled, as if from a nightmare, but there is no dream, only the question: How did I get here? Why am I living with these Utes, these descendants of Spanish settlers? I used to be Irish, a Kansas dairy farmer's daughter until I was thrown out of my home. So, what am I—an immigrant, a refugee, an expatriate?

Over the years she struggled with those questions, but now they are mostly resolved. What helped her, was to notice how many people in this world have left home. Some have fled war to live in refugee camps, others are seeking asylum, some crossed the southern border of the U.S.—without documentation, as they say today—risking their actual life for a better life for themselves and their children.

Her home imploded with her father's fatal heart attack and before that with his dismissive anger. She landed at Horseshoe Ranch, and if Wayne had sent her away when he found out she was pregnant, she would have been truly homeless, pushing her belongings in a grocery cart, with Norma Lou stuffed in her backpack, begging at an intersection. What if Carlos had not been persistent in his love for her?

It is a small price she has paid to have lost her home, to have no childhood residence to return to, no place to evoke nostalgia or homesickness, because she found a wonderful home that makes her very happy. She realizes that many people choose to leave their home, to go to study, to capitalize on a promotion, or just to try out a new place to live. So, there are many people like her, just not so many that were actually shoved out the door by their father.

When she stops to think of it, she remembers that the Utes actually migrated to Colorado from someplace further west and the Old Spanish actually left Spain to settle here. Some of those ancestors just wandered in, like she did. She realizes that a lot of people through the ages have awakened startled asking: How did I get here? And isn't that what every newborn baby feels but has no words to ask? When she realizes how widely asked that question is, she stops asking it.

One afternoon while Carmencita and Molly were emptying the dishwasher in the main house and setting the table for a family dinner, Carmencita asked Molly about her experience growing up in the Catholic Church. At first Molly thought she wouldn't have much of anything to say, but as they talked, she remembered the classes taught by the old priest and realized that his teaching had had a significant impact on her, certain images and beliefs having been drummed into her head without her quite realizing it. Molly told Carmencita that she hadn't attended church in her childhood because her father was so negative about the priests. So, she wasn't a very good Catholic.

Carmencita smiled and asked if she would go to church with her on the following Sunday. As Carlos babysat, she went off to church with her mother-in-law on a clear warm day in late September right before the potato harvest. Carmencita took her to the San Juan Catholic Spiritual Center, a short drive from the farm on dusty back roads to a spot near a little town called La Garita. The Center, Molly discovered from signs in both English and Spanish, was intended as a place of peace, prayer, and reflection, dedicated to honoring the courageous Hispano people, priests, and sisters, who settled the San Luis Valley, bringing the Catholic way of life from Old Spain. Services were held only on special feast days, and of course Carmencita knew this was one of them.

Molly found the church to be indescribably beautiful, a simple white stucco structure with arched windows framed in red brick and a reddish-brown peaked roof. A plain white picket fence spread across the front although it was difficult for Molly to tell what was being fenced in or out.

The roof had a cupola with a small six-armed cross at the top. No spire, no bells. The inside of the church was plain and peaceful with an oak floor and natural pine pews, everything bathed in light. It is called *La Iglesia de San Juan Bautista,* but Molly ended up thinking of it as "the little church on the prairie" because it stood out from the barren landscape and could be seen from several miles away as they approached. The priest that day was having a challenge maintaining a sense of the holy because there was a family there with a whole raft of children—Carmencita counted eight—and even though the children were well disciplined, they were after all squirmy, wiggly children of all ages sitting through a church service.

Afterward, Carmencita and Molly took a walk through the graveyard. There on the tombstones were some of the family names of the first Hispano settlers of the Valley: Romero, Archuleta, Baca, Rivera, and Sandoval. She remembered *abuela* mentioning some of those names. To Molly, it seemed that everywhere she stepped there was history, and the ground seemed hallowed as she thought about the ancestors of both sides of her family walking here long before she arrived.

That night she told Carlos all about their trip and how much she had enjoyed her time with his mother, not only the visit to the church itself but the talks they had had about religion while they were traveling back and forth. He nodded proudly. Then she asked him if it was difficult having different religions in the family. He smiled at her question and thought for a moment before he spoke. "When the Mormons came west under Brigham Young, they were hell bent on converting the Utes, which they did without much trouble, except that the Utes kept their old beliefs in the Great Spirit and went right on with life as usual as Mormons." Then he smiled and reminded Molly that Chief Ouray was actually raised by a Catholic family and that later in life he was a Methodist. "Ouray," he told her, "is famous for the saying, 'If one religion is good, two religions are much better.'"

Carlos and Molly had begun contemplating more seriously the prospect of adoption. One day when she took Lulu in for a check-up with Doctor Archuleta—he must also be a descendant of old Spanish settlers—she told him about their interest. Naturally he remembers why, and she can see in his eyes that he is doing a mental search of the entire Valley for some child he remembers who needs a home. She tells him that she and Carlos don't really want to be foster parents and that if possible, they don't want to adopt a baby, but a child more the age of Lulu. Molly forgets that Norma Lou is old enough now to listen in to adult conversations, so from that day forward she keeps asking when she is going to get her little brother. Lulu can't understand why they don't just make a baby like other parents do, and Molly doesn't try to explain.

The next week, Doctor Archuleta calls and says that he has been thinking of a family with foster children up in La Garita. Naturally Molly wonders if it is that family with the raft of children at the Saint John the Baptist Church the day that she attended several months ago with Carmencita. Small world here in the Valley. The Doctor tells Molly that foster parents receive a small stipend for their efforts, so that poor families sometimes see this as a way of "making a living." In fact, their expenses usually outstrip their resources, and they sometimes find themselves in dire financial straits, willing to let go of a child they have come to love but can't support. He says that this family has a young boy about the age of Lulu, but he thinks he remembers the boy as having a medical condition, a problem with his foot. He arranges a visit with the family for Molly and Carlos to meet the child and foster parents.

Ricky's story is a heart-breaker. The foster parents tell them that he had been left at the door of the fire station in Alamosa, wrapped in that same little blanket that he holds wherever he goes. No one had a clue where he had come from and the agency in Pueblo where he eventually landed had no idea what his background might be: Ute, Hispano, Mexican, African-American, or some blend that made identification of his parental heritage impossible.

Doctor Archuleta takes a look at Ricky's foot, as Carlos and Molly learn from Paula and Marco that they are certain that he needs surgery and equally sure that they can't afford either the time or the money to fix his foot even with the assistance they might get from the government. They say that Ricky's full name is Ricardo and until the time when they took him on, the agency had been referring to him as *pie torcido*, which Molly and Carlos both understand to mean "crooked foot." Carlos winces and looks away. Molly has the sense as she listens to the foster parents that they are sincerely-motivated, good Christian people, but well over their head with these former babies now growing into young children. She arrived at their house a bit apprehensive about taking away a child they had grown to love, but she was feeling now that their giving up this boy would actually be a relief to them, especially if the child might get the help he needs.

At the suggestion of Doctor Archuleta, they get permission from the adoption agency to make an excursion to The Children's Hospital in Denver to consult with a pediatric orthopedic surgeon to find out more about the scope of the problem with Ricky's foot. They leave Lulu behind this time and focus all of their attention on Ricardo, who appears to have mastered the art of adult conversation and acts like they are his old friends. Molly tells Carlos that with Ricardo's being bounced around so much, he could either end up extremely insecure or highly adaptable, and after watching him for a while they both agree that it is the latter. To Ricky, maybe they are just one more set of foster parents taking him to one more examination of his twisted foot, and he is not missing permanent parents because he has never had any, and the idea of permanent has not occurred to him by age five. Consequently, Ricardo seems ready for whatever is to come next, already an expert, Molly notes, in expecting the unexpected. The doctor in Denver, the one who worked on Selena's foot, agrees to being Ricardo's surgeon and suggests the name of a top-notch family law firm to help them through the adoption.

A few nights after the trip to Denver, Carlos invites Molly to go outside to gaze at the stars. Sometimes the two of them will slip on jackets and sit on the loveseat glider on the back porch of his parents' house to just swing and talk, but when the sky is clear, they will often step out into the backyard to see if they can find the constellations or just enjoy the grand sweep of the Milky Way spreading between the two mountain ranges, a great nocturnal panorama of twinkling light. This is another bonus to living in the Valley: an unhampered view of the breathtaking splendor of the bright night sky free of light pollution from a big city. Molly finds the Big Dipper standing out from the curve of the galaxy and the two pointer stars directing her to the North Star. When she sees it, always in its same place, due north, guiding travelers on land and sea, she says to Carlos, "That's how I think of you, as my North Star, my steady reliable guide." He seems bashful, not knowing how to take her compliment. "I've noticed that you don't have a native name. What if I just start calling you North Star?"

"Well, it would be an honor," he says slowly, nodding thoughtfully. "But what if we gave that name to Ricky?" He puts an arm around Molly. "I'm sensing that there is something special in that child with all that he's been through. He has carried a heavy basket without stumbling. We need to watch him, listen to him, and learn from him about adaptability, inner courage, hope. He may guide us in ways we could never imagine."

"Lulu Lobo and North Star? Those names sound nice together," she says. So, they agree to call their new son Ricardo North Star Ouray, which may turn into Ricky North if he chooses an acting career in TV or film.

It took many weeks, reams of forms, a probing visit to their home by the adoption services, a lot of signed paperwork from the lawyer, and constant worry about the effects of the delay on Ricky's life and health, but finally it is finished. They are ready to pick up their adopted son from his foster home in La Garita and bring him home. Naturally they tell Carmencita and Standing Elk every detail, and of course Diego and Peta are standing ready to help even though she is expecting male twins. Selena is eager to meet her new nephew. So when Molly and Carlos arrive home with Ricardo, the whole family is assembled in the living room waiting to greet him. Even *abuela* has come out of her bedroom, clutching a feather of honor, entering the room unsteadily sliding along with her walker, but needing guidance now being almost blind. Red Dog sits down beside her on the floor at the dining table, thrashing his tail as if he senses that he will soon have a newcomer to protect.

Lulu Lobo has gone with her parents to pick up her brother and when they get out of the new Pathfinder, Lulu comes around to Ricardo's door to help him out. She takes Ricky by his little brown hand to steady him across the gravel walkway, up onto the porch, and in through the big double doors of the old homestead, her red pony tail bobbing from side to side with the awkward lurching of their gait. What a touching sight it is for the family to see Lulu helping Ricky like that. Each one comes up to give Ricky a hug and welcome him into the family. He stands there, his weight on one leg, full of composure, *abuela's* feather tucked into his dark hair over one ear, holding onto Lulu with one hand, his tattered blanket folded over his arm.

Peta comes to greet him last, maybe because she was the last to join the family, and bending down to hug him, she asks, "Where did you get that blanket, sweetie?" He clutches it a little tighter as if to make sure she won't take it away from him. Molly explains that this is the blanket they found him wrapped in as an infant when he was abandoned at the fire station and that it goes with him wherever he goes. "It's a Ute blanket," Peta points out confidently. "Unmistakable. Definitely a Ute pattern."

"He's one of us," Standing Elk says proudly.

Molly smiles and feels happy tears running down her face as she glances over at Carlos beaming down at his son. Yes, one of us. One more member of the family of man blessed to dwell in this home of loving people. Lulu Lobo's brother, North Star.

Molly's life has settled into a busy but pleasant routine balanced comfortably among work in the potato fields, raising Lulu Lobo and Ricky North Star, and working three days a week at the Social Services Center. Her pony-tail is gone and she no longer wears her darkening red hair long, and in a clip, but cut shorter and brushed back across the sides, layered and styled. When she looks in the mirror, she sees the person Carlos calls a mature woman, no longer a teen-age girl. In spite of the faithful use of sunscreen, she thinks she sees the hint of wrinkles in the corners of her eyes.

She likes her work and is taking courses toward her master's degree in counseling psychology at the university. She is more confident about how she relates to clients, focusing, as she has been taught, on the identification of the client's feelings and reflecting them back. But sometimes she confronts their feeble defenses and actually tells them what she thinks they should do. She believes she has seen just about everything and heard the saddest of stories, and she's sure now that nothing will surprise her at work. But then one day, it happens.

Her door is open and she hears the receptionist say, "Welcome to the Social Services Center." Poor lady, there is a whistle in her "s" that everyone employed there accepts, listening to it all day long, but first-time visitors hearing it as "Sssossial Ssservisses Ssscenter" sometimes smile or laugh. Molly hears a low giggle. She looks out and thinks she sees a familiar face, and before she can object to their entry, she is being presented her new clients.

She is sure that it is Jimmy Joe, but who is he with and what are they doing here? Do they have guns? Is he planning to kidnap her? Molly controls a fleeting moment of panic. She is certain of his identity, the guy who shot the bison over at Horseshoe Ranch, kidnapped Selena, and signed the confession when the amigos hung him in the well. How long ago was that? But Jimmy Joe is not letting on that he recognizes Molly. Does he, or doesn't he? Surely, he has reasons to remain anonymous. So, she decides to play his game, pretending she doesn't know him. This ought to be fun.

"Please be seated and let's get acquainted," she says in her most professional voice, noticing that Jimmy Joe does not remove his telltale white cowboy hat.

Jimmy Joe squirms and speaks first, "I'm James." Then he introduces the person who is with him as Doreen.

Molly nods, prevents a smirk, and gives Doreen a pleasant smile. There is the typical long silence before anyone says anything, which gives Molly a moment to size up Doreen. Clearly, Doreen is not a woman, but a transvestite dressed in a tight red suit and a blond wig, fully made up, with polish on the nails of his long bony fingers. She is the guy's guy, pretending, not very well, to be a woman. But why is Jimmy Joe back in the Valley? Was he not prosecuted? Did his Daddy find a way to get him released? Finally, she asks, "Are you two from the Valley?" as she waves a forefinger back and forth at them.

Jimmy Joe searches Doreen's eyes for some indication that he can speak. "Not originally," he begins. "As you will be able to tell from my accent, I was raised in Texas. I'd been in the San Luis Valley some years ago and just fell in love with the place, so when I returned for a visit, I stopped in at a Cantina downtown that I had been in years before, and that's where I met Doreen. A relationship developed, and I decided to settle here."

It was Pepe's Cantina where he had deceived Selena, and the little weasel has the nerve to bring it up under the guise that he doesn't recognize Molly and she doesn't recognize him. She musters the discipline not to reach across the desk and smack him in the face. For a split second she wonders if Doreen is Sonny, that creep at Pepe's who unintentionally brought Carlos into her life. No definitely not Sonny. "And where do you work, James?"

"From home. I'm in investments."

Molly nods. So, Daddy transferred some stocks to Jimmy Joe in exchange for his promise to never set foot in Texas again. That's her guess. If only Daddy could see him now. "What help are you seeking?" she asks.

Jimmy Joe finally removes his large white cowboy hat and points to a long gash on his forehead, recently stitched together, but healing. "She hit me," he complains.

The whine in his voice is unmistakable, and if Molly had any doubts about his identity, they are gone now. "How did it happen?" she asks.

Doreen answers, "A Texas Rangers baseball bat we keep around the house. I lost my temper. I don't want it to happen again. We have guns, too."

"She needs help," Jimmy Joe adds, sounding discouraged.

"But he provokes me," Doreen grumbles.

"She can't control herself."

"He can be so incredibly annoying."

"She's like a grenade waiting to explode."

"He pulls my pin."

And so, the accusations fly back and forth, a familiar exchange between men and women, the kind Molly has heard many times before in this office, but between two gay men? This is new to her, but certainly understandable. She's not sure she can help or even wants to. She tries not to admit to herself that the baseball bat may be the best solution. "Have you thought of splitting up? Going your separate ways?"

"Oh, No," Doreen says in a low firm voice. "That's the problem, I don't have anywhere to go."

Molly ponders that situation for a moment and says to Jimmy Joe, "You might consider a safe house. I could recommend one."

"For me? They're for women."

"For battered women." She means to be serious and only recognizes the pun on *bat* when it is out of her mouth.

They talk more. She listens intently. They both acknowledge they need help. It's her opening.

Molly leans forward to make a strong recommendation. "You both could profit from some hi-grade, top-quality professional help. You won't find that here in the Valley. You need to go to a big city, probably not even here in Colorado, maybe California. Professional psychotherapy, rehabilitation, psychiatrists, perhaps psychoanalysis. It's not cheap, but I assume you have the resources. If you plan to stay together and live happy lives, you need to learn how to resolve your conflicts. That's my advice."

They look at each other and nod their heads, slowly at first, then more vigorously, seeming to agree both with Molly and each other. They stand up, ready to leave. Jimmy Joe puts on his white cowboy hat and adjusts it to the proper angle as Doreen stumbles in her high heels on the way to the door.

"A big city?" Doreen says to Jimmy Joe, as she takes his arm. "That sounds exciting."

"On the West coast," James replies. "Maybe San Francisco."

"Frisco would be good," Molly says, standing beside her desk. Then she hollers out clear, unmistakable instructions, "Just don't come back here, Jimmy Joe."

Did Jimmy Joe hear his name? Did it register with him that she knows it? They leave quietly as she closes the door behind them. She wants to laugh out loud. She stretches her elbows back a few times, rotates her neck in circles, and rises on her toes to stretch out her legs. She's eager to get home and tell Carlos about her encounter with Jimmy Joe, the game he played, and her parting shot.

She sits down at the computer behind her desk, thinking she should jot a few notes as she usually does, but decides not to enter any record of this odd encounter. Those two will never return. She swivels back, staring at the empty chairs and thinks for a moment of the many clients who have been seated across from her, remembering their sad faces. Abuse. Sometimes physical, sometimes emotional. Often from an uncontrolled urge or desire. Loss of respect. Hurt feelings. The defense of pride through power. Violence. More pain and more suffering. Now she must add to her gallery of faces, the images of Jimmy Joe and Doreen. For a moment she feels bad for Jimmy Joe, stuck in his life, still suffering, and for poor mixed-up Doreen, who without help, will only inflict more pain on Jimmy Joe. It appears that JJ's second chance isn't working out so well. Then Molly wonders if she is playing the role of the Pied Piper, leading the vermin from the Valley. Well, yes, but she also sincerely hopes they will find help.

Why is it so hard for people to get along? The abusers need to get themselves under control and the abused need to...well, they need to do a lot of things, but once it has happened, to recover and see that it never happens again. Recover? Carlos calls her "gritty." Standing Elk says she is "strong." Carmencita uses the word "resilient." Selena calls her "my feminist hero." Diego simply says she is "tough." She's all of those things now. She has her own safe home, only it's a real home, a happy home with a loving husband and sweet kids. She definitely got her second chance. But most important, she's in charge of herself, clear about what to do and not afraid to do it.

On bad days she still remembers everything all over again, the grove of trees, the stream, being forced down into the rotting leaves. On good days she remembers the people who helped her: Wayne, Rainbow, Bonnie, Carlos, the amigos. She says good-night to the receptionist and finds the car in the mall parking lot. Carlos sold her rickety old truck and bought her a new AWD Rogue sedan for her commute. On the way out of town, she recalls again what Carlos and the amigos did to Jimmy Joe after he had kidnapped Selena, weird memories of an abandoned well, creepy spiders, and imaginary butterflies. They make her laugh. But then the laugh turns into a smile that seems to linger in place while she travels the dusty roads, edged in golden prairie sunflowers, making her way home. This was a good day. She's having pleasant memories of Horseshoe Ranch, that ranch without cowboys.

READERS GUIDE

1. At first, Molly didn't understand that she had been raped. What was confusing her?

2. If rape is the worst, what else is on the continuum of abuse for women? What major and minor offenses would you put on the list? Is there, or should there be, a sexual abuse list for men and children?

3. Molly certainly had an "unwanted pregnancy." How can that affect the birth process and the experience of motherhood?

4. Who and what contributed to Molly's recovery? What motivated Wayne and Rainbow to help her? Why was Savannah unable to contribute much?

5. When Molly's father died, she couldn't rebuild the relationship as she had hoped. Her counselor told her that some things just go unresolved. Can you provide an example of something in your life, or the life of an acquaintance, where things simply went unresolved?

6. Molly's mother and father communicate poorly. How did that affect Molly and her brother Danny?

7. Molly gained strength from her horse O'Grady. Can animals help people rehabilitate? How?

8. Who were the good men in this story? What makes them good? Are good men hard to find in real life?

9. Molly found an unexpected home with Carlos, Standing Elk, Carmencita, Running Deer, and Diego. What matters, and what doesn't matter, in a happy home?

10. Carlos and the amigos play a special role in bringing about justice for Tommy Dawson and Jimmy Joe Richardson. Were they operating outside the law, within the law, or both?

11. When Molly learns that Carlos can't have children, she understands better why he is able to raise a child that is not his own, but she is suddenly perplexed about whether he truly loves her as well as her baby. Have you ever been in an ambiguous situation where you weren't sure what people thought of you?

12. The title *Ranch Without Cowboys* can be taken as a metaphor or symbol with some larger meaning. What do you think it could mean?

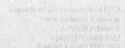

CPSIA information can be obtained
at www.ICGtesting.com
Printed in the USA
LVHW031335200921
698273LV00015B/865